U0015829

美國《世界日報》連載10年最受歡迎英語學習專欄作家

美國實用
英語文法

懷中◎著

Practical English Grammar for Chinese Speakers

用最生活化的文字，幫你建立最正統的美語文法觀念

序

聯經出版公司出版了我的兩本書：《美國最新口語》及《美國常用生活會話》，兩岸三地的讀者反應不錯，也進入美國世界書局的暢銷排行榜前 10 名。現在聯經公司又同意出版這本文法書，我很高興。

《世界日報》是美加兩國最有名氣、銷售量最大的中文報，我有幸能在該報的〈世界週刊〉寫了 10 年的「實用英語專欄」。這本書可說是集專欄中文法篇章之大成。

本書的特點是：我以許多的例句去解釋生活上的英語文法，並用淺白易懂的字句加以說明，使一般中國人都能充分了解，即使英文程度欠佳，也能建立觀念，獲得助益。

我講求實際，也認為一本書該讓讀者以內容作為評價的基礎。雖然一本書很難人人稱好，可是我只想做到應盡的努力。

出書是一般從事教育者的心願，也是一件苦差事。但只要能得到讀者的認可，也就感到幸運了。

在出書過程中，我仍然要感謝〈世界週刊〉前後任主編蘇斐玫與常誠容女士，經過她們的編審，我的文稿生色不少。同時也要感謝世界書局周才博總經理的賞識，由於他的推薦，我和聯經才有了密切的合作。

我也非常謝謝聯經發行人林載爵先生對我文稿的興趣，以及編輯何采嬪小姐與林雅玲小姐細心的處理。

序

　　專攻英美文學史、寫作功力深厚、也是我一直以來非常敬佩的 James Thrash 教授，更是在我有疑問時，適時提出精闢見解的良友。

　　家人對我的鼓勵，給了我寫作的力量。

　　最後，我要謝謝恩師趙麗蓮教授啟發了我用「懷中」這個筆名。這二十幾年來我在各報投稿，愛用「懷中」作為筆名，是因為趙教授當年對我們台大外文系畢業生的離別贈言：「到了國外，千萬不可忘記自己是中華的兒女。」其次，在做人處事上，我也以「中庸之道」自勉。這兩種思想長懷我心。

　　我的三本書，如對文化交流與讀者學習美語有些幫助的話，那就是我最大的喜樂。

懷中

目次

懷中 >>

序

i

一、詞類

CHAPTER >> **1-1**

談名詞

001

CHAPTER >> **1-2**

代名詞與其先行詞

023

CHAPTER >> **1-3**

動詞的形式

041

CHAPTER >> **1-4**

動詞時態和用法

061

CHAPTER >> **1-5**

動詞的語氣和語態

085

CHAPTER >> **1-6**

動詞與主詞的一致

101

CHAPTER >> **1-7**

形容詞的用法

115

目次

CHAPTER >> **1-8**

副詞的用法 **139**

CHAPTER >> **1-9**

介詞的用法 **159**

CHAPTER >> **1-10**

連接詞和感嘆詞 **175**

CHAPTER >> **1-11**

分詞的用法 **191**

CHAPTER >> **1-12**

不定詞的用法 **205**

CHAPTER >> **1-13**

動名詞用法 **221**

CHAPTER >> **1-14**

冠詞的用法 **233**

二、句子結構

CHAPTER >> **2-1**

句型和結構 **253**

CHAPTER >> **2-2**

句子的組合 　　　　　　　　　　　　**269**

CHAPTER >> **2-3**

容易弄錯的句子 　　　　　　　　　　**291**

CHAPTER >> **2-4**

直接引語和間接引語 　　　　　　　　**333**

CHAPTER >> **2-5**

談句子不同的開頭 　　　　　　　　　**347**

CHAPTER >> **2-6**

多寫簡短易懂的字句 　　　　　　　　**367**

三、片語與子句

CHAPTER >> **3-1**

談片語的種類 　　　　　　　　　　　**383**

CHAPTER >> **3-2**

談子句的種類 　　　　　　　　　　　**399**

目次

四、其他

CHAPTER >> **4-1**
大寫字母的用法
417

CHAPTER >> **4-2**
常見的英文縮寫
431

CHAPTER >> **4-3**
標點符號的用法
447

CHAPTER >> **4-4**
撇號的用法
465

CHAPTER >> **4-5**
受詞和補語
479

1-1

談名詞

名詞(noun)，係來自拉丁文 nomen，意思是名字(name)，其主要功用是稱呼人名、動物名、地名、事物、思想或觀念。

通常一個句子可包括一個名詞或多個名詞。

例如：

◉ The man went to the store with his son.
（man, store, son 都是名詞）

現在我把名詞幾個重要觀念，分別說明。

一、名詞的種類

一般來說，名詞可分為：

1. 普通名詞(common nouns)

是指任何人、地、物的名稱，是一般性，也就是看得到，摸得到的具體東西，在句中不必大寫。

例如：

◉ Mr. A is not only a writer but also a professor.
A 先生不但是作家，也是教授。
（writer 和 professor 是一般性，故是普通名詞）

◉ Do you consider Mr. Chen a statesman or a politician?
你認為陳先生是政治家，還是政客？
（statesman 和 politician 都是普通名詞）

◉ His uncle is his only immediate relative.
他叔叔是他唯一的至親。
（uncle 和 relative 都是普通名詞。immediate＝close）

◉ There is a tall building on the corner of the street.
在馬路的角落有座高樓。
　(building, corner street 都是普通名詞)

其他又如：

指具體東西：store 店鋪、bicycle 單車、kite 風箏、wheat 小麥、refrigerator 冰箱、garlic 大蒜、bruise 瘀青、document 文件、bumblebee 大黃蜂等等。

指人名：sailor 水手、pilot 飛行員、neighbor 鄰居、horseman 騎師、teacher 教師、astronaut 太空人等等。

指地名：college 大學、beach 海邊、garden 花園、library 圖書館、hotel 旅館、river 河流、theater 電影院等等。

2. 專有名詞(proper nouns)

指特別的人、地、物的名稱，通常要大寫。

例如：

◉ Wang Chunghua is a Chinese student here.
王中華是這裡的中國學生。
　(Wang Chunghua 是專有名詞)

◉ My children graduated from Parkside High School.
我孩子從 Parkside 高中畢業。
　(Parkside High School 是專有名詞)

◉ The White House immediately denied the story.
白宮立即否認這篇報導。
　(White House 也是專有名詞)

其他又如：Canada 加拿大、Ohio 俄亥俄州、Uncle Jen 任叔叔、John 約翰、Amazon River 亞馬遜河、Neptune 海王星，Spring Street 春日街等等。

有時特別指定的人，或對家人直接稱呼，也算是專有名詞。

例如：

◉ For twenty years, Auntie Margaret has worked at this school.
瑪格麗特阿姨在這學校服務了20年。
（Auntie Margaret 是特別指定的人，算是專有名詞）

但 My auntie was a high school teacher.
（這裡的 auntie，是普通名詞，不必大寫；auntie 比 aunt 親暱些）

◉ Please tell me something, Son, about your trip to California.
兒子，請告訴我一些有關你到加州旅行的情形。
（這裡的 Son，是指直接稱呼，也屬專有名詞）

如果不是專有名詞的一部分，則不必大寫：

例如：

◉ the state of Maryland 馬里蘭州
the city of San Francisco 三藩市
the eastern part of China 中國東部
（eastern 不必大寫，而 state 與 city 過去有人大寫，現在可以小寫）

指人的專有名詞，如果加上冠詞，係指許多位中的一位。

例如：

◉ The John Smith who came here yesterday bought a new car.
昨天來這裡的那位 John Smith，買了部新車。
（指許多叫 John Smith 中的一位）

（The John Smith＝one of the men called John Smith）

◉ A Robert Anderson talked to me about his business.
一位名叫 Robert Anderson 的人跟我談到他的生意。

（A Robert Anderson＝a certain Robert Anderson）

3. 複合名詞(compound nouns)

名詞有時與另一個字或兩個以上的字，連在一起，指一件事，當作一個名詞用。複合名詞有的是分開的，有的是連在一起，也有是用連字號(hyphen)連在一起。

分開的複合名詞：

例如：

◉ Most people hate the dog days of summer.
許多人討厭酷熱的天氣。
(dog days of summer 意思是酷熱的天氣，雖是分開的複合名詞，但指一件事，必須連用，其中 of summer 常被省去)

◉ The mail carrier left a small package in my mailbox.
郵差把一個小包裹放進我的信箱裡。
(mail carrier 雖是分開的複合名詞，但指一個人，必須連用)

◉ We lunched on meat loaf, string beans and fruit salad.
我們午餐吃肉捲、四季豆和水果沙拉。
(meat loaf, string beans 和 fruit salad 雖然都是分開的複合名詞，但都指一種食物，有特別意義)

◉ Being a flight attendant is certainly not an easy job.
空服員肯定不是一份簡單的差事。
(flight attendant 雖是分開兩個字，但指某種職業)

其他又如：landing gear 起落架，station wagon 旅行車，jump suit 傘兵服或連身服，boarding pass 登機證，test tube 試管，scarlet fever 猩紅熱，post office 郵局，junior high school 國中等等。雖然都是分開的複合名詞，但都另有其意，必須放一起。

注意

exercise machine, winter coat, college students, factory workers 等字雖然都是兩個名詞，但前一個名詞 exercise, winter, college, factory 皆當作形容詞使用，不一定要連用。

用連字號的複合名詞：

例如：

◉ Her sister-in-law bought a basketful of apples.
她的弟媳買了一籃蘋果。

◉ An attorney-at-law is needed on the committee.
委員會需要一位律師加入。
(用 attorney-at-law 比 lawyer 正式)

◉ Mary wore her older sister's hand-me-downs until she was 16.
Mary 穿她姐姐的舊衣服穿到十六歲。
(hand-me-down 是指傳下來的舊衣服或舊東西)

注意：

◉ His 80-plus-year-old father wanted to marry a young woman.
他八十多歲的老父，想娶一名年輕女子。

◉ Mr. Bush stands by his stay-the-course strategy for the war in Iraq.
布希先生對伊拉克戰爭，堅守貫徹始終的政策。

（stay-the-course 是奮力貫徹始終的意思）（以上的 80-plus-year-old 和 stay-the-course 都是當形容詞用，修飾名詞 father 和 strategy；非修飾連字號的複合名詞）

其他又如：jack-in-the-box 驚奇箱、commander-in-chief 總司令、jack-of-all-trades 雜而不精的人（什麼都會一點，但都不精通）等等。

至於兩個字，諸如：cure-all 治百病的靈藥，bulls-eye 靶的中心等等，也有美國人寫成一個字，不用連字號。

連在一起的複合名詞：

例如：

◉ The chairperson was really just a figurehead.
主席只是一位名義上的領袖。
（chairperson 是由 chair 和 person 連在一起；figurehead 也是由 figure 和 head 連在一起的複合名詞）

◉ The salesperson sold her a new computer.
推銷員賣一台新電腦給她。
（salesperson 是由 sales 和 person 連在一起的複合名詞）

◉ Playing basketball seems to be a popular activity for young people.
打籃球似乎是年輕人流行的活動。
（basketball 也是由 basket 和 ball 連在一起的複合名詞）

◉ Mr. A does a little bit of writing as a sideline.
A 先生把寫文章當作一種副業。
（sideline 也是由 side 和 line 連成的複合名詞）

其他又如：sleepwalker 夢遊者、snowshoes 雪鞋、eyewitness 目擊者或見證人、housekeeper 女管家、firefighter 消防隊員，

dragonfly 蜻蜓、eardrum 耳膜、stockholder 股東、grandparents 祖父母等等。

4. 抽象名詞(abstract nouns)

這是指看不到、摸不到，或五官不能察覺得到(perceive)的名詞。通常是指思想(idea)、感情(emotion)、行為(action)、情況(condition)或特性(quality)等。

（例如：）

◎ Excitement is to be expected at a party.
在宴會中，興奮是可預料的。
（excitement 就是抽象名詞）

◎ Genuine friendship is always appreciated.
誠摯的友誼非常可貴。
（friendship 是抽象名詞）

◎ Imagination is a necessary quality for an inventor.
想像力是發明家必備的特質。
（imagination 是抽象名詞）

其他又如：Patience 忍耐、strength 力量、justice 公正、charm 魅力、ability 能力、courage 勇氣、fear 恐懼、success 成功、failure 失敗等等。

有的是由字尾 -dom, -ism, -ment, -ness, -ship, -hood 而形成的：loneliness 孤單，willingness 樂意，illness 生病，freedom 自由，leadership 領導，entertainment 娛樂，horsemanship 騎術，nationalism 民族主義，terrorism 恐怖主義，brotherhood 兄弟關係等等。

有的是由形容詞形成的：friendly/friendliness 友善，high/height 高度，pure/purity 純潔，thoughtful/thoughtfulness 關懷等等。

5. 集合名詞(collective nouns)

這是指一個群體(一般指人和動物)，當做一個單位(unit)來看待，所以是單數，動詞也用單數。

例如：

◉ The jury has reached a verdict today.
陪審團今天作出裁定。
(把 jury 當個整個單位，是單數，所以動詞也用單數 has)

◉ The cast gives a wonderful performance every night.
那表演團體每晚都有精采的演出。
(把 cast 當做一個單位，是單數，動詞也用單數 gives)

◉ The committee meets every Monday morning at 10.
委員會每周一上午十點開會。
(把 committee 視為一個整體，是單數，動詞也用單數 meets)

其他又如：council 議會、orchestra 管弦樂隊、team 隊伍、staff 職員、army 軍隊、family 家庭、panel 小組、company 公司、band 樂隊、assembly 集會、squad 小隊／小組、delegation 代表團、faculty 教師團、entourage 隨行人員等等。

註：

這些集合名詞，英國人多半當作複數用，現在也有美國人認為如果是指單位中的成員，就可當複數。不過為了讓句子明白起見，使用複數時，最好加上 members。

- The jury members express their concern for the defendant.
  陪審團的成員對被告表示關切。
  （這裡的 jury members 是複數，動詞也用複數 express）

如指單數，就是：

- The jury expresses its concern for the defendant.

- The cast members of the play are rehearsing their lines.
  這表演團體正在排練他們劇本的台詞。
  （cast members 是複數，動詞也用複數 are rehearsing）

如指單數，就是：

- The cast of the play is rehearsing its lines.
  這部戲的演員正在對台詞。

不過，以上這些集合名詞，美國人當作複數時，往往不加
members。

注 意
有些集合名詞包括多種東西，本身不用複數，但是將其中的東西
區分出來的話，就有單、複數之分了。

例如：

Food 食物（包括 vegetables, apples, noodles 等）

Furniture 家俱（包括 chairs, tables, beds, desks 等）

Mail 郵件（包括 letters, postcards, packages 等）

Clothing 衣服（包括 dresses, pants, sweaters 等）

Money 金錢（包括 dollars, dimes, nickels 等）

Fruit 水果（包括 apples, grapes, bananas 等）

Jewelry 首飾（包括 necklaces, bracelets, rings 等）

Makeup 化妝品（包括 lipstick, rouge, eye shadow 等）

Homework 作業（包括 compositions, reading, writing 等）

以上括弧內的細項就可以用單、複數。

6. 多數型的名詞，但意義上是單數

多半指學科方面或新聞上或某種疾病，字尾有 s，看起來像複數，實際上是單數，所以動詞也用單數。

（例如：）

◉ Social studies becomes Mr. A's major in college.
社會學變成 A 先生的大學主修。
(social studies 是一種學科，是單數，動詞也用單數 becomes)

◉ Measles is a dangerous disease for children.
麻疹對孩子是種危險的疾病。
(動詞用單數 is)

◉ Today's news seems encouraging.
今天的新聞令人振奮。
(news 是單數，動詞也用單數 seems)

◉ Is politics an honorable profession?
從事政治是個高尚的職業嗎？
(politics 的動詞用單數 is)

◉ It seems that ethics is neglected by our society today.
現今，道德倫理似乎被我們社會所忽視。
(ethics 後面動詞用單數 is)

其他又如：linguistics 語言學、phonetics 語音學、economics 經濟學、physics 物理學、mathematics 數學、genetics 遺傳學、acoustics 聲學、electronics 電子學、dynamics 力學、optics 光學、statistics 統計學、mumps 腮腺炎、arthritis 關節炎等等。

有些學科（subject）名稱通常也只用單數，諸如：art, history, grammar, biology, chemistry, geometry 等等。

二、名詞單、複數的變化

以下是幾種讓單數變成複數的方法：

1. 有些單數名詞，不論最後字母發音或不發音，通常只加 s，就成為複數。

例如：office/offices 辦公室、vote/votes 選票、race/races 賽跑或種族，lip/lips 嘴唇、flag/flags 旗幟、pad/pads 墊子、ruler/rulers 統治者或直尺、pin/pins 別針等等。

月份和星期也可在字尾加 s，成為複數：

Monday（Mondays）, Friday（Fridays）, June（Junes）, September（Septembers）（不過月份極少用複數）

所以可以說：

- ◉ I spent two Mondays working on my articles last month.
  上個月我用了兩個星期一的時間寫文章。

- ◉ Mr. A spent two Julys in Taiwan over the past three years.
  過去三年來，A 先生有兩年的七月份都在台灣。

2. 單數名詞，最後字母是 ch, sh, s, x, z 時，通常加 es，就變成複數。

例如：bus/buses 公車、buzz/buzzes 嗡嗡聲、fox/foxes 狐狸、mass/masses 一團或一堆、watch/watches 監視、dish/dishes 碟盤、bush/bushes 叢林等等。

3. 單數名詞，最後字母是 y，如果 y 前面字母是母音(即 a, e, i, o, u)時，加 s 就成為複數。

例如：attorney/attorneys 律師、boy/boys 男孩、day/days 日子、survey/surveys 調查等等。

但是，單數名詞最後字母是 y，如果 y 前面字母是子音，把 y 改為 i，再加 es 就成為複數。

例如：city/cities 城市、lady/ladies 女士、baby/babies 嬰孩、story/stories 故事、berry/berries 莓果、country/countries 國家、puppy/puppies 小狗、quantity/quantities 數量等等。

4. 單數名詞最後字母是 f 或 fe，通常把 f 或 fe 改為 v，再加 es 就成為複數。

　　leaf/leaves 葉子、wolf/wolves 狼、shelf/shelves 書架、half/halves 一半、loaf/loaves 一條麵包、life/lives 生命、knife/knives 刀、wife/wives 妻子等等。

　　但有些例外，只加 s 就會成為複數：roof/roofs 屋頂、chief/chiefs 首領、belief/beliefs 信仰、cuff/cuffs 袖口等等。

5. 單數名詞最後字母是 o，如果 o 前面字母是子音，加 s 或 es 就會成為複數。

　　例如：solo/solos 獨奏、ego/egos 自我、hero/heroes 英雄、piano/pianos 鋼琴、echo/echoes 回音、veto/vetoes 否決、potato/potatoes 馬鈴薯、cello/cellos 大提琴、embargo/embargoes 禁運、torpedo/torpedoes 魚雷、two/twos 兩個等等。

　　所以可以說：

◉ They came out in twos and threes.
　他們三三兩兩地出來。

　　但是最後字母是 o，而 o 前面是母音，加 s 就成為複數。

　　例如：radio/radios 收音機、zoo/zoos 動物園、studio/studios 工作室、video/videos 錄影帶、cameo/cameos 浮雕寶石、portfolio/portfolios 文件夾或投資組合等等。

6. 有些單數名詞變成複數時,是不規則的。

例如:man/men 男人、woman/women 女人、child/children 小孩、foot/feet 腳或英尺、tooth/teeth 牙齒、goose/geese 鵝、ox/oxen 公牛、mouse/mice 老鼠、louse/lice 蝨子、die/dice 骰子、serviceman/servicemen 軍人、clergyman/clergymen 神職人員、clergywoman/clergywomen 女神職人員、person/people 或 persons 人們等等。

7. 有些名詞只用複數,不用單數,所以動詞也用複數。

例如:cattle 牲畜/牛、clothes 衣服、remains 遺體、proceeds 由某種活動得來的收入、riches 財富、(eye)glasses 眼鏡等等。

這類包括由兩個部分組成的複數,例如:pajamas 睡衣、pants 褲子、trousers 長褲、blue jeans 牛仔褲、pliers 鉗子、scissors 剪刀、shears 大剪刀等等。

注意

由兩個部分或一對所組成的複數名詞,如果前面有 a/the pair 的字眼,動詞就得用單數,否則用複數。

例如:

◎ The pair of pliers is on the bench.
那把鉗子在工作台上。
(動詞用單數 is)

◉ Be careful, the pliers are very sharp.
小心，那把鉗子很利。
（動詞用複數 are）

◉ Generally, a pair of blue jeans costs 30 dollars.
一般而言，一件牛仔褲要價 30 塊美金。
（動詞用單數 costs）

◉ Blue jeans have become popular in the US.
牛仔褲在美國已很流行。
（動詞用複數 have）

8. 有些名詞單、複數型式都相同。

sheep/sheep 羊、deer/deer 鹿、swine/swine 豬、bison/bison 野牛、species/species 生物種類、series/series 一系列、corps/corps 部隊等等。

corps 發音是/kor/，而 corpse（死屍）發音是/korps/不可弄錯。

9. 連字號的單數複合名詞，只要改變其中一個主要的字，就成為複數。

例如：

brother-in-law/brothers-in-law 姐夫、妹婿，editor-in-chief/editors-in-chief 主編，lady-in-waiting/ladies-in-waiting 女王或公主的女侍者，attorney-general/attorneys-general 司法部長或首席檢察官等等。

所以可以說：

⊚ Several attorneys-general were fired by the president.
數位首席檢查官遭總統解職。

⊚ The princess had five ladies-in-waiting in the palace.
這位公主在王宮中有五位女侍。

10. 有些單數名詞，是來自拉丁文或希臘文，把字尾的-on 或-um，改為 a；或把字尾的-sis，改為-ses，就成為複數。

例如：criterion/criteria 準則、尺度、phenomenon/phenomena 現象、memorandum/memoranda 備忘錄、datum/data 詳細資料、bacterium/bacteria 細菌、basis/bases 基本原則、crisis/crises 危機、hypothesis/hypotheses 假設、parenthesis/parentheses 括弧、analysis/analyses 分析（analyze＝analyse 是動詞）、synopsis/synopses 大綱、提要等等。

至於平時的稱呼，變成複數時，倒要小心。（一般用在正式的邀請）

Mr.（Messrs.）
Mrs.（Mmes.）（因為 Mmes 無法發音，故讀成 mesdames）

Miss（Misses）
Ms.（Mses.）小姐或太太（用在婚姻狀況不明或不願提及婚姻狀況時）

所以：

Messrs. Wang and Lee（正式）＝Mr. Wang and Mr. Lee（不正式）

Mmes. Wang and Lee＝Mrs. Wang and Mrs. Lee

Misses Wang and Lee＝Miss Wang and Miss Lee

Mses. Wang and Lee＝Ms. Wang and Ms. Lee

三、不可數名詞（uncountable nouns）

是指某些元素很難分割出來，只好當作一個整體看待，所以沒有複數。

諸如：water, milk, soup, coffee, butter, meat, iron 等等。也包括抽象名詞，諸如：time, experience 等等。

另一種物質，本是一堆或一團（mass），其組織的成份太多或太小，很難去數，也不值得去數，故沒有複數。諸如：hair, rice, sand, dirt, dust, sugar, grass, flour, salt, corn, wheat, pepper 等等。

但是為了表示這些不可數名詞的數量，也可用以下方法計算：

1. 用某種容器表示：

a glass of water 一杯水、a cup of coffee 一杯咖啡、a bottle of water 一瓶水、a carton of milk 一盒牛奶、a bag of flour 一袋麵粉、a bowl of soup 一碗湯、a can of soda 一罐汽水、a jar of peanut butter 一罐花生醬（以上的容器，都可用複數，例如：two glasses of water, three cartons of milk 等）

2. 用表面的形狀表示：

a piece of meat 一塊肉、a piece of cake 一片蛋糕、a sheet 或 piece of paper 一張紙、a strip of bacon 一條培根、a slice/piece of bread 一片麵包、a scoop of ice cream 一球冰淇淋、a slice of pizza 一片披薩、a loaf of bread 一條麵包、an ear of corn 一根玉米、a head of lettuce 一顆萵苣、a tube of toothpaste 一條牙膏、a bar of soap 一塊肥皂(以上 piece, strip, slice, ear 等都可以用複數)

3. 用容量、重量表示：

諸如：an ounce of sugar 一盎司白糖、a quart of oil 一夸脫的 油、a pound of meat 一磅肉、a gallon of milk 一加侖牛奶、a pint of cream 一品脫奶油(以上 ounce, quart, pound 等都可用複數)

> **注 意**
>
> 不可數名詞(包括抽象名詞)有時也可作為可數名詞(countable nouns)。

◉ Many women use irons to press clothes.
許多女人用熨斗熨衣服。
(iron 指「鐵質」時本是不可數的名詞，這裡當「熨斗」，就可以數)

◉ Bob had many exciting experiences on his trip to China.
Bob 的中國之行有許多刺激的經驗。
(experience 本為不可數，這裡指多種不同的經驗，就可以加 s，成為複數)

- John has to write two papers today.
  John 今天必須寫兩篇文章。
  (paper 本是不可數的名詞，這裡當文章解釋，就可以數)

- At the restaurant, Mr. A ordered two coffees.
  A 先生在餐廳點了兩杯咖啡。
  (coffee 本來不可數，這裡 two coffees＝two cups of coffee)

4. 不可數名詞，表示數量很多時，常用 much, a lot of 或 too much；表示數量很少，則用 little, a little 或 very little，但意義上有些不同。

（例如：）

- Mrs. A has much housework, but Mrs. B does not have a lot (of housework).
  A 太太有很多家務要做，但 B 太太沒有很多。
  (much＝a lot of。a lot 後面的 of housework 可省去)

不過 a lot of 也可指可數的名詞：

- I have a lot of friends living in Maryland.
  我有很多朋友住在馬里蘭州。

- There is too much competition in the business world.
  商場的競爭太激烈。
  (competition 是不可數名詞，帶有負面的意思)

- Elementary school students in Taiwan have too much homework.
  台灣的小學生有太多功課要做。
  (帶有負面的意思)

指可數的名詞，用 too many 時，也有負面的意味：

◉ Mr. Chang has too many girlfriends.
張先生有太多女友了。
(意味張先生太「花」了，不好)

◉ John needs (a) little assistance.
John 需要一些幫忙。
(如果只用 little，表示幾乎不需要幫忙)

◉ Mr. B. has a little money.
B 先生有一點點錢。
(表示 B 先生雖然錢不多，但仍有一些，比較正面意思)

◉ Mr. C has very little money.
C 先生幾乎沒什麼錢。
(表示 C 先生錢太少，買不起東西，有負面意味)

◉ He cannot help her, because he has very/too little time.
他無法幫她，因為他沒什麼時間。
(表示他根本沒有時間幫她忙，帶有負面意思)

至於可數名詞，表示數量很少時，通常用 few, a few 和 too few，但意義也有些不同。

例如：

◉ Mr. Lee has a few friends.
李先生有幾個朋友。
(表示李先生朋友不多；但還有幾位，有正面意味。a few＝several)

◉ Mr. Wang has too few friends.
王先生沒什麼朋友。
(指王先生朋友很少，很孤單；有負面意味)

可見，使用 much, many, a lot of , a little, a few 都有正面意味；但用 too much, too many 或 too little, too few 都有負面味道。

所以可以說：

- Mr. A is unhappy, because he has too many troubles.
  A 先生不快樂，因為他有太多煩惱。

但不能說：

Mr. A is happy, because he has too many friends.

因為 too many 有負面意味，與句中 happy 不搭調；要把 too many 改為 many 或 a lot of 才是正面意思。

1-2

代名詞與其先行詞

　　顧名思義，代名詞就是代替名詞。使用代名詞的目的，就是避免句中名詞的重覆而令人厭煩。

　　我們不說：

Mr. Wang said Mr. Wang lost Mr. Wang's new bike.
而說：

◉ Mr. Wang said he lost his new bike.
　王先生說他弄丟了他的新腳踏車。
　(he 和 his 就是代替名詞 Mr. Wang)

　　在談代名詞的使用前，要先知道先行詞是什麼，因為先行詞決定了需要使用那一種代名詞。

一、先行詞（antecedent）

　　先行詞就是代名詞所代替的名詞。它可能代替一個字、一個片語或一個句子，通常放在句中代名詞的前面。例如上句 Mr. Wang 就是代名詞 he 和 his 的先行詞。

◉ I saw John and spoke to him.
　我看到 John，並且跟他說話。
　(John 就是 him 的先行詞)

◉ California is popular because it has a mild climate.
　加州因氣候溫暖而令人喜愛。
　(California 就是代名詞 it 的先行詞)

◉ When the Wangs moved back to Taiwan, they gave their cat to John.
　王家人搬回台灣時，把貓送給了 John。
　(the Wangs 指王家的人，是代名詞 they 和 their 的先行詞)

◉ The father and husband brought his family from Taiwan to the U.S.
爸爸／老公帶著全家從台灣搬來美國。
(the father and husband 指一個人，當集合名詞，是代名詞 his 的先行詞。如果是 the father and the husband, 則是兩個人，代名詞就要用多數 their families)

◉ The workers' union is ready to strike for the new contract that its members have been promised.
工會準備罷工以要求資方履行承諾新的合約。
(union 是代名詞 its 的先行詞；把工會當為一個單位，所以代名詞也用單數的所有格)

◉ Trying to write a good article is hard work; it takes years of practice.
想寫一篇好文章不容易，需要多年的練習。
(trying to write a good article 是片語，也是代名詞 it 的先行詞；把寫好文章當成一回事，故用單數 it，真正的主詞是 trying)

◉ Taking care of elderly persons can be rewarding, but it requires a lot of kindness and patience.
照料老年人是蠻有意義的事，不過需要許多的愛心和耐心。
(taking care of elderly persons 是片語，是代名詞 it 的先行詞；把照顧老人當成一件事，故用單數 it)

◉ I hear that Mr. A is sick and this really worries me.
我聽說 A 先生病了，真令我擔心。
(that Mr. A is sick 是附屬句，也是代名詞 this 的先行詞；this 代替 A 先生病了這件事，故用單數，也可用 it)

◉ As the data are obsolete, we can't use them any longer.
由於資料陳舊，我們不能再用。
(data 是代名詞 them 的先行詞，是複數，所以也用複數代名詞) (data 的單數是 datum，通常都用多數)

◉ The tennis team left their seats and moved toward the court.
網球隊員離開座位，走進球場。
(team 是代名詞 their 的先行詞；因為 team 本是集合名詞，但這裡指隊員們，係複數，所以代名詞也是複數)

◉ Most dogs behave intelligently if they are well trained.
大多數的狗如果好好訓練，舉止都很聰明。
(dogs 是代名詞 they 的先行詞)

◉ Research and development had its budget slashed this semester.
這學期研發部門的經費被縮減。
(research and development 是代名詞 its 的先行詞，當作一個 unit，所以是單數，代名詞也用單數)

有時，先行詞也可以放在代名詞的後面：

◉ Because of its climate, Florida is Mr. A's favorite place.
因為天氣的關係，佛州是 A 先生喜愛的地方。
(先行詞 Florida 是放在代名詞 its 的後面)

◉ In his report, Mr. B explained the action taken by the legislature.
在他的報告中，B 先生解釋立法當局所採取的行動。
(先行詞 Mr. B 放在代名詞 his 的後面)

但有時代名詞沒有先行詞：

例如：

◉ Who will represent our school？
誰會代表我們的學校？
(代名詞 Who，沒有指定什麼人，所以沒有先行詞)

◉ Everything was destroyed in the fire.
火災燒毀了一切。
(代名詞 everything，沒有特指什麼，故無先行詞)

從上述的許多例句中可以知道：代名詞的單複數、陽性、陰性或中性，都必須與其先行詞一致。這點，在下面談代名詞的用法時，也會提及。

二、代名詞的種類

代名詞大致可歸類為六種。

1. 人稱代名詞(personal pronouns)

這是最常用的代名詞，也就是指自己，指他人或指其他事物。

第一人稱單數：I, me, my, mine
第一人稱多數：we, us, our, ours
第二人稱單複數相同：you, your, yours
第三人稱單數：he, him, his；she, her, hers；it, its
第三人稱多數：they, them, their, theirs

例如：

◉ Miss A brought her friends a cake for their party.
A 小姐為她朋友的宴會帶了一個蛋糕。
(her 和 their 都是人稱代名詞所有格)

◉ The movie does not live up to its ads, but it has an interesting ending.
電影不如廣告所說的那麼好，但結局變有趣。
(its 是代名詞所有格；it 是代名詞主格；movie 是先行詞)

人稱代名詞的主格、所有格、受格後面再談。

2. 反身代名詞(reflexive pronouns)

就是用 -self 或 -selves 表示在句中所指的名詞或代名詞。

第一人稱單數：myself（多數是 ourselves）

第二人稱單數：yourself（多數是 yourselves）

第三人稱單數：himself, herself, itself（多數是 themselves）

例如：

⊚ The boy keeps telling himself he is not afraid of dogs.
這男孩一直對自己說他不怕狗。
（himself 是反身代名詞；boy 是先行詞）

⊚ John and Bob bought two tickets for themselves.
John 和 Bob 為他們自己買了兩張票。
（themselves 是反身代名詞；John & Bob 是先行詞）

有時反身代名詞的使用，只是為了加強名詞或代名詞的意思，有人稱之為加強語氣代名詞(intensive pronoun)。如果不用，也不影響句子的意思，這種加強語意的代名詞多半緊跟著先行詞。

例如：

⊚ I myself have never questioned his honesty.
我本身從未懷疑過他的誠實。
（myself 只是加強代名詞 I 的語氣，緊跟著先行詞 I，也可以省略）

⊚ The college president himself attended the meeting.
大學校長親自參加開會。
（himself 只是加強語氣，緊跟著先行詞 president）

有時也可放在句尾：

◉ John fixed the computer himself.
John 自己修理電腦。
(himself 指先行詞 John，只是加強語氣)

◉ Mr. and Mrs. B wallpapered their bedroom themselves.
B 先生夫婦自己貼了臥房的壁紙。
(themselves 是指先行詞 Mr. and Mrs. B 只是加強語氣)

3. 指示代名詞 (demonstrative pronouns)

就是指人、地、物；也可放在先行詞的前或後。

單數	多數
this	these
that	those

this 和 these 多半指較近的；that 和 those 多半指較遠的。

例如：

◉ This is the picture I like.
這是我喜歡的圖畫。
(指示代名詞 this 放在先行詞 picture 的前面，指較近的圖畫)

◉ These are the tomatoes from Jen's garden.
這些番茄來自任氏菜園。
(指示代名詞 these，放在先行詞 tomatoes 前)

◉ I need to buy some sugar and salt; those are essential to the taste.
我要買些糖和鹽；那些是調味的要素。
(指示代名詞 those，放在先行詞 sugar and salt 之後)

4. 關係代名詞(relative pronouns)

就是引導句中附屬子句和主要子句的連接之用。

關係代名詞有：that, which, who, whose, whom

例如：

- Here is the book that I like to read.
  這是我喜歡讀的那本書。
  (由 that 所引導的附屬子句 that I like to read 與主要子句 here is the book 連接起來)

- He bought an old car which needs some repairs.
  他買了一部需要修理的舊車。
  (由 which 所引導的附屬子句 which needs some repairs 和主要子句 he bought an old car 連接起來)

- The woman whom you met last night is my friend.
  你昨晚遇到的那個女生是我朋友。
  (由 whom 所引導的附屬子句 whom you met last night 與主要子句 the woman is my friend 連在一起)

- Mr. B, whose house you just passed, is a lawyer.
  B 先生是律師；你剛從他家門口經過。
  (由關係代名詞 whose 所引導的附屬子句 whose house you just passed 與主要句 Mr. B is a lawyer 連接起來)

以上句中的附屬子句，其實也是形容詞子句。

5. 疑問代名詞(interrogative pronouns)

就是指 what, which, who, whose, whom。

例如：

⊙ What do you take me for?
你把我當成什麼？

⊙ What do you mean by that?
你是什麼意思？
(以上兩句，都沒有先行詞，因為沒有指定什麼東西)

⊙ Who will go with you to the party?
誰要跟你去參加宴會？
(沒有先行詞)

⊙ Whom did you want to speak to?＝To whom did you want to speak?
你要跟誰說話？
(沒有先行詞)

⊙ Which is the shortest way to the post office?
到郵局哪一條路最近？
(way 是 which 的先行詞)

疑問代名詞，除 which 多半有先行詞外，其餘很少有先行詞。

6. 不定代名詞(indefinite pronouns)

也是指人、地、物，有時沒有指定那一個；有時也沒有先行詞。最常用的不定代名詞有：

指單數：another, anybody, anyone, anything, each, every, either, everybody, everyone, everything, little, much, neither, nobody, no one, nothing, one, other, somebody, someone, something

指多數：both, few, many, others, several

指單數或多數：all, any, more, most, none, some

例如：

◉ Anyone can volunteer to work in the nursing home.
任何人都可以在養老院當義工。
(不定代名詞 anyone，沒有指定那個人，所以沒有先行詞)

◉ Few are willing to donate money.
很少人願意捐款。
(few 是複數的不定代名詞，沒有先行詞)

◉ Somebody has brought his guitar to the party.
有人帶自己的吉他到宴會。
(不定代名詞 somebody 指單數，人稱代名詞也用單數所有格 his 或 her)

◉ None of my friends wished me a happy birthday.
我的朋友都沒有祝我生日快樂。
(不定代名詞 none，可指單數或複數)

◉ Anyone is welcome to try out his skills.
歡迎任何人試試他的能力。
(不定代名詞 anyone，指單數，動詞也用單數 is)

◉ Either of the articles is satisfactory to him.
隨便哪篇文章，他都滿意。
(不定代名詞 either，指單數，所以動詞也用單數 is)

◉ Neither of the teachers attends the birthday party.
沒有一位老師參加生日宴會。
(不定代名詞 neither，指單數，所以動詞也用單數 attends)

◉ Each of the proposals has been accepted.
每個提議都被接受。
(不定代名詞 each，是單數，動詞也用 has)

三、人稱代名詞有三種格：

也就是主格、所有格和受格。

1. 主格(nominative case)

用做句子的主詞或表語主格（predicate nominative）也叫表語名詞。

單數是：I, you, he, she, it; 多數是：we, you, they

例如：

◉ Mr. A and I are good friends.
A 先生和我是好友。
(I 與 Mr. A 都是主詞，故用主格)

◉ The Lins and we live near the park.
林家和我們都住在公園附近。
(we 和 the Lins 都是主詞，故用主格)

◉ Our college president for ten years has been he.
十年來，我們大學的校長一直都是他。
(he 是主詞 president 的表語主格，說明校長是誰)

◉ The person who helped us is she.
幫忙我們的人是她。
(she 是主詞 person 的表語主格，說明主詞是誰)

◉ It was he who wrote the article for the magazine.
為雜誌寫文章的就是他。
(he 是主詞的 it 表語主格，故是主格)

但在口頭上，也有人用受格：

It was me/her/us/them who....

其實應該用主格，才合乎文法：

It was I/she/we/they who....

例如：

⊙ It seems to have been they who made the proposal.
提出建議的似乎是他們。
(不用受格 them)

⊙ It must have been he who raised the question.
提出問題的一定是他。
(不用受格 him)

為了禮貌起見，要先提別人，再提自己：

例如：

⊙ John and I will not attend the party.
約翰和我將不會參加宴會。
(不說 I and John)

⊙ You and we should get together sometime.
你和我們改天應該聚聚。
(不說 we and you)

2. 所有格(possessive case)

表示對名詞的所有權。

單數：my, mine; your, yours; his; her, hers; its

多數：our, ours; your, yours; their, theirs

例如：

◉ Is this sofa his or hers?
這沙發是他的還是她的？
（his 和 hers 都是所有格）

◉ The lion escaped from its cage.
獅子從籠子裡跑了。
（its 指獅子所用的所有格，也修飾 cage；不能寫成 it's）

◉ The conference room is ours for tomorrow afternoon.
明天下午，會議室是屬於我們使用的。
（ours 是所有格，指使用的所有權，不能寫成 our's）

◉ The white station wagon is theirs.
這輛白色旅行車是他們的。
（theirs 指所有權，不能寫成 their's；theirs＝their station wagon）

◉ Ours is the first house on the right.
我們的房子是右邊第一棟。
＝The first house on the right is ours.
（不能寫成 our's；ours＝our house）

◉ Hers was the best article in the writing contest.
寫作比賽中，她的文章最好。
＝The best article in the writing contest was hers.
（不能寫成 her's；hers＝her article）

因為所有格能修飾名詞，所以也能修飾動名詞(gerund)：

例如：

◉ Did Miss Lee notice his waiting outside?
李小姐知道他在外面等著嗎？
（所有格 his 修飾動名詞 waiting，著重 waiting 的動作）

如果說：

◉ Did Miss Lee notice him waiting outside?
李小姐有注意到他在外面等著嗎？
(這裡的 waiting 是現在分詞，修飾受詞 him，著重 him 這個人)

◉ What do you think of John's singing?
你覺得 John 歌唱得如何？
(所有格 John's，修飾動名詞 singing，著重唱歌的行為)

◉ Can you imagine John singing?
(這裡的 singing 是現在分詞，修飾 John，表示懷疑 John 能唱歌)

3. 受格(objective case)

作動詞的直接受詞、間接受詞和介詞受詞。

單數用：me, you, him, her, it

多數用：us, you, them

例如：

◉ In public, Mrs. Wang's high-pitched voice embarrassed me and him.
王太太在公共場合，尖銳的說話聲讓我和他都感到難為情。
(me 和 him 作動詞 embarrassed 的直接受詞，故用受格)

◉ Mr. A sent us and them a care package respectively.
A 先生分別寄給我們和他們一份禮物包裹。
(us 和 them 是動詞 sent 的間接受詞，故用受格；package 是直接受詞)

◉ Everyone laughed except her and me.
除了她和我外，每個人都笑了。
(her 和 me 是介詞 except 的受詞，故用受格)

◉ With you and them on our team, I am sure we will win.
有你和他們在我們隊上，我相信我們會贏。
(you 和 them 是介詞 with 的受詞，故用受格)

四、注意事項

1. who 是主格，whom 是受格，使用時也要小心。

who 和 whom 是關係代名詞，也是疑問代名詞

例如：

◉ Who will be the next president of our college?
誰是我們大學下屆的校長？
(who 是主詞，做疑問代名詞，故是主格)

◉ Who was the captain of the team?
誰是隊長？
(who 是主詞，故是主格；是直接問句)

◉ She asked who the captain of the team was.
她問誰是隊長。
(who 是附屬句的主詞，也是主格；是間接問句)

◉ John is somebody whom I have confidence in.
我對 John 這個人有信心。
＝John is somebody in whom I have confidence.
(whom 是介詞 in 的受詞，故是受格。somebody 也可用 the one 代替)

◉ Mr. A is a teacher who I know is reliable.
A 先生是一位老師，我知道他很可靠。
＝Mr. A is a teacher I know (that) he is reliable.
(who 和 he 都是指 teacher，所以是主格)

◉ Mr. A is a teacher whom I know to be reliable.
　＝Mr. A is a teacher. I know him to be reliable.
　(意思同上句，但本句的whom 和 him 都是指 teacher，故是受格)

◉ Whom did you get the package from?
　＝From whom did you get the package?
　你從誰那裡取得包裹？
　(whom 是介詞 from 的受詞，故是受格；介詞放在句首較好)

2. its 是指事物的所有格，而 it's 是 it is。

例如：

◉ The family needed help with its problem.
　這個家庭的問題需要幫忙。
　(its 指家庭，是所有格，修飾 problem，不是 it's)

◉ The election results are in; it's all over.
　選舉的結果出來，選舉就結束了。
　(it's＝it is；it 指選舉這件事)

3. 使用代名詞 it, him, her 時，必須清楚地指明是什麼，不可模擬兩可。

例如：

◉ If the cat does not eat the food, take it away.
　貓不吃的話，就把它拿走。
　(it 可指 cat，也可指 food，故不清楚)

　應該說：Take the cat away if it does not eat the food. (it 指 cat)
　或：Take the food away if the cat does not eat it. (it 指 food)

◉ When Mr. Wang visited John, he had a good time.
王先生拜訪 John 時，他玩得很愉快。
(he 可指 Mr. Wang 也可指 John，故不清楚)

應該說：When he visited John, Mr. Wang had a good time.
或：John had a good time when Mr. Wang visited him.
(he 指 Mr. Wang；him 指 John)

◉ In this book, it talks about Chinese politics.
這本書談到中國的政治。
(在這裡，in 是多餘的，it 也不指任何東西)

只要說：The book talks about Chinese politics 就行了。

4. 遇到句子作比較時，在 than 和 as 後面的代名詞，是否用主格或受格，多半要看句中的意思以及省了什麼字後，再作決定。

例如：

◉ Mr. A visited her more than (he visited) me.
A 先生拜訪她比他拜訪我多。

◉ Mr. A visited her more than I (visited her).
A 先生拜訪她比我拜訪她多。
(上面兩句，如把括號裡的字省去，就能知道用受格 me，或主格 I，但意思不同)

◉ He runs faster than you or I (run).
他跑得比你我都快。

也就是：

◉ He runs faster than you (run) or I (run).
(把 run 省略，就知道用主格 you 和 I；但用 me 就不通)

◎ Mr. B played basketball as often as I (played basketball).
　B 先生跟我一樣常打籃球。
　(用 me 就不行)

◎ They blamed John as much as (they blamed) us.
　他們責備 John 和責備我們一樣。

◎ They blamed John as much as we (blamed John).
　他們責備 John 和我們責備他一樣。
　(如把括號裡的字省略，就知道用 us 或 we，但意思不同)

1-3
動詞的形式

在英語裡，動詞最重要，因為沒有動詞，就沒有句子。動詞是指一個動作（action），一個狀態（condition）或一種存在（existence）。

動詞通常有五種形式：動作動詞、及物和不及物動詞、連綴動詞、助動詞、語氣助動詞。

一、動作動詞（action verb）

大部分的動詞，都屬於動作動詞。就是表示某人或某物如何施行（perform）一個動作。但動作動詞又包括可以看見的動作（visible action）和看不見的，只在腦子裡的心理活動（mental action）。

可以看見的動詞諸如：run, swim, eat, smile, jump, walk, open, chase, rip, strike, jog, file, sprout 等等。

例如：

◎ Mr. A jogs two miles every morning.
A 先生每天早上慢跑兩哩路。
(指主詞 A 先生施行跑的動作)

◎ The dog chased the cat in my backyard.
狗在我家後院追著貓。
(說明主詞 dog 追的動作)

◎ Mrs. B filed the bill in the wrong file.
B 太太把帳單存錯檔案。
(指主詞 B 太太存檔的動作)

◉ Lightning struck the building last night.
昨晚閃電打到了建築物。
(指主詞 lightning 所施行的動作)

◉ Weeds sprouted all over my garden this summer.
今夏野草長滿了我的菜園。
(說明了主詞 weeds 的動作)

只在心裡，看不見的動詞，諸如：think, learn, hope, worry, remember, believe, appreciate, dream, wonder, consider, decide, understand, expect, feel, love, dislike 等等。

例如：

◉ Mrs. Wang dreamed of her family in China.
王太太夢見她在中國的家人。
(dreamed 就是看不見的動詞)

◉ Mr. A believes in justice and freedom for all.
A 先生相信大家都有公義和自由。
(believes 就是心理的動詞)

◉ I appreciate your assistance and understanding.
我感謝你的協助和諒解。
(appreciated 也是看不見的動作)

◉ His uncle remembers many terrible events from World War Ⅱ.
他叔叔記得二次世界大戰許多可怕的事情。
(remember 是心理的動詞)

◉ For several days Captain A and his crew have been worrying about not being able to reach land.
幾天來 A 船長和船員為無法登陸而煩惱。
(worried 也是心理的動詞)

二、及物和不及物動詞(transitive and intransitive verb)

及物動詞就是動作涉及某人或某物,所以有受詞(object),也可變成被動語態。而不及物動詞,不涉及他人或事物,故沒有受詞,也不能變成被動語態。換句話說,能回答 whom 或 what 的動詞,就是及物動詞,否則,就是不及物動詞。

及物動詞:

例如:

◉ Bob opened the window with difficulty.
Bob 開窗戶有困難。
(opened 是及物動詞;window 是 open 的直接受詞,回答了開了什麼)

◉ A stray cat followed me home.
流浪貓跟我回家。
(followed 是及物動詞;me 是 followed 的直接受詞,回答了跟誰)

◉ Mrs. Wang planted many flowers along her driveway.
王太太沿著停車道,種了許多花。
(planted 是及物動詞;flowers 是 planted 的直接受詞,回答種了什麼)

◉ Later in the week, Mr. B prepared the entire report.
該週稍後,B 先生準備整個報告。
(prepared 是及物動詞;report 是 prepared 的直接受詞,回答準備了什麼)

◉ Mr. J wrote an article for *World Journal*.
J 先生為《世界日報》寫了篇文章。
(wrote 是及物動詞;article 是直接受詞)

也可變成被動語態：An article was written for World Journal by Mr. J.

◉ Amy gave her mother a box of cookies.
　Amy 給她媽媽一盒餅乾。
　＝Amy gave a box of cookies to her mother.

可見及物動詞後面的名詞或代名詞能回答「給誰？」（to whom?）或「為誰？」（for whom?）的字眼，就是間接受詞。

上句及物動詞是 gave；給的對象是 mother，故是間接受詞；給的物品是 cookies，故是直接受詞。

有直接和間接受詞時，也可改為被動語態：

A box of cookies was given to her mother by Amy.
（直接受詞當主詞）
＝Her mother was given a box of cookies by Amy.
（間接受詞當主詞）

不及物動詞：

例如：

◉ Mrs. Lin sings at church every Sunday.
　林太太每星期天在教堂唱歌。
　（不能回答唱什麼，沒有受詞，所以 sings 是不及物動詞；church 是介詞 at 的受詞）

◉ My daughter frequently smiles at the baby in her arms.
　我女兒常常對著她懷裡的嬰兒微笑。
　（smiles 是不及物動詞，沒有受詞；baby 是介詞 at 的受詞）

⦿ John continually complains about his job.
John 不斷地埋怨他的工作。
(complains 是不及物動詞，沒有受詞；job 是介詞 about 的受詞)

也可以說，不及物動詞，加上介詞後，就有受詞了。

然而許多的動作動詞(action verb)，可作及物動詞，也可作不及物動詞，要看句子的意思而定。

例如：

⦿ Mr. J reads World Journal every day.
J 先生每天都看《世界日報》。
(reads 是及物動詞，World Journal 是直接受詞)

⦿ Mrs. Wang reads to her child at bedtime.
王太太在孩子睡前唸書給他聽。
(reads 是不及物動詞，沒有受詞；child 是介詞 to 的受詞)

⦿ Mary walked her dog before going to work.
Mary 上班前遛狗。
(walked 是及物動詞；dog 是直接受詞)

⦿ Mary walked to the podium and gave a speech.
Mary 走到講台，發表演說。
(walked 是不及物動詞，沒有受詞；podium 是介詞 to 的受詞)

三、連綴動詞(linking verb)

連綴動詞不表示動作，它只是一種狀態或存在。它可以把主詞和另一個名詞、代名詞、形容詞或介詞片語等連繫在一起。最常用的連綴動詞是 be，也就是 be 動詞。
參閱："verb to be" 的型式(form) P.060

例如:

◉ John is the winner.
John 是得勝者。
(連綴動詞 is,把 John 和另一個名詞 winner 連在一起,說明主詞是什麼)

◉ An oral recommendation will be enough.
口頭推薦就夠了。
(will be 是連綴動詞;把主詞 recommendation 和形容詞 enough 連接起來)

◉ I am always the last person in line.
排隊時,我總是最後一位。
(am 是連綴動詞,把主詞 I 和名詞 person 連在一起,說明了主詞是什麼)

◉ He is being rude.
他蠻無禮的。
(is being 是連綴動詞,把主詞 he 與形容詞 rude 連接起來,修飾了主詞;用進行式 is being,表示無禮是暫時性的)

◉ This group of actors had been successful on the stage.
這群演員在台上表演得很成功。
(had been 是連綴動詞,把主詞 group 和形容詞 successful 連在一起,說明了主詞)

◉ The cutting board should be in the kitchen.
切菜板應該在廚房。
(should be 是連綴動詞,把主詞 cutting board 和介詞片語 in the kitchen 連在一起,說明主詞)

連綴動詞除 be 動詞之外,還有以下幾個動詞,也屬連綴動詞,其用法與 be 動詞一樣。

諸如：appear, become, feel, grow, look, remain, seem, smell, sound, stay, taste, turn

例如：

◉ Mr. Chen feels a little lonely at times.
陳先生有時候會感到有點寂寞。
(feels 是連綴動詞，把主詞 Mr. Chen 和形容詞 lonely 連在一起，說明主詞)

◉ They have remained good friends all their lives.
他們一輩子都是好朋友。
(remain 是連綴動詞，把主詞 they 和 friends 連起來，修飾主詞)

◉ The weather turned suddenly colder during the day.
白天天氣突然變冷。
(連綴動詞 turned，把主詞 weather 和形容詞 colder 連在一起，說明主詞)

◉ His father grew tired from the long walk.
他爸爸走了遠路後，覺得疲倦。
(grew 是連綴動詞，連繫 father 和 tired，修飾主詞)

◉ At this moment, Mary appears cheerful.
此刻 Mary 顯得興高采烈。
(appears 是連綴動詞，把主詞 Mary 和形容詞 cheerful 連在一起，修飾主詞)

◉ The white sandy beach looks inviting.
白色的沙灘看來很吸引人。
(looks 是連綴動詞，把主詞 beach 和形容詞 inviting 連接起來，說明主詞)

◉ Mr. A sounded happy about the results.
A 先生對結果似乎很高興。
(連綴動詞 sounded，連接 Mr. A 和 happy，修飾主詞)

⊙ The fried chicken stayed fresh and crisp.
炸雞保持新鮮和酥脆。
(stayed 是連綴動詞，連接主詞 chicken 和形容詞 fresh and crisp，修飾主詞)

　　不過，這些連綴動詞，有時也當做動作動詞。要想區分出連綴動詞和動作動詞，可用 am, was, is, are 來代入句中，如果合理，就是連綴動詞，否則就是動作動詞。

例如：

⊙ The apple tasted sweet.
蘋果嚐起來很甜。
(如果把 tasted 改為 is 或 was，還是合理，故是連綴動詞)

⊙ I tasted the apple.
我嚐了蘋果。
(如把 tasted 改為 am 或 was，就不合理，故是動作動詞)

⊙ The tree has grown very tall.
樹長得很高。
(如把 has grown 改用 is，也合理，故是連綴動詞)

⊙ Mr. J grows tomatoes every year.
J 先生每年種番茄。
(如把 grows 改為 is 或 was 就不通，故是動作動詞)

⊙ Mr. B felt unhappy yesterday.
B 先生昨天不高興。
(felt 可用 was 代替，故是連綴動詞)

⊙ The doctor of Chinese medicine felt my pulse.
中醫量我的脈搏。
(如把 felt 用 was 代替就不通，故是動作動詞)

四、助動詞（helping verb）

又稱輔助動詞（auxiliary verb 或 auxiliaries）。

助動詞加在主要動詞前面，形成動詞片語，進一步表達動作的細節。

除了 be 動詞可當助動詞外，其他常見助動詞還有：do, does, did, has, have, had, shall, should, will, would, can, could, may, might, must。

例如：

- He is writing an article for the magazine.
  他正在為雜誌寫文章。
  （is 是連綴動詞，這裡當助動詞，writing 是主要動詞）

- He will be working on his car tomorrow afternoon.
  明天下午他將修理汽車。
  （will be 是連綴動詞，這裡當助動詞；working 是主要動詞）

- The bus will have arrived tonight at 10:00.
  今晚十點，公車將已到達。
  （will have 是助動詞，放在主要動詞 arrived 前面，形成一種動詞片語；如果只用 arrived，意思就不同）

- The party may have ended by now.
  宴會也許已經結束了。
  （may have 是助動詞，ended 是主要動詞，如果只用 ended，意思就不同）

- That teacher would have been hired by the school.
  那位老師原本會被學校聘用。
  （would have been 是助動詞，hired 是主要動詞）

- The street must be ploughed after a snowstorm.
  暴風雪過後，一定要清除路上的雪。

  (must be 是助動詞，ploughed 是主要動詞；如果只用 ploughed，意思就不同，可見助動詞是幫助動詞的意義。ploughed＝plowed)

- Mr. B has worked here for ten years.
  B 先生已在這裡工作十年了。

  (has 是助動詞，worked 是主要動詞)

注意

助動詞 do, does 和 did，有時只用於加強語氣，不可與真正的助動詞弄錯。

例如：

- I do agree with you on this issue.
  在這問題上，我確實同意你的看法。

  (do 只是加強語氣，表示「確實」，也可以不用；agree 是真正動詞)

- I do not agree with you on this issue. (否定)
  或 Do you agree with me on this issue? (疑問)
  (這裡的 do 是真正的助動詞，不能省去)

- Mr. Wang does need to know about the problem.
  王先生的確需要知道這個問題。

  (does 是加強語氣，可以不用；need 是真正動詞)

- Mr. Wang does not need to know about the problem. (否定)
  或 Does Mr. Wang need to know about the problem? (疑問)
  (這裡的 does 是真正的助動詞，不能省去)

- Mary did send the letter to her father.
  Mary 真的有寄信給她爸爸。

  (did 是加強語氣、也可以不用；send 是真正動詞)

◉ Mary did not send the letter to her father. (否定)

或 Did Mary send the letter to her father? (疑問)

（這裡 did 是真正的助動詞，不能省去）

助動詞後面須接原形動詞；此外，助動詞與主要動詞未必都連在一起，有時也會被其他的字眼分開。

(例如：)

◉ Mr. A will definitely not be going with her.

A 先生一定不會與她一同去。

（definitely not 把動詞片語 will be going 分開了）

◉ He had carefully arranged his trip a month in advance.

他在一個月前就細心安排他的旅程。

（carefully 把 had arranged 分開）

◉ John should not even have attempted that risky game.

John 甚至不該嘗試那種危險的遊戲。

（not even 把 should have attempted 分開）

其他分開動詞片語的字，最常用的還有：probably, often, also, not yet, slowly 等等。

五、語氣助動詞（modal auxiliary）

以下這些字，有人歸類為語氣助動詞：may（might）, can（could）, will（would）, shall（should）, had better, must。其用法如下：

might:
本是 may 的過去式，意思是可能、也許、多半。

例如：

◉ She might be at her office.
她可能在她的辦公室。
(但不能確定)

◉ It might be around five o'clock.
也許是五點左右了。
(但不確定)

may:

意思與 might 相同外，還有允許的涵義。

例如：

◉ He may be at home or he may be at school.
他也許在家，也許在學校。
(只是 might 的可能性較少)

◉ May I ask you a question?
我能問你一個問題嗎？
(表示請求對方的許可。非正式時，也可用 can)

can:

表示能力或許可，與 be able to 意義相似。

例如：

◉ Mr. Chen can speak English, but he can't speak it well.
陳先生會說英文，但他說得不好。
(表示說英文的能力)

- Mr. B can swim well.
  ＝Mr. B is able to swim well.
  B 先生游得很好。
  (表示能力)

- Mr. C cannot write well.
  ＝Mr. C is unable/not able to write well.
  C 先生寫得不好。
  (表示能力)

- Can I（或 may I）open the door?
  我能開門嗎？
  (請求對方的許可)

---

could:

本是 can 的過去式，表示客氣的請求或建議，也可指過去的能力或用在假設語態的條件句。

例如：

- Could I borrow your pen for a minute?
  我能借你的筆用一會兒嗎？
  (禮貌的要求)

- You could get a part-time job at the store.
  你可以在店裡找份兼職工作。
  (表示建議)

- When he was young, he could speak French.
  他年輕時會說法文。
  (指過去有說法文的能力)

⦿ If he had 10,000 dollars, he could buy a new car.
假如他有一萬元，他就能買部新車。
（假設語態的條件句）

有時 could 也可用 was/were able to 代替，表示過去的能力。

例如：

⦿ Yesterday, I could find my watch.
＝Yesterday, I was able to find my watch.
或 Yesterday, I was not able（或 unable）to find my watch.

---

will:

用在第二、三人稱時，表示未來式；用在第一人稱時，表示決心或意願，也可用在請人幫忙。

例如：

⦿ What will you do if it rains?
假如下雨，你要做什麼？
（表示未來式）

⦿ I will try to write better articles this year.
今年我要寫更好的文章。
（表示意願或決心）

⦿ Will you help me with this heavy box?
你能幫我搬這個重的箱子嗎？
（請求幫忙）

有時指將來計劃好的事情，也可用 be＋ going to。

例如：

◉ I am going to visit my friend in the hospital.
我要去醫院看我的朋友。
（表示計劃好要去探望）

◉ She is going to shop for a birthday present.
她要去買一份生日禮物。
（表示計劃好要買）

> **would:**
> 本是 will 的過去式，表示禮貌的請求。

例如：

◉ Would you mind turning down the volume on your TV.?
你能把電視的聲音調小聲一點嗎？
（表示客氣的請求，有時也用 do，但不用 will）

◉ Would you drive me there to pick up my car?
你能送我到那裡取我的車嗎？
（表示客氣的請求）

但表示一種 offer 或 invite 時，多半與 would you like 連用。

例如：

◉ Would you like some hot tea?
你要一些熱茶嗎？

◉ What would you like to do now?
你現在想要做什麼呢？

> **shall:**
> 用在第一人稱時，表示未來式；用在第二、第三人稱時，表示按照某種法規。

例如：

◎ I shall see Mr. A tomorrow at 10 a.m.
明早十點，我將見到 A 先生。
(指未來式)

◎ The company shall provide safety equipment for its employees.
公司要為員工提供安全設備。
(指按照法律)

◎ You shall not wear T-shirts in class.
教室裡不能穿短袖汗衫。
(指按規定)

◎ The furniture shall be delivered on Tuesday at 9 a.m.
家具要在星期二早上九點送達。
(指按契約)

should:

本是 shall 的過去式，表示勸告、建議；或對某事的期望、責任、義務、必要或應該。與 ought to 意思相似。

例如：

◎ You should take some medicine for your headache.
＝You ought to take some medicine for your headache.
你頭痛應該服藥。
(表示勸告)

◎ You should not have said that.(較常用)
＝You ought not to have said that.(較少用)
你不應該說那些話。

◉ He should call her and set up an appointment.
他應該打電話給她約個時間。
（表示建議）

◉ The weather should be warmer in March.
三月天氣應該會暖和些。
（表示期望）

◉ You should recommend Mr. Wang for promotion.
你應該推薦王先生晉升。
（表示有義務或責任）

當然，在假設語態裡也用 could, would, might, should 表示條件句。（參見「動詞的語態」）

---

had better:

口語時只用（had）better，與 should 的意思相似，也表示忠告或建議，但比 should 語氣較強，幾乎有「警告」的味道。所以下屬對上級，子女對父母，最好不用，否則不禮貌。

例如：

◉ You（had）better go (to或and) see a doctor; you might need some medication.
你應該去看醫生；你也許需要服藥。
（較強的建議）（go和see之中，省去to或and）

◉ You'd better study harder or you might fail the test.
你應該更努力讀書，否則考試會不及格。
（較強的忠告。you'd better＝you had better; had 也可省去）

---

must:

表示依照規定的一種義務或需要，一般用在正式書面上。也表示對某種情況的推斷。

例如：

◉ All students must register for new semester before September 4.
新學期，所有學生必需在九月四日前註冊。
(表示依照規定)

◉ Applicants for this program must be over 18 years old.
要申請這個計畫，必須要年滿 18 歲。
(按照規定)

◉ You must not use a pencil for this test.
這個考試不可使用鉛筆。
(按照規定)

也有人用 have/has to 代替 must，表示一種義務。但 must 沒有過去式，只能用 had to 去代替。

例如：

◉ Every student has to register before September 5.
每位學生必須在九月五日前註冊。

◉ You have to be sixteen to get a driver license.
你必需年滿 16 歲，才能取得駕駛執照。

◉ It is only 4:30, so he must be at work.
現在才四點半，所以他一定還在上班。
(對情況的判斷)

◉ This big musical center must have a good selection of CDs.
這個大型音樂中心一定有完善的 CD 收藏。
(對情況的判斷)

附註：

"verb to be" 有以下的型式(form):

am, is, are, was, were,

am being, are being, is being,

was being, were being,

can be, could be, may be, might be, must be,

shall be, should be, will be, would be,

have been, has been,

had been, could have been, may have been,

might have been,must have been,

shall have been, should have been,

will have been, would have been

1-4

動詞時態和用法

　　動詞時態(verb tense)在句子裡很重要，因為它說明動作發生的時間是現在、過去或將來，下面介紹平時所用的動詞時態與用法：

一、動詞時態(在此以動詞原式 write 為例)

(一)簡單式

1. 現在簡單式(simple present)：用動詞原式

　　⊙ He writes for a living.
　　　他以寫作謀生。
　　　(因為第三人稱單數，故用 writes)

2. 過去簡單式(simple past)：用動詞過去式

　　⊙ He wrote a book last year.
　　　他去年寫了一本書。

3. 未來簡單式(simple future)：shall/will＋動詞原式

　　⊙ He will write a book next year.
　　　他明年將要寫一本書。

(二)完成式

1. 現在完成式(present perfect)：have/has＋過去分詞

　　⊙ He has written many articles for the magazine.
　　　他已經為雜誌寫了許多文章。

2. 過去完成式(past perfect)：had＋過去分詞

- He had written his first book by the time he was fifty.
  他在 50 歲前寫了第一本書。

3. 未來完成式(future perfect)：shall/will＋have＋過去分詞

- He will have written two books by May 2008.
  他在 2008 年 5 月前將會寫完兩本書。

(三)進行式

1. 現在簡單進行式(simple present progressive)： is/are＋現在分詞

- He is writing an article now.
  他現在正在寫一篇文章。

2. 過去簡單進行式(simple past progressive)： was/were＋現在分詞

- He was writing his article when I entered his room.
  當我走進他房間時，他正在寫文章。

3. 未來簡單進行式(simple future progressive)： shall/will＋be＋現在分詞

- He will be writing an article next month.
  下個月他將要寫一篇文章。

4. 現在完成進行式(present perfect progressive)：
   have/has＋been＋現在分詞

   ◉ He has been writing articles for years.
   他寫了多年的文章。

5. 過去完成進行式(past perfect progressive)：
   had＋been＋現在分詞

   ◉ He had been writing articles when he was in Taiwan.
   他在台灣時就在寫文章。

6. 未來完成進行式(future perfect progressive)：
   shall/will＋have＋been＋現在分詞

   ◉ He will have been writing articles for six years by the end of this September.
   到今年 9 月底，他就寫了六年文章了。

   可見動詞有以下常用的四個形式：

   1. 現在式(present tense)。如：write(用在現在和未來簡單式)

   2. 現在分詞(present participle)。如：writing(用在進行式)

   3. 過去式(past tense)。如：wrote(用在過去簡單式)

   4. 過去分詞(past participle)。如：written(用在完成式)

二、動詞的變化

大部分動詞的變化是規則的(regular)，只要在動詞原式(root form)後面加上 d 或 ed 就行了。但是不規則(irregular)動詞的變化很不一樣，必須熟記。

1. 規則動詞：

例如：

動詞原式	過去式	過去分詞	現在分詞
live	lived	lived	living
play	played	played	playing
save	saved	saved	saving
skip	skipped	skipped	skipping
stop	stopped	stopped	stopping
type	typed	typed	typing
wave	waved	waved	waving
work	worked	worked	working

　　動詞原式前面加 to，就是不定詞(infinitive)。live 變成 living 時，後面的 "e" 可省去。skip, stop 變成過去式、現在分詞或過去分詞時，最後的一個子音(consonant)要多加一個 "p"，其他有類似情形的動詞同樣比照辦理。

2. 不規則動詞：

　　以下都是平時最常用的，必須記住。

　　過去式和過去分詞都一樣。

例如：

動詞原式	過去式	過去分詞	現在分詞
bind	bound	bound	binding
build	built	built	building
bring	brought	brought	bringing
buy	bought	bought	buying
catch	caught	caught	catching
fight	fought	fought	fighting
find	found	found	finding
get	got	got/gotten	getting
hold	held	held	holding
keep	kept	kept	keeping
lay	laid	laid	laying
lead	led	led	leading
leave	left	left	leaving
lose	lost	lost	losing
pay	paid	paid	paying
say	said	said	saying
send	sent	sent	sending
sit	sat	sat	sitting
sleep	slept	slept	sleeping

spend	spent	spent	spending
spin	spun	spun	spinning
stand	stood	stood	standing
stick	stuck	stuck	sticking
sting	stung	stung	stinging
swing	swung	swung	swinging
teach	taught	taught	teaching
win	won	won	winning
wind	wound	wound	winding

三個時態都一樣。例如：

動詞原式	過去式	過去分詞	現在分詞
bet	bet	bet	betting
bid	bid	bid	bidding
burst	burst	burst	bursting
cost	cost	cost	costing
cut	cut	cut	cutting
hit	hit	hit	hitting
hurt	hurt	hurt	hurting
let	let	let	letting
read	read	read	reading

put	put	put	putting
set	set	set	setting
shut	shut	shut	shutting
spread	spread	spread	spreading

bet, bid, cut, hit, let, put, set, shut 變成現在分詞時，最後的子音，都要重複。

三個時態都不一樣。例如：

動詞原式	過去式	過去分詞	現在分詞
arise	arose	arisen	arising
be	was were	been	being
bear	bore	born	bearing
blow	blew	blown	blowing
break	broke	broken	breaking
choose	chose	chosen	choosing
do	did	done	doing
draw	drew	drawn	drawing
eat	ate	eaten	eating
fall	fell	fallen	falling
fly	flew	flown	flying
freeze	froze	frozen	freezing

give	gave	given	giving
go	went	gone	going
grow	grew	grown	growing
know	knew	known	knowing
lie	lay	lain	lying
ride	rode	ridden	riding
rise	rose	risen	rising
see	saw	seen	seeing
shake	shook	shaken	shaking
speak	spoke	spoken	speaking
steal	stole	stolen	stealing
strive	strove	striven	striving
swear	swore	sworn	swearing
take	took	taken	taking
tear	tore	torn	tearing
throw	threw	thrown	throwing
wear	wore	worn	wearing
write	wrote	written	writing

註：

以上的過去分詞多半是 n 或 en 結尾。

還有一些動詞原式中有 i 時，變成 a，成為過去式；變成 u，成為過去分詞。例如：

動詞原式	過去式	過去分詞	現在分詞
begin	began	begun	beginning
drink	drank	drunk	drinking
ring	rang	rung	ringing
shrink	shrank	shrunk	shrinking
sing	sang	sung	singing
sink	sank	sunk	sinking
spring	sprang	sprung	springing
swim	swam	swum	swimming

有少數動詞的原式和過去分詞一樣。例如：

動詞原式	過去式	過去分詞	現在分詞
become	became	become	becoming
come	came	come	coming
run	ran	run	running

三、動詞時態的用法

(一)簡單式

1. 現在簡單式：用動詞的原式

(1)表示現在的動作或情況。

例如：

◉ I see what you meant by that remark.
我了解你所說的意思。
(表示現在了解了)

◉ The apples are rotten.
蘋果爛了。
(表示現在爛了)

◉ The old man lives alone.
這名老人獨居。
(表示現在情況；第三人稱單數故用 lives)

(2)表示經常發生的動作或情況。

例如：

◉ Mr. Wang works every day from 8 to 5.
王先生每天八點到五點上班。
(表示經常的行為)

◉ He always arrives late for meetings.
他經常開會遲到。
(表示他的經常的毛病)

◎ It rains a lot in spring.
春天下很多雨。
(表示經常的情況)

◎ Mrs. Wang eats a light lunch every day. (或 Mrs. Wang eats light lunches.)
王太太午餐吃得很少。
(日常的習慣)

(3)表示一般不變的事實或是科學上的根據。

例如：

◎ Human blood is red.
人類的血液是紅色的。
(是事實)

◎ The sun rises in the east.
太陽從東方昇起。
(是事實)

◎ The physician warned us that too many sweets are not good for our health.
醫生警告我們吃太多甜食對健康不好。
(雖然前面用過去式動詞 warned，但後面還是用現在式動詞 are，因為這是科學上的根據)

◎ Young people need eight hours of sleep every day.
年輕人每天需要八小時的睡眠。
(這是醫學上的根據)

2. 過去簡單式：用動詞的過去式

表示動作或情況已經發生，或在過去某一時間內發生一次或多次，也許一分鐘前，也許 10 年、20 年、50 年前，但不延續到現在。

> **例如：**

- ⦿ He went home last week.
  他上星期回家。

- ⦿ Mr. Wang wrote a book five years ago.
  王先生五年前寫了一本書。

- ⦿ Many people saw the accident.
  許多人看到這個意外事件。
  ＝The accident was seen by many people.（被動）

也可用 used to 代替：

- ⦿ Mr. Wang used to work here.
  王先生過去在這裡工作過。
  ＝Mr. Wang formerly worked here.
  ＝Mr. Wang worked here.
  ＝Mr. Wang did work here.（加強語氣）
  王先生的確曾經在這裡工作過。

3. 未來簡單式：shall/will＋動詞原式

表示未來某個時間的動作或情況。

> **例如：**

- ⦿ He will be home next week.
  他下星期回家。

- ⦿ Mr. Wang hopes that we shall go there with him tomorrow.
  王先生希望我們明天跟他一起去那裡。

⊚ His new job will begin in July.
他的新工作將在 7 月開始。

有時也可以用 going to 或 about to 代替：

⊚ He is going to buy a new car next week.
下星期他將買一部新車。
＝He will buy a new car next week.
＝He is about to buy a new car next week.
＝The new car is to be bought (by him) next week.（被動）

(二)完成式

1. 現在完成式：have/has＋過去分詞

　　表示一種動作或情況在過去發生，直到說話為止，已經結束或完成。（也可能動作或情況還在持續，但可能性較少）

（例如：）

⊚ Mr. Chang has finished his project.
張先生已經完成他的方案。

⊚ I have waited here for two hours.
我在這裡已經等了兩小時。
（可能繼續等下去）
但是 I have been waiting here for two hours.
（強調我還在繼續等下去）

⊚ How long has Mrs. Lin been here?
林太太在這裡多久了？

2. 過去完成式：had＋過去分詞

表示過去一個動作或情況，發生在另一個過去的動作或情況之前。

例如：

⊚ I had left before he did.
我比他先離開。
(我離開的動作在先，他離開的動作在後。did＝left)

⊚ Mr. A had been healthy before he caught T.B.
A 先生在得肺結核之前很健康。
(健康在先，得肺結核在後)

⊚ After I had washed the car, it rained very hard.
我洗完汽車後，下起大雨。
(洗車在先，下雨在後)

可見，如果要表示過去兩個動作或情況的先後，那麼用過去完成式較好。否則，也可用過去簡單式。

例如：

⊚ He talked to his wife before the meeting started.
他在開會前與太太談話。
(雖然談話在先，開會在後，但沒有強調動作的先後次序)

3. 未來完成式：shall/will＋have＋過去分詞

表示在將來某一個時間裡，可以完成某項事情或狀況。

例如：

- I will have left by the time you arrive.
  你到達時，我將已經離開。
  (雖然到達時間也是未來，但不用 will arrive)

- We shall have been up for hours before you call.
  你打電話給我們以前，我們將已起床幾個小時了。
  (也不用 you will call)

- After he buys the new car, he will have spent all his money.
  他買新車之後將會把錢花光。
  (也不用 he will buy)

由於美國人現在喜歡使用簡短的句子，所以有人用將來簡單式代替將來完成式。

例如：

- My boss will read the report by Friday.
  我老闆星期五就會看過報告。
  (因為 will read 比 will have read 更簡單)

(三)進行式的用法

1. 現在簡單進行式：(is/are＋現在分詞)

表示動作或情況，現在正在進行中。

例如：

- He is working on his dissertation.
  他正在寫他的論文。

- It is raining very hard, so I am staying at home.
  雨下得很大，所以我留在家裡。

但是 am, is, are＋going＋不定詞也可代替未來簡單式。

（例如：）

◉ What are you going to do next weekend?
　＝What will you do next weekend?
　下週末你要做什麼？

◉ I am going to write a letter tomorrow.
　＝I will write a letter tomorrow.
　我明天要寫一封信。

要注意的是：動作動詞（action verb），才能用進行式。不是動作動詞，例如 own, possess, like, need, seem, prefer,等，不能用進行式。

不能說：I am owning two cars.

只能說：I own two cars.

如果 have 的意思是 possess，也不能用進行式。

不說：I am having a new car.

只說：I have a new car.

假如：have 的意思是 do some kind of action，那麼可以用進行式。例如：

◉ I am having a good time.
　我玩得很開心。

◉ He is having a party/a problem
　他正舉行派對／正有個麻煩。

2. 過去簡單進行式：(was/were＋現在分詞)

指某一個動作或情況在過去的某一時間內進行中。

例如：

◉ Mr. A was walking in the park around 5 p.m. yesterday.
昨天下午大約五點鐘，A 先生正在公園裡走路。

◉ He was working on a book last summer.
去年暑假，他正在寫書。

◉ Bob was being agreeable yesterday on that topic.
昨天 Bob 對那個話題，沒有提出反對意見。

至於動詞 be，一般容易弄錯，其實它的基本形式就是：

(to) be, being, was(were), (have 或 has)been；「be 動詞」不是 動作動詞通常不用進行式，但表示「暫時性」時就可以用。

諸如上句：Bob was being agreeable...(說不定，過後又反對了)

◉ Am I being silly?
我這樣做愚蠢嗎？
(即使愚蠢，也是指一時，不是長久的)

be 的其他時態是：

He is a student.(現在簡單式)

He was a student.(過去簡單式)

He will be a student.(未來簡單式)

He has been a student.(現在完成式)

He had been a student.(過去完成式)

He will have been a student. (未來完成式)

3. 未來簡單進行式：shall 或 will＋be＋現在分詞

指一個動作或情況，將在未來某一個時間內進行，

- ◉ I will be working as a volunteer after my retirement.
  我退休後要當義工。

- ◉ Mr. Wang will be seeing his old friend next week.
  王先生下星期將見到老朋友。

但是許多美國人喜歡用未來簡單式代替未來簡單進行式。所以上面兩句就成為：

I will work as a volunteer after my retirement.

Mr. Wang will see his old friend next week.

4. 現在完成進行式：(have 或 has＋been＋現在分詞)

表示過去一個動作或情況，一直延續到現在說話的時候，而且還在延續中。

例如：

- ◉ I have been living in this house for 30 years.
  我住在這棟房子已經 30 年了。
  (強調還在住)

比較：

I have lived in this house for 30 years.
(可能不再住了)

⊚ He has been reading a novel for five weeks.
五星期來，他都在看一本小說。
(強調還在看)

比較：

He has read a novel for five weeks.
(可能不再看了)

⊚ What has he been studying all this week?
他這週都在唸什麼？

⊚ He has been studying English all this week.
他這週都在唸英文。
(以上兩句都是強調「一直繼續下去」的行為)

5. 過去完成進行式：had＋been＋現在分詞

表示過去某一動作或情況，雖然當時還在進行，但在某種程度上，已經完成。現在許多人多用過去簡單進行式代替。

例如：

⊚ I had been sleeping when he called. (不常用)
他打電話來時，我那時候正在睡。
不過：I was sleeping when he called. (較常用)

⊚ He had been grading papers when I came. (不常用)
我來的時候，他正在改考卷。
不過：He was grading papers when I came. (較常用)

6. 未來完成進行式：shall/will＋have＋been＋現在分詞

指未來某一個動作或情況；將在另一個動作或情況之前繼續進行。現在許多人用未來完成式替代。

例如：

◉ When we meet next week, he will have been practicing tennis for five months.
下星期我們見面時，他將已練習網球五個月。（不常用）

不過：When we meet next week, he will have practiced tennis for five months.（較常用）

◉ By the time the new semester starts, I will have been working here for two years.
在新學期開始的時候，我將已在這裡工作兩年了。（不常用）

不過：By the time the new semester starts, I will have worked here for two years.（較常用）

◉ By the time I retire, I will have been working here 30 years.
等我退休時，我就在這裡工作 30 年了。

可見現在美國人很少使用過去完成進行式和未來完成進行式，也許這是因為大家講求句子簡短明瞭的緣故。

四、注意

1. 動詞時態，有時也要前後一致，不能隨意改變。

例如：

◉ Mr. Wang resigned from his job, but later realized he made a mistake.
王先生辭職過後就了解自己錯了。
（前面動詞用過去式 resigned，後面動詞也要用過去式 realized 和 made）

⊙ He went to college where he became interested in chemistry.
他進了大學後，對化學產生了興趣。
（前面動詞用過去式 went，後面的動詞也用過去式 became）

但是表示時間上的不同，亦可改變。

例如：

⊙ Mr. Chen moved to New York where he now manages a grocery store.
陳先生搬到紐約，現在經營一家雜貨店。
（雖然用過去式 moved，但現在還在做，故用現在式 manages）

⊙ I admire the courage that Mr. Lin showed.
我欽佩林先生表現出來的勇氣。
（雖然他勇氣的表現是用過去式 showed，但我至今還在欽佩，故用現在式 admire）

2. 假如過去有兩個動作或情況發生時間不分先後，則用過去簡單式，例如：

⊙ Mr. A bought the material and repaired the house.
A 先生買材料修房子。
（不在乎買材料和修房子的先後）

⊙ After I came home, it rained cats and dogs.
我回家後，下起了傾盆大雨。
（不在乎回家和下雨時間的先後）

但是如果要強調過去兩個動作有先後發生的次序，那麼先發生的動作，用過去完成式；後發生的動作，用過去簡單式。

例如：

◉ Mr. A repaired the house after he had bought the material.
A 先生買了材料後，修了房子。
(表示買材料在先，修房子在後)

◉ After I had come home, it rained very hard.
我回家之後，雨下得很大。
(表示回家在先，下雨在後)

3. 句中的完成式，如果第二個動詞的助動詞也是 have、has
或 had 時，那麼可以省去。

(例如：)

◉ The cup had fallen from the shelf and (had) broken.
杯子從架上掉下來並打破了。
(第二個 had 可省去)

◉ He has taken the car and (has) driven to the mall.
他牽車並開到購物中心。
(第二個 has 可省去)

1-5
動詞的語氣
和語態

動詞裡的語氣（mood）和語態（voice）也是平時常用的。本章要談的，主要是假設語氣（subjunctive mood）和主動與被動語態（active and passive voice）。

動詞裡的語氣，通常分為三種：陳述語氣（indicative mood）、祈使語氣（imperative mood）和假設語氣。我們平常所用的多半是陳述語氣。而祈使語氣，只用於祈求或命令句裡。

(例如：)

◉ Be polite to others all the time.
時時以禮待人。

◉ Give me a cup of tea.
給我一杯茶。

◉ Please reply to my letter at your convenience.
請你方便時回我的信。

一、假設語氣

有人認為假設語氣是一種條件句（conditional sentence），因為它們都包括一個主要子句（main clause）和一個附屬子句（subordinate clause）。現分述如下：

1. 假設語氣，有時可用陳述句的條件方式來表達。

(例如：)

◉ If he has the money, he will buy a house.
假如他有錢，他就會買房子。
(if 句放在前面時，其後加逗點)

⊙ If it rains, I will stay home.
如果下雨，我就會待在家。

　＝If it happens to rain, I'll stay home.

　＝I will stay home if it rains.
(if 句放在後面，就不加逗點)

⊙ When/if/whenever she washes the dishes, her husband dries them.
她洗碗時，老公就把碗擦乾。

⊙ If I should do this, I will do it well.
假如我做這件事，我就會做得好。

　＝Should I do this, I will do it well.

⊙ If Mr. Lee is intelligent, then you are Albert Einstein.
假如李先生算聰明的話，那麼你就是愛因斯坦了。
(表示李先生不聰明)

⊙ I hope (that) Mr. Wang finishes/will finish his project soon.
我希望王先生很快完成他的方案。

⊙ He hopes (that) she will attend/attends the meeting.
他希望她會參加會議。

2. 前面子句是「情緒動詞」(emotive verb)時，也用現在條件句，表示「要求」、「建議」、「堅持」等等，希望達到某種目的。這時用原形動詞，第三人稱單數亦同。

以下是一些常用的情緒動詞：ask, command, demand, determine, insist, move, order, pray, prefer, propose, recommend, request, require, suggest, urge, wish 等。

例如：

◉ We ask that everyone be silent at the meeting.
我們要每個人在開會時保持安靜。(未必能保持安靜)
(前面動詞是 ask，所以 that 子句裡用 be；不用 is 或 will be)

◉ Mr. A moves that the contract be approved.
A 先生提議批准合同。(未必能批准)
(前面動詞是 move，所以 that 子句裡的動詞用 be，不用 is 或 will be)

◉ The law requires that you be sixteen before you drive.
法律規定你要滿十六歲才能開車。(未必大家都能遵守法律)
(前面動詞是 require，故條件句裡的動詞用 be，不用 are 或 will be)

◉ I demand that they be punctual.
我要求他們準時。(未必能準時)
(前面動詞是 demand，故條件句動詞用 be，不用 are 或 should be)

◉ The teacher prefers that Miss Wang write a descriptive essay.
老師比較希望王小姐寫篇描寫文。
(前面動詞是 prefer，故後面 that 子句動詞不用 writes)

◉ The judge ordered that the defendant stand trial tomorrow.
法官命令被告明天出庭。
(前面動詞是 ordered，所以後面動詞 stand 不加 s)

◉ I suggested that Mr. A establish a financial department.
我建議由 A 先生成立財務部門。
(前面動詞是 suggested，所以後面 that 子句動詞不用 establishes)

◉ The committee recommends that water quality testing continue.
委員會建議繼續進行水質檢測。
(前面是 recommend，所以 that 子句的動詞 continue 不加 s)

◉ The new teacher insists/insisted that every student attend class.
新老師堅持每位學生都要上課。
(前面動詞是 insist，所以 that 子句的動詞不用 attends)

◉ Her parents propose that she stay with them.
她的父母建議她與他們住在一起。
(前面動詞是 propose，所以 that 子句的動詞 stay 不加 s)

3. 與現在事實相反的假設語氣：(較常用)

也就是在 if 或 that 引導的子句裡，表示一種願望、意志、目的等，但並沒有發生在現在的實際生活中。動詞和助動詞都用過去式，但 be 動詞不論是什麼人稱，不論是單複數，都用 were。

（1）wish＋ 子句

◉ I wish (that) I were able to solve this problem.
我真盼望我能解決這個問題。（但我無能為力）
(不用 hope，因為 hope 是較有可能的希望，但 wish 指希望渺茫)

◉ He wishes he were a millionaire.
他盼望他是百萬富翁。（但他現在不是富翁，而且希望太小）
(wishes 後面的 that，一般都省去)

（2）

If	were	+	would	+	原形動詞
			should		
	過去式		could		
			might		

◉ If I were a rich person, I could help many poor people.
假如我是有錢人，我就能幫助許多窮人。（但我不是有錢人）
＝Were I a rich person, I could help many poor people.
(助動詞除 could 外，也可用 would, should 或 might，但意義略有不同)

＝I could help many poor people were I a rich person.
(主要子句放在前面時，後面不加逗點)

⊙ If he had the time, he would/might go to Taiwan.
假如他有時間，他會去台灣。（但他現在沒有時間）
＝Had he the time, he would go to Taiwan.

⊙ If I could fly, I would see you every day.
假如我能飛，我要每天見到你。（但我不能飛）
＝Could I fly, I would（或 could）see you...

⊙ If it should rain, I would stay home.
假如下雨，我就會待在家。（但是現在不下雨）
＝Should it rain, I would stay home.

⊙ If it were up to me, I would（＝I'd）not do that.
假如由我決定，我就不會去做那件事。（但不是由我決定）
＝Were it up to me, I would not do that.

⊙ If there were a concert tonight, I would go.
假如今晚有音樂會，我會去參加。（但沒有音樂會）
＝Were there a concert tonight, I would go.

⊙ I would not marry her if/even if she were the last woman on earth.
即使她是世上最後一個女人，我也不會娶她。
＝If (even if) she were the last woman on earth, I would not marry her.（但她不可能是世上最後一個女人。）
＝Were she the last woman on earth, I would...
(on earth 是指「人世間」，earth 前不加 the)

⊙ If Mr. Wang were here, he would be able to help.
假如王先生在這裡，他就能幫忙。（但他不在這裡）
＝Were Mr. Wang here, he would be...

⊙ If she practiced piano more often, she could be a better player.
假如她更常練習鋼琴，她就會彈得更好。（但她不常練習）
(不能把 practiced 放在句首)

- If she had the money, she could (would) buy a house.
  假如她有錢，她會買棟房子。(但她沒有錢)
  ＝Had she the money, she could buy a house.

- If they should arrive today, I would be happy to see them.
  假如他們今天到達，我會很高興見到他們。(但他們今天不能到達)
  ＝Should they arrive today, I would be...

- If you were I, what would you do under such circumstances?
  假如你是我，在此情況下，你會怎麼做？(你不可能是我)

也可寫為：

  Were you I, what would you do...(但較少用)

- If I were you, I would save more money.
  假如我是你，我會存更多錢。

也可寫成：

  Were I you, I would save more money.(較少用)

- If he were taller, he could join the basketball team.
  假如他長得高一點，他就能參加籃球隊。(但他不高)
  ＝Were he taller, he could join...

as though 或 as if 所引導的子句中，be 動詞皆為 were，表示與現在事實相反。

(例如：)

- He talks as though he were my boss.
  他說起話來，像是我的老闆。(但他不是我的老闆)

- Mr. Lee spoke to her as if she were an idiot.
  李先生把她當笨蛋一樣跟她說話。(但她不笨)

4. 與過去事實相反的假設語氣：(較常用)

If	had + p.p	+	would should could might	+	have p.p
	過去完成式				

在 if 或 that 的子句裡用 had+過去分詞，主要子句裡用 should/would/could/might＋have＋過去分詞。

- ◉ If he had arrived earlier, he would not have missed the dinner.
  假如他早點到，他就不會錯過晚餐。

  ＝Had he arrived earlier, he would not have missed the dinner.
  (與過去事實相反，因為他遲到了，所以錯過了晚餐)

- ◉ If Mr. Wang had been here, I could have explained everything.
  假如王先生在這裡，我就會向他解釋一切。

  ＝Had Mr. Wang been here, I could have...
  (但是當時王先生不在這裡，與過去事實相反)

  ＝I could have explained everything had Mr. Wang been here.
  ＝I could have explained everything if Mr. Wang had been here.
  (也可用 would、should 或 might，但意思略有不同)

- ◉ If Mr. Chang had had the time, he would have gone to Taiwan.
  假如張先生有時間，他老早就去台灣了。

  ＝Had Mr. Chang had the time, he would have gone to Taiwan.
  (與過去事實相反。因為他沒時間，所以沒去台灣)

⊙ If Mr. Wang had stayed in Taiwan, he would have become an influential politician.
假如王先生留在台灣，他早已成為一位有影響力的政客。

= Had Mr. Wang stayed in Taiwan, he would...

= Mr. Wang would have become an influential politician if he had stayed in Taiwan.
(這也是與過去事實相反，因為他沒有留在台灣)

⊙ If I had known that, I would not have made any comments.

= Had I known that, I would not...
假如我知道那回事，我就不會作出任何評論。
(因為我不知道，所以作出評論。與過去事實相反)

⊙ What would you have done about Iraq if you had been the President?
假如你當時是總統，你會怎麼對付伊拉克？

= Had you been the President, what would you have done about Iraq?

= What would you have done about Iraq had you been the President?

= If you had been the President, what would you have done about Iraq?

⊙ If I had been the President, I might not have gone to war.
假如我當時是總統，我也許不會開戰。

⊙ If he had been invited, he would have attended the wedding.
假如他當時受邀，他就會去參加婚禮。
(但他沒有被邀請，故與過去事實相反)

= He would have attended the wedding had he been invited.

= Had he been invited, he would have attended the wedding.

⊙ If I had been you, I would not have done that.
假如我那時是你，我就不會做那件事。
(但我過去也不可能是你)
＝Had I been you, I would not have done that.

如果與現在事實相反，就可改為：

If I were you, I would not do that.

二、主動和被動語態(**active and passive voice**)

1. 主動時，主詞在執行動作(perform an action)；被動時，
主詞就會變成受詞，接受動作(receive the action)。帶有動
作的動詞(action verb)都能有主動或被動語態。及物動詞
(transitive verb)都可用在被動語態。

例如：

⊙ The car hit a dog.(主動)
汽車撞到一隻狗。
(hit 是過去式，也是及物動詞；dog 是直接受詞)
→ A dog was hit by the car.(被動)

⊙ I introduced the new professor.(主動)
我介紹了新教授。
→ The new professor was introduced by me.(被動)
(變成被動時，受詞 dog 和 professor 變成主詞；而主詞 car 和 I 變成介
詞 by 的「受詞」)

2. 句子裡有直接和間接受詞時(direct and indirect object)，可用任何一個受詞當被動語態的主詞。

例如：

◉ Mr. Wang gave her some candies.（主動）
王先生給她一些糖果。
（her 是間接受詞；candies 是直接受詞）
→ She was given some candies by Mr. Wang.（被動）
＝Some candies were given（to）her by Mr. Wang.
（to 可省去）

◉ He has sent his girlfriend a letter.（主動）
他寄一封信給他的女友。
（girlfriend 是間接受詞；letter 是直接受詞）
→ A letter has been sent to his girlfriend by him.（被動）
＝His girlfriend has been sent a letter by him.
（被動和主動的動詞時態，要互相配合。例如第一句主動句的動詞是過去式 gave，被動句也要用 was 或 were given）

被動句較常用的時態如下：

Many toys are made in China.（現在簡單式）

Many toys were made in China.（過去簡單式）

Many toys will be made in China.（未來簡單式）

Many toys have been made in China.（現在完成式）

Many toys had been made in China.（過去完成式）

Many toys will have been made in China.（未來完成式）

Many toys are being made in China.（現在進行式）

Many toys were being made in China.（過去進行式）

也有人用 be 動詞 + going to 代替未來簡單式：

Many toys are going to be made in China.

＝Many toys will be made in China.

被動句在非正式的口語裡，也有人用 get 代替 be。

例如：

⊙ Mr. Wang got invited to the party.
王先生受邀參加宴會。
＝Mr. Wang was invited to the party.（較好）

⊙ This bed has/had not got slept in.
這張床還未被睡過。
＝This bed has/had not been slept in.（較好）

3. 盡量多用主動句，少用被動句。因為主動比被動簡短、
直接而有力。

例如：

⊙ God helps those who help themselves.（主動）
天助自助者。（簡短）
如用被動：Those who help themselves are helped by
God.（不好）

⊙ Everyone expected an exciting baseball game, but no one
predicted a victory.（主動）（短而有力）
每個人都在期待一場激烈的棒球賽，但沒人預料誰能得勝。
如用被動：An exciting baseball game was expected by
everyone, but a victory was predicted by no one.（不夠直接
有力）

　　如果認為動作的執行者(performer of action)不重要或不需要，那麼只用主動語態。

例如：

◎ The bank opens at 9 and closes at 3(for business).
銀行九點開門，三點關門。
(誰開誰關不重要)

如果說：

◎ The bank is opened at 9 and is closed at 3.
(意思只是開門和關門，未必是營業)

◎ The balloon suddenly burst.
氣球突然破了。

如果說：

◎ The balloon suddenly was burst.
(意思是有人故意弄破)

◎ I was reading the newspaper when the door opened.
我在看報時，門開了。
(怎麼開的並不重要)

◎ Gas prices increase because of many factors.
汽油因為許多因素而漲價。
(是誰讓它漲價，倒不重要)

　　遇到以下動詞時，要用主動，不用被動：appear, disappear, happen , occur , seem , take place 等。

例如：

- He appeared to be sad yesterday.
  他昨天看起來很傷心。
  (不用 was appeared)

- The snake disappeared in the wood.
  蛇在森林中消失了。
  (不用 was disappeared)

- The incident occurred before I knew the real situation.
  在我知道實際情形之前這件事就發生了。
  (不用 was occurred)

- She seems happy every day.
  她似乎每天都很高興。
  (不用 is seemed)

4. 如果是強調動作的接受者(receiver of action)，而不是動作的執行者也可用被動語態。

例如：

- The expensive painting was damaged by the storm.
  昂貴的畫作被暴風雨損壞了。
  (強調 painting，故放在句首當主詞)

- His best friend was struck by a truck yesterday.
  他最好的朋友昨天被卡車撞到。
  (強調 best friend，故放在句首當主詞)

- The special effects were developed by a team of workers.
  一組工作人員研發出特效。
  (強調 special effects)

- Mr. A has been selected to the committee.
  A 先生被推選加入委員會。
  (強調 Mr. A 這個人)

假如以上各句的主詞並不是你強調的對象,當然也可變成主動語態:

- The storm damaged the expensive painting.
- A truck struck his best friend yesterday.
- A team of workers developed the special effects.
- The committee selected Mr. A.

5. 如果不知道誰是動作的執行者(performer of action),還是認為執行者不重要或不想讓別人知道誰是執行者,也可用被動語態。

例如:

- The bank was robbed last night.
  昨晚銀行被搶了。
  (不知道誰搶的)

當然也可以說:

 Someone robbed the bank last night.
 ＝There was a bank robbery last night.

- A car was abandoned near the library.
  一部汽車被遺棄在圖書館附近。
  (不知道誰遺棄的)

也可以說:

 Someone abandoned a car near the library.

- The painting was stolen sometime at night.
  那幅畫是在晚上被偷的。
  (不曉得誰偷的)

也可以說：

⊙ Someone stole the painting sometime at night.

⊙ The truck will be sold at the auction tomorrow.
明天卡車將在拍賣場出售。
(誰是執行者，倒不重要)

⊙ This report should be submitted to the higher authority.
這份報告應送到更高當局。
(誰去送，倒不重要)

⊙ The concert will be held on May 10 this year.
音樂會將在今年 5 月 10 日舉行。
(誰舉辦，倒不重要)

⊙ It is/was said that Mr. A is impolite and arrogant.
據說 A 先生無禮和傲慢。
(不願說是誰說的)

⊙ Some mistakes have been made in that article.
那篇文章有些錯誤。
(不願說是誰出錯)

⊙ An error was found in the figures.
數字裡發現有錯。
(不願說是誰發現)
＝Someone found an error...

但不能說：

That article has made some mistakes.

也不能說：

The figures found an error.
(因為 article 和 figures 都不能擔任動作的執行者)

1-6

動詞與主詞
的一致

英語裡，動詞與主詞要一致（verb and subject agreement），也就是說，主詞如果是單數或多數，動詞也要與其一致。這在動詞的用法中常常被誤用。

在此特別舉出一些例句，供讀者參考。

1. 介詞的受詞，不可誤認為主詞：

例如：

◉ The arrival of two pandas from China has caused much excitement at the zoo.
中國兩隻熊貓的到來，讓動物園的人都很興奮。
(這句的主詞是 arrival，是單數，所以動詞也用現在式單數 has，不用複數 have。而 pandas 不是主詞，只是介詞 of 的受詞。of two pandas from China 是介詞片語，修飾 arrival)

◉ Mr. Wang with his children is/was standing in front of the park.
王先生和他的孩子站在公園前面。
(這句的主詞是 Mr. Wang，是單數，所以動詞也要用單數 is 或 was。children 不是主詞，只是介詞 with 的受詞；with his children 是介詞片語，當形容詞，修飾 Mr. Wang，所以動詞不能用複數 are 或 were)

◉ The books on the shelf have all been cataloged.
書架上的書全部都已編目完成。
(主詞是 books，是多數，所以動詞也用多數 have been; shelf 只是介詞 on 的受詞；on the shelf 是介詞片語，修飾 books)

◉ A long row of tall, well-constructed apartments stands at the end of the street.
一長排建築精良的高樓公寓座落於馬路盡頭。
(這句的主詞是 row，是單數，因此動詞也用現在式單數 stand 後加 s；而 apartments 不是主詞，只是介詞 of 的受詞。of tall, well-constructed apartments 係介詞片語，修飾 row)

⦿ The fresh air and bright sunshine of this area make his parents cheerful.
這個地方的新鮮空氣和燦爛陽光使他父母高興。
(這裡的主詞是 air 和 sunshine，是複數，所以動詞也用複數 make，不用現在式單數 makes；而 area 不是主詞，只是 of 的受詞；of this area 是介詞片語，修飾主詞)

⦿ The manual on developing one's writing skills is very helpful to her.
這本培養寫作技巧的手冊對她很有用。
(這句的主詞是 manual，是單數，所以動詞也用單數 is，而 skills 只是介詞 on 的受詞；on developing one's writing skills 是介詞片語，修飾主詞)

⦿ A Chinese painting of flowers and trees hangs in my living room.
我的客廳裡掛著一幅有花有樹的中國畫。
(這句的主詞是 painting，是單數，所以動詞也為現在式單數 hangs；而 flowers and trees 只是介詞 of 的受詞，所以動詞不能用複數 hang)

⦿ The desks that were in the storage room have been moved to the office.
儲藏室裡的桌子已經搬到辦公室。
(這裡的主詞是 desks，是多數，因此動詞也要用多數 have；room 只是介詞 in 的受詞，故不用單數動詞 has；that were in the storage room 是形容詞子句，修飾主詞)

2. 兩個或兩個以上的單數主詞(singular subject)，若是用 either... or 或 neither... nor 連接時，動詞用單數。

例如：

⦿ Either Mr. Chang or Mr. Wang is going to help her.
不是張先生就是王先生會幫助她。
(Mr. Chang 和 Mr. Wang 都是單數主詞，所以動詞也要用單數 is 或 was)

但是句子裡，如果一個主詞是單數，另一個主詞是複數，被 either... or, neither... nor, not only... but also 所連接時，動詞是跟最靠近的主詞一致。

例如：

◉ Neither the students nor their teacher was/is waiting for us in the auditorium.
學生和他們的老師都沒有在禮堂裡等我們。
(因為最靠近的主詞 teacher 是單數，故動詞也用單數 is 或 was)

◉ Not only the labor leader but also the socialists believe in the supremacy of the working class.
不只工會領袖人，連社會主義者也相信工人階級的優越性。
(這句最靠近的主詞 socialists 是多數，所以要用複數動詞 believe，不用現在簡單式的動詞 believes)

◉ At this store neither the prices nor the quality has changed.
這家店的價格與品質都沒變。
(這句最靠近的主詞是 quality，是單數，所以動詞也用單數 has)

◉ Either one book or several articles are sufficient for my research.
不是一本書或是幾篇文章就夠我研究之用。
(這裡最靠近的主詞是 articles，是複數，所以動詞也用複數 are)

如果把兩個主詞的位置互相調換，動詞也須變動，如下句所示：

Either several articles or one book is sufficient for my research.

如果句子裡只有 neither 或 either 時，動詞用單數。

例如：

◉ Neither of the students has finished his/her homework.
兩位學生都沒有完成作業。
（因為 neither＝not one，所以動詞用單數 has）

◉ Either of these two dishes is delicious.
這兩道菜中的任何一道都好吃。
（因為 either＝one，所以動詞用單數 is）（也就是 Both dishes are delicious.）

但是兩個或兩個以上的單數主詞用 or 連接時，動詞用單數；兩個或兩個以上的複數主詞用 or 連接時，動詞用多數。

例如：

◉ Mr. Chang or Mr. Wang raises the question.
張先生或王先生提出這個問題。
（動詞是單數現在式 raise 後加 s）

◉ The Changs or the Wangs come on a trip with us.
張家或王家會加入我們的旅行。
（因為張家和王家都是多數，所以動詞也用多數 come，後不加 s）

3. 兩個或兩個以上的主詞用 and 連在一起，在習慣上被視為一個整體或無法分開，其動詞是用單數。

例如：

◉ Bacon and eggs is a popular breakfast in the U.S.
在美國，培根蛋是人氣早餐。
（這裡的 bacon 和 eggs，被當做一種分不開的食品，所以動詞用單數 is）

⊙ Peanut butter and jelly seems to be the favorite combination for many Americans.

對許多美國人而言，花生醬加果醬是他們最喜歡的組合。

(這裡的 peanut butter 和 jelly，在習慣上已經被老外認為是不能分開的，所以動詞 seem 後要加 s，成為單數)

⊙ Spaghetti and meatballs was served last night at the party.

昨晚宴會吃的是肉丸義大利麵。

(spaghetti 和 meatballs 也被認為是不可分開的，所以動詞用單數 was)

此外，還有 "bread and butter", "bow and arrow" 等。

4. 在詩詞裡，往往把主詞顛倒，放在動詞之後，那麼主詞與動詞的單複數，也要一致。

例如：

⊙ Along the fence are growing some Chinese vegetables.

沿著籬笆種著一些中國蔬菜。

(主詞是 vegetables，所以動詞也用複數 are)

一般說法：Some Chinese vegetables are growing along the fence.

⊙ Across the lake appears the tall building.

湖的對岸出現一座高樓。

(building 是主詞，所以動詞也用單數 appears)

一般說法：The tall building appears across the lake.

除此之外，主詞放在動詞後面的倒裝句，還有用 there, here 作句子的開端字（sentence starter）或當副詞用。其他還有用 where, what, which, why, how 開頭，也是把主詞放在動詞後面形成問句。

例如：

- There are many pencils in the box.
  ＝Many pencils are in the box. 盒子裡有很多鉛筆
  (there 是開端字或當副詞用，修飾 are。主詞 pencils 是多數，動詞也要用多數 are)

- What are the main ideas in his stories?
  他故事的主旨是什麼？
  (照理說＝The main ideas in his stories are what? 但在文法上不能這麼說，一定要把 What 放在句首。ideas 是主詞且為複數名詞，所以動詞也要用複數 are)

同理：

- Why has he called me so late in the evening?
  為什麼他要三更半夜打電話給我？
  不能說成：He has called me so late in the evening why?
  (只能把 Why 放在句首，成為問句)

- Where are the keys to the house?
  這屋子的鑰匙在哪？
  不能說成：The keys to the house are where?
  (主詞是 keys，故動詞用多數 are)

- How many times has John filled his plate?
  John 裝了幾次盤？
  不能說成：John has filled his plate how many times?
  (how many times 在問句時，還是要放在句首)

5. 遇到句首有 anyone/anybody、everyone/everybody、someone/somebody 或 nobody 時，動詞用單數。

例如：

◉ Everyone in the first two rows was delighted by the play.
前兩排的每個人都喜歡這齣戲。
(句首是 everyone，動詞用單數 was 有時為了加強語氣，也可寫成
every one)

◉ Everybody was frightened by the film.
每個人都被這部片嚇到了。

◉ Nobody is allowed to do as he/she likes.
沒有人可以隨心所欲。

很少人把上面分開寫成：any one, every one, some one, any
body, every body, some body，尤其 nobody 不能分開寫，否則 body
會被誤認為屍體。例如：

No body was found. (body＝corpse)
沒有屍體被尋獲。

但遇到 all, most, some, none 在句首時，有時動詞用單數，有
時用複數，要看句子的含意而定。

例如：

◉ All of the ice cream has melted.
所有冰淇淋都已融化。
(動詞用單數 has。有時 ice cream 也可用多數，例如：I have had three
ice creams.)

◉ All of the teachers have attended the meetings.
所有老師都參加了這個會議。
(動詞用複數 have)

◉ Most of the story was written from a teacher's point of view.
大部分的故事是以老師的觀點寫成的。
(動詞用單數 was)

◉ Most of the students have not spelled "Mississippi" correctly.
大部分學生都沒能正確地拼出「Mississippi」這個字。
(動詞用多數 have)

至於在句子前有 every 或 each 時，動詞用單數。

例如：

◉ Every/each student receives a textbook.
每個學生都拿到了課本。
(動詞現在式，單數用 receives)

加強語氣時，可以說：

◉ Each and every teacher gets a raise this year.
每一位老師今年都會加薪。
(動詞仍用單數 gets)

◉ Every boot, shoe, and belt in this store is made of leather.
這間店的每一雙長靴、每一雙鞋子和每一條皮帶，都是皮製的。
(動詞單數 is)

◉ Each of his examples was from his own ideas.
他舉的每一個例子都是出自他個人的意思。

6. 集合名詞(collective noun)當作一個整體單位時，動詞用單
數；當作整體中每位個體時，動詞用多數。

例如：

◉ The class with the highest marks receives a prize.
分數最高的班級會得到一個獎品。
(把 class 視為一個班級，所以動詞用單數 receives)

◉ The class ask many questions on current politics.
班上學生詢問許多關於當今政治的問題。
(指班上的學生，所以動詞用多數 ask)

◉ My family are all well and healthy.
我的家人都很好很健康。
(指全家，故動詞用多數 are)

◉ The committee has already held its first meeting of the year.
此委員會已舉行了它今年的第一場會議。
(把委員會當作一個單位，所以動詞用單數 has)

◉ The committee are going to vote for their chairperson.
委員們將選出他們的主席。
(指委員會中的委員們投票選主席，所以動詞用多數 are)

表示多數時，最好在 class, family, committee 後面，加上 members，以免造成混淆。

此外，還有 audience, commune, majority, minority, team, herd, flock 等都是集合名詞。

7. 有些指科學知識等普通名詞或指地名、書名、報紙名等專有名詞，字尾雖然有 s，但動詞仍用單數。

例如：

◉ No news is good news.
沒有消息就是好消息。
(news 後面的動詞，用單數 is)

◉ Physics seems to be a difficult subject for many students.
物理對許多學生而言似乎是個困難的學科。
(physics 後面動詞用單數 seems)

◉ Acoustics is a branch of science that is growing fast.
聲學是科學的一支,正在快速發展中。

◉ Measles is no longer common in the U.S.
在美國麻疹不再普遍了。

◉ The *Daily Times* has the largest circulation in this area.
《每日時報》在此區的發行量最大。
(Daily Times 是報紙名稱,動詞用單數 has)

此外,還有 athletics 體育課,civics 公民課,ethics 倫理學,mathematics 數學,economics 經濟學,mumps 腮腺炎,Wales 威爾斯(英國的一部分)等,都要用單數動詞。

至於指距離、金錢、時間、重量等相關字彙,雖然也是複數,但視為一個單位,所以動詞也用單數。

(例如:)

◉ One hundred miles is a long distance.
100 英里是很長的距離。
(把 100 miles 當做 one unit 看待,動詞仍用單數;同時,在句首的數字,通常都拼寫出來)

◉ Two million dollars is a lot of money.
兩百萬美元是一大筆錢。

◉ Five years seems a long time to spend on an M.A. thesis.
寫一篇碩士論文要花五年時間似乎很長。
(動詞 seems 也是單數)

◉ Four weeks has been the checkout time for our library book(s).
我們圖書館的書籍借閱時間一直都是四個禮拜。
(four weeks 當作一個單位,動詞也用單數 has)

8. 分數或小數(fractions)或百分比(percentages)，以及算術的
加、減、乘、除，動詞都常用單數。

例如：

◉ One-half(或 fifty percent)of the toxic waste has escaped.
毒氣已漏出一半。
(動詞用單數 has)

◉ Two-thirds of the students is satisfied with his class.
三分之二的學生對他的課程感到滿意。

◉ Forty-five percent of the teachers has received a pay raise.
百分之 45 的老師得到加薪。
(把 forty-five percent 當做一個整體，動詞仍用單數 has)

◉ One plus one is/equals two.
一加一等於二。

◉ Four minus two is/equals two.
四減二等於二。

◉ Ten divided by two is/equals five.
十除二等於五

◉ Two times two is/equals four.
二乘二等於四

此外，遇到有 pair of, the number of, in addition to, together
with, as well as, along with 時，動詞用單數。

例如：

◉ A pair of trousers is on the chair.
椅子上有條褲子。

但是 His trousers are on the chair.
(trousers 單獨使用時，動詞用複數。通常由兩部分組成的東西，還有 scissors, shoes, eyeglasses 等)

◉ This pair of shoes needs to be repaired.
這雙鞋需要修了。
(動詞用單數 needs)

但是 My shoes need to be polished.（動詞用多數 need）

◉ The U.S., together with China, has made many contributions to world civilization.
美國和中國對世界文明做出了許多貢獻。
(動詞還是用單數 has)

◉ His advice, in addition to his kindness, really helps her self-esteem.
他的勸告，加上他的仁慈，對她的自尊真的有很大的幫助。
(動詞仍然用單數 helps)

◉ The number of students in our college is six thousand.
我們大學的學生人數是六千人。

但是：

◉ A number of pages are badly torn.
很多頁破損嚴重。
(a number of＝many，所以動詞要用多數 are)

注意

假如遇到句中有："one of those (students) who..."，或 "one of the best (games) that..." 或 "only one of the (stories) which..." 時，關係代名詞 who, that, which 如果是指 one，就用單數動詞，否則就用多數動詞。

例如：

◉ This is the only one of the stores which remains open all night.
這家是這些店中唯一一家整晚營業的。
(因為是指唯一的一家商店，所以 which 是修飾 one，故動詞用單數 remains)

1-7

形容詞的用法

一個句子裡，有了名詞(或代名詞)和動詞，多半就能表達意思。但為了描寫得更明確、更仔細，就需要形容詞和副詞了。所以它們也稱為修飾語(modifier)。

一、形容詞放置的位置

形容詞只能修飾名詞或代名詞。通常是放置在名詞或代名詞前面，有時也放在句中或句尾，但不可與所修飾的名詞或代名詞相距太遠，以免造成誤會。

例如：

◉ Mrs. Lin is a beautiful and intelligent lady.
林太太是位美麗聰明的女性。
(形容詞 beautiful 和 intelligent，都是修飾名詞 lady，說明她是什麼樣的女人)

◉ He is tactful in his interaction with others.
他與人互動很圓滑。
(形容詞 tactful 修飾代名詞 he)

◉ We consider Mr. A cunning.
我們認為 A 先生很狡猾。
(形容詞 cunning，修飾 Mr. A)

◉ The narrow and dark room frightened the girl.
又窄又黑的房間使女孩害怕。
(形容詞 narrow 和 dark 都是修飾名詞 room)

也可以說：

The room, narrow and dark, frightened...
但不要說：The room frightened the girl, narrow and dark.
(因為形容詞 narrow 和 dark 與要修飾的 room 相距太遠)

◉ Slim and strong, he is the picture of health.
他瘦而壯，是健康的寫照。
(形容詞 slim 和 strong，有時也可放在句首，都是修飾代名詞 he)

也可以說：

He is slim and strong, the picture of health.
或：He is the picture of health, slim and strong.
(因為 picture of health 就是 healthy；與 slim and strong 有相關的意思，不會使人迷糊)

◉ The tall and beautiful building burned down yesterday.
那棟又高又美的大樓昨天燒掉了。
(形容詞 tall 和 beautiful，都是修飾名詞 building)

也可以說：

The building, tall and beautiful, burned...
(也有人認為形容詞放在句中，語氣較弱)

但不要說：The building burned down yesterday, tall and beautiful.
(因為形容詞與要修飾的名詞 building 相距太遠)

◉ Mrs. B was heartbroken by the divorce.
B 太太因為離婚而心碎。
(形容詞 heartbroken 修飾 Mrs. B)

可以說：

Heartbroken by the divorce, Mrs. B started a new career.
因離婚而心碎，B 太太開始了新的事業。

但不要說：Mrs. B started a new career, brokenhearted by...
(因為形容詞與要修飾的 Mrs. B 相距太遠)

◉ Large and colorful flowers bloomed in my front yard.(較好)
大而艷麗的花朵在我的前院盛開。
(形容詞 large 和 colorful 都是修飾名詞 flowers)

如果說：Flowers, large and colorful, bloomed in... (較弱)

但不要說：Flowers bloomed in my front yard large and colorful.
(因為會被誤解是修飾名詞 yard)

◉ The small, cute, and long-haired dog performed many unusual tricks.(較好)
這隻小小可愛的長毛狗耍出了許多不尋常的把戲。
(形容詞 small, cute, long-haired 都是修飾名詞 dog；而 many, unusual 又修飾 tricks)

如果說：The dog, small, cute, and long-haired, performed...(較弱)

但不要說：The dog performed many unusual tricks, small, cute and long-haired.
(因為與要修飾的名詞 dog，相距太遠)

◉ A string of red, yellow, black, and blue beads was given to my daughter.
有人送一串有紅、黃、黑、藍色的珠子給我女兒。
(形容詞 red, yellow, black, blue 都是修飾名詞 beads，可見許多形容詞，可以修飾同樣一個字)

也可以說：

A string of beads, red, yellow, black, and blue, was given...

但不要說：

A string of beads was given to my daughter, red, yellow, black, and blue.
(因距離要修飾的名詞 beads 太遠，似乎在修飾 daughter)

　　至於多個不同的形容詞，修飾一個名詞時，其排列次序雖無嚴格規定，但通常是以冠詞開頭，名詞結尾。形容詞排列順序大致為：

　　冠詞(或代名詞)→大小→年歲→顏色→分詞→專有形容詞→名詞當形容詞→名詞

例如：

◉ The large, ancient, red Chinese flower vase may be worth a lot of money.
這個古代中國紅色大花瓶，可能值很多錢。
(要修飾的名詞是 vase)

◉ That big, blue American sports car is expensive.
那部大型藍色美國跑車價格昂貴。
(要修飾的名詞是 car，也就是：代名詞→大小→顏色→專有形容詞→名詞當形容詞→名詞)

◉ The tiny, black frightening field mouse showed up in my backyard.
一隻令人害怕的黑色小田鼠出現在我家後院。
(也就是：冠詞→大小→顏色→分詞→名詞當形容詞→名詞；要修飾的名詞是 mouse)

◉ My wife bought a small, fashionable, pink silk shirt yesterday.
我太太昨天買了一件小號時髦的粉紅絲襯衫。
(要修飾的名詞是 shirt。排列順序為：冠詞〔a〕→大小〔small〕→年歲〔fashionable〕→顏色〔pink〕→名詞當形容詞〔silk〕→名詞〔shirt〕)

二、形容詞的種類

1. 名詞當形容詞：

也就是把普通名詞，當作形容詞用，去修飾另外的名詞。

例如：

◉ Mr. Wang likes apple/orange juice.
　　王先生喜歡蘋果／柳橙汁。
　　(apple 或 orange 都是普通名詞，當形容詞用，修飾另一個名詞 juice，說明了哪一種果汁)

◉ I bought a winter jacket last week.
　　我上周買了一件冬天穿的夾克。
　　(winter 是普通名詞，修飾另一個名詞 jacket，說明了哪一種夾克)

◉ My wife took long grocery lists to the store.
　　我太太帶了長長的採購清單到商店去。
　　(普通名詞 grocery，是修飾另一個名詞 lists)

通常是由意義次要的名詞：apple, orange, winter, grocery 去修飾意義較為重要的名詞：juice, jacket, lists。

其他如同：desk lamp, dinner party, evening meal, brick wall, highway sign 等等。

也可用兩個以上的名詞，修飾另一個名詞。

例如：

◉ Mr. A tracks gas prices through credit card purchases.
　　A 先生用信用卡帳單來追蹤汽油價格。
　　(嚴格的說，credit 是修飾 card，但這兩個名詞都是修飾另一個名詞 purchases)

⊚ Mrs. Wang received a baby shower invitation from her cousin.
王太太自她表妹那裡收到一份嬰兒送禮會的邀請。
(雖然 baby 是修飾 shower，但這兩個名詞，都是修飾另一個名詞 invitation)

註：

baby shower 是為了表示友愛，親友在嬰兒誕生前贈送嬰兒用品的聚會。

⊚ I attended the Maryland State University 1990 class reunion last month.
我上個月我參加馬里蘭州立大學 1990 年同學會。
(雖然 1990 是修飾 class, Maryland State University 也是修飾 class，但整個來說，都是修飾另一個名詞 reunion)

以上名詞所修飾的，都是句中重要的名詞：purchases, invitation, reunion。

至於專有名詞，也可當做形容詞，變成專有形容詞。

例如：

⊚ Many students are learning the French language.
許多學生在學法文。
(France 是專有名詞，French 就是專有形容詞，修飾另一個名詞 language)

⊚ My wife bought a piece of Danish porcelain.
我太太買了一件丹麥的瓷器。
(Denmark 是專有名詞，Danish 是專有形容詞，修飾另一個名詞 porcelain)

⊚ I saw a Shakespearean comedy at the college.
我在大學裡看了一齣莎士比亞的喜劇。
(Shakespeare 是專有名詞，Shakespearean 是專有形容詞，修飾另一名詞 comedy)

◉ Many immigrants in the U.S. come from African nations.
美國許多移民來自非洲國家。
(Africa 是專有名詞，African 是專有形容詞，修飾另一個名詞 nations)

有時也可直接使用專有名詞做為形容詞：

諸如：a California newspaper, a Chicago family, April showers, Monday evening, Boston(或 Bostonian)architecture, San Francisco streets 等等。

2. 複合形容詞(Compound adjectives)

就是把幾個字，用連字號(hyphen)連在一起，當形容詞用。不過，有時也不用連字號。

例如：

◉ A well-known surgeon will perform(an) open-heart surgery tomorrow on Mr. A.
一位知名外科醫師明天要為 A 先生做開心手術。
(well 和 known 用連字號連接，成為形容詞，修飾名詞 surgeon；open 和 heart，用連字號連接，修飾 surgery)

◉ The hit-and-run driver was captured last night.
肇事逃逸的駕駛員昨晚被捕。
(hit, and, run 三個字用連字號連接，當形容詞，修飾 driver)

◉ Many physicians have a high-and-mighty attitude.
許多醫生的態度都很高傲自大。
(high, and, mighty 三個字連起來，當形容詞，修飾名詞 attitude；也有人不用連字號)

◉ After five-and-a-half hours of deliberation, the jury reached a
  verdict.
  經過五個半小時的討論後，陪審團作出了裁決。
  (five-and-a-half 是修飾 hours；也有人不用連字號)

◉ Mr. B is actually a real joke-around kind of guy.
  B 先生其實是位愛開玩笑的人。
  (joke-around 當形容詞，修飾名詞 kind)

◉ Living on the farm is a back-to-nature experience.
  在農場生活是一種回歸大自然的經驗。
  (back-to-nature 當形容詞，修飾 experience)

◉ This young woman has a peaches-and-cream complexion.
  這名年輕女子皮膚細如凝脂。
  (peaches-and-cream 當形容詞，修飾名詞 complexion；也有人不用連
  字號)

◉ That is an ill-conceived project.
  那是個安排欠佳的計畫。
  (ill-conceived＝badly managed，修飾 project)

其他例子：(有人不用連字號)

long-term commitment 長久的承諾
lifelong friendship 終生的友誼
crossword puzzle 填字遊戲
farsighted leaders 有遠見的領導者(不用連字號)
not-too-distant future 不久的將來
salt-and-pepper beard 斑白的鬍鬚
absent-minded professor 健忘的教授

rank-and-file workers 普通工人	
one-sided opinion 單方面意見	
so-called expert 所謂的專家(要用連字號)	
under-paid employees 低薪員工	
high-pitched voice 高而尖銳的聲音	
over-the-counter medicine 不需處方,隨時可買到的成藥(要用連字號)	
well-informed mayor 消息靈通的市長	
worn-out clothes 破舊的衣服	
nearsighted teacher 近視的老師(不用連字號)	

可見人們使用複合形容詞的目的是要精簡文句。

例如:

past-due bill＝the bill that is past due 逾期帳單

blue-grey bedroom set＝a bedroom set that is blue grey 藍灰色寢具

3. 代名詞當形容詞(pronouns used as adjectives)

(1)人稱代名詞的所有格當形容詞

也就是：my, your, his, her, its(單數)

　　　　our, your, their(多數)

例如:

◎ John is ready to meet his responsibilities as a manager.
John 已準備好擔任經理的職責。

(his 是人稱代名詞所有格,當形容詞,修飾名詞 responsibilities)

- They were late and did not keep their appointments.
  他們遲到了而不能守約。
  (their 是 they 的人稱代名詞所有格，當形容詞，修飾名詞 appointments)

- Please put the books back on their shelves.
  請把書放回書架上。
  (their 是指 books 的代名詞所有格，修飾名詞 shelves)

- China is trying to build up its（或 her）economic strength.
  中國正試圖擴大其經濟力量。
  (its 或 her 是 China 的代名詞所有格，修飾名詞 strength；形容詞 economic 也修飾 strength)

(2)指示代名詞，當形容詞(demonstrative adjectives)

也就是：this, that（單數）

these, those（多數）

例如：

- This book and these pencils belong to me.
  這本書和這些鉛筆是我的。
  (this 和 these 都是指示代名詞，當形容詞用，修飾 book 和 pencils)

- That test will take him two hours.
  那場考試要花他兩小時。
  (that 是指示代名詞，當形容詞，修飾名詞 test)

- I feel sorry for those people caught in the flood.
  我為那些受困水災的人感到難過。
  (those 是指示代名詞，修飾名詞 people)

但是：

◉ How did you do this?
你如何做這件事？

◉ That will take me three hours.
那要花我 3 小時。

◉ I told him I would not bring these (those).
我告訴他我不會帶這 (那) 些東西。

以上三句中的 this, that, these 或 those，後面都沒有名詞可以修飾，只是代替已經提過的名詞，所以還是代名詞，不是形容詞。

(3) 疑問代名詞，當形容詞 (interrogative adjectives)

也就是：which, what, whose

例如：

◉ Which book do you think she will choose?
你想她會選那一本書？
(which 是疑問代名詞，當形容詞，修飾名詞 books)

◉ What type of skirt does she prefer?
她喜歡那一種裙子？
(what 是疑問代名詞，當形容詞，修飾 type)

◉ Whose jacket is black?
誰的夾克是黑色的？
(whose 是疑問代名詞，當形容詞，修飾名詞 jacket)

但是：

◉ Which do you think she will choose?
你想她會選哪個？

⊙ What happened yesterday at your office?
昨天你的辦公室裡發生了什麼事？

⊙ Whose is this?
這是誰的？

以上三句中的 which, what, whose 後面都沒有名詞可以修飾，只是代替已經提過的名詞，所以還是代名詞，不是形容詞。

(4)不定代名詞當形容詞(indefinite adjectives)

可修飾單、複數的名詞。

修飾單數名詞的有：another, each, either, much, neither, one

例如：

⊙ Each book costs twenty bucks.
每本書花費 20 元。
(each 是不定代名詞，當形容詞，修飾單數名詞 book)

但是：

⊙ He bought one of each.
他每一樣都各買一個。
(each 後面沒有名詞可以修飾，只是代替提過的名詞，所以還是代名詞，不是形容詞)

⊙ Please give Mr. B another chance.
請再給 B 先生一次機會。
(another 是不定代名詞，當形容詞，修飾名詞 chance)

但是：

⊙ you need to send me another.
你需要寄另一個給我。
(another 只是代替已經提過的名詞，故是代名詞，不是形容詞)

◉ Mr. A sent me only one letter.
A 先生只寄給我一封信。
(one 是不定代名詞，修飾單數名詞 letter，故是形容詞)

但是：

◉ We will choose one.
我們將會選出一個。
(one 是代替已經提過的名詞，所以只是代名詞)

修飾複數名詞的有：both, few, many, several

例如：

◉ Few people will sign the petition.
很少人會簽名請願。
(few 是不定代名詞，當形容詞，修飾多數名詞 people)

但是：

◉ Few remembered the old man's name.
很少人記得這位老先生的名字。
(few 的後面沒有名詞可以修飾，只是代替已經說過的名詞，所以還是代名詞，不是形容詞)

◉ Several students competed for scholarships.
有幾個學生爭取獎學金。
(several 是不定代名詞，當形容詞，修飾複數名詞 students)

但是：

◉ Several understood our real problem.
有幾位了解我們真正的問題。
(several 後面沒有名詞可以修飾，只是代替已經提過的名詞，故是代名詞，不是形容詞)

修飾單數或複數的名詞有：all, any, more, most, other, some

例如：

- Mr. A does not need any assistance.
  A 先生不需要任何協助。
  （any 是不定代名詞，當形容詞，修飾名詞 assistance）

但是：

- Mr. B does not want any.
  B 先生什麼都不要。
  （any 後面沒有名詞可以修飾，只是取代提過的名詞，所以還是代名詞）

- When I was in Taiwan, I bought some books.
  我在台灣時買了一些書。
  （some 修飾複數名詞 books，故是形容詞）

但是：

- I need some for the future.
  我需要一些以備不時之需。
  （some 後面沒有名詞可以修飾，只是取代提過的名詞，所以還是代名詞，不是形容詞）

4. 表語形容詞(predicate adjectives)

這種形容詞，通常放在連綴動詞(linking verb)的後面，當主詞的補語。

常用的連綴動詞是：be 動詞, become, grow, look, feel, smell, taste, sound, stay, turn, remain。

例如：

⊚ I was tired and thirsty after a long walk.
走了很久後我又累又渴。
(tired 和 thirsty 都是表語形容詞，放在連綴動詞 was 的後面，作為主詞 I 的補語)

⊚ Mr. A became impatient, because you were taking too long to respond.
你遲遲不回答讓 A 先生不耐煩了。
(impatient 是表語形容詞，在連綴動詞 became 後面，作主詞 Mr. A 的補語)

⊚ During the argument, John remained calm.
John 在爭吵中保持鎮定。
(calm 是表語形容詞，在連綴動詞 remained 後面，作主詞 John 的補語)

⊚ My wife seems healthy and rested after her vacation.
我太太度完假後看起來健康有精神。
(healthy 和 rested 都是表語形容詞，在連綴動詞 seems 後面，修飾主詞 wife，作主詞補語)

⊚ This small room grew crowded and stuffy.
這個小房間變得擁擠又悶熱。
(crowded 和 stuffy 都是表語形容詞，放在連綴動詞 grew 後面，修飾主詞 room，作主詞補語)

5. 分詞當作形容詞(participles used as adjectives)

包括現在分詞和過去分詞。

例如：

⊚ The trip to Taiwan was both exhausting and rewarding.
台灣行累人但有收穫。
(exhausting 和 rewarding 都是現在分詞，當形容詞，修飾主詞 trip)

- The sleeping baby looked so lovely.
  正在睡覺的嬰兒看起來真可愛。
  (sleeping 是現在分詞，當形容詞，修飾主詞 baby)

- Mr. B handed me his completed report.
  B 先生將寫完的報告交給我。
  (completed 是過去分詞，當形容詞，修飾名詞 report)

- Tired and discouraged, Mr. A dropped out of the marathon.
  因為疲憊和洩氣，A 先生退出了這場馬拉松賽。
  (tired 和 discouraged 都是過去分詞，當形容詞，修飾 Mr. A)

注意：

- The ringing bell at church was loud.
  教堂的鐘聲很響亮。
  (ringing 是現在分詞，修飾 bell)

但是：

The bell at church was ringing loudly.
(was ringing 是動詞過去進行式)

- The waxed piano shines.
  上過蠟的鋼琴閃閃發亮。
  (waxed 是過去分詞，修飾 piano)

但是：

My wife waxed the piano last week.
上周我太太人將鋼琴上蠟。
(waxed 只是動詞過去式)

三、形容詞的比較：

形容詞有三種比較：原級（positive）、比較級（comparative）和最高級（superlative）。

通常比較級是在形容詞原級後面加 er（或在其前加上 more/less），多半是比較兩個人，兩個地方或兩件事物。最高級是在形容詞原級後面加 est（或在其前加上 the most 或 the least），是比較兩個以上的人、地和事物。

例如：

⊙ Mr. A is tall.
A 先生很高。
(不與他人相比，故是原級)

⊙ Mr. B is taller than Mr. A.
B 先生比 A 先生高。
(兩人相比，故是比較級)

⊙ Mr. C is the tallest (of all).
C 先生是所有人中最高的。
(兩人以上相比，故是最高級)

⊙ The trip was more enjoyable than the last one.
這次旅行比上次更愉快。

⊙ Ms. Chang is the pickiest person in her family.
張小姐是她家最挑剔的人。

⊙ Mr. F is the most dependable person I have ever known.
F 先生是我認識最可靠的人。

四、形容詞比較的一般規則：

(1)遇到一個或兩個音節（syllable）時，通常在形容詞原級後面加 er，變成比較級；加 est，變成最高級。

例如：

單字	比較級	最高級
mean 刻薄的	meaner	the meanest
dull 乏味的	duller	the dullest
bright 明亮的	brighter	the brightest
plain 簡單明瞭的	plainer	the plainest
nice 美好的	nicer	the nicest
blue 沮喪的	bluer	the bluest（後面有 e，只加 r 或 st）
tiny 微小的	tinier	the tiniest
funny 好笑的	funnier	the funniest（後面有 y，把 y 改為 i，再加 er 或 est）

　　(2)形容詞原級有三個或三個以上音節時，通常在原級前面加 more/less，變成比較級；加 the most/the least 為最高級。

例如：

單字	比較級	最高級
delicate 精緻的	more delicate	the most delicate
affectionate 溫柔親切的	more affectionate	the most affectionate
ambitious 有野心的	more ambitious	the most ambitious
incredible 難以置信的	more incredible	the most incredible
terrible 糟糕的	more terrible	the most terrible

enthusiastic 熱心的	more enthusiastic	the most enthusiastic
generous 慷慨的	more generous	the most generous
responsible 負責任的	more responsible	the most responsible

(3)有時一個或兩個音節的形容詞，如果在原級後加 er 或 est 聽起來會很奇怪，所以也可以在前面加 more/less 變成比較級；加 the most/the least 成為最高級。

例如：

單字	比較級	最高級
vicious 邪惡的	more vicious	the most vicious
pleasing 令人高興的	more pleasing	the most pleasing
famous 出名的	more famous	the most famous
charming 迷人的	more charming	the most charming
obese 肥胖的	more obese	the most obese
moving 動人的	more moving	the most moving

(4)以下是最常用的不規則形容詞比較級和最高級，必須記住：

原級	比較級	最高級	注意事項
bad 壞的	worse	the worst	
good 好的	better	the best	

far 遠的	farther	the farthest	表示距離
	further	the furthest	表示程度
late 晚的	later	the latest	
little 少的	less	the least	指數量
many 許多的	more	the most	指可數的
much 大量的	more	the most	指不可數的

至於 less 和 least，也是形容詞的比較級和最高級，其實就是 more 和 most 的相反意義。

例如：

⊙ Mr. A is less ambitious than his younger brother.
A 先生不如他弟弟有野心。

⊙ Mr. B is the least ambitious in his family.
B 先生是他家裡最沒有野心的。

五、容易弄錯的形容詞比較：

1. 使用比較級時，不可把自己也包括在內，否則就不合理。

例如，不能說：

Mr. Wang's speech was shorter than any in the contest.

應該說：

⊚ Mr. Wang's speech was shorter than any other in the contest.
演講比賽中，王先生講的比任何人都短。
(在 any 後面加 other，成為「任何其他人」，才不會把王先生自己也包括在內)

同理，不能說：

Mary is more talkative than anyone/anybody in class.

應該說：

⊚ Mary is more talkative than anyone/anybody else in class.
Mary 在班上比任何人都愛講話。
(在 anyone 或 anybody 後面加 else，成為「任何其他人」，才不會把她自己也包括在內)

2. 使用比較時，不可用不同性質或不相關聯的東西(unrelated items)相比較，否則也是不合理。

例如，不能說：

⊚ John's article was longer than Mr. A.
(因為「文章」並不能與「A 先生」這個人作比較，否則不合理)

應該說：

⊚ John's article was longer than Mr. A's〔article〕.
John 的文章比 A 先生長。
(最後的 article 可省去)

也可以說：John's article was longer than that of Mr. A.
(that＝article)

或者說：John's article was longer than the one Mr. A wrote.
(較弱)

不能說：

The houses in Taipei are more expensive than in Maryland.

應該說：

◉ The houses in Taipei are more expensive than those in Maryland.
台北的房子比馬里蘭的貴。
(因房子本身不能與馬里蘭州相比，否則不合理)(those 是指 houses；單數時，就用 that)

3. 有些形容詞的本身意義，已經很完整，不宜相比。這種字，叫做「絕對修飾字」(absolute modifier)。

例如：eternal 永久的，fatal 致命的，infinite 無限的，mortal 會死的，final 最後的，perfect 完美的，unique 獨特的等等，其本身都有「絕對」的意義，所以通常不用 more、most 去比較。有時可用副詞 almost、nearly、quite 修飾。

不要說：

This will be his more (或 the most) final chance to win the race.
(因為沒有「比較最後」或「最最後」的說法，所以要把句中的 more 或 the most 刪去)

不要說：

By revising his composition, Mr. A made it more perfect.
(把句中 more 改為 nearly 或 almost，較為恰當)

但加強語氣時，可以說：

◉ What could be more perfect than Springtime!
還有什麼比春天更完美！

不要說：

This is the most unique vase in his antique collection.
這是他古董收藏裡最獨特的花瓶。
(把句中的 the most，改為 quite 或 nearly 或 almost 較恰當)

1-8

副詞的用法

副詞(adverb)與形容詞一樣，均修飾(modify)另一個字，使其意義顯得更特別、更明確(more specific)。

副詞通常是修飾動詞、形容詞或其他副詞；也就是回答：何處(where)、何時(when)、為何(how)或為什麼(why)。

副詞不論是單字、片語或子句，其用法和功用大致一樣。現分別說明：

一、單字副詞(single-word adverb)修飾動詞

1. 指 where 的單字副詞：

例如：

◉ The dictionary is right there.
字典就在那兒。
(副詞 there，是修飾動詞 is，說明何處)

◉ The wind scattered the newspaper everywhere.
風把報紙吹得到處都是。
(everywhere 是副詞，修飾動詞 scattered，說明何處)

◉ My daughter put her baby upstairs.
我女兒把她的寶寶放在樓上。
(upstairs 是副詞，修飾動詞 put，說明何處)

◉ Mr. A is trying to push his career forward.
A 先生試圖衝刺他的事業。
(forward 是副詞，修飾動詞 push，說明何處)

表示「何處、位置」的常見單字副詞還有：here, where, wherever, across, around, backwards, in, out, over, sideways, through, under, near 等。

2. 指 when 的單字副詞

例如:

◉ Mr. Wang will leave here soon for Taiwan.
王先生即將離開前往台灣。
(soon 是副詞,修飾動詞 leave,說明何時)

◉ Chung-hua Lee always likes to sign his name with "Dr."
李中華簽名時,總是喜歡冠上「博士」字樣。
(always 是副詞,修飾動詞 likes,說明常常喜歡,指何時)

◉ The ads for his new book finally appeared in the *World Journal*.
他的新書廣告最後在《世界日報》出現。
(finally 是副詞,修飾動詞 appeared,說明何時)

其他指「何時、時間、頻率等」的常見單字副詞還有:when, whenever, while, as, after, before, since, until, never, now, once, forever, seldom, weekly, monthly, yearly, frequently, eventually, occasionally 等。

3. 指 how 的單字副詞

例如:

◉ The police cautiously approached the angry crowd.
警察小心地接近憤怒的群眾。
(cautiously 是副詞,修飾動詞 approached 說明如何靠近)

◉ Mary speaks well in front of many people.
Mary 在眾人面前很會說話。
(well 是副詞,修飾動詞 speaks,說明如何說話)

◉ Many Chinese talk noisily at the table.
許多華人吃飯的時候說話很大聲。
（noisily 是副詞，修飾 talk，說明如何說話；at the table 在美式口語指「吃飯時」或「在吃飯」，dining table 則指家裡的餐桌）

◉ After finishing the exam, Mr. A was cheerfully humming to himself.
考完試後，A 先生自個兒愉快地哼著歌。
（cheerfully 是副詞，修飾動詞片語 was humming，說明如何哼歌）

◉ If you want to help someone, you need to do so willingly.
假如你要幫助人，你就需要樂意去做。
（willingly 是副詞，修飾 do，說明 how）

◉ Many people eagerly awaited news about Mr. A's visit to Cuba.
許多人渴望地等待A先生訪問古巴的消息。
（eagerly 是副詞，修飾 awaited，說明如何等待）

◉ No matter what a person's occupation is, we should treat him/her equally.
不論一個人從事何種職業，我們都該平等對待。
（equally 是副詞，修飾動詞 treat，說明如何對待）

◉ In order to keep herself slim, Miss Wang hardly eats.
為了保持身材苗條，王小姐很少吃東西。
（hardly 是副詞，修飾動詞 eats 說明程度）

◉ The Japanese government has angrily ignored complaints about its World War II crimes.
關於在二次世界大戰所犯下的罪行遭到抗議，日本政府憤怒地不予理會。
（angrily 是副詞，修飾 has ignored，說明如何不理）

◉ When she heard of her friend's passing away, she almost cried.

她聽到她朋友去世的消息，幾乎哭了。
（almost 是副詞，修飾動詞 cried，說明 how）

　其他指「程度，方法」的單字副詞，最常用的又如：sincerely 誠摯地，handily 靈巧地，hotly 熱切地，tirelessly 持久地，entirely 完整地，luckily 恰巧地，orderly 秩序地，mildly 溫和地，excessively 過分地，thoroughly 徹底地，scarcely 幾乎不等等。

二、單字副詞修飾形容詞

　一般放在形容詞前，表示到什麼程度（to what degree）

例如：

◉ Mr. B was completely surprised by his blood test results.
B 先生對他的抽血檢查結果感到十分驚訝。
（completely 是副詞，修飾形容詞 surprised，說明驚訝的程度）

◉ In my judgment, Mr. C's answer was roughly correct.
依我判斷，C 先生的回答大致正確。
（roughly 是副詞，修飾形容詞 correct，說明正確的程度）

◉ Mr. A was frequently absent from the meetings.
A 先生開會常常缺席。
（frequently 是副詞，修飾形容詞 absent，說明缺席程度）

◉ His boss was somewhat satisfied with his performance.
他的老闆對他的表現頗感滿意。
（somewhat 是副詞，修飾形容詞 satisfied，強調滿意的程度）

◉ After the heart surgery, Mr. B looked very weak.
B 先生開過心臟手術後，看起來非常虛弱。
(very 是副詞，修飾形容詞 weak，強調虛弱的程度)

◉ Your solution to the pay-raise issue was quite reasonable.
你解決加薪問題的方式相當合理。
(副詞 quite 修飾形容詞 reasonable，強調合理的程度)

◉ Most Americans seem extremely friendly at least on the surface.
大部分美國人至少在表面上顯得極為友善。
(extremely 是副詞，修飾形容詞 friendly，強調友善的程度)

◉ The water was absolutely still when we were in the fishing boat.
我們在漁船上時，海水完全平靜無波。
(副詞 absolutely 修飾形容詞 still，說明水平靜的程度)

◉ John is remarkably knowledgeable about high technology.
John 對高科技有卓越的知識。
(副詞 remarkably，修飾形容詞 knowledgeable，強調對知識了解的程度)

◉ My professor has a really profound knowledge of English.
我的教授對英語有相當淵博的知識。
(副詞 really 修飾形容詞 profound，強調淵博的程度)

◉ Our family was especially excited to see our old friend Mr. Huang.
我家人見到老友黃先生特別興奮。
(especially 是副詞，修飾形容詞 excited，說明興奮的程度)

◉ Are you nearly ready for your overseas trip?
你出國旅行大致準備好了嗎？
(副詞 nearly 修飾形容詞 ready，說明準備的程度)

常見單字副詞修飾形容詞的例子有：extremely beautiful 極漂亮，supremely confident 極度有自信，somewhat cold 有點寒冷，definitely wrong 絕對地錯，rather fluent 頗流利等等。

三、單字副詞修飾另一副詞

當副詞修飾另一副詞時，就是對另一個副詞的意義加以闡釋（to sharpen the meaning of another adverb）。

例如：

◉ The committee accepted my proposal surprisingly quickly.
委員會接受我提議的速度，出乎意料地快。
(副詞 surprisingly 修飾另一個副詞 quickly，加強了快速的程度)

◉ What you are thinking is not exactly what I meant yesterday.
你所想的不完全是我昨天的意思。
(副詞 exactly，修飾另一個副詞 not，強調真正的意義)

◉ Many Americans speak English too rapidly for foreigners to understand them.
許多美國人說英文說得太快，外國人很難聽懂。
(副詞 too 修飾另一個副詞 rapidly，強調快的程度；them 指 Americans)

◉ I believe that most editors can write extremely well.
我相信大部分的編輯文筆非常好。
(extremely 是副詞，修飾另一副詞 well，加強了好的程度)

◉ His girlfriend very happily accepted his marriage proposal.
他的女友非常高興地接受他的求婚。
(副詞 very 修飾另一副詞 happily，強調高興的程度)

⊙ Mr. C climbed the tree rather cautiously.
C 先生相當小心地爬樹。
(副詞 rather 修飾另一副詞 cautiously，加強小心的程度)

⊙ Please move the desk farther forward.
請把書桌往前移。
(副詞 farther 修飾另一副詞 forward，加重往前的程度)

⊙ Mrs. A is quite easily talked into changing her mind.
A 太太很容易被人說服而改變主意。
(副詞 quite 修飾另一副詞 easily，強調容易的程度)

⊙ I felt only slightly tired after a long walk.
走了很遠的路以後，我只覺得有一點累。
(副詞 only 修飾另一副詞 slightly，加重稍微的程度)

⊙ Mr. Chou told me that he would see me relatively soon.
周先生告訴我他很快就會來看我。
(副詞 relatively 修飾另一副詞 soon，加強快的程度)

⊙ My wife looked almost everywhere for my watch.
我太太為了我的手錶，幾乎到處都找遍了。
(副詞 almost 修飾另一副詞 everywhere，而 everywhere 又修飾動詞 looked)

⊙ He awaited the news somewhat nervously.
他等消息時有點緊張。
(副詞 somewhat 修飾另一副詞 nervously，加強希望的程度)

其他單字副詞修飾另一副詞的，又如：rather suddenly, too early, very swiftly, not completely, too willingly, less loudly, most enthusiastically, fairly well, almost always 等等。

四、介詞片語當副詞用：

它與單字副詞一樣，可以修飾動詞、形容詞或其他副詞，也可回答 where, when, how，所以也叫副詞片語。

例如：

◉ The committee members met in my office.
委員會成員在我的辦公室會面。
（in my office 是介詞片語，當副詞，修飾動詞 met 說明何處）

◉ A young woman ran into the street and screamed for help.
年輕女子跑到馬路上大聲求救。
（into the street 是介詞片語，當副詞，修飾動詞 ran，說明何處）

◉ I made a long-distance call at six o'clock.
6 點鐘時，我打了一通長途電話。
（at six o'clock 是介詞片語，修飾動詞 made，說明何時）

◉ I always write my articles with great care.
＝I always write my articles carefully.
我寫文章一直很細心。
（with great care 是介詞片語，當副詞，修飾動詞 write，說明如何寫）

◉ After supper, my wife and I took a walk.
晚餐後，我太太和我去散步。
（after supper 是介詞片語，當副詞，修飾動詞 took，說明何時）

◉ Mr. J writes articles for his own pleasure.
J 先生因自身興趣而寫文章。
（for his own pleasure 是介詞片語，當副詞，修飾動詞 write，說明為什麼要寫）

◉ Mr. A's writing is famous for its simplicity and clarity.
A 先生的寫作因文筆簡潔明晰而聞名。
(for its simplicity and clarity 是介詞片語,當副詞,修飾形容詞 famous。通常片語都放在形容詞後面)

◉ The little girl seems to be afraid of the strangers.
小女孩似乎害怕陌生人。
(of the strangers 是介詞片語,當副詞,修飾形容詞 afraid)

◉ That article is full of practical experience.
那篇文章滿是實用的建議。
(of practical experience 是介詞片語,當副詞,修飾形容詞 full)

◉ Mr. F wrote several books late in life.
F 先生晚年寫了幾本書。
(in life 是介詞片語,修飾另一副詞 late)

◉ The noise can be reduced only by sound-proofing.
此噪音只有用隔音設備才能減低。
(by sound-proofing 是介詞片語,修飾另一副詞 only)

五、從屬子句(subordinate clause)當副詞子句用:

副詞子句與單字副詞一樣,可修飾動詞、形容詞或其他副詞,也回答 when,where,how 或 why。但這種子句,通常以從屬連接詞(subordinating conjunctions)引導。最常用的從屬連接詞是:after, before, although, as, as if, as long as, as soon as, because, as though, if, since, so that, in order that, than, provided that, though, unless, until, when, whenever, where, wherever, while 等。

例如:

◉ The baseball game will start when the rain stops.
當雨停了，棒球賽就會開始。
（when the rain stops 是附屬子句，也是副詞子句，修飾動詞 start，回答何時）

◉ Mr. Lee spoke as though he knew everything.
李先生說起話來一副什麼都懂的樣子。
（as though he knew everything 是副詞子句，修飾動詞 spoke，回答如何說話）

◉ Please put the package wherever you can find a place.
只要你能找到地方放包裹，就請把它放在那兒。
（wherever you can find a place 是副詞子句，修飾動詞 put，回答何處）

◉ He will help with your thesis whenever you ask.
不論你何時需要，他都會幫你寫論文。
（whenever you ask 是副詞子句，修飾動詞 help，說明何時）

◉ Sit where I can see you.
坐在我看得到你的地方。
（where I can see you 是副詞子句，修飾動詞 sit，說明何處）

◉ Unless you hurry, you will be late for the meeting.
你要快一點，否則開會會遲到。
（unless you hurry 是副詞子句，修飾形容詞 late，說明如何行動）

◉ Mr. A was glad, because I helped him finish the project.
A 先生很高興，因為我幫他完成這計畫。
（because I helped him finish the project 是副詞子句，修飾形容詞 glad，說明為什麼高興）

◉ I was tired after I had walked for two hours.
我走了兩小時後，覺得累了。
（after I had walked for two hours 是副詞子句，修飾形容詞 tired，說明為何疲累）

⊙ The movie lasted longer than I had expected.
電影放映時間比我預料的長。
（than I had expected 是副詞子句，修飾另一副詞 longer，說明時間程度）

⊙ We arrived at the theater early so that we could find better seats.
我們提早到電影院，是為了找比較好的座位。
（so that we could find better seats 是副詞子句，修飾另一副詞 early，說明為何提早）

六、名詞當作副詞用

有些名詞，可當副詞用，多半說明 when 或 where，常用的有：home, today, yesterday, tomorrow, morning, evening, day, night, year, Monday, Tuesday 等。

例如：

⊙ I saw Mr. Wang yesterday.
我昨天看到了王先生。
（yesterday 本是名詞，現當副詞用，修飾動詞 saw，說明何時）

⊙ After school, the boy ran home.
放學後，這個男孩跑回家去。
（home 本是名詞，現當副詞用，修飾動詞 ran，說明何處）

⊙ Mr. B attends school days and works nights.
B 先生白天上學，晚上工作。
（days 和 nights 當副詞用，修飾動詞 attends 和 works，說明何時）

⊙ The Huangs are leaving for Taiwan tomorrow.
黃家明天動身前往台灣。
（tomorrow 本是名詞，現當副詞用，修飾 are leaving，說明何時）

◉ Mr. C must definitely see a doctor today.
C 先生今天一定要看醫生。
（名詞 today，當副詞用，修飾動詞 see，說明何時；另一副詞 definitely 也修飾 see）

◉ Saturdays and Sundays, Mary usually baby-sits for her neighbor.
每週六與週日，Mary 常幫鄰居看小孩。
（Saturdays 和 Sundays 原本都是名詞，現當副詞用，修飾動詞 baby-sits，說明何時）

◉ I walked approximately three miles Thursday.
星期四我大約走了三哩路。
（Thursday 當副詞用，修飾動詞 walked，說明何時；如果 Thursday 前加上介詞 on，那麼不但加強語氣，也變成副詞片語了）

但不可與真正的名詞弄錯。

例如：

◉ To me, Monday was a good day, but what happened Thursday was better.
對我來說，星期一是美好的一天，但星期四發生的事更好。
（Monday 是真正的名詞；Thursday 是副詞，修飾動詞 happened）

七、副詞放置的位置

1. 單字副詞多半可放在句首、句中或句尾。但介詞片語當副詞時，一般要放在所修飾的字旁邊。從屬子句當副詞時，因放在句中顯得彆扭，所以美國人並不常用，故少用為妙。

例如：

◉ Silently, John approached the classroom.
　＝John silently approached the classroom.
　＝John approached the classroom silently.
　John 靜靜地走近教室。

◉ Immediately, Mr. A answered her question.
　＝Mr. A immediately answered her question.
　＝Mr. A answered her question immediately.
　A 先生很快就回答她的問題。
　(副詞 silently 和 immediately 修飾動詞 approached 和 answered)

◉ Mr. B left the office without a word.
　＝Without a word, Mr. B left the office.
　B 先生一聲不響地離開辦公室。
　(without a word 是介詞片語，當副詞，修飾動詞 left)

◉ My student wrote his composition with great care.
　＝With great care, my student wrote his composition.
　我學生非常用心地寫他的文章。
　(with great care 是介詞片語，當副詞，修飾動詞 wrote)

◉ Mr. Wang is happy about his academic achievements.
　王先生對他學術上的成就感到高興。
　(about his academic achievements 是介詞片語，當副詞，修飾形容詞 happy；不宜放在句首或句中，因為要盡量靠近所修飾的字)

◉ Many new immigrants in the U.S. are dissatisfied with their financial situations.
　美國許多新移民對他們的經濟情況感到不滿意。
　(with their financial situations 是介詞片語，當副詞用，修飾形容詞 dissatisfied，不宜放在句首或句中，因為與所修飾的形容詞距離太遠時，顯得彆扭)

- The picnic will be canceled if it rains.
  ＝If it rains, the picnic will be canceled.
  如果下雨，野餐就會被取消。
  (副詞子句 if it rains，修飾動詞 canceled)

注意

> 副詞子句放在句首時，要加逗點；放在句尾，則不必。

2. 表示「地點」或「時間」的副詞或副詞片語，通常把「較小」的，放在前面，「較大」的，放在後面。

例如：

- Mr. B lives in a ranch house on Smith Street.
  B 先生住在 Smith 街的一棟平房裡。
  (in a ranch house 和 on Smith Street 都是介詞片語，當副詞用。Ranch 比 street 小，多半放在前面)

- The package was placed on the desk in my room.
  有人把包裹放在我房間的書桌上。
  (on the desk 和 in my room 都是副詞片語，也是介詞片語，但 desk 比 room 小，多半放在前面)

- I had a doctor appointment at 10 a.m. on Monday.
  星期一早上10點我去看醫生。
  (at 10 a.m. 和 on Monday 都是副詞片語，但 10 a.m. 比 Monday 小，多半放在前面)

遇到句中有兩個副詞，一個指「地點」，另一個指「時間」時，那麼通常把指地點的副詞放在前面。

例如：

⊚ Mr. B was studying at our college last semester.
上學期 B 先生在我們大學修課。
(at our college 指地點的副詞片語，last semester 指時間的副詞，都是修飾動詞 was studying，所以把指地點的，放在前面)

⊚ Mr. C works at the store every day.
C 先生每天在店裡工作。
(at the store 是指地點的副詞片語，故放在前面；every day 是指時間的副詞，放在後面)

如果說：At the store, Mr. C works every day.(不好)

⊚ I watched a TV show here last night.
昨晚我在這裡看電視節目。
(here 是指地點的副詞，故放在前面；last night 是指時間的副詞，故放在後面)

如果說：I watched a TV show last night here.(不好)

3. 表示「頻率」的副詞(frequency adverbs)，多半是放在普通動詞的前面，但是往往放在連綴動詞的後面。最常用的頻率副詞是：always, usually, often, rarely, almost, finally, never, generally, occasionally, seldom 等。

例如：

⊚ Mr. A always arrives(或 arrived)on time.
A 先生都準時到達。
(副詞 always 放在普通動詞 arrives 前面)

⊚ Mrs. Lin is always cheerful.
林太太總是開朗的。
(always 放在 be 動詞 "is" 的後面)

副詞的用法 >> 1-8

- Mr. Wang often came home late.
  王先生常常很晚回家。
  (副詞 often 放在普通動詞 come 前面)

- I never intended to be a leader; I am always a helper.
  我從來都不想當老大，我只要當助手。
  (副詞 never 放在普通動詞 intended 前面；而 always 放在 be 動詞
  "am" 的後面)

- Is Mr. Wang usually punctual for work?
  王先生平時上班守時嗎？
  (副詞 usually 放在 is 的後面)

- Did he finally finish his project?
  他終於完成計畫了嗎？
  (副詞 finally 放在普通動詞 finish 前面)

八、連接副詞（conjunctive adverbs）

有些副詞可把兩個意思不同的句子，順利地連接起來。最常
用的是：accordingly, also, anyway, besides, however, consequently,
furthermore, indeed, incidentally, instead, moreover, nevertheless,
otherwise, then, thus, therefore, meanwhile, still, again, next 等。

例如：

- Mr. A worked hard, so he succeeded.
  A 先生工作努力，因而他成功了。
- Our school has issued a dress code; we must dress accordingly.
  我們學校公布了服裝規定，所以我們要照規定穿。
  (accordingly 多半放在句尾)

⊙ Eat your breakfast, then, go to school.
吃早餐，然後去上學。

⊙ Mr. B had some unpleasant experience with his friends, hence/therefore, he trusts nobody.
B 先生跟朋友有過不愉快的經驗，因此他不相信任何人。

⊙ He saw the show, however, he did not enjoy it.
他看了表演，但並不喜歡。

⊙ Mr. J has retired, nevertheless, he keeps writing articles for the magazine.
J 先生已退休，但他仍然為雜誌寫稿。
（nevertheless＝nonetheless）

⊙ His car broke down; consequently, he had to walk home.
他的汽車壞了；結果必須走路回家。

⊙ Mr. Wang came late, furthermore, he forgot to bring me the book.
王先生遲到了，而且忘了帶書給我。

九、注意事項

1. 副詞的比較，也有原級、比較級和最高級，與形容詞相似。

不過副詞的比較，多半用動作動詞（action verb），而形容詞的比較，多半用連綴動詞（linking verb）。副詞最高級前的 the，往往可省去，但形容詞最高級前的 the 則不能省去。

例如：

副詞比較：

- He smiled pleasantly in front of us. (原級)
  他在我們面前笑得很開心。

- He smiled more pleasantly when he met her. (比較級)
  他遇見她時笑得更開心。

- He smiled (the) most pleasantly when he got a date. (最高級)
  當他有約會時，笑得最開心。
  (smiled 是動作動詞；最高級前的 the 可省去)

形容詞比較：

- He was pleasant in front of us. (原級)
  他在我們面前很開心。

- He was more pleasant when.... (比較級)
  他遇見她時更開心。

- He was the most pleasant when.... (最高級)
  他有約會時最開心。
  (was 是連綴動詞；最高級前的 the，不能省去)

2. 副詞比較時，與形容詞一樣，也不能把自己包括在內，
   所以要加 other 或 else。

   例如：

- John runs faster than anyone/anybody else in the competition.
  John 在這場比賽中跑得比任何人都快。

- He wrote his term paper more carefully than any other student
  in the class.
  他比班上其他任何一位學生都更仔細地寫他的學期報告。

3. 雖然多半副詞是由形容詞後面加 ly 而來，但有 ly 的字未
必都是副詞，有時也是形容詞。

例如：

⦿ Mr. Lee is an elderly man.
李先生是位老人。
（elderly 是形容詞）

⦿ He offered his girlfriend some brotherly advice.
他給女友一些兄長般的忠告。
（brotherly 是形容詞；fatherly, motherly, sisterly 都是形容詞）

⦿ The young lady gave me a neighborly wave.
年輕女子對我友善的招手。
（（neighborly 是形容詞）

⦿ Mr. A married a homely woman with a kind heart.
A 先生娶了一位其貌不揚，但心地善良的太太。
（homely 是形容詞）

⦿ Miss Wang's stately performance on stage surprised us.
王小姐在台上表現莊重，令我們吃驚。
（stately 是形容詞）

其他又如：lonely man 孤單的男子，lovely personality 可愛
的個性，ugly scene 可怕的場面，kingly feast 國王般的宴席，
leisurely speed 悠閒的速度，friendly smile 友善的笑容，daily
exercise 每天的運動，timely decision 及時的決定等等。

1-9
介詞的用法

使用介詞(preposition)可以表達字與字間的關係，也就是表達句子裡名詞(或代名詞)與其他字的關係。以下即以最常用的介詞，舉例說明。

一、用不同的介詞，句子就有不同的意義

例如：

⊙ The airplane flew toward the tall building.
飛機飛向高樓。
(說明了 flew 與 building 間的關係。如果把介詞 toward 改用其他介詞 above 或 around 或 into 或 in back of，那麼意思就不同了)

⊙ We were walking through the park.
我們正走過公園。
(說明 walking 與 park 間的關係。假如把介詞 through 改為 around 或 near 或 toward 或 from，意義就不同了)

同理：

⊙ He was at Mr. Wang's house yesterday.
他昨天在王先生家。
(用介詞 at 表示已經在王先生家)

⊙ He went to Mr. Wang's house yesterday.
他昨天去王先生家。
(用 to 表示朝王先生家走)

⊙ He walked by Mr. Wang's house yesterday.
他昨天經過王先生家。
(用 by 表示經過王先生家)

常用的介詞：about, above, across, after, against, along, among, around, at, before, behind, below, beneath, beside, besides, between, beyond, but(＝except), by, down, despite, during, except, for, from, in, inside, into, like, near, of, off, on, opposite, out, outside, over, past, since, through, to, toward（＝towards）, under, underneath, until(＝till), up, upon, with, without 等。

例如：

⊙ He sat beside his wife during the banquet.
宴會時，他坐在太太旁邊。
(beside＝next to 或 at the side of)

⊙ The committee chose two members besides me for the budget problem.
由於預算問題，除了我之外，委員會還選了兩位委員。
(besides＝in addition to)

⊙ The votes were divided between Mr. A and Mr. B.
選票由 A 先生、B 先生兩人瓜分。
(表示兩者之間用 between)

The votes were divided among Mr. A, Mr. B, and Mr. C.
選票由 A 先生、B 先生和 C 先生三人所瓜分。
(表示兩者以上用 among)

⊙ You may come to see me any day but Sunday.
除了星期天以外，你任何日子都可以來看我。
(but＝except)

⊙ Statewide contributions for 2008 exceeded those of 2007 by 10%.
全州的捐款，2008 年比 2007 年多了 10%。

◎ Despite his limited income, he is still willing to help others.
雖然他收入有限，他還是願意幫助別人。
（＝Although his income is limited, he is...）

◎ Of all the major powers, the U.S. has the most experience in guerrilla warfare.
在所有強國中，美國對游擊戰最富經驗。
（of＝among）

◎ She pulled the chair out from under the table.
她從桌子下面拉出椅子。
（為了精確表示出從桌子下拿出來的動作，可用兩個介詞 from 和 under；out 只是副詞，修飾動詞 pulled）

常用的複合介詞：according to, ahead of, apart from, aside from, as of, because of, by means of, in the name of, in addition to, in back of, in case of, in front of, in place of, in regard to, instead of, in spite of, in view of, next to, on account of, on top of, out of, owing to, prior to, with a view to 等。

例如：

◎ A slow truck was ahead of my car.
我的車前面有輛慢吞吞的卡車。

◎ Apart from being beautiful, she is smart and helpful.
除了美麗之外，她還很聰明又樂於助人。
（apart from＝besides＝in addition to）

◎ He does not know many people in this community aside from the Wangs.
除了王家外，他在這社區沒有認識很多人。
（aside from＝except）

◉ His resignation will take effect as of mid-July.
他的辭職將自 7 月中旬起生效。
（as of＝from）

◉ In view of his success in business, he was asked to run for the company presidency.
由於他在商界很成功，他被要求角逐公司總裁職務。
（in view of＝considering）

◉ He bought this old car with the intention of rebuilding its engine and reselling it for a profit.
他買這部舊車是為了要改裝引擎，轉手賣出得利。
（with the intention of＝for the purpose of）

◉ Owing to a staff shortage, all buses are running late.
由於人手不足，所有公車都脫班了。
（owing to＝on account of）

◉ The man by the name of Wang Chunghua was a teacher.
這位男士名叫王中華，是位教師。

但是：

◉ In the name of the law, I order you to stop doing that.
我依法命令你停止這個行為。
（in the name of＝in the cause of）

◉ In case of emergency, call the police for help.
遇到緊急情況時，打電話向警察求助。
（in case of＝in the event of）

但是：

◉ In the case of John vs. Smith, the judge ruled in favor of Smith.
（比較常用）
關於 John 與 Smith 的案子，法官判決 Smith 勝訴。
（in the case of＝in the matter of＝in the legal case of，通常指法律特別案件）

◉ He is sitting in the back of the room.
他坐在房間內最後頭。

但是：

◉ He is sitting in back of the room.
(指他坐在房間後面，也可能是房間之外)

二、介詞和副詞的分別

介詞只是介詞片語(prepositional phrase)的一部分，並且有名詞或代名詞為受詞。但副詞是獨立使用，沒有受詞(object)。

例如：

◉ The teacher talked to his students before the game.
遊戲開始前老師和他的學生講話。
(before 是介詞，game 是介詞的受詞，before the game 就是介詞片語)

◉ I have never seen this person before.
我從來沒有見過這個人。
(before 是副詞，修飾 seen，沒有受詞)

◉ The fishing boat was found underneath the bridge.
漁船是在橋下找到的。
(underneath 是介詞，bridge 是介詞的受詞)

◉ To repair the car, the mechanic crawled underneath.
為了修理汽車，技師爬到車子下面。
(underneath 是副詞，修飾動詞 crawled，沒有受詞)

◉ His father told her about his war experience.
他爸爸告訴她有關他作戰的經驗。
(about 是介詞，experience 是介詞的受詞)

◉ As he was upset, he walked about for a few minutes.
他因為苦惱而閒逛了幾分鐘。
(about 是副詞，修飾 walked；for a few minutes 是副詞片語，也修飾
動詞 walked)

◉ The students played football behind the school yard.
學生在學校操場的後面踢足球。
(behind 是介詞，yard 是介詞受詞)

◉ Just leave your worries behind when you go on vacation.
度假時就要把煩惱都拋到腦後！
(behind 是副詞，修飾 leave；when you go on vacation 是附屬子句，也
當副詞用，修飾動詞 leave)

也可以說：

Just leave behind your worries...

◉ The library is two blocks further on the right.
再走兩條街，右手邊就是圖書館。
(on 是介詞，right 是介詞的受詞)

◉ Please turn on the light before it gets dark.
天黑前請開燈。
(on 是副詞，修飾動詞 turn；before it gets dark 是副詞子句，也修飾
turn)

三、介詞片語當形容詞用（也叫形容詞片語）

　　片語是不含主詞和動詞的。介詞片語，也只是一個介詞搭
配名詞或代名詞組成。介詞片語不論長短，就像單字的形容詞一
樣，可修飾主詞的名詞或代名詞，直接或間接受詞以及主詞的補
語。

1. 介詞片語，有時可改成單字形容詞(single-word adjective)，修飾名詞。

不過介詞片語要放在所修飾字的後面，而單字形容詞，通常放在所修飾字的前面。

（例如：）

● The boys in the neighborhood have formed a baseball team.
社區的男孩已組成一支棒球隊。
(in the neighborhood 是介詞片語，修飾主詞的名詞 boys，但要放在 boys 的後面)

也可以說：

The neighborhood boys have formed a baseball team.
(neighborhood 形容 boys，但放在 boys 前面)

● Twenty children in good health participated in the study.
20 個健康的孩子參加了該項研究。
(in good health 是介詞片語，形容 children，放在 children 後面)

也就是：Twenty healthy children participated in...
(healthy 形容 children，放在 children 前面)

● The father with angry face punished his son.
臉上帶有怒氣的父親處罰了他的兒子。
(with angry face 是介詞片語，形容 father，放在 father 後面)

也可以說：

The angry-faced father punished his son.
(face 後面要加 d 當形容詞，修飾 father)

● The girl with blue eyes and brown hair is pretty.
這個棕髮碧眼的女孩很漂亮。
(with blue eyes and brown hair 是介詞片語，修飾 girl)

也可勉強說：

The blue-eyed, brown-haired girl is pretty.（用介詞片語較好）

◉ He bought a car with power windows and airbags.
他買了一輛配有自動車窗和安全氣囊的汽車。（較好）

不能說：He bought a power-windowed and air-bagged car.

形容詞片語，修飾主詞補語(subject complement)時，也不能使動詞與補語相距太遠。動詞多半是連綴動詞。

(例如：)

◉ Mr. Chou is a man of fine character.（較好）
周先生是位品格高尚的人。

Mr. Chou is a fine-charactered man.（不好）
(man 是主詞 Mr. Chou 的補助語，of fine character 是形容詞片語，修飾 man)

◉ Mr. Chang's opinion is of no value.
張先生的意見沒有價值。
(opinion 是主詞，of no value 是形容詞片語，修飾主詞)

也可以說：Mr. Chang's opinion is valueless.

◉ This is another book by the same author.
這是同一位作者的另一本書。
(book 是主詞 this 的補助語，by the same author 是形容詞片語修飾 book)

但不能說：This is the same author another book.因為動詞 is 與主詞補助語 book 相距太遠。

- He seems to be a man without money, health, or companionship.
  他似乎是個沒錢、沒健康又沒朋友的男人。
  (man 是主詞 he 的補助語，without money, health, or companionship 是形容詞片語，修飾 man)

  但不能說：He seems to be a without money, health, or companionship man. 因為主詞 he 的補助語 man，與動詞 seems 相距太遠。

2. 介詞片語，當形容詞可修飾直接或間接受詞，也可修飾句中相同或不同的名詞。

  例如：

- I wrote a report for students and faculty.
  我為學生和教授們寫了一篇報告。
  (for students and faculty 是形容詞片語，修飾直接受詞 report)

- He does not like people with neither ability nor aspirations.
  他不喜歡既沒能力又沒抱負的人。
  (with neither ability nor aspirations 是包括連接詞 neither... nor 的形容詞片語，修飾直接受詞 people)

- Our university awarded Mr. Wang from Taiwan a doctorate.
  我們大學授予博士學位給來自台灣的王先生。
  (from Taiwan 是形容詞片語，修飾間接受詞 Mr. Wang)
  ＝Our university awarded a doctorate to Mr. Wang from Taiwan.

- The teacher gave his students with high scores less homework.
  老師給分數高的學生較少作業。
  (with high scores 是形容詞片語，修飾直接受詞 students)
  ＝The teacher gave less homework to his students with high scores.

- The bouquet of roses on the table arrived today.
  桌上的這束玫瑰是今天送達的。
  (句中兩句介詞片語 of roses 和 on the table 都是修飾主詞 bouquet)

- The grocery store near the entrance to the subway sells sandwiches.
  靠近地鐵入口的雜貨店有賣三明治。
  (near the entrance 是形容詞片語，修飾 store，而 to the subway 又是修飾 entrance)

- The carton of eggs on the bottom of the pile was crushed.
  這堆東西最下面的這盒雞蛋被壓破了。
  (形容詞片語 of eggs 和 on the bottom 都是修飾主詞 carton；但 of the pile 又是修飾 bottom)

四、介詞片語當副詞用（也叫副詞片語）

　　介詞片語當作副詞用時，就像單字的副詞一樣，可修飾動詞、形容詞或其他副詞。

1. 副詞片語，有時可改為單字副詞：

例如：

- Please drive with care.
  請小心開車。
  (介詞片語 with care，當副詞，修飾動詞 drive)

  可改為：Please drive carefully.

- The basketball team played with great skill.
  籃球隊打球很有技巧。
  (副語片語 with great skill，修飾動詞 played)

可改為：The basketball team played well.

但不能說：The basketball team well played.

◉ Many Chinese often talk in a loud voice.
許多中國人說話嗓門大。
(介詞片語 in a loud voice，當副詞，修飾 talk)
可改為：Many Chinese often talk loudly.
(副詞 loudly 修飾 talk；在非正式時，也有人用 loud，不用 loudly)

但有的副語片語，沒有單字副詞可以代替。

(例如：)

◉ I traveled by train.
我乘火車旅行。
(介詞片語 by train，沒有單字副詞可以代替)

(同理：)

◉ She sang in our church.
她在我們教堂唱歌。

◉ Suddenly, a fly landed on my head.
突然間，有一隻蒼蠅停在我頭上。
(in our church 和 on my head 都不能用單字副詞代替)

2. 介詞片語，當副詞用(即副詞片語)，可以修飾相同的動詞，形容詞或其他副詞。

(例如：)

◉ On Sundays, Mr. Hsu studies at the library.
每週日，徐先生都在圖書館讀書。
(on Sundays 和 at the library 都是副詞片語，修飾動詞 studies)

◉ In his spare time, Mr. Wang wandered through the woods.
王先生閒暇時在樹林中漫步。
(in his spare time 和 through the woods 都是副詞片語，修飾動詞
wandered)

◉ After the baseball game, the team left without delay to the
restaurant.
棒球賽比完後，隊員立即到餐廳去。
(after the baseball game, without delay, to the restaurant 都是副詞片語，
修飾動詞 left)

◉ The boy was sleepy during the football game.
男孩看足球賽時打瞌睡。
(during the football game 是副詞片語，修飾形容詞 sleepy)

◉ Mr. Wang was very upset at her refusal.
王先生對她的拒絕很不高興。
(at her refusal 是副詞片語，修飾形容詞 upset)

◉ Mr. Lee was mean toward (to) either me or Mr. A.
李先生對我還是 A 先生都不友善。
(toward either me or Mr. A 是副詞片語，修飾形容詞 mean; toward＝
towards)

◉ We discussed it late into the midnight.
我們討論到三更半夜。
(late 是副詞，修飾動詞 discussed；而副詞片語 into the midnight 修飾 late)

◉ He finished the project earlier in the week.
他在本週稍早時就完成了該計畫。
(earlier 是副詞，修飾動詞 finished；而副詞片語 in the week 則是修飾
earlier)

五、一般形容詞片語，要靠近所形容的字眼，但副詞片語，可放在句首或句後，有時也可放在句中。

> 例如：

◉ In a well-prepared speech, Mr. Wang explained his point of view.
在一次準備充分的演講裡，王先生解釋了他的觀點。

可放在句後：Mr. Wang explained his point of view in a well-prepared speech.

如果放在句中：Mr. Wang, in a well-prepared speech, explained his point of view. 文法上可以接受，但不好，因為主詞 Mr. Wang 與動詞 explained 相距太遠。

◉ With the assistance of his loyal and helpful employees, the boss finally finished the project.
老闆在他忠誠又有幫助的員工協助之下，終於完成了計畫。

可放在句後：The boss finally finished the project with the assistance of his loyal and helpful employees.

如放在句中：The boss, with the assistance of his loyal and helpful employees, finally finished the project. 文法上可以接受，但不好，因為主詞 The boss 和動詞 finished 相距太遠。

◉ Without any help, his wife canned a dozen apples.
他老婆在沒有任何協助之下將一打蘋果裝罐。

放在句尾：His wife canned a dozen apples without any help.

如果放在句中：His wife, without any help, canned a dozen apples. 文法上可以接受，但不好。

◉ Despite their increasing representation in the work force, the income of women has failed to approach that of men.
儘管女性在職場上的表現提昇，收入仍然趕不上男性。

可放在句尾：The income of women has failed to approach that of men despite their increasing representation in the work force.

如果放在句中：The income of women, despite their increasing representation in the work force, has failed to approach that of men. 主詞 The income 與動詞 failed 相距太遠，故不好

有時為了加強語氣，多半把副詞片語放在句首。

例如：

◉ In his bare feet, he ran the ten-mile race from the school through the park to the finish line.
他赤著腳，從學校穿越公園，跑了 10 哩到達終點。
(因為強調的是 in his bare feet，所以不放在句尾)

1-10

連接詞和感嘆詞

一般來說，連接詞（conjunction）要比感嘆詞（interjection）重要。在此，先談連接詞（也叫連詞）。

一、連接詞

連詞是用來連接單字、片語或句子。可分為四類來說明。

1. 對等連接詞(coordinating conjunction)

連接兩個或兩個以上的相等詞類、片語或句子。最常用的對等連接詞有：and, but, for, nor, or, so, yet, while 等。

連接名詞或代名詞：

⦿ The teacher and his student designed this project.
老師和他的學生設計了此企畫。
(and 連接了兩個名詞 teacher 和 student)

⦿ Will you have a hot dog or a hamburger?
你要熱狗還是漢堡？
(or 連接兩個名詞 hot dog 和 hamburger)

⦿ She and he seldom agree on anything.
她和他鮮少意見一致。
(and 連接了代名詞 she 和 he)

連接動詞：

⦿ The dog barked but wagged its tail.
這隻狗邊叫卻邊搖著尾巴。
(but 連接兩個動詞 barked 和 wagged；動詞時態：wag, wagged, wagging＝waggle, waggled, waggling)

◉ Did you fly or drive to New York?
你去紐約是搭飛機還是開車？
(or 連接兩個動詞 fly 和 drive)

◉ Some teenagers laughed, sang, and danced last night.
昨晚一些青少年歡笑、歌唱和跳舞。
(and 連接動詞 laughed, sang 和 danced)

連接形容詞：

◉ The pork chop was tender and large, yet tasteless.
豬排很嫩又大塊，但沒味道。
(yet 連接形容詞 tender, large 和 tasteless)

◉ Mrs. Lin's dress is beautiful but expensive.
林太太的洋裝很美但很貴。
(but 連接形容詞 beautiful 和 expensive)

◉ Mrs. Lin wore a simple and elegant outfit.
林太太穿了一套簡單又高雅的套裝。
(and 連接形容詞 simple 和 elegant)

連接副詞：

◉ He wrote an article slowly and carefully.
他寫文章慢工出細活。
(and 連接了兩個副詞 slowly 和 carefully)

◉ Mr. A responded quickly but incorrectly.
A 先生回答得很快，但不正確。
(but 連接了兩個副詞 quickly 和 incorrectly)

◉ John ran the marathon swiftly and easily.
John 跑馬拉松跑得又快又輕鬆。
(and 連接了副詞 swiftly 和 easily)

連接介詞片語：

◉ You may leave the box on the desk or in the closet.
你可以把盒子放在書桌上或放進衣櫥裡。
(or 連接了兩個介詞片語 on the desk 和 in the closet)

◉ The old man followed the trail up the hill and along the river.
老人沿著小徑走上小山丘，並順著河邊往前走。
(and 連接介詞片語 up the hill 和 along the river)

◉ Several cars were parked in the street and in the driveway.
有幾輛車停在路邊和車道上。
(and 連接介詞片語 in the street 和 in the driveway)

連接獨立句或附屬子句：

◉ John likes basketball, but he prefers to play baseball.
John 喜歡籃球，但他更喜歡打棒球。
(but 連接兩個獨立子句 John likes basketball 和 he prefers to play baseball；but 的前面，要加逗號)

◉ I went to bed early, for I was exhausted.
我早早就上床睡覺，因為我累死了。
(for 連接兩個獨立子句 I went to bed early 和 I was exhausted；for 的前面，要加逗號)

◉ You may consider this proposal, or you may ignore it.
這個提案，你可以考慮也可以不予理會。
(連詞 or，連接兩個獨立子句 you may consider this proposal 和 you may ignore it)

◉ I waited for an hour, yet no one showed up.
我等了一小時，但沒有人出現。
(yet 連接兩個獨立子句 I waited for an hour 和 no one showed up)

- Their team was not well-trained, while ours was highly trained. (while＝but; ours＝our team)

  他們的隊伍訓練不足，但我們隊卻訓練有素。

  (while 連接了兩個獨立子句 their team was not well-trained 和 ours was highly trained。所以使用對等連接詞連接兩個獨立子句時，連接詞前要加逗號，但連接單字或片語時，則不必加逗號)

- Mr. A had not succeeded before, nor was he likely to succeed now.

  A 先生過去沒有成功，現在也不太可能成功。

  (以 nor 連接兩個獨立子句時，第一句多半是含有 not 的否定句，第二句因為 nor 放在句首，所以用倒裝句型，亦即動詞常移到在主詞前面)

- Mr. B told me that he had enjoyed the trip but that he caught a cold.

  B 先生告訴我他這次旅行玩得很愉快，不過感冒了。

  (but 連接兩個附屬子句 that he had enjoyed the trip 和 that he caught a cold)

- I knew (that) it was late and that I had to hurry.

  我知道時間不早了，所以要快一點。

  (and 連接兩個附屬子句 that it was late 和 that I had to hurry；第一個 that 可省，但第二個 that 通常不能省)

2. 相關連接詞(correlative conjunction)

與上述對等連接詞相似，相關連接詞也是連接相等或相似的詞類、片語或句子。不過它們多半都成對或成雙(in pairs)使用。

最常用的有五對：both... and, either... or, neither... nor, not only... but (also), whether... or。

例如：

連接名詞或代名詞：

◉ Both shirts and ties are on sale.
襯衫和領帶都在拍賣。
(Both... and 連接兩個名詞 shirts 和 ties)

◉ Mr. B owns neither a car nor a house.
B 先生既沒有汽車，也沒有房子。
(neither... nor 連接兩個名詞 car 和 house)

◉ Neither the quality nor the prices have changed.
品質和價格都沒有改變。
(neither... nor 連接了兩個名詞 quality 和 prices；但動詞要與最靠近的 prices 一致，故用複數 have，如果 nor 後面是 quality，那麼動詞就要用單數 has)

◉ Either he or you have to prepare a speech.
不是你就是他要準備好演講。
(either... or 連接代名詞 he 和 you 時，動詞通常與最靠近的代名詞 you 一致，故用 have；但口語往往不受此限制)

◉ His book was neither a bestseller nor a complete failure.
他的書既不是暢銷書，卻也不全然是失敗之作。
＝His book was not a bestseller, nor was it a complete failure.

◉ It is hard to say whether he or she is the better student.
很難講他或她誰是比較好的學生。
(whether... or 連接了兩個代名詞 he 和 she)

◉ Mr. A is not only a professor but (also) a politician.
A 先生不但是位教授，也是一位政治人物。
(not only... but also 連接兩個名詞 professor 和 politician；有人也把 also 省去)

◉ Mr. B enjoys both writing and reading.
B 先生喜歡寫作和閱讀。
(both... and 連接兩個動名詞 writing 和 reading)

連接副詞：

◉ Mr. A finished the sketch not only effortlessly but also masterfully.
A 先生完成了素描，不但不費力還很熟練。
(not only... but also 連接兩個副詞 effortlessly 和 masterfully)

◉ Ms. Wang draws both skillfully and creatively.
王小姐畫畫既有技巧又有創造力。
(both... and 連接兩個副詞 skillfully 和 creatively)

連接動詞：

◉ He will either walk or run to the park.
他到公園不是走路，就是跑步。
(either... or 連接兩個動詞 walk 和 run)

◉ Every morning Mr. J both reads and writes.
J 先生每天上午既讀書又寫作。
(both... and 連接兩個動詞 reads 和 writes)

連接形容詞：

◉ The weather was not only cold but also windy.
天氣不但很冷，而且風還很大。
(not only... but also 連接了兩個形容詞 cold 和 windy)

◉ The negotiations were neither hostile nor friendly.
這些協商雖無敵意，卻也不友善。
(neither... nor 連接兩個形容詞 hostile 和 friendly)

連接介詞片語:

◉ You may put my book either on the table or beside the telephone.
你可以把我的書放在桌上或電話旁邊。
(either... or 連接兩個介詞片語 on the table 和 beside the telephone)

◉ I don't know whether Mr. B will come by bus or by plane.
我不知道 B 先生是要坐公車還是搭飛機來。
(whether... or 連接兩個介詞片語 by bus 和 by plane)

◉ He looked neither to the right nor to the left.
他既不看右邊,也不看左邊。
(neither... nor 連接介詞片語 to the right 和 to the left)

連接句子:

◉ Either we leave now or (we) don't go at all.
我們要不就現在離開,要不就乾脆別去。
(either... or 連接兩個獨立子句 we leave now 和 we don't go at all;因為主詞一樣,都是 we,所以第二個 we 可省去)

◉ It is not important whether Mr. A comes himself or he sends a representative.
A 先生親自來或派代表來,都無關緊要。
(whether... or 連接兩句 Mr. A comes himself 和 he sends a representative)

◉ Neither did Mr. B forget the appointment nor was he sick.
B 先生既沒忘了約會,也沒生病。
(neither... nor 連接兩個句子 Mr. B forget the appointment 和 was he sick)

◉ Not only was he a fine student, but he was also a good athlete.
他不但是好學生,也是好運動員。
(not only... but also 連接兩個句子 he was a fine student 和 he was a good athlete;not only 放在句首時,因為是否定,所以要把動詞倒置在主詞前,成為 was he... 而不是 he was...;但 but also 可分開使用,寫作 but he was also... ,也可寫成 but also he was... ,而且不必把動詞放在主詞前)

其實也就是：

He was not only a fine student but （also）a good athlete.
（此句連接兩個名詞 student 和 athlete；有人也把 also 省去）

再舉幾個例子：

◉ Not only did we go to the fair, but we also won a prize.
我們不但去了市集，還贏了一個獎品。
（not only 放在句首時，要把助動詞放在主詞前，成為 did we go to the fair，像是問句；但在 but also 句裡，就不必把主詞與動詞倒裝）

◉ Not only can she sing, but she can also dance.
＝Not only can she sing, but （also）she can dance.
她不但會唱歌也會跳舞。
（but also 連用時，also 常被省去，但分開使用時，則不省去）

3. 從屬連接詞(subordinating conjunction)

就是利用從屬連接詞所引導出來的附屬子句與主要子句連接起來（通常附屬子句就是副詞子句）。

常用的從屬連接詞有：

指原因或目的	as, because, so that, since, in order that, as long as
指對比或讓步	although （though）, even though, as though, even if
指條件	as if, if, in case, unless, when, whether, provided, now that
指地點	where, wherever
指時間	after, before, as soon as, since, until （till）, when, while, whenever

例如:

- Let's go home before the rain starts.
  我們在下雨前回家吧。
  (附屬子句 before the rain starts 是由從屬連接詞 before 引導出來的,連接主要子句 Let's go home)

- As soon as Mary heard about the sale, she rushed to the store.
  Mary 一聽到有拍賣,就衝去那家店。
  (附屬子句 as soon as Mary heard about the sale 是由從屬連接詞 as soon as 引導出來的,再與主要子句 she rushed to the store 連接。附屬子句可放在主要子句之前或之後,放在前面時,要加逗點,放在後面則不必)

- We can start the class Monday provided the textbooks arrive.
  ＝Provided the textbooks arrive, we can start the class Monday. (provided＝if)
  假如教科書送來了,我們星期一就能開課。
  (附屬子句 provided the textbooks arrive 是由從屬連接詞 provided 引導出來後,再與主要子句 We can start the class Monday 連接起來)

- I go to the library whenever I have time.
  ＝Whenever I have time, I go to the library.
  我只要有時間就會去圖書館。
  (附屬子句 whenever I have time 是由從屬連接詞 whenever 引導出來,再與主要子句 I go to the library 連接)

- Now that the harvest is behind them, the farmers can relax.
  既然都收割完了,農夫可以輕鬆一下。
  (從屬連接詞 now that 引導附屬子句 now that the harvest is behind them,與主要子句 the farmers can relax 連接;now that＝because＝since＝as)

◉ You should eat different kinds of fruits and vegetables since they are good for your health.
你應該多吃不同的水果和蔬菜,因為對健康有益。
(附屬子句 since they are good for your health 是由從屬連接詞 since 引導出來,再與主要子句 you should eat different kinds of fruits and vegetables 連接)

◉ Even though Mr. B has little experience, I will hire him for this position.
即使 B 先生沒有什麼經驗,我還是要聘請他擔任這項職務。
(附屬子句 even though Mr. B has little experience 是由 even though 引導出來,再與主要子句 I will hire him for this position 連接)

◉ I have to take a detour because the street is being repaired.
＝Because the street is being repaired, I have to take a detour.
我必須繞路,因為那條街正在整修。
(從屬連接詞 because 所引導的附屬子句 because the street is being repaired 與主要子句 I have to take a detour 連接起來)

after, before, since, until (till), when等,可以作從屬連接詞,也可作副詞。不過作從屬連接詞時,是連接兩個句子,但作副詞時,是修飾動詞或作介詞片語。

例如：

◉ John started to run before the signal was given.
起跑訊號發出前,John 就起跑了。
(before the signal was given 是附屬子句,所以 before 是從屬連接詞)

◉ John never works before 8 o'clock a.m.
John 在早上 8 點前從不工作。
(before 8 o'clock a.m.是介詞片語,當副詞用,修飾動詞 works)

⊙ John has never ridden a horse before.
John 從未騎過馬。
(before 是副詞，修飾動詞 has ridden)

⊙ Don't stand under a tree when there is lightning.
閃電時不要站在樹下。
(when there is lightning 是附屬子句，所以 when 是從屬連接詞；when 也可用 while 代替)

另外，從屬連接詞 as，意思與 like 相似，但不能互相替代。因為 as 是連接兩個句子；而 like 只作介詞或形容詞。

例如：

⊙ Mr. Wang speaks English as a native does.
王先生的英語說得跟母語人士一樣好。
＝Mr. Wang speaks English like a native.
(as a native does 是附屬子句，所以 as 是從屬連接詞，不能用 like 代替。而 like 是介詞，後接名詞 native)

⊙ Mr. Lee is very hospitable as many Chinese are.
李先生就像許多中國人一樣很好客。
＝Mr. Lee is very hospitable like many Chinese.
(as many Chinese are 是附屬子句，所以 as 是從屬連接詞，不能用 like 代替。而 like 是介詞，後接名詞 Chinese)

4. 副詞連接詞(adverbial conjunction)

本來是副詞，但能把獨立句子連接起來，使其意義有連貫性或有轉折性，所以也稱為連詞副詞(conjunctive adverb)、句子連接詞(sentence connector)或轉折語(transitional terms)。

常用的副詞連接詞單字有：accordingly, again, also, anyway, besides, certainly, consequently, finally, furthermore, hence, however, incidentally, indeed, instead, likewise, meanwhile, moreover, nevertheless（＝nonetheless）, still, otherwise, then, therefore, thus, similarly, undoubtedly 等。

常用的轉折片語有：after all, as a result, at any rate, at the same time, by the way, even so, for example, in addition, in fact, in other words, on the contrary, on the other hand 等。

例如：

◉ Mr. A is reliable, moreover, he is punctual.
A 先生很可靠，而且很守時。
＝Mr. A is reliable. Moreover, he is punctual.
（moreover 把這兩個獨立子句連接起來連成一句時，在 moreover 前後都要加逗號）

◉ I had waited for two hours, finally, the physician showed up.
我等了兩個小時後，醫生終於出現了。
（finally 把兩個獨立句連接起來，使其意義有連貫性）

◉ The book was interesting, thus, I read it all day.
這本書很有趣，因此我看了一整天。
（thus 把兩個獨立子句連接起來）

◉ The bus arrived late, therefore, he missed dinner.
公車誤點，所以他錯過了晚餐。
（therefore 把兩個獨立子句連接起來）

◉ It rained until the baseball field was soggy, consequently, the game was postponed.
大雨淋濕球場，結果球賽延期了。
（consequently 只是把兩個主要子句 it rained 和 the game was postponed 以及一個附屬子句 until the baseball field was soggy 連貫起來，但不修飾任何一句）

- We took your advice, as a result, we had a nice experience.
  我們聽了你的建議，因此我們有了一次滿意的經驗。
  (as a result 作兩個獨立句的轉折語，雖然也可放在句尾，但較不好)

- Mr. B teaches at a high school, in addition, he works in the evening.
  B 先生在高中教書，另外他晚上也工作。
  (in addition 當做兩個獨立子句的轉折片語)

- Mr. A doubted the effectiveness of the medication; however, he wanted to try it.
  A 先生懷疑這種藥品是否有效，但是他還是想嘗試一下。
  (把 however 放在句中 he wanted, however, to try it，或放在句尾都也可以，但較不好)

注意

使用對等連接詞時，位置不能移動。

例如：

- Mr. A doubted the effectiveness of medication, but he wanted to try it.
  (對等連接詞 but 不能移動位置)

二、感嘆詞

用來表達一種情緒、感受或興奮(emotion, feeling, or excitement)或引起別人的注意。它在句子裡是獨立的，與其他字沒有關係，很少用在正式公文或商業上，多半用在廣告、私人信件、小說或非正式場合。

在此，以下分兩方面說明：

1. 表示較強的情緒時，其後接感嘆號(exclamation mark)。

例如：

- Ouch! This pan is still very hot.
  哎喲！平底鍋還很燙。(也可用 Ow!)
  (表示突然的傷痛，故用感嘆號！；This 的第一個字母要大寫)

- Hurray! My watch is not missing.
  好耶！我的手錶沒有弄丟。
  (表示高興的喊聲，後用感嘆號！；My 的第一個字母要大寫)

- Gosh! We made it just in time for the meeting.
  啊！我們剛好趕上開會耶。
  (另外，Oh, my gosh! 則常譯為「我的天啊！」，這裡的 gosh 是 God 的委婉語)

其他還有：

Wow!	哇！	(表示驚奇、欽佩或喜歡)
Ugh!	唷！	(表厭惡，不喜歡)
Oops!	哎喲！	(表不小心做錯事)
Hey!	嘿！	(表驚訝或喚起別人注意)
Golly!	天哪！	(表驚訝，也是 God 的委婉字)
Darn!	該死！	(表憤怒或失望)(是 damn 的委婉語)

美國人生氣時常說 Damn it!，就是「該死」或「他媽的」，故少用為妙。

Yuck!	呸！	（表厭惡或反感）
Gee!	哎呀！	（表喜悅＝My goodness!）
Tsk!	嘖嘖！	（表可惜）＝Tsk-tsk

2. 表示溫和的感嘆(mild interjection)時，後面只用逗號與主
   要子句隔開。

   例如：

   ◉ Hooray, our team won the game.
     好棒啊，我們隊贏了。
     （hooray 後只用逗號，our 也不必大寫）

   ◉ Hey, don't forget to bring me the book.
     嘿，別忘了帶書給我。
     （hey 後面只用逗號，don't 第一個字母也不必大寫）

   ◉ My, this was an exciting news.
     啊，這是令人興奮的消息。

   其他還有：good grief（糟糕），well（好啦），表示不以為然。
   其實感嘆的強烈或溫和，因人而異，所以後面用感嘆號或逗號並
   沒有一定的規則。

1-11

分詞的用法

英語裡的分詞(participle)常常遭到混淆與誤用,因此使用時須相當小心。

一、現在分詞(**present participle**)

就是在原形動詞(verb root form)後面加 ing,當形容詞用,一般也可放在句首、句中,甚至句尾,但要緊跟在所形容的名詞或代名詞的旁邊。

(例如:)

◉ Shouting, the man walked down the river.
這男子邊大叫,邊沿著河邊走。
(現在分詞 shouting 是形容主詞 man,就是原形動詞 shout 後面加 ing)

也可放在句中:
The man, shouting, walked down the river.
或放在句尾:
The man walked down the river, shouting.
較不好,因為與所修飾的名詞 the man 相距太遠。

◉ The barking and lunging dog frightened the girl.
那隻狗邊吠邊撲過來,把女孩嚇壞了。
(現在分詞 barking 和 lunging 都是修飾 dog,從動詞 bark 和 lunge 而來)

也可放在句中:
The dog, barking and lunging, frightened the girl.
如果放在句尾:
The dog frightened the girl, barking and lunging.
分詞就會像是在形容 girl 而產生誤解。

- The young woman, complaining and weeping, told her story to her friend.
  那個年輕女子邊抱怨邊哭泣，向朋友訴說她的故事。
  (現在分詞 complaining 和 weeping 都修飾 woman，由動詞 complain 和 weep 而來)

也可放在句首：
Complaining and weeping, the young woman told her story to her friend.
但不能放在句尾：
The young woman told her story to her friend, complaining and weeping. 因為分詞所要修飾的名詞不清楚，可能讓人誤以為是形容 friend。

二、現在分詞片語（present participle phrase）

由於分詞是由動詞演變而來，故仍保有動詞的性質，故可用副詞修飾，也可以接受詞（object），構成分詞片語。

例如：

- Gently lifting the window, the burglar slipped into the house.
  竊賊輕輕地拉起窗戶，溜進屋裡。
  (這裡 gently 是副詞，修飾現在分詞 lifting；而 lifting the window 是分詞片語，修飾 burglar)

也可放在句中：
The burglar, gently lifting the window, slipped into the house.

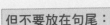

> **但不要放在句尾：**
>
> The burglar slipped into the house, gently lifting the window.
> 因為會像是先溜進房屋，再拉起窗戶，並不合理，而且與修飾的主詞 burglar 相距太遠，不合文法規定。

◉ Carrying a suitcase, Mr. Chang boarded the bus.
  張先生拿著手提箱上了公車。

  (carrying 是現在分詞，suitcase 是受詞；而 carrying a suitcase 又是現在分詞片語，修飾 Mr. Chang)

> **也可放在句中：**
>
> Mr. Chang, carrying a suitcase, boarded the bus.
>
> **放在句尾：**
>
> Mr. Chang boarded the bus, carrying a suitcase. （較不好）

◉ Living on his pension and thinking about his future, the old man worries a great deal.
  這個老先生靠退休金生活，想到將來，不勝擔憂。

  (這裡的分詞片語 living on his pension 和 thinking about his future 都是修飾 old man)

> **如果放在句中也可：**
>
> The old man, living on his pension and thinking about his future, worries a great deal.

◉ Trembling with excitement, Mr. Wang waited for his girlfriend.
  王先生興奮得發抖，等著他的女友。

  (with excitement 是副詞片語，修飾 trembling，而分詞片語 trembling with excitement 又是修飾 Mr. Wang)

也可放在句中：
Mr. Wang, trembling with excitement, waited for his girlfriend.

但不能放在句尾：
Mr. Wang waited for his girlfriend, trembling with excitement. 因為分詞片語，似乎是修飾 girlfriend，語意不清。

　　遇到連綴動詞（linking verb），如 be, become, look, smell, sound, grow, stay, turn 等時，現在分詞也可用名詞或形容詞作為補語，進而形成分詞片語。

例如：

◉ Being an invalid, he could not climb the mountain.
他身有殘疾無法爬山。
（being 就是連綴動詞 be 加 ing；invalid 為名詞；being an invalid 就是現在分詞片語，修飾 he）

也可放在句中：
He, being an invalid, could not climb the mountain.

最好不要放在句尾：
He could not climb the mountain, being an invalid. 因為距離要修飾的 he 太遠了。

◉ Becoming weary, Mr. Lee sat down to rest.
李先生累了而坐下休息。
（becoming 的原形動詞為 become，形容詞 weary 修飾 becoming；而 becoming weary 是分詞片語，修飾 Mr. Lee）

也可放在句中：
Mr. Lee, becoming weary, sat down to rest.

> **如果放在句尾：**
>
> Mr. Lee sat down to rest, becoming weary.
> 句子語氣就會太弱而不理想。

三、過去分詞（past participle）：

　　過去分詞，一般是在原形動詞後面加 d, ed, t, n, en 等，還有不規則的動詞如：drunk, gone, sung, written 等等。也當形容詞用，多半帶有一點「被動」的意味。同時也像現在分詞，可放在句首、句中或句尾，端看是否與修飾的名詞緊靠在一起，以及句子的意義是否清楚合理。

例如：

⊚ The child, frightened, slept with his mother.
　＝The frightened child slept with his mother.
　受驚的孩子與媽媽同睡。
　(過去分詞 frightened 是由原形動詞 frighten 而來，修飾主詞 child)

> **如果放在句尾就不好：**
>
> The child slept with his mother, frightened.
> 因為 frightened 會像是在修飾 mother，易生混淆。

⊚ The soiled and torn curtains lay on the floor.
　弄髒且破損的窗簾被放在地上。
　(過去分詞 soiled 和 torn，是由原形動詞 soil 和 tear 而來，都是修飾主詞 curtains)

> **也可放在句中：**
>
> The curtains, soiled and torn, lay on the floor.

如果放在句尾就不好：
The curtains lay on the floor, soiled and torn.
因為句意也許是地板髒了，不能與所要修飾的主詞相距太遠。

四、過去分詞片語（past participle phrase）：

過去分詞與現在分詞一樣，也可用副詞修飾，構成過去分詞片語。

例如：

◉ Remodeled recently, the house looks very attractive.
這房子最近重新裝潢過，看起來很漂亮。
（recently 是副詞，修飾過去分詞 remodeled，而過去分詞片語 remodeled recently 修飾 house）

也可放在句中：
The house, remodeled recently, looks very attractive.
如果放在句尾就不好：
The house looks very attractive, remodeled recently.
因為句子語氣會太弱，並且與所修飾的主詞 house 相距太遠。

◉ His car, burned almost beyond recognition, was on the side of the street.
他的車子燒得面目全非，停在路邊。
（almost beyond recognition 是副詞片語，修飾過去分詞 burned，而過去分詞片語 burned almost beyond recognition 修飾主詞 car）

也可放在句首：
Burned almost beyond recognition, his car was on the side of the street.
放在句尾：
His car lay beside the street, burned almost beyond recognition. 雖然與修飾的主詞 car 相距較遠，但不會誤以為是修飾 street，因為馬路不會燒得面目全非。

◉ The bird, frightened by the cat, flew away.
這隻鳥被貓一嚇就飛走了。
(by the cat 是副詞片語，修飾 frightened；而整個過去分詞片語 frightened by the cat 修飾主詞 bird)

也可放在句首：
Frightened by the cat, the bird flew away.
放在句尾也行：
The bird flew away, frightened by the cat.

◉ Encouraged by his wife and assisted by his friends, Mr. Wang restarted the business.
王先生受到老婆的鼓勵與朋友的協助，事業東山再起。
(過去分詞片語 encouraged by his wife 和 assisted by his friends 都是修飾 Mr. Wang)

也可放在句中：
Mr. Wang, encouraged by his wife and assisted by his friends, restarted the business.
如果放在句尾：
Mr. Wang restarted the business, encouraged by his wife and assisted by his friends. 與所修飾的主詞 Mr. Wang 相距太遠，較不理想。

◉ Forgotten too long by history, millions of Chinese victims of the Japanese invasion should be remembered today.

應該在今日受到紀念的數百萬日本侵華下的受害者，長久以來卻遭到歷史遺忘。

(too long by history 在此當副詞片語用，修飾 forgotten；而分詞片語 forgotten too long by history 修飾 Chinese victims)

也可放在句中：
Millions of Chinese victims of the Japanese invasion, forgotten too long by history, should be remembered today.
放在句尾會非常勉強，因為分詞片語與修飾詞相距太遠：
Millions of Chinese victims of the Japanese invasion should be remembered today, forgotten too long by history.

◉ Designed by an architect and decorated by an artist, the new house is beautiful.

新房子在建築師的設計和藝術家的裝飾下美輪美奐。

(過去分詞片語 designed by an architect 和 decorated by an artist 都是修飾 new house)

也可放在句中：
The new house, designed by an architect and decorated by an artist, is beautiful.
如果放在句尾：
The new house is beautiful, designed by an architect and decorated by an artist. 句子語氣顯得太弱且與修飾的主詞 house 相距太遠。

五、完成式分詞（perfect participle）

就是在過去分詞前面加 having，而形成完成式分詞。諸如：

having seen, having written, having finished 等等。完成式分詞也當形容詞用。因為它有動詞性質，所以仍然可以有受詞，也可用副詞修飾。

例如：

◉ Having finished the article, I put it in a folder.
我寫完文章後，把它放在檔案夾裡。
(having finished 是完成式分詞，article 是受詞；完成式分詞片語 having finished the article 當形容詞，修飾主詞 I)

也可放在句中：
I, having finished the article, put it in a folder. 也有人在 having 前面加 after，但多被省去。
放在句尾，顯得勉強：
I put it in a folder, having finished the article. 因為與所修飾的主詞 I 相距太遠。

◉ Having swum to the shore, Mr. Chang came out of the water.
張先生游到岸邊後，從水裡出來。
(to the shore 當副詞片語用，修飾 swum；而完成式分詞片語 having swum to the shore，修飾 Mr. Chang)

也可放在句中：
Mr. Chang, having swum to the shore, came out of water.
放在句尾，因為與修飾的 Mr. Chang 相距太遠，也很勉強：
Mr. Chang came out of water, having swum to the shore.

◉ Having recovered completely and having exercised regularly, Mr. Wang stays in good health.
王先生完全康復後定期運動，身體保持得很健康。

(completely 和 regularly 都是副詞，分別修飾 recovered 和 exercised；而完成式分詞片語 having recovered completely 和 having exercised regularly 都是修飾 Mr. Wang)

也可放在句中：
Mr. Wang, having recovered completely and having exercised regularly, stays in good health.
放在句尾會比較勉強：
Mr. Wang stays in good health, having recovered completely and having exercised regularly.

◉ Having been a writer for years and having edited many articles for magazines, she knows how to write well.
當了多年作家且為雜誌編輯了許多文章，她知道如何寫出好文章。
(句裡的 having been a writer for years 和 having edited many articles for magazines 都是完成式分詞片語，都是修飾主詞 she)

也可放在句中：
She, having been a writer for years and having edited many articles for magazines, knows how to write well.
放在句尾較為勉強：
She knows how to write well, having been a writer for years and having edited many articles for magazines.

六、錯置修飾詞（misplaced modifier）：

也稱「虛懸修飾語」（dangling modifier），是指句子裡的分詞或分詞片語，所修飾的主詞不明確或不合理，令人混淆。這是常犯的錯誤，必須小心。

例如：

不能說：

Walking through the park, a wallet was picked up.

(walking through the park 不能修飾 wallet，因為 wallet 並不會 walking)

故應改為：

◎ Walking through the park, I picked up a wallet.
我走過公園時，撿到一個錢包。
(主詞可用任何人)

不能說：

Jumping into the water, the boy was rescued by the lifeguard.

(這裡的分詞片語 jumping into the water 似乎是修飾 boy；其實是 lifeguard 跳進水裡，救了孩子)

所以要改為：

◎ Jumping into the water, the lifeguard rescued the boy.
救生員跳進水裡，救了男孩。
＝The lifeguard, jumping into the water, rescued the boy.

不能說：

Angered by the driver, the windshield of the taxi was smashed with a cane.

(這裡的過去分詞片語 angered by the driver 似乎是修飾 windshield〔擋風玻璃〕，其實 windshield 是不會生氣的)

故應改為：

◉ Angered by the driver, the man smashed the windshield of the taxi with his cane.
這名被計程車司機激怒的男子用拐杖打碎擋風玻璃。
＝The man, angered by the driver, smashed the windshield of the taxi with his cane.

不能說：

Discouraged by low grades, dropping out made sense.
(這裡過去分詞片語 discouraged by low grades 不能修飾主詞 dropping out.)

故應改為：

◉ Discouraged by low grades, he thought dropping out made sense.
他因為成績不好感到洩氣，所以想退學是合情合理的

不能說：

Having stopped for some snacks, the journey was continued.
(這裡的完成分詞片語 having stopped for some snacks 不能修飾 journey)

故要改為：

◉ (After)having stopped for some snacks, we continued the journey.
我們停下來吃些點心後再繼續旅行。
(句首的 after，通常都省去，這裡用上較好)
＝We, having stopped for some snacks, continued the journey.

有些人把分詞片語與名詞連在一起，獨立使用，在文法上與主詞沒有什麼關連，故少用為妙。

例如：

⊙ The sun having set, the farmers decided to go home.
太陽下山後，農夫決定回家。
(這裡分詞片語 having set 是修飾名詞 the sun，獨立使用，與句子其他部分在文法上並沒有太多關係)

其實最好說：

⊙ When the sun set, the farmers decided to go home.

⊙ The bus being late, we all missed the train.
公車遲到了，我們都沒趕上火車。
(這裡分詞片語 being late 是修飾名詞 the bus，也是獨立使用，不是修飾句子其他部分)

其實最簡單的說法是：

⊙ Because the bus was late, we all missed the train.

總之，現代一般美國人喜歡使用簡單明白的句子，讓對方能充分理解。

1-12
不定詞的用法

　　不定詞（infinitive）與分詞和動名詞一樣，都是由動詞演變而來，它不是真正的動詞，只能當作其他詞類使用，但仍然帶有動詞的特性。

　　不定詞是在動詞原形（verb root form）前加 to，這個 to，只是符號，而不是介詞。它可當名詞、形容詞或副詞用。當名詞時，可作為主詞、受詞、表語主格和同位語。

　　如果不定詞裡含有修飾語（modifier）或補語（complement），那麼就成為不定詞片語（infinitive phrase），它與單一的不定詞一樣，具有以上的功用。現舉例說明。

一、當主詞（subject）

例如：

◉ To succeed is his goal.
　成功是他的目標。
　（to succeed 是不定詞，作動詞 is 的主詞）

◉ To apologize requires courage and humility.
　道歉需要勇氣和謙遜。
　（to apologize 是不定詞，作動詞 requires 的主詞；注意：humidity 是
　「濕氣」的意思，勿與 humility 混淆）

◉ To fly scares some people.
　有些人怕飛行。
　（to fly 作動詞 scares 的主詞）

◉ To wait for the bus seems troublesome sometimes.
　有時候等公車似乎很煩。
　（to wait for the bus 是不定詞片語，作主詞用；for the bus 是介詞片
　語，修飾 to wait）

- To capture the pretty scenery requires a good camera.
  捕捉美景需要一部好相機。
  (to capture the pretty scenery 是不定詞片語，當動詞 requires 的主詞；
  the pretty scenery 是補語)

- To write good articles beautifully would require a long time of practice.
  要寫出好文章需要長時間的練習。
  (to write articles beautifully 是不定詞片語，作 require 的主詞；articles beautifully 是不定詞的補語)

- To listen carefully to the speaker is important.
  仔細聽演講者說話很重要。
  (to listen carefully to the speaker 是不定詞片語，作 is 的主詞；carefully to the speaker 是修飾 to listen)

- To stroll along the beach at sunset appears relaxing.
  黃昏時在海邊散步似乎很愜意。
  (to stroll along the beach at sunset 是不定詞片語，作 appears 的主詞；along the beach at sunset 是修飾 to stroll；也可用動名詞 strolling 代替 to stroll)

- To get home during the storm was difficult.
  狂風暴雨時要回家很困難。
  (to get home during the storm 是不定詞片語，作 was 的主詞；during the storm 是修飾 to get；也可用動名詞 getting 代替 to get)

- To graduate a year earlier became his goal.
  提早一年畢業成為他的目標。
  (to graduate a year earlier 是不定詞片語，作 became 的主詞；a year earlier 是修飾 to graduate；也可用動名詞 graduating 代替 to graduate)

- To keep the Taiwan Strait peaceful has been/is the effort of many people. (可用 keeping 代替 to keep)
  維持台海兩岸和平一直是許多人努力的目標。
  (to keep the Taiwan Strait peaceful 是不定詞片語，作 has been 的主詞；the Taiwan Strait peaceful 是補語)

註：

> 雖然文法上不定詞與動名詞多半可以互相替代，但有時涵義會稍有不同。

二、當受詞（object）

多半作動詞的受詞，偶爾也作介詞的受詞，但機會不多。

例如：

◉ Mr. A loves to swim.
A 先生喜愛游泳。
(to swim 是不定詞，作動詞 loves 的直接受詞)

◉ I like to write when I have time.
我有時間就愛寫東西。
(to write 是不定詞，作動詞 like 的直接受詞)

◉ With two days off, Mr. Wang planned to relax.
王先生打算藉著休假兩天來放鬆。
(to relax 是不定詞，作 planned 的直接受詞)

◉ His father would like to buy John a new computer.
他爸爸想為 John 買台新電腦。
(to buy John a new computer 是不定詞片語，作動詞 like 的受詞)

◉ Mr. Wang wants to know the price of this car.
王先生想知道這部車的價格。
(to know the price of this car 是不定詞片語，作動詞 wants 的受詞。不用動名詞 knowing 代替 to know)

◉ Mr. Smith hopes to become a professor and a writer.
Smith 先生希望成為教授和作家。
(to become a professor and a writer 是不定詞片語，作動詞 hopes 的受詞；這裡的不定詞 to become，就不能用 becoming 代替)

- She decided to lend her boyfriend some money.
  她決定借點錢給她的男友。
  (to lend her boyfriend some money 是不定詞片語，作動詞 decided 的受詞。這裡的不定詞 to lend 不能用動名詞 lending 代替)

- Some people do not like to travel by airplane.
  有些人不喜歡搭飛機旅行。
  (to travel by airplane 是不定詞片語，作動詞 like 的受詞；這裡不定詞 to travel，可以用動名詞 traveling 代替)

- During the test, our professor permitted (us) to use our dictionaries.
  教授允許我們考試時用字典。
  (to use our dictionary 是不定詞片語，作動詞 permitted 的受詞。這裡的 to use 可用 using 代替)

不定詞很少作為介詞的受詞，通常只在 about 或 but(＝except)後面出現。

例如：

- She was about to sing.
  她快要唱歌了。

- They do nothing except (to)argue.
  他們光會吵架而已。

三、當表語主格(predicate nominative)

也就是不定詞和連綴動詞(linking verb)同時出現作表語主格，說明了主詞。

例如：

◉ His hobby is to write.（＝To write is his hobby.）
他的嗜好是寫作。
(to write 與連綴動詞 is 在一起，說明了主詞 hobby 是什麼。也可用動名詞 writing 代替 to write)

◉ This semester, all he wants to do is to pass the exams.
他這學期只希望能通過考試。
(to pass the exams 是不定詞片語，與連綴動詞 is 在一起，說明主詞 hope，成為表語主格，或主詞補語)
＝This semester, to pass the exam is all he wants to do.
(也可用動名詞 passing 代替 to pass)

◉ Our plan was to reach the airport by 5 p.m.
我們的計畫是下午 5 點前抵達機場。
(to reach the airport by 5 p.m.是不定詞片語，與前面連綴動詞 was 在一起，作為表語主格，說明主詞 plan 是什麼，也就是主詞補語)
＝To reach the airport by 5 p.m. was our plan.

◉ Mr. J's dream is to establish some scholarships for poor students.
J 先生夢想為貧窮學生設立獎學金。
(to establish some scholarships for poor students 是不定詞片語，與連綴動詞 is 在一起，說明主詞 dream 是什麼。也可以說是主詞的補語或表語主格)
＝To establish some scholarships for poor students is Mr. J's dream.
(也可用 establishing 代替 to establish)

◉ One of Mr. J's goals in life has been to learn more English and to write good essays.
J 先生的畢生目標之一是要多學英語和寫好文章。
(to learn more English 和 to write good essays 都是不定詞片語，與連綴動詞 has been 在一起說明主詞 one of Mr. J's goals 是什麼，也算是表語主格或主詞補語)

＝To learn more English and to write good essays has been one of Mr. J's goals in life.

(也可用 learning 和 writing 代替 to learn 和 to write)

有時也可以用表語形容詞(predicate adjective)當主詞補語。

例如：

◎ Despite his failure, Mr. Lee's ambition remains/is to become powerful and rich.

儘管失敗了，李先生的野心仍然是爭權和致富。

(to become powerful and rich 是不定詞片語；powerful 和 rich 是形容詞，當主詞 ambition 的補助語，也是表語形容詞)

＝To become powerful and rich remains/is Mr. Lee's ambition despite his failure.

四、當同位語(**appositive**)

例如：

◎ Her goal, to diet, only lasted two weeks.

她的目標是節食，只維持了兩星期。

(不定詞 to diet，就是說明主詞 goal，故為同位語)

◎ Mr. Wang's plan, to live abroad for a year, has not been realized.

王先生住在國外一年的計畫尚未實現。

(to live abroad for year 是不定詞片語，就是解釋主詞 plan 是什麼，故為同位語)

◎ Miss Chang finally has achieved her dream—to become a famous writer.

張小姐最後達成她的夢想──成為名作家。

(to become a famous writer 是不定詞片語，說明名詞 dream 是什麼。句中的 dream 後面可用破折號或逗點)

◉ Mr. Smith's proposal, to borrow money from the bank, was turned down by the committee.

Smith 先生向銀行貸款的建議，被委員會拒絕。

(to borrow money from the bank 是不定詞片語，說明主詞 proposal 是什麼，故是同位語)

五、當形容詞

也就是說，不定詞可以修飾名詞：

例如：

◉ Mr. Chen lacked the patience to wait.

陳先生缺少等待的耐性。

(to wait 是修飾名詞 patience，說明什麼樣的耐心)

◉ You may ask your supervisor's permission to leave.

你可以詢問上司能否離開。

(不定詞 to leave 是修飾名詞 permission，說明什麼樣的許可)

◉ The right person to contact for assistance will be Mr. Wang.

尋求協助時應該找的人是王先生。

(to contact for assistance 是不定詞片語，修飾名詞 person)

◉ My wife bought a new dress to wear for the party.

我太太買了新洋裝好穿去參加宴會。

(to wear for the party 是不定詞片語，修飾名詞 dress)

◉ Mr. Smith was known for his ability to predict the future.

Smith 先生以預測未來的能力聞名。

(to predict the future 是不定詞片語，修飾名詞 ability)

六、當副詞用

也就是說，不定詞可修飾動詞、形容詞和其他副詞，多半是表示行動的原因、目的或程度。

例如：

- We all live to learn.
  活著就要學習。
  (to learn 是不定詞，修飾動詞 live，說明生活的目的)

- The traveler stopped on the roadside to rest.
  旅客停在路邊休息。
  (to rest 是修飾動詞 stopped，說明停下的原因)

- Mr. A's article is difficult to understand.
  A 先生的文章很難懂。
  (to understand 是修飾形容詞 difficult，說明程度)

- Impossible to miss, the post office is on the right of the street.
  郵局就在這條街的右邊，不可能找不到。
  (不定詞 to miss，修飾形容詞 impossible)

- Effectively to describe the problem was the main purpose of this meeting.
  有效地描述問題是這次會議的主要目的。
  (不定詞 to describe 修飾副詞 effectively)

不過，不定詞表示原因或目的時，也可放在句首。

例如：

- To protect yourself, you need to sign this paper.
  為了保護自己，你需要在紙上簽名。

◉ To prove my point, I will have to tell him the story.
為了證明我的論點，我要告訴他事情的真相。

◉ To tell（you）the truth, Mr. B is not competent.
老實說，B 先生並不適任。

◉ Not to be outdone, he wanted to work harder.
因為不甘示弱，所以他想更努力工作。
（not to be outdone 意思是：not let someone do better 動詞時態：outdo, outdid, outdone）

◉ To be（very）frank/honest with you, I don't care what he said.
老實告訴你，我不在乎他說什麼。

七、當虛詞（expletive）

在句子的開頭，用 it 做填補的虛詞。

例如：

◉ It always pays to tell the truth.
講真話總是值得的。
＝To tell the truth always pays.
（主詞也可用動名詞 telling）

◉ It is your responsibility to protect your children.
保護你的孩子是你的責任。
＝To protect your children is your responsibility.
（主詞也可用 protecting）

◉ It is advisable to drive carefully.
開車小心是明智的。
＝To drive carefully is advisable.
（主詞也可用 driving）

由於不定詞還有動詞的性質，所以可用副詞或副詞片語去修飾。

 例如：

⊚ Mr. A wants to leave early.
A 先生要早些離開。
(副詞 early 修飾 to leave)

⊚ Her goal is to sing well and to dance gracefully.
她的目標是歌唱得好，舞跳得優雅。
(副詞 well 和 gracefully 是修飾 to sing 和 to dance)

⊚ The couple love to walk through the park in the afternoons.
這對夫婦喜歡每天下午走過公園。
(through the park in the afternoons 修飾 to walk)

注意

(1)不定詞前面的to與介詞to，不可弄錯。

⊚ He loves to read.
他愛看書。
(to 只是不定詞前面的符號，後面跟動詞原式 read)

⊚ The boy goes to school.
這個男孩上學。
(to 是介詞，後面 school 是名詞)

⊚ He gave the book to her.
他給她一本書。
(to 是介詞，後面是代名詞 her)

⊙ I am looking forward to meeting you.
我期待見到你。

(to 是介詞，meeting 是動名詞)(可見介詞後面要用名詞、代名詞或動名詞，而不定詞後面是用動詞)

注意

(2)下面的動詞，如果用在主動語態，那麼後面不定詞符號to可省去：bid, dare, do, feel, hear, help, let, make, need, please, see, watch

例如：

⊙ They bid us beware.
他們告訴我們要小心。

＝They told us to be careful.
(在 bid 後面，不用 to beware。bid 的動詞時態：bid, bid, bid)

但被動語態時，就要加 to：We were bid to beware.

⊙ The young lady does not dare stay home alone.
這個年輕小姐不敢單獨在家。
(在 dare 後面不用 to stay)

⊙ I saw Mr. Wang enter the house.
我看到王先生進屋了。
(在 saw 後面，不用 to enter)

⊙ He will help Mrs. Chen carry the baggage.
他會幫陳太太提行李。
(在 help 後面，不用 to carry)

⊙ Let us go to the movies.
我們一起去看電影。
(Let us＝Let's。let 後面不用 to go)

◉ Please call me tomorrow.
  (在 please 後面，不用 to call)

◉ She made the boy sit still for the photographer.
  她要男孩坐著不動，讓攝影師拍照。
  (在 made 後面不用 to sit)

但被動時，就要加 to，例如上句可改寫為：The boy was made to sit still for the photographer.

注意

(3)不定詞的時態(tense)有兩種：
  to write (現在簡單式，主動)
  to be written (現在簡單式，被動)
  to have written (現在完成式，主動)
  to have been written (現在完成式，被動)

遇到句子前面的動詞是 hope, plan, intend, expect, want 等，表示未來的意味，通常只用簡單式不定詞。

例如：

◉ He intends to write an article about this topic.
  他想寫篇關於此議題的文章。
  (不用 to have written)

◉ I expect Mr. A to finish up this project by this week.
  我期待 A 先生本周內完成這項計畫。
  (不用 to have finished)

◉ He wants to publish an article.
  他要發表一篇文章。
  (不用 to have published)

但要表示不定詞的動作是發生在主要動詞之前，那麼就用不定詞完成式。

例如：

◉ Mr. Wang seemed/seems to have enjoyed his trip to Taiwan.
王先生赴台旅行，似乎玩得愉快。
(to have enjoyed 發生在 seemed 或 seems 之前)

◉ I feel/felt sorry to have taken so much of your time.
我很抱歉花了你這麼多時間。
(to have taken 發生在 feel 或 felt 之前)

◉ He is/was happy to have seen his old friend.
他很高興見到老友。
(to have seen 發生在 is 或 was 之前)

注意

(4)不可輕易用副詞分開(split)不定詞。

例如：

　　John asked me to immediately return his book.

最好說成：

◉ John asked me to return his book immediately.
John 要我立刻還他書。
(不要用副詞 immediately 把 to return 分開)

The police are determined to carefully investigate the murder.

最好說成：

◉ The police are determined to investigate the murder carefully.

＝The police are determined to investigate carefully the murder

警察決心仔細調查這起謀殺案。

(副詞 carefully 不可把不定詞 to investigate 分開)

1-13

動名詞用法

動名詞（gerund）與分詞（participle）、不定詞（infinitive）一樣，都是由動詞構成，但不能當成真正的動詞，只能作為其他詞類用。

動名詞，就是在原形動詞後面加 ing，當名詞用，所以與一般名詞一樣，可以作句子裡的主詞、動詞的受詞、介詞的受詞、表語主格和同位語。

由於動名詞還有動詞的本質，所以也可用副詞來修飾。

如果動名詞含有形容詞、受詞、介詞或副詞片語，作為補語（supplement）或修飾語（modifier），那麼就成為動名詞片語（gerund phrase）。

動名詞片語與單一的動名詞一樣，當名詞用時，也有上述的功用。在此舉例說明。

一、當主詞（subject）

（例如：）

◎ Writing is Mr. Wang's hobby.
寫作是王先生的嗜好。
（writing 是動名詞，由原形動詞 write 而來，當主詞用）

◎ Gardening and fishing can be enjoyable.
園藝和釣魚可說是愉快的活動。
（garden 和 fish 也可以當動詞用，後面加 ing，成為動名詞，作為句子的主詞）

◎ Speeding will lead to the loss of one's driver's license.
超速開車會導致吊銷駕照的下場。
（speeding 是動名詞，當主詞用）

⊙ To me, swimming and walking are always fun.
對我而言，游泳和走路一直很好玩。
(swimming 和 walking 都是動名詞，由原形動詞 swim 和 walk 形成，作 are 的主詞)

⊙ He told students that good writing needs a lot of practice.
他告訴學生，文章要寫得好需要多多練習。
(writing 是動名詞，作動詞 needs 的主詞)

⊙ Cleaning the office is one of Mr. Smith's daily duties.
清掃辦公室是 Smith 先生每天的職責之一。
(cleaning the office 是動名詞片語，作動詞 is 的主詞。the office 是 cleaning 的受詞補語)

⊙ Speaking loudly in public may irritate other people.
在公共場合大聲說話可能會惹惱他人。
(speaking loudly in public 是動名詞片語，作動詞 irritate 的主詞。loudly in public 修飾 speaking)

⊙ Jogging through the park has become a routine of mine.
慢跑穿過公園已成為我慣常從事的活動。
(Jogging through the park 是動名詞片語，作動詞 has become 的主詞；而 through the park 是介詞片語，作副詞用，修飾 jogging)

⊙ Bringing children to a party without the host's permission is not always welcome in the US.
在美國，未經主人許可而帶孩子參加宴會，未必受歡迎。
(bringing children to a party without the host's permission 是動名詞片語，當動詞 is 的主詞。children 是 bringing 的受詞；to a party 和 without the host's permission 都是句中的修飾語，修飾 bringing)

⊙ Telling your boss the truth seems a better way to solve the problem.
告訴老闆真相似乎是解決問題比較好的方法。
(telling your boss the truth 是動名詞片語，作動詞 seems 的主詞。your boss 是 telling 的間接受詞，the truth 是 telling 的直接受詞)

⊙ Bragging about one's advanced degree is not an endearing quality.
吹噓高學位不是受人喜愛的特質。
(about one's advanced degree 是修飾語，修飾 bragging；而 bragging about one's advanced degree 是動名詞片語，作 is 的主詞)

⊙ Hoarding cash under the mattress seems an unsafe way to save money.
在床墊下藏現金似乎不是安全的存款方法。
(cash 是 hoarding 的受詞，而 under the mattress 是修飾語，形容或修飾 hoarding；所以 hoarding cash under the mattress 是動名詞片語，當動詞 seems 的主詞)

⊙ Complimenting your children occasionally will make them happy.
偶而誇獎你的小孩會讓他們開心。
(complimenting your children occasionally 是動名詞片語，當動詞 make 的主詞。happy 是受詞 them 的補語)

二、當受詞（object）

1. 作動詞的受詞

例如：

⊙ His wife enjoys cooking.
他太太喜歡做菜。
(cooking 是動名詞，作動詞 enjoys 的直接受詞)

⊙ After several years, Mr. A stopped writing.
過了幾年，A 先生不再寫文章了。
(writing 是動名詞，作動詞 stopped 的直接受詞)

- I gave gardening all my attention.
  我全心投入園藝工作。
  (gardening 是動名詞,是動詞 gave 的間接受詞;attention 是 gave 的直接受詞)

- Mr. Wang just finished writing an article.
  王先生剛寫完一篇文章。
  (writing an article 是動名詞片語,作動詞 finished 的受詞)

- Some people do not like speaking before crowds of people.
  有些人不喜歡在人群面前演講。
  (speaking before crowds of people 是動名詞片語,作動詞 like 的受詞)

- The nurse stopped the bleeding from the cut in his leg.
  護士為他的腿傷止血。
  (bleeding from the cut in his leg 是動名詞片語,作動詞 stopped 的受詞)

- My plans for this summer include painting my house.
  我今年的暑期計畫包括粉刷房子。
  (painting my house 是動名詞片語,作動詞 include 的受詞)

- I suggested sending Mr. Wang a letter.
  我建議寄封信給王先生。
  (sending Mr. Wang a letter 是動名詞片語,作動詞 suggested 的受詞)

- Our boss tried giving Mr. Chang a promotion.
  我們老闆試過要拔擢張先生。
  (giving Mr. Chang a promotion 是動名詞片語,作動詞 tried 的受詞)

2. 作介詞的受詞

(例如:)

- Please turn off the light before leaving.
  離開前請把電燈關掉。
  (leaving 是動名詞,作介詞 before 的受詞)

◉ Mr. B applied for a job in programming.
B 先生申請程式設計的工作。
(programming 是動名詞，作介詞 in 的受詞)

◉ Many Chinese in the US earn a living by working in restaurants.
在美國，許多中國人靠著在餐館工作謀生。
(working in restaurants 是動名詞片語，作介詞 by 的受詞)

◉ Whenever they get together, they talk about making a lot of money.
他們每次聚在一起就會談到賺很多錢的事。
(making a lot of money 是動名詞片語，作介詞 about 的受詞)

◉ Mr. Smith passed the bar exam by burning the midnight oil every night.
Smith 先生每天熬夜才通過了律師考試。
(burning the midnight oil every night 是動名詞片語，作介詞 by 的受詞)

◉ I am sorry to learn of his being sick（或 I was sorry to learn of his having been sick）.
聽到他生病，我很難過。
(being sick 或 having been sick 是動名詞片語，作介詞 of 的受詞。前者指現在生病；後者指過去生病)

◉ Mrs. Smith gave her son a choice between hearing a story and playing a game.
Smith 太太讓她兒子選「聽故事」或「玩遊戲」。
(hearing a story 和 playing a game 都是動名詞片語，作介詞 between 的受詞)

三、當表語名詞（predicate noun）

也有人稱為表語主格（predicate nominative），就是名詞或代名詞與連綴動詞（linking verb）在一起，說明句子的主詞。

連綴動詞是指「沒有動作」的動詞，它只是把主詞連在一起。平時最常用的連綴動詞是 be 動詞 (am, is, are, was, were)，become, remain, seem, has been, have been, would be 等等。

例如：

◉ Mr. Lee's worst habit is lying.
李先生最壞的習慣是撒謊。
(動詞也可用 has been 或 remains。lying 是動名詞，與連綴動詞 is 在一起，說明主詞 habit 是什麼，就是表語主格或主詞補語)
＝Lying is Mr. Lee's worst habit.
(這時，動名詞變成主詞；動詞也可用 has been 或 remains)

◉ John's hobbies are fishing and reading.
John 的嗜好是釣魚和看書。
(fishing 和 reading 都是動名詞，與 are 在一起，說明主詞 hobbies 是什麼，也就是表語主格)
＝Fishing and reading are John's hobbies.
(這時，動名詞變成了主詞)
(上句的連綴動詞，除了用 are 外，也可用 have been、were 或 remain)

◉ Mr. Lee's major concern has become/is the losing of his popularity.
李先生最擔憂的是失去他的人氣。
(losing of his popularity 是動名詞片語，與連綴動詞 is 或 has become 在一起，說明主詞 concern 是什麼，也就是表語主格)
＝The losing of his popularity has become/is Mr. Lee's major concern.
(動名詞片語變成主詞)

◉ His only fault remains/is complaining about others.
他唯一的毛病就是埋怨別人。
(complaining about others 是動名詞片語，與連綴動詞 remains 或 is 在一起，說明主詞 fault 是什麼，也就是表語主格)

＝Complaining about others remains/is his only fault.
(這時，動名詞片語，也就變成主詞了。)

◎ My favorite pastime has always been writing articles for the World Journal Weekly.
我最喜愛的消遣一直都是替《世界周刊》寫稿。
(writing articles for the World Journal Weekly 是動名詞片語，作連綴動詞 has been 的表語主格，說明主詞 pastime 是什麼)
＝Writing articles for the World Journal Weekly has always been my favorite pastime.
(這時，動名詞片語就變成句子的主詞。因為主詞是 writing，不是 articles，所以動詞用單數 has been)

◎ A qualification for this position was/is/would be having a degree in computers.
這份工作的條件之一是要有電腦學位。
(having a degree in computers 是動名詞片語，與連綴動詞 was 或 is 或 would be 在一起，說明主詞 qualification 是什麼，故是表語主格)
＝Having a degree in computers was/is/would be a qualification for this position.
(這時，動名詞片語變成主詞了)

四、當同位語（appositive）

例如：

◎ Mrs. Wang has a new hobby, cooking.
王太太有個新嗜好——做菜。
(cooking 是動名詞，說明了 hobby 是什麼)

◎ Her pastime, drawing, gives her much satisfaction.
她繪畫的興趣帶給她很大的滿足感。
(drawing 是動名詞，說明主詞的 pastime)

- Mrs. Chang brought her talent, arranging flowers, into full play.
  張太太將她插花的天分發揮地淋漓盡致。
  (arranging flowers 是動名詞片語，說明了名詞 talent)

- His job, wiretapping for the Secret Service, can be stressful and unpleasant.
  他為特勤局擔任竊聽工作，可謂是壓力大又很煩人。
  (wiretapping for the Secret Service 是動名詞片語，說明主詞 job)

- John's work, buying and selling property, earns him $60,000 a year.
  John 買賣房地產的工作，年收入六萬美金。
  (buying and selling property 是動名詞片語，說明主詞 work)

由於動名詞當名詞用，所以可以用形容詞去修飾；又因為動名詞還有動詞的本質，因此也可以用副詞去修飾。

例如：

- The audience applauded Ms. Chang's graceful dancing.
  觀眾為張小姐優美的舞蹈鼓掌。
  (graceful 是形容詞，修飾動名詞 dancing)

- Her husband's loud snoring annoyed her.
  她丈夫打鼾很大聲惹她厭煩。
  (loud 是形容詞，修飾動名詞 snoring)

- Mr. Chen's loud, high-pitched talking in public places is irritating.
  陳先生在公共場合高聲、尖銳的談話，令人不舒服。
  (形容詞 loud, high-pitched，修飾動名詞 talking)

- Waiting for the train has exhausted his patience.
  等火車耗掉了他的耐心。
  (for the train 本是介詞片語，當形容詞，修飾 waiting)

◉ Answering too quickly is not always a good idea.
太快回答未必好。
(副詞 quickly，修飾動名詞 answering，而副詞 too 又修飾 quickly)

◉ My son's morning routine includes showering leisurely.
我兒子每天早上都會悠閒地沖澡。
(副詞 leisurely 修飾 showering)

◉ Many people forbid shouting in the house.
許多人家裡禁止大聲喊叫。
(in the house 修飾 shouting)

注 意

動詞、分詞和動名詞，不可弄錯。

◉ Mr. Wang is traveling in Taiwan.
王先生正在台灣旅行。
(is 或 was traveling 是動詞進行式)

◉ A traveling circus came to our city last week.
上周一個巡迴表演的馬戲團來到我們城裡。
(traveling 是現在分詞，當形容詞，修飾 circus)

◉ Traveling will tire me out.
旅行將會讓我疲憊不堪。
(traveling 是動名詞，當主詞用)

◉ Mr. Wang's hobby is traveling.
王先生的嗜好是旅行。
(這裡的 traveling 是動名詞，當表語主格，說明主詞 hobby 是什麼)

五、動名詞前面，要用名詞或代名詞的所有格（possessive case）

例如：

- His mother objected to his playing on the football team.
  他媽媽反對他參加足球隊。
  (在動名詞 playing 前，要用代名詞所有格 his，而不是用受格 him，因為反對的是 playing，而不是 him)

- The dog's barking at night upset the neighbors.
  夜晚的狗叫聲使鄰居不高興。
  (dog's 是名詞所有格，當形容詞，修飾動名詞 barking)

六、使用動名詞片語時，要注意主詞與動詞間的合理性

例如：

- Upon receiving the bad news, he decided to cancel the party.
  接到壞消息後，他決定取消宴會。
  (因為主詞 he，才是收到壞消息者)

不能說成：

Upon receiving the bad news, the party was cancelled.
(因為 party 不是收到壞消息者)

當然也可以把介詞片語改成附屬句：

- After he had received the bad news, he cancelled the party.

◉ By running very fast, Mr. A reached the finish line.
A 先生因為跑得很快而抵達了終點。

不能說成：

By running very fast, the finish line was reached.

但也可改成附屬句：

◉ Mr. A was running very fast, when he reached the finish line.

◉ After climbing the mountain, the tour guide suggested a rest
(for us).
爬完山後導遊建議（我們）休息一下。

不能說：

After climbing the mountain, a rest was suggested by the tour
guide.

但可以說：

◉ After we had climbed the mountain, the tour guide suggested a
rest.

1-14

冠詞的用法

冠詞(article)在文法裡算是較為複雜的項目，因為有些用法取決於說話者的意思，而非遵循某種規則。

有人把冠詞 a, an, the 歸類為形容詞，不過多數人把 a, an 稱為不定冠詞(indefinite article)，而稱 the 為定冠詞(definite article)。

名詞的性質也會影響到冠詞的用法。換言之，名詞屬於普通名詞、專有名詞、抽象名詞或集合名詞等，乃至可數或不可數名詞、單數或複數名詞，都是影響冠詞用法的因素。現在分述如下：

一、不定冠詞的用法

1. 不定冠詞 a, an，是用在單數的普通名詞前，係指一般性的人、地或物。

   (例如:)

   ◎ You can find a history book in the bookstore.
      你可以在書店裡找到歷史書。
      (指任何一本歷史書，沒有特別指定那一本；a 也修飾 history book)

   ◎ Mr. A is a student in this college.
      A 先生是這所大學的學生。
      (只是一個學生而已，沒有特指那一個；a 也修飾 student)

   ◎ A study reveals that we may get too much iron in our diet.
      研究顯示，我們在飲食中也許攝取了過多鐵質。
      (只是一項研究而已，沒有特指那一種；a 修飾 study)

也有人把 some 列入不定冠詞裡，修飾可數或不可數名詞（count or non-count noun）。

例如：

- I bought some apples and some oranges yesterday.
  昨天我買了一些蘋果和柳橙。
  （apples 和 oranges 都是可數複數普通名詞；some 修飾 apples 和 oranges）

- Mr. A likes to listen to some music while working.
  A 先生做事的時候喜歡聽點音樂。
  （music 是不可數的普通名詞；some 修飾 music）

2. 不定冠詞 a，其後所接字詞的首字母為子音(consonant sound)，而 an 其後所接字詞的首字母則是母音(vowel sound)。(母音：a, e, i, o, u，其餘都是子音，也叫輔音)

例如：

- He stayed in a hotel outside the city.
  他住在城外的一個旅館裡。
  （hotel 的首字母是子音 h，故用 a）

- Mr. B told me an interesting story.
  B 先生告訴我一個有趣的故事。
  （interesting 的首字母是母音 i，故用 an）

- There are an ax and an empty can on the porch.
  門廊上有一把斧頭和一個空罐。
  （ax 的首字母是母音 a；empty 的首字母是母音 e，故都用 an）

- I ate an egg, an orange, and an apple today.
  我今天吃了一顆蛋、一個柳橙和一個蘋果。
  （egg, orange 和 apple 的首字母都是母音 e, o, a，故都用 an）

◉ Don't forget to take an umbrella with you.
別忘了隨身帶把傘。
（umbrella 的開頭字是母音 u，故用 an）

冠詞為 an 的常見字詞還有：an eraser, an angry look, an opportunity, an old map, an opinion, an ear, an only child, an endless task, an evergreen tree, an account, an elephant, an idea, an uncle, an unusual title, an omelet, an article, an early retirement 等。

3. 使用 a 或 an 時須特別注意的發音。

例如：

◉ Mr. J is an honest person.
J 先生是誠實的人。
（honest 的首字母 h，不發音，是以第二個字母 o 為準，故用 an）

◉ It will take an hour to drive from here to your house.
從這裡開車到你家要一個小時。
（hour 的首字母 h 不發音，故以第二個字母 o 為準）

◉ There is a university in this city.
這座城裡有所大學。
（university 的首字母 u 的發音是子音 /ju/ ，故用 a）

◉ A union worker wanted to go on strike.
一名工會工人想要罷工。
（union 的首字母雖是母音 u，但發子音 /ju/ 的短音，故用 a）

◉ Friendship is not a one-way street.
友誼不是單方面的。
（one 的開頭字雖是母音 o，但發音為 /w/ ，故用 a）

◉ Mr. Chen is pushing his son to be an M.D.
陳先生逼他兒子當醫生。
(m 發音是 /ɛm/，故用 an；M.D.是 medical doctor 的縮寫)

◉ He missed an E and an F in that long word.
他在那個很長的單字中漏掉了 E 和 F。
(E 發音為 /i/，故用 an，而 F 發音為 /ɛf/，故也用 an)

其他又如：

a useful article, a unit, a unique design（u 的發音為 /ju/ ）

an X-ray（X 的發音為 /ɛks/ ）

a European trip（Eu 的發音為 /ju/ ）

a once-in-a-lifetime opportunity（once 發音為 /wʌns/，故用 a）

二、定冠詞的用法

1. 單數普通名詞，是指特定的人、地、物時，前面要加 the。

（例如：）

◉ Mr. Wang is the person to see.
王先生是你要見的人。
(隱含「因為只有他能夠幫你的忙」。the person 是指特定要看的人)

◉ The tiger escaped from the zoo.
老虎逃出動物園了。
(the tiger 和 the zoo 都是指特定的動物和地點)

◉ The agent has shown me several houses.
仲介讓我看了幾棟房子。
(the agent 是指特定帶我看房子的房屋仲介)

- The fruit I bought was very fresh.
  我買的水果很新鮮。
  (the fruit I bought 指明是「我」買的水果)

2. 從一般性變成特定性

英文中，通常一般性的人、事、物第一次出現時，用不定冠詞 a 或 an；但之後再度或多次提及同一個人、事、物時，就要用定冠詞 the。(也就是從一般性變成特定性)

例如：

- Mr. B left a book on my desk; he returned to get the book.
  B 先生在我桌上留了一本書；他回來拿那本書。
  (第一次用 a book，是指一般的書；但第二次再提時，變成 the book，是指特定的那本書)

- My wife bought a cake and some ice-cream; we ate the cake and the ice-cream for dessert.
  我太太買了一個蛋糕和一些冰淇淋；我們吃那個蛋糕和冰淇淋當甜點。
  (第一次用 a cake 和 some ice-cream 指一般性，但再提 the cake 和 the ice-cream 時，就變成特定性)

- I saw a car in my driveway; my friend got out of the car.
  我看到有輛車在我的車道上；我朋友下了那輛車。
  (第一次用 a car，指一般性；再提及時就變成特定性，故用 the car)

- I had a banana and an apple; I gave the banana to John.
  我有一根香蕉和一個蘋果；我把香蕉給了 John。
  (第一次用 a banana，指一般性；再提及時就變成特定性，故用 the banana)

3. 當可數的單數普通名詞用以表示說者和聽者彼此都知道、熟悉或期待的事物時，就用定冠詞 the。

例如：

◉ Please close the window in the kitchen.
請把廚房裡的窗戶關上。
(聽者也知道 window 和 kitchen 在那裡，故加 the)

◉ When you leave, be sure to turn off the light.
你離開時一定要關燈。
(聽者也知道 light 在那裡；light＝lamp)

◉ Mary came into the kitchen and put a bag on the table.
Mary 走進廚房，把一個包包放在桌上。
(聽者知道廚房裡有桌子，故用 the table)

◉ When John heard a phone ring, he picked up the receiver.
John 聽到電話鈴響時拿起了聽筒。
(說者預料到 John 會拿起 receiver，故加 the)

◉ The newspaper is over there on the couch.
報紙在那邊的沙發上。
(聽者也明白 newspaper 和 couch 在那裡，故加 the)

4. 普通名詞後面有修飾語(modifier)時，那麼就從一般性變成特定性，所以要加 the。

例如：

◉ The flowers in this vase are beautiful.
這花瓶裡的花很美。
(片語 in this vase 修飾 flowers，把花限定了，故用 the flowers)

- I like the house that Mr. A owns.
  我喜歡 A 先生擁有的那棟房子。
  (子句 that Mr. A owns 修飾 house，把房子限定了，故用 the house)

- He will pick her up at the corner of Smith Street and Hall Drive.
  他將在 Smith 街和 Hall 路的轉角接她。
  (of Smith Street and Hall Drive 修飾 corner，限定了那一個轉角，故用 the corner)

但是也可以說：

- I like a house that is not too big.
  我喜歡不太大的房子。
  (則是指任何一棟房子，只要不太大，就夠了)

- He likes a wine that is not too sweet.
  他喜歡不太甜的酒。
  (指任何一瓶或一杯酒，只要不太甜就好了)

所以要看說話者的口氣以及句子的含義，如指一般性，就用 a 或 an。

5. 如果指一般人都熟悉的場所或地點，諸如旅館、餐館、圖書館、體育館、郵局等，前面要加 the。

例如：

- He stayed at the Holiday Inn near the art museum.
  他住在美術館附近的假日飯店。

- Mr. B goes to the post office every two weeks.
  B 先生每隔兩星期去一趟郵局。

⊙ John studies at the library once a week.
John 每週去圖書館讀書一次。

⊙ There are many old people in the mall.
購物中心有許多老人。

(以上 Holiday Inn, art museum, post office, library, mall 都是大家耳熟能詳的地方，所以要加 the)

6. 指群山、群島、海洋、沙漠等專有名詞以及帶有 united, kingdom, republic 等字眼的國家名稱之前，要加 the。

例如：

⊙ The United States is an immigrant country.
美國是個移民國家。

⊙ The United Kingdom is a favorite travel destination for many people around the world.
英國是全球許多人最愛的旅遊地點。

⊙ Mr. A has visited the Philippines and the Gulf of Mexico.
A 先生去過菲律賓和墨西哥灣。

(Philippines 也可稱為 Philippine Islands，指菲律賓群島)

⊙ The Republic of China is also known as Taiwan.
中華民國又名台灣。

其他又如：

| The Rocky Mountains＝the Rockies 落磯山脈 |
| The Himalayas＝the Himalaya Mountains 喜馬拉雅山脈 |
| The Alps 阿爾卑斯山脈 (後面通常不加 mountains) |
| The Andes 安第斯山脈 (後面不加 mountain) |

The Gobi Desert 戈壁沙漠

The Black Sea 黑海(Sea 不能省略)

The Mississippi (River)密西西比河

The Panama Canal 巴拿馬運河

The Suez (Canal)蘇伊士運河

The Pacific (Ocean)太平洋

the Indian Ocean 印度洋

The Caribbean (Sea)加勒比海

The Mediterranean (Sea)地中海

但是，如果指單獨的山，以及一般的國家、城市、州等名稱，則屬專有名詞，前面不加冠詞。

例如：

◉ Has anyone in this college ever climbed Mt. Everest or Mt. Washington?
這所大學裡有人爬過聖母峰或華盛頓山嗎？
(Mt.＝Mount＝Mountain)

◉ Many students in the US come from Canada, Great Britain, Nigeria, and Switzerland.
許多在美國念書的學生來自加拿大、英國、奈及利亞和瑞士。

◉ The number of crimes in New York City has declined in recent years.
近幾年來，紐約市的犯罪數字已經降低。

三、不用冠詞的情況

1. 專有名詞(proper noun)，指人名、地名或機關名稱，通常首字母大寫，不用冠詞。

例如：

- John Smith is a professor in our college.
  John Smith 是我們大學的教授

- Stanford University is a well-known school.
  史丹佛大學是一所名校。

- I have been living on Aberdeen Road for years.
  我多年來都住在 Aberdeen 路。

- MAG Technology Company in Taiwan makes a lot of computers.
  台灣的 MAG 科技公司製造大量電腦。

但是，有時專有名詞，被修飾語限定範圍時，則可用冠詞。

例如：

- The John Smith who came here yesterday is not his relative.
  昨天來這裡的那位 John Smith 並不是他的親戚。
  (who came here yesterday 限定了 John Smith)

- He feels National Taiwan University is the Harvard University of Taiwan.
  他覺得台大是台灣的哈佛大學。
  (Harvard University 被 of Taiwan 所修飾，受到限制，故可用 the)

2. 可數的一般性複數名詞，前面不加冠詞。

例如：

- Physicians believe that soybeans are a healthful food.
  許多醫生相信黃豆是健康食品。
  (Physicians 是可數複數名詞，指一般性)

- Computers have become more common and more powerful.
  電腦已變得更普遍、功能也更強。
  (computers 是可數的複數名詞，也指一般性)

- Modernizing kitchens and bathrooms is usually expensive.
  打造現代化的廚房和廁所通常很昂貴。
  (kitchens 和 bathrooms 都是可數的，指一般性的複數名詞。主詞
  modernizing 是單數，故用 is)

- Shopping malls take away business from old stores.
  購物中心搶走了老店的生意。
  (malls 是可數的一般性複數名詞)

- Schools generally have many activities.
  學校通常有許多活動。
  (schools 也是一般性可數的名詞)

但是，如果有修飾語就會受到限制，變成特指的，可加
the。

例如：

- The schools in some areas are unsafe places for kids to go.
  某些地區的學校對孩童來說並不是可以安全就讀的地方。
  (in some areas 修飾 schools，把學校限定了，指特定的學校，故加
  the)

- Due to snow, the malls in Salisbury are closed today.
  由於下雪，Salisbury 的購物中心今天不開。
  (in Salisbury 修飾 malls，把 malls 限定了，故加 the)

3. 語言和課程(course of study)前面通常不加冠詞。

例如：

◉ Learning Chinese has become popular in the US.
在美國學中文變流行了。

◉ English is a foreign language for him.
英語對他而言是外語。

其他又如：French, Russian, Arabic 等等。

◉ Not many students like to study physics.
沒有很多學生喜歡物理。

◉ Literature became his major in college.
文學成為他在大學的主修。

其他又如：chemistry, poetry, psychology, engineering, biology, history, music, anthropology 等等。

但是：

◉ The Chinese that many Americans are learning seems difficult.
許多美國人正在學的中文好像很難。
(that many Americans are learning 修飾 Chinese，把中文限定在美國人所學的範圍內，故可加 the)

4. 自然界的現象不加任何冠詞。

諸如天氣、陽光、雷雨等等(lightning, daylight, moonlight, sunshine, fog, gravity, snow, hail, energy, dew, humidity, light, heat, fire...)是不可數名詞，所以當然不加任何冠詞。

例如：

⊚ Sunlight is a good source of vitamin D.
陽光是維他命 D 良好的來源之一。

⊚ Thunder, wind, and rain all started at the same time yesterday.
昨天同時開始打雷、颱風和下雨。

⊚ Weather is unpredictable sometimes.
天氣有時難以預測。

⊚ Darkness is frightening to many children.
對許多孩子而言，黑暗很恐怖。
(以上的 sunlight, thunder, wind, rain, weather, darkness 都屬自然現象，不加冠詞)

但是遇到修飾語受到限定時，就可加 the：

例如：

⊚ The weather in Maryland is nice.
馬里蘭州的氣候宜人。
(in Maryland 修飾 weather，所以天氣被限定了，故可加 the)

⊚ The darkness in your room frightens the child.
你房間暗暗的嚇到孩子了。
(修飾語 in your room，限定了 darkness，故加 the)

5. 流質或氣體

如：juice, wine, coffee, tea, blood, honey, soup, oil, shampoo, smoke, steam 等，都是不可數名詞不加任何冠詞。

例如：

⊚ Water consists of hydrogen and oxygen.
水包括氫和氧。

- Man cannot live without air.
  人類沒有空氣無法生存。
  (以上 hydrogen, oxygen, air 都屬氣體)

- Milk and cream are major dairy products.
  牛奶和奶油是主要的乳製品。

- Gasoline is very important for all Americans.
  汽油對所有美國人而言都很重要。
  (以上 milk, cream, gasoline 都屬流質)

但是遇到修飾語受到限定時，即可加 the。

例如：

- The water in this area is very clean.
  這裡的水很乾淨。
  (in this area 修飾水，把 water 限定了，故加 the)

6. 物質的原料名稱

如：silver, paper, wool, silk, wood, glass, plastic, rubber, cotton, copper, tin 等，不加任何冠詞。

例如：

- Paper currency is backed by gold.
  紙幣有黃金做後盾。

- Iron is a type of metal.
  鐵是金屬的一種。

- Cement is a vital material in construction.
  水泥是建築主要的原料。

- I got sand in my shoes.
  我鞋子裡有沙子。
  (以上 gold, iron, cement, sand 都是物質原料的名稱)

但是受到修飾語所限制時，則可加 the。

例如：

- The iron we use at this factory is of high quality.
  我們在這間工廠裡所使用的鐵，品質很好。
  (we use at this factory 把鐵限定了，故可加 the)

- The sand in the boy's eyes needs to be removed.
  男孩眼裡的沙子必須取出。
  (in the boy's eyes 限定了 sand，故加 the)

7. 食品名稱前面，不加任何冠詞。

例如：

- Butter is a dairy product.
  奶油是一種乳製品。

- We had meat for supper yesterday.
  我們昨天晚餐吃肉。

- Bread is made of flour.
  麵包是麵粉製成的。

- Most Americans love beef, ham, lamb, and pork.
  大部分美國人喜歡牛肉、火腿、羊肉和豬肉。

以上的 butter, meat, bread, beef, ham, lamb, pork 都屬食物名稱，前面不加任何冠詞。其他又如：rice, cheese, sugar, bacon, chicken, fish, corn 等等。

但是有了修飾語，受到限制時，則可加 the。

例如：

⊙ The butter on this bread is delicious.
這個麵包上的奶油很可口。
(on this bread 限定了 butter，故加 the)

⊙ The meat we ate last night came from overseas.
我們昨天晚上吃的肉來自國外。
(we ate last night 把 meat 限定了，故加 the)

8. 抽象名詞(abstract noun)前面，不加任何冠詞。

例如：

⊙ Many people have to pay a high price for popularity.
許多人為了出名必須付出很高的代價。

⊙ Mr. Bush has enormous influence on the Iraq War.
布希先生對伊拉克戰爭有重大的影響。

⊙ Happiness consists in contentment.
幸福在於滿足。（知足常樂）
(以上 popularity, influence, happiness 都是抽象名詞)

但是受到限制時，則可用冠詞 the。

例如：

⊙ The popularity of Mr. A is beyond description.
A 先生的聲望言語難以形容。
(of Mr. A 限定了 popularity，所以加 the)

⊙ The happiness of writers depends on the response of their readers.
作者的快樂與否取決於讀者的反應。
(of writers 修飾 happiness，故加 the)

其他抽象名詞如：confidence, courage, cowardice, enjoyment, greed, honesty, generosity, hospitality, ignorance, intelligence, justice, patience, knowledge, poverty, pride, wealth, stupidity, career, violence, progress, nationalism 等，都屬看不見、摸不到、沒有實質型態且不可數的抽象名詞。

9. 由個體組成的集合名詞(collective noun)前不加冠詞。

不加任何冠詞，也不用複數。但可用 some, a lot of, too much 或 a little 去修飾。

例如：

⊙ I bought some furniture.
我買了一些家具。
(furniture 是由桌、椅、床等個體所組成的集合名詞，故不加冠詞，也不用複數)

但指明是何種家具時，可用複數：

⊙ I bought some chairs and several tables.
我買了一些椅子或桌子。

如果 furniture 被限定了，也可用冠詞 the：

⊙ I bought the furniture for my living room.
我買了客廳的家具。
(修飾語 for my living room 限定了 furniture)

同理：

◉ Mr. A got some mail today.
A 先生今天收到了一些信。
（mail 也是由信件、明信片等組成的集合名詞，故不加任何冠詞，也不用複數）

但指個體時，就能用複數：

◉ Mr. A got a few letters and some postcards.
A 先生收到一些信件和明信片。

◉ Mrs. B loves to buy some jewelry every so often.
B 太太偶爾喜歡買些首飾。
（jewelry 係由 ring, bracelet, necklace 等組成的集合名詞，故不加任何冠詞，也不用複數）

但指個體時，可用複數：

◉ Mrs. B bought many bracelets and several rings.
B 太太買了許多手鐲和幾只戒指。

如果有修飾語受到限定，也可加冠詞 the：

◉ The jewelry that Mrs. B bought costs $1,000.
B 太太買的首飾價值一千美元。
（that Mrs. B bought 修飾 jewelry，被限定了，故加 the）

◉ John has a lot of/lots of money.
John 有很多錢。
（money 由 dollar, quarter, nickel 等組成的集合名詞，故不用不定冠詞，也不用複數）

但指錢的幣值及種類時，可用複數：

◉ He has ten quarters and twenty nickels.
他有 10 個兩毛五和 20 個五分硬幣。

若特指某一筆錢時，也可用冠詞 the：

◉ I gave John $100, so he has the money.
我給了約翰 100 元，所以他有那筆錢了。

其他常見集合名詞如：traffic, clothing, equipment, homework, fruit, hardware, garbage, scenery, information, stuff 等等。

 註：

單數普通名詞前加冠詞a, an, the時，與複數普通名詞意義相同，都指一般性。

例如：

◉ A dog is a loyal animal.
＝The dog is a loyal animal.
＝Dogs are loyal animals.
狗是忠實的動物。
(指一般的狗)

◉ An apple is a healthful food.
＝The apple is a healthful food.
＝Apples are a healthful food.
蘋果是健康食品。
(a＝a kind of)

◉ An American is a law-abiding person.
＝The American is a law-abiding person
＝Americans are law-abiding people.
美國人很守法。
(泛指一般人都安分守己)

2-1

句型和結構

在英文中，每個句子都要有主詞和動詞(有時也要補語)才能表達完整的意思。

一、五大句型(sentence pattern)

1. 主詞＋動詞(S＋V)：

例如：

◉ The phone rang.
電話響了。
(phone 是主詞，rang 是動詞)

◉ A bird nested in the tree.
一隻鳥在樹上築巢。
(bird 是主詞，nested 是動詞)

◉ Many people swim daily.
許多人每天游泳。
(people 是主詞，swim 是動詞)

以上的主詞和動詞，只有一個，所以也叫做簡單主詞和簡單動詞(simple subject and simple verb)；可以用連接詞 and、or 或 but 等，把簡單主詞和簡單動詞變成複合主詞和複合動詞(compound subject and compound verb)。也就是，兩個或兩個以上的主詞有共同的動詞，就是複合主詞；兩個或兩個以上的動詞，有共同的主詞，就是複合動詞。

例如：

◉ Jim and Amy are brother and sister.
Jim 和 Amy 是兄妹。
(主詞 Jim 和 Amy，用 and 連接，其共同的動詞是 are，故為複合主詞)

⊙ His daughter or Bob will represent the school.
他女兒或 Bob 將代表學校。
(主詞 daughter 和 Bob，用 or 連接，其共同的動詞是 represent，故為複合主詞)

⊙ My boss smiles often and frowns occasionally.
我老闆常常面帶微笑，偶爾才皺個眉。
(動詞 smiles 和 frowns，用 and 連接，有一個共同的主詞 boss，故為複合動詞)

⊙ The program may succeed or fail within a year.
這個計畫在一年內也許就知成敗。
(動詞 succeed 和 fail，用連接詞 or 連接，其共同的主詞是 program，故為複合動詞)

⊙ Mary sings well but dances poorly.
Mary 歌唱得很好，但舞跳得很差。
(動詞 sings 和 dances，用連接詞 but 連接，只有一個共同的主詞 Mary，故為複合動詞)

2. 主詞＋動詞＋直接受詞(S＋V＋DO)：

例如：

⊙ Mr. Wang sells furniture.
王先生販賣家俱。
(Mr. Wang 是主詞，sells 是動詞，furniture 是直接受詞；furniture 是家俱總稱，不加 s)

⊙ My wife baked an apple pie.
我太太烤了一個蘋果派。
(wife 是主詞，baked 是動詞，pie 是直接受詞)

⊙ Her father carefully wrote, revised, and typed his letter.
她父親仔細撰寫、修改和打他的信件。

(father 是主詞，wrote, revised 和 typed 是複合動詞，letter 是直接受詞。加上直接受詞後句子意思才完整)

也可用連接詞 and, or, but 等連接，把簡單直接受詞，變成複合直接受詞。

例如：

◉ My wife prepared some cookies and green tea.
我太太準備了一些餅乾和綠茶。
(wife 是主詞，prepared 是動詞，cookies 和 tea 是複合直接受詞)

◉ Mrs. Wang and her daughter cooked eggs, pancakes, and sausage.
王太太和她女兒煎了蛋、煎餅和烤香腸。
(Mrs. Wang 和 daughter 是複合主詞；cooked 是動詞；eggs, pancakes 和 sausage 是複合直接受詞)

3. 主詞＋動詞＋間接受詞＋直接受詞(S＋V＋IO＋DO)：

例如：

◉ Mr. A offered her a job.
A 先生給了她一份工作。
(her 是間接受詞；job 是直接受詞)

◉ Teacher handed Mary a dictionary.
老師遞了一本字典給 Mary。
(Mary 是間接受詞；dictionary 是直接受詞)

◉ Mr. B sent Mary and Lucy letters.
B 先生寄信給 Mary 和 Lucy。
(Mary 和 Lucy 都是間接受詞；letters 是直接受詞)

◉ We gave John and Bob some books and pens.
我們給了 John 和 Bob 一些書和筆。
(John 和 Bob 是間接受詞；books 和 pens 是直接受詞；可見間接受詞
通常放在直接受詞前面)

4. 主詞＋動詞＋直接受詞＋受詞補語(S＋V＋DO＋OC)：

一般是用名詞或形容詞去修飾直接受詞，作受詞補語。

例如：

◉ I called Mr. Chang uncle.
我叫張先生叔叔。
(Mr. Chang 是直接受詞；uncle 是名詞，也是修飾 Mr. Chang 的補語)

◉ His father painted his garage yellow.
他爸爸把車庫漆成黃色。
(garage 是直接受詞；yellow 是形容詞，修飾 garage，作為直接受詞
的補語)

◉ The teacher appointed Jim captain of the team.
老師任命 Jim 為隊長。
(Jim 是直接受詞；captain 是名詞，作為 Jim 的補語)

◉ The jury found the defendant guilty.
陪審團判定被告有罪。
(defendant 是直接受詞；guilty 是形容詞，作為直接受詞的補語)

5. 主詞＋連綴動詞＋主詞補語(S＋LV＋SC)：

通常也用名詞或形容詞修飾主詞，作為主詞補語。而連綴
動詞只是連接一個字與主詞之間的關係，並非行動動詞(action
verb)。

最常用的連綴動詞是：be（am, is, are, was, were, been）, appear, grow, seem, stay, become, look, smell, taste, feel, remain, sound, get（＝become）

例如：

- Mr. Wang is a computer programmer.
  王先生是電腦程式設計師。
  （Mr. Wang 是主詞；is 是連綴動詞；programmer 是名詞，修飾主詞，與主詞互為相等關係，故為主詞補語。這種名詞補語，也叫 predicate noun）

- Mr. B was a teacher and an interpreter.
  B 先生身兼老師和口譯員兩職。
  （Mr. B 是主詞；teacher 和 interpreter 都是名詞；was 是連綴動詞，與主詞是相等關連的，故為主詞補語）

- The waves seemed powerful and dangerous.
  海浪似乎又大又危險。
  （waves 是主詞；seemed 是連綴動詞；powerful 和 dangerous 都是形容詞，修飾主詞，作為主詞補語。這種形容詞補語，也叫 predicate adjective）

- The old man looks healthy and happy.
  老人看來健康快樂。
  （man 是主詞；looks 是連綴動詞；healthy 和 happy 都是形容詞，修飾主詞，作為主詞補語）

- Many passengers remained calm.
  許多旅客保持鎮靜。
  （passengers 是主詞；remained 是連綴動詞；calm 是形容詞，修飾主詞，故為主詞補語）

二、句子的結構（sentence structure）

談到句子的結構前，先要知道子句(clause)有兩種：獨立子句(independent clause)和附屬子句(subordinate clause)，雖然兩者都有主詞和動詞，但獨立子句能表達完整的思想，可以獨立存在；而附屬子句，不能表達完整的思想，不能獨立存在。獨立子句又稱主要子句(main clause)。

例如：

◉ After Mr. Wang left his office...
王先生離開辦公室後……
(然後呢？意思不完整，故為附屬子句)

◉ He went swimming.
他去游泳。
(意思完整，可以獨立存在，故為獨立子句)

句子通常有四種基本的結構：

1. 簡單句(simple sentence)

簡單句裡只能有一個獨立子句(不能多於一個)，也不能有任何附屬子句。

當然簡單句也可以把主詞或動詞變成複合主詞或複合動詞；也可以添加直接受詞，不定詞或分詞、介詞片語或補語。

例如：

◉ Mary and Lucy both sing and dance.
Mary 和 Lucy 兩人都又唱又跳。
(Mary 和 Lucy 是複合主詞；sing 和 dance 是複合動詞)

◉ Leo passed chemistry, but failed English.
Leo 通過了化學考試，但英文沒過。
(passed 和 failed 是複合動詞；chemistry 和 English 是直接受詞)

◉ A man, two boys, and a girl appeared at my door and asked for a Mr. Chen.
一個男人、兩個男孩和一個女孩出現在我家門口，要找一位陳先生。
(man, boys 和 girl 是複合主詞；appeared 和 asked 是複合動詞；at my door 和 for a Mr. Chen 是介詞片語)

◉ At supper, Mr. Wang gave us the news about the victory.
晚餐時，王先生告訴我們有關勝利的消息。
(At supper 和 about the victory 都是介詞片語，us 是間接受詞，news 是直接受詞)

◉ Mr. A went to the baseball game and to the dinner party afterward.
A 先生去看棒球賽，之後再去聚餐。
(to the baseball game 和 to the dinner party 都是介詞片語)

◉ Remembering the time, his son ran to school.
他兒子想起了時間，跑去學校。
(remembering the time 是現在分詞片語，進一步說明主詞 son；ran 是動詞；to school 是介詞片語)

◉ Melting quickly, snow from the mountains flooded the village.
山上的雪快速融化淹沒了這座村莊。
(melting quickly 是現在分詞片語，進一步說明主詞 snow；from the mountains 是介詞片語，flooded 是動詞，village 是直接受詞)

◉ Mr. B produced, directed, and sometimes acted in his own plays.
B 先生自製自導，有時也在他自己的戲裡軋上一角。
(produced, directed 和 acted 是複合動詞；in his own plays 是介詞片語)

- Neither the father nor the son heard or saw the car accident.
  父子倆都沒聽說，也沒目睹車禍事故。
  (father 和 son 是複合主詞；heard 和 saw 是複合動詞；car accident 是直接受詞)

- To support Mr. B or not (to support him) is a dilemma.
  要不要支持 B 先生真是兩難。
  (to support Mr. B 和 not to support him 是不定詞片語，用 or 連接，當主詞；is 是動詞；dilemma 是主詞補語。not 後面的 to support him 可省去)

- Destroyed by fire, the store was not rebuilt.
  被火燒毀的商店還未重建。
  (destroyed by fire 是過去分詞片語，修飾主詞 store)

可見簡單句可添加其他不同修飾語，但不能有附屬子句，也不能有另一個獨立子句。

2. 複合句 (compound sentence)

複合句裡包括兩個(或兩個以上)的獨立子句，但沒有附屬子句。

通常複合句的兩個獨立子句(即兩個簡單句)是由一個逗點和另一個對等連接詞 (coordinating conjunction) 連接起來。有時也可用分號 (semicolon) 相連。

常用的對等連接詞是：and, but, for, nor, or, so, yet

例如：

- The sky became dark, and it began to rain.
  天色變暗並開始下雨了。
  (the sky became dark 和 it began to rain 都是獨立子句。即使不用逗號和對等連接詞 and，也能各自獨立)

◉ Mr. Chang may visit our college, or he can tour the library.
張先生可以參觀我們的大學，或者看看圖書館。
(Mr. Chang may...和 he can tour...都是獨立子句，用逗號及對等連接詞 or 連接)

◉ Mr. B is interested in special education, so he reads many books on the subject.
B 先生對特殊教育有興趣，所以他看了許多那方面的書。
(Mr. B is interested...和 he reads many...都是獨立子句，用逗號和對等連接詞 so 連接起來)

◉ I would like to help him, but/yet I know very little about computer science.
我很想幫他忙，但我對電腦科學懂得很少。
(I would like to...和 I know very...都是獨立子句，用逗號和對等連接詞 but 或 yet 連接)

◉ Your argument is weak, for you have no proof to support your ideas.
你的論點薄弱，因為沒有證據可以支持你的觀點。
(your argument is...和 you have...都是獨立子句，以逗號和對等連接詞 for 連接起來)

如果使用分號，一般是連接兩個意思有所關連(related idea)的獨立子句。

例如：

◉ I swim often; water relaxes my muscles.
我常游泳，水會使我的肌肉放鬆。
(這兩個獨立子句的意思是有關連的)

◉ Mrs. Wang wrote cook books; she also illustrated them.
王太太寫烹飪書，並親自畫插圖。
(這兩個獨立子句意思也有關連)

但使用 however 或 moreover 時，後面還要加個逗點。

例如：

- Their team worked hard; however, they lost by a staggering margin.
  他們的隊伍打得很賣力，但在分數上以非常大的落差輸了。
  (however 後面要加逗點)

3. 複雜句(complex sentence)

複雜句裡包括一個獨立子句(即主要子句)和一個(或一個以上的)附屬子句(即形容詞子句或副詞子句)。

例如：

- Many people who know Mr. Wang admire him.
  許多認識王先生的人都很欣賞他。
  (many people admire him 是獨立子句；who know Mr. Wang 是附屬子句，當形容詞，修飾 people)

- This is the university that she described in her letter.
  這就是她在信中所描述的那所大學。
  (this is the university 是主要子句，也叫獨立子句；that she described是附屬子句，當形容詞，修飾 university)

- The package which I had mailed never arrived.
  我寄出的包裹，一直沒有送達。
  (the package never arrived 是主要子句；which I had mailed 是附屬子句，當形容詞，也叫形容詞子句，修飾 package)

- Many people do not go to college because it costs too much.
  許多人不能上大學，因為費用太高。
  (many people do not...是主要子句；because it costs...是附屬子句，當副詞用，修飾動詞 go)

◉ Mrs. Wang carries pepper spray wherever she goes.
王太太不論到哪裡，都帶著一個胡椒噴霧器。
(Mrs. Wang carries...是主要子句；wherever she goes 是附屬子句，當副詞用，修飾動詞 carries)

◉ I helped paint the house although Mr. Wang did most of the work.
我幫忙油漆房子，雖然大部分是王先生漆的。
(I helped...是主要子句；although Mr. Wang...是附屬子句，當副詞用，修飾動詞 helped。也可以說：Although I helped paint the house, Mr. Wang did most of the work. 這時 Mr. Wang did...變成主要子句；although I helped...變成附屬子句，當副詞，修飾動詞 did)

◉ When the fog lifted, we continued our trip.
＝We continued our trip when the fog lifted.
霧散後，我們繼續旅行。
(we continued our trip 是主要子句；when the fog lifted 是附屬子句，當副詞用，修飾動詞 continued)

◉ If you are unhappy with his work, you can wallpaper the room yourself.
＝You can wallpaper the room yourself if you are unhappy with his work.
假如你覺得他做得不好，你可以自己幫這間房間貼壁紙。
(you can wallpaper...是主要子句；if you are...是附屬子句，當副詞用，修飾動詞 wallpaper)

注意

名詞子句當主詞時，雖然它本身會有附屬子句的味道，但還是簡單句。

例如：

⊙ That Miss A wanted to leave this department has bothered her boss.
A 小姐想離開這個部門,讓她的老闆很困擾。

(that Miss A wanted to leave this department 是名詞子句,當主詞用,動詞是 bothered;boss 是受詞,所以還是簡單句,不是複雜句)

4. 混合句 (compound-complex sentence)

混合句裡包括一個複合句和一個複雜句;也就是包括兩個(或兩個以上的)獨立子句,和一個(或一個以上的)附屬子句。

例如:

⊙ Mr. A planned to drive to work, but he could not do so until the snowplows cleared the streets.
A 先生想開車去上班,但要等到掃雪車清好馬路才能上路。

(Mr. A planned to...和 he could not... 都是獨立子句;until the snowplows... 是附屬子句)

⊙ As Mr. B left for the office, he remembered to take his lunch, but he forgot the report that he finished last night.
B 先生去上班時,記得要帶午餐卻忘了帶昨晚寫好的報告。

(he remembered to take his lunch 和 he forgot the report 都是獨立子句;as Mr. B left for office 和 that he finished last night 都是附屬子句)

⊙ Mr. F was the professor whom I liked best, but he hasn't taught since he became sick.
F 先生是我最喜歡的教授,但他自從生病後就不再教書了。

(Mr. F was the professor 和 he hasn't taught 都是獨立子句;whom I liked best 和 since he became sick 都是附屬子句)

⊙ Because Mr. Wang was late from the meeting, he called home, but no one answered.
王先生因為開會晚了而打電話回家,但沒有人接。

(he called home 和 no one answered 都是獨立子句;because Mr. Wang was late from the meeting 是附屬子句)

不少美國人為求簡單明瞭而不愛使用冗長的混合句，因為主詞不同時，往往容易造成困擾與混淆，所以大多愛用簡單句、結合句或複合句。

例如：

⊙ If you can pack quickly, you may come with me, but I have to leave within an hour.（混合句）
假如你能快點打包，你也許可以跟我一起走，但我必須在一個小時內出發。

也可改為簡單句和複合句：

I have to leave within an hour. You may come with me if you can pack quickly.

⊙ The football game is fun, but I prefer basketball because it is safer.（混合句）
足球賽很好玩，但我比較喜歡打籃球，因為比較安全。

也可改為簡單句和複合句：

The football game is fun. I prefer basketball because it is safer.
（句中的 it 顯然是指 basketball，比上句明白）

⊙ The streets were closed after the storm struck, and they are still dangerous.（混合句）
颱風侵襲過後，道路封鎖但依然危險。

可以改為複雜句：

The streets, which are still dangerous, were closed after the storm struck.
（混合句中的 they，是否指 streets，也許會造成誤會，不如刪去，更為明白）

　　總之，現代人生活繁忙，分秒必爭，許多美國人主張文字應該簡單明瞭，避免使用長句和難字，讓一般人都能充分理解，達到溝通目的。

2-2
句子的組合

把句子組合起來的目的，就是把一些短句或「支離破碎」的句子連接起來，使句子更好、更有連貫性。以下把一般常用的句子組合方法，舉例說明：

1. 把簡單型(simple form)的主詞、動詞、受詞或補助語連接起來，成為複合型(compound form)。

例如：

- ◉ Mr. Wang is applying for this position.
  王先生正在申請這個職位。
- ◉ Mr. Lee is also applying for this position.
  李先生也在申請這個職位。

  → Mr. Wang and Mr. Lee are both applying for this position.
  (把 Mr. Wang 和 Mr. Lee 用 and 連接，成為複合主詞)

- ◉ My wife read for an hour last night.
  昨晚我太太看了一小時的書。
- ◉ She also wrote a letter.
  她也寫了一封信。
- ◉ In addition, she cooked a nice dinner.
  而且，她煮了一頓美味的晚餐。

  → Last night my wife read for an hour, wrote a letter, and cooked a nice dinner.
  (由於主詞相同，所以可把三個動詞 read, wrote 和 cooked，以逗號和對等連接詞 and 連接，形成複合動詞)

- ◉ The school gave Mr. Chang extra credits for his field work.
  學校因張先生的實地考察給予額外學分。

◉ Mr. Lee was given extra credits as well.
李先生也得到了特別褒揚。

→ The school gave Mr. Chang and Mr. Lee extra credits for their field work.

(先把第二句的被動 was given 改為主動後，再把間接受詞 Mr. Chang 和 Mr. Lee 連接起來)

◉ The old man sat at a roadside stand.
這位老先生坐在路邊攤。

◉ He sold vegetables to passing drivers.
他把蔬菜賣給路過的駕駛人。

→ The old man sat at a roadside stand and sold vegetables to passing drivers.

(把動詞 sat 和 sold 用 and 連接，成為複合動詞)

◉ Mr. A called Mr. B a scholar.
A 先生稱呼 B 先生學者。

◉ He also called Mr. B a philanthropist.
他也稱呼 B 先生是位慈善家。

◉ Finally, Mr. A called Mr. B a wonderful man.
最後，A 先生認為 B 先生是個大好人。

→ Mr. A called Mr. B a scholar, a philanthropist and a wonderful man.

(把受詞補助語 scholar, philanthropist 和 wonderful man 用逗號分開，再用 and 連成一個簡單句。在 and 的前面，通常不加逗號)

◉ The college library cost five million dollars.
大學圖書館造價五百萬美元。

◉ It took five years to complete.
它花了五年的時間才完工。

→ The college library cost five million dollars and took five years to complete.

(因為 it 也指圖書館，所以可把直接受詞 dollars 和 years 連接起來)

◉ Mr. Chen will bring a camcorder to the party.
陳先生會帶錄影機去參加派對。

◉ One of his friends will also bring a camcorder to the party.
他的一位朋友也會帶錄影機參加派對。

→ Both Mr. Chen and one of his friends will bring camcorders to the party.

(上面兩句不同的主詞，可用 both...and 連接，成為複合主詞)

◉ The faculty members elected John (as the) chairperson.
全體教師選 John 當主席。

◉ They also named Bob (as the) secretary.
他們也指定 Bob 當祕書。

→ The faculty members elected John chairperson and Bob secretary.

(動詞 elected 和 named 意義相似，故可省去一個。把受詞補語 chairperson 和 secretary 用 and 連接起來。可把 as the 省去)

◉ In the fitting room, Mary tried on the swimsuit.
Mary 在試衣間裡試穿泳衣。

◉ She looked in the full-length mirror.
她在全身鏡前照著。

◉ She then smiled.
然後她笑了。

→ In the fitting room, Mary tried on the swimsuit, looked in the full-length mirror and smiled.

(由於主詞都一樣，所以可省去其他的 she)

- Mr. Wang's article stressed the terrible working conditions in some Chinese factories.
  王先生的文章強調一些中國工廠裡不良的工作環境。
- It also described the cramped housing in the surrounding areas.
  該文也描述四周擁擠的住宅。
- Finally, it pointed out the filthy environment there.
  最後，該文指出那裡不衛生的環境。

  → Mr. Wang's article stressed the terrible working conditions in some Chinese factories and described the cramped housing and filthy environment in the surrounding areas.

  (動詞 described 和 pointed out 意義相似，但與動詞 stressed 意思不同。為了保持原意，仍然要用兩個不同的動詞)

2. 利用對等連接詞(coordinating conjunction)和帶有連接詞作用的副詞(conjunctive adverb)，把意義相近的獨立句，連接起來，成為複合句。

常用的對等連接詞如：but, or, so, for, therefore, because, nor, either... or, neither... nor, yet 等。

帶有連接詞作用的副詞如：besides, furthermore, otherwise, consequently, accordingly, thus, notwithstanding, still, whereas 等。

例如：

- John will go to a piano lesson.
  John 要去上鋼琴課。
- Mary will stay home to baby-sit her brother.
  Mary 要在家照顧弟弟。

→ John will go to a piano lesson and Mary will stay home to baby-sit her sister.

(把這兩個獨立句,用 and 或 but 連接,成為複合句)

◉ Rain had soaked the football field.
下雨使足球場濕透了。

◉ The game was rescheduled.
比賽的日期改了。

→ Rain had soaked the football field; therefore, the game was rescheduled.

(把上面兩句獨立句,用 therefore 或 so 連接,成為複合句)

◉ They were the last to leave the house.
他們是最後離開房子的。

◉ No one remembered to lock the door.
沒人記得鎖門。

→ They were the last to leave the house, but no one remembered to lock the door.

(把上面兩句獨立句,用 but 連接,成為複合句)

◉ Unlike his friends, Mr. Lee enjoys his sideline job.
跟他的朋友不一樣,李先生樂於從事他的副業。

◉ He likes to work seven days a week.
他喜歡一星期工作七天。

→ Unlike his friends, Mr. Lee enjoys his sideline job; because he likes to work seven days a week.

(上面兩句用 because 或 therefore 連接,成為複合句。當然,用不同的連接詞,意思就有所不同)

◉ John will not attend the meeting.
John 不會去開會。

◉ Bill will not go to the movie.
Bill 不會去看電影。

→ John will not attend the meeting, nor will Bill go to the movie.
(用 nor 連接時，記得要倒裝，也就是把主詞 Bill 放在助動詞 will 的後面)

◉ Bob lost his history notes.
Bob 把他的歷史筆記弄丟了。

◉ He had to spend all of Sunday copying his girlfriend's work.
他整個星期天都得在抄他女友的功課。

→ Bob lost his history notes; consequently, he had to spend all of Sunday copying his girlfriend's work.
(以上兩句，用 consequently 連接，成為複合句)

◉ My wife felt strongly about the need for a trip to California.
我太太強烈認為需要去一趟加州。

◉ We took one two years ago.
我們兩年前去了加州一趟。

→ My wife felt strongly about the need for a trip to California; accordingly, we took one two years ago.
(以上兩句，用 accordingly 連接成為複合句)

◉ I made other plans for tonight.
今晚我有其他計畫了。

◉ I have already seen that movie.
我已經看過那部電影。

→ I made other plans for tonight; besides, I have already seen that movie.
(這兩句用 besides 連接，意思更能連貫)

3. 在獨立句中，加上附屬字(subordinating words)或關係代名詞(relative pronoun)，使其變成附屬子句；再與主要子句連接，成為複雜句(complex sentence)。

最常用的附屬字如：if, as if, as though, because, since, as, so that, unless, although, while, whenever, after, before 等。

主要關係代名詞如：which, who, whose, whom, that 等。

例如：

◉ My wife served the food.
我太太端上菜餚。

◉ I entertained the guests.
我招待客人。

→ My wife served the food, while I entertained the guests.
(while I entertained the guests 為附屬子句，全句就是複雜句，served 和 entertained 兩個動作，幾乎同時發生)

◉ John received a package in the mail.
John 收到一個寄來的包裹。

◉ He opened it quickly.
他很快就打開了它。

→ When John received a package in the mail, he opened it quickly.
(when John... 是附屬子句；he opened... 是獨立子句)

◉ The room was very quiet.
  房間很安靜。

◉ I still could not concentrate on my work.
  我仍然不能聚精會神地工作。

→ Although the room was very quiet, I still could not concentrate on my work.

(用 although 或 even though 或 though，變成附屬句。通常較不重要的，成為附屬句)

◉ Vitamin C tablets may reduce your chance of getting a cold.
  維他命 C 錠也許能減少罹患感冒的機會。

◉ They are taken regularly.
  定期服用。

→ Vitamin C tablets, if (they are) taken regularly, may reduce your chance of getting a cold.

(在附屬句裡，they 是指 tablets，因兩句主詞相同，可省去 they are。
if taken regularly 雖可放在句尾或句首，但放在句中較好)

◉ The murderer admitted his guilt.
  兇手認罪了。

◉ The innocent man was killed.
  這名無辜的男子被殺了。

→ After the innocent man was killed, the murderer admitted his guilt.

(附屬句 after the innocent...放在句首，表示較為重要；放在句尾，表示較不重要)

◉ Suppose there are no hamburgers.
  假如沒有漢堡。

- Suppose there are no hot dogs.
  假如沒有熱狗。
- Can a picnic really be fun?
  野餐還會好玩嗎?
- The picnic is this Saturday.
  本周六要野餐。

  → If there are no hamburgers or hot dogs, can the picnic this Saturday really be fun?
  (在附屬句中,可用 if 或 in the event that,意思大致相同)

- More colleges are creating loan plans to aid students from middle-income families.
  更多的大學制訂貸款計畫來協助中等收入家庭的學生。
- Middle-income families are too poor to pay rising college costs.
  中等收入的家庭太窮,不能支付大學日益昂貴的費用。
- Many middle-income families are still too rich to qualify for assistance.
  中等收入家庭仍然太過富有,而沒有資格申請補助。

  → Even though more colleges are creating loan plans to aid students from middle-income families, many families are still either too poor to pay rising college costs or are too rich to qualify for assistance.
  (加上 even though 形成附屬句 Even though more colleges...;主要子句裡用 either...or 連接)

- Many officials took bribes from citizens.
  許多官員收受百姓的賄賂。
- They abused public trust.
  他們濫用了大眾的信任。

→ Many officials, who took bribes from citizens, abused the public trust.

（who took bribes from citizens 是附屬句，當形容詞，修飾 officials）

◉ This man will head the trade delegation.
這位男子將率領貿易代表團。

◉ We met him last week.
我們上周見過他。

→ The man whom we met last week will head the trade delegation.

（whom we met last week 就是附屬句，當形容詞，修飾 man；因為 whom 是動詞 met 的受詞，故用受格）

◉ The idea is still catching on.
這種想法還很流行。

◉ Mr. Wang approved the idea.
王先生同意這種想法。（approved＝agreed）

→ The idea which Mr. Wang approved is still catching on.

◉ The project turned out successfully.
這計畫的結果很成功。

◉ He worked on the project for months.
他花了好幾個月在這計畫上。

→ The project on which he worked for months turned out successfully.

（on which he worked for months 是附屬句，當形容詞，修飾 project。
On 放在 which 前，要比放在 worked 後面好）

⊙ The customer left this morning.
顧客今早離開了。

⊙ His coat had been stolen.
他的大衣被偷了。

→ The customer whose coat had been stolen left this morning.
(whose coat had been stolen 是附屬句，修飾 customer)

4. 使用同位語(appositives)，不但能減少字數，也可將句中
的名詞或代名詞解釋得更為清楚。

(例如：)

⊙ Mr. A used to teach（at the）high school.
A 先生過去在這所高中教書。

⊙ He is our new professor.
他是我們的新教授。

→ Mr. A, our new professor, used to teach（at the）high school.
(our new professor 就是解釋 Mr. A。teach high school 是指教高中的程度；而 teach at the high school 是指在某一高中教書)

⊙ Many students in the school play basketball.
學校裡許多學生打籃球。

⊙ Basketball is a popular sport in the United States.
籃球在美國是流行的運動。

→ Many students in the school play basketball, a popular sport in the United States.

也可用子句：

◉ Many students in the school play basketball which/that is a popular sport in the United States.
(用 which 或 that 形成附屬句，修飾 basketball)

◉ Some African-American leaders viewed equal opportunity as the most important civil rights issue.
一些非洲裔領袖將平等機會視為人權最重要的議題。

◉ They are especially the more conservative.
那些人更為保守。

→ Some African-American leaders, especially the more conservative, viewed equal opportunity as the most important civil rights issue.
(有時同位語可用 namely, in other words, for example, including, especially, particularly, notably, mainly 來引導句子)

◉ Her school denied a speaking permit to Mr. Lee.
她的學校拒發演說許可給李先生。

◉ He is an outspoken politician.
他是一位說話直率的政客。

→ Her school denied a speaking permit to Mr. Lee, an outspoken politician.

＝Mr. Lee, an outspoken politician, has been denied a speaking permit by her school.

＝A speaking permit to Mr. Lee, an outspoken politician, has been denied by her school.

＝An outspoken politician, Mr. Lee, has been denied a speaking permit by her school.
(同位語應靠近要解釋的名詞或代名詞；如上句 an outspoken politician 放在靠近 Mr. Lee)

同位語可用逗號、斜線或冒號與主要子句隔開。

comma (,)：說話者照實說出，不會令人驚訝。

dash (-)：加重語氣。

colon (:)：較正式與嚴肅。

⊙ My daughter bought a beautiful vase for Jenny, her best friend.
我女兒買了一個很美的花瓶給她最好的朋友 Jenny。
(也可用 —— 或 :)

5. 使用介詞或介詞片語(preposition or prepositional phrase)，
把句子連接起來。

例如：

⊙ A dog barked at me as I walked across the street.
我過馬路時，一隻狗對著我吠。

⊙ The dog was in my neighbor's yard.
那隻狗在我鄰居的院子裡。

→ A dog in my neighbor's yard barked at me as I walked across the street.
(in my neighbor's yard 是介詞片語，修飾主詞 dog)

⊙ The secretarial pool's schedule was full.
秘書室很忙。

⊙ No one could type this article right away.
沒有人有空馬上打這篇文章。

→ Because of the secretarial pool's full schedule, no one could type this article right away.
(也可用介詞片語 due to 或 on account of，修飾主詞 one)

- Snakes have a fearsome appearance.
  蛇的外表可怕。
- They are not really dangerous if you leave them alone.
  假如你不去招惹牠們的話，牠們其實不危險。

  → Despite their fearsome appearance, snakes are not really dangerous if you leave them alone.
  (也可用 in spite of 的介詞片語，修飾 snakes)

- He complied with the local law.
  他遵守當地法律。
- He paid a $100 fine because he drank beer in a public area.
  他因為在公共場所喝啤酒而繳了一百美元的罰款。

  → In compliance with the local law, he paid a $100 fine for drinking beer in a public area.
  (也可用 according to、under 或 within)

- Many Chinese believe that all Americans are wealthy.
  許多中國人認為所有的美國人都很富有。
- There are millions of Americans still in poverty.
  還是有數百萬的美國人很貧窮。

  → Contrary to the belief of many Chinese that all Americans are wealthy, there are millions of Americans still in poverty.
  (belief 不用複數，表示 one same belief)

6. 利用現在分詞片語(present participial phrase)。也就是在原形動詞後加 ing 當形容詞，修飾最靠近的主詞，並且帶有主動的味道，表示一個動作與另一個動作，幾乎同時發生。

例如：

- Mrs. Wang sat on the porch.
  王太太坐在門廊上。
- She watched the sunrise.
  她看著日出。

  → Sitting on the porch, Mrs. Wang watched the sunrise.
  (sitting on the porch 是現在分詞片語，修飾 Mrs. Wang；這時 sat 與 watched 兩個動作，幾乎同時發生)

- His wife came to the dinner party.
  他太太來參加晚餐宴會。
- She was wearing her new dress.
  她穿著她的新禮服。

  → Wearing her new dress, his wife came to the dinner party.
  ＝His wife, wearing her new dress, came to...
  (句中的分詞片語，不能放在句尾，因為與修飾的主詞 wife 相距太遠)

- The dog was barking angrily.
  狗叫得很兇。
- The dog raced after the car.
  狗追著汽車跑。

  → Barking angrily, the dog raced after the car.
  ＝Racing after the car, the dog barked angrily.
  (分詞片語修飾主詞 dog)

- The theater closed for good.
  戲院關門大吉。
- The theater showed its last movie.
  戲院放映最後一部電影。

→ Having shown its last movie, the theater closed for good.

(showed 的動作比 closed 動作早，故用過去完成式的分詞型態)

◉ He went from door to door.

他挨家挨戶地走。

◉ He reminded people to vote.

他提醒人們去投票。

→ Reminding people to vote, he went from door to door.

＝Going from door to door, he reminded people to vote.

◉ He thought that the envelope was empty.

他以為信封是空的。

◉ He threw it away.

他把它扔了。

→ Thinking that the envelope was empty, he threw it away.

◉ The newspaper printed his letter.

報紙刊登了他的信。

◉ It gave both sides of the argument.

它提出兩方的論點。

→ The newspaper printed his letter, giving both sides of the argument.

(it 是指 letter；所以片語要修飾 letter，不是修飾 newspaper。不能說成：Giving both sides of...,the newspaper printed his letter.)

◉ He was climbing the ladder.

他爬著梯子。

◉ He struck his head on the ceiling.

他的頭撞到天花板。

→ Climbing the ladder, he struck his head on the ceiling.

不能說：

Climbing the ladder, his head struck...
（片語是修飾 he，不是 head）

也不能說：

Striking his head on..., he climbed...
（因為不合理）

◉ Mr. Hsu was born in Taiwan.
徐先生在台灣出生。

◉ He now serves as a computer designer.
他現在是電腦設計師。

◉ He was educated at Stanford University.
他在史丹福大學受教育。

→ Serving as a computer designer, Mr. Hsu was born in Taiwan and educated at Stanford University.

＝Mr. Hsu, serving as..., was born in...
（分詞片語不能放在句尾，因為與所修飾的主詞 Hsu 相距太遠）

◉ Mr. Chen expects a letter from his girlfriend.
陳先生期待女友的來信。

◉ He constantly checks his mailbox.
他常常看他的信箱。

→ Expecting a letter from his girlfriend, Mr. Chen constantly checks his mailbox.

＝Mr. Chen, expecting a letter..., constantly checks his mailbox.

＝Checking constantly his mailbox, Mr. Chen expects a letter...

＝Mr. Chen, checking constantly..., expects a letter...

7. 使用過去分詞片語(past participial phrase)，也就是動詞後面有 ed, en 或 n，以及不規則動詞。有「被動」的味道。其動作可能與另一動作同時發生或更早發生。

例如：

⊙ Mr. A gave the speech.
A先生發表演說。

⊙ He was cheered by the audience.
他受到觀眾歡呼。

→ Cheered by the audience, Mr. A gave the speech.
(把第二句的 He was 刪去)

＝Mr. A, cheered by..., gave the speech.
(cheered by the audience 是過去分詞片語，當形容詞，修飾主詞 Mr. A。把片語放在句尾也不好，因為與主詞 Mr. A 相距太遠。這與現在分詞片語的原則相同)

⊙ The ship was badly damaged by the storm.
船遭到暴風雨嚴重破壞。

⊙ The ship finally reached a safe harbor.
最後船抵達一處安全的港口。

→ Badly damaged by the storm, the ship finally reached a safe harbor.
(badly damaged by the storm 修飾主詞 the ship)

＝The ship, badly damaged..., finally reached a safe harbor.

⊙ The gift was wrapped in red paper.
禮物用紅紙包著。

⊙ Miss Chen accepted the gift.
陳小姐接受了禮物。

→ Ms. Chen accepted the gift wrapped in red paper.
(可見句中的 be 動詞，都可刪去，變成過去分詞片語。wrapped in red paper 是修飾 gift，故不能放在句首，否則變成修飾 Ms. Chen，就不合理了)

◉ Her daughter has been discouraged by her poor grades.
她女兒因成績不好而洩氣。

◉ She does not want to go to school.
她不想上學了。

→ Discouraged by her poor grades, her daughter does not want to go to school.
＝Her daughter, discouraged by..., does not...
(分詞片語不能放在句尾，否則會變成修飾 school)

◉ The swimming pool is operated by the YMCA.
游泳池由 YMCA 管理。

◉ It is open only to its members.
它只對會員開放。

→ Operated by the YMCA, the pool is open only to its members.
＝The pool, operated by..., is open...
(但分詞片語不能放在句尾，否則變成修飾 members)

◉ The shirt was spattered with red paint.
襯衫濺到了紅漆。

◉ It could not be worn.
不能再穿了。

→ Spattered with red paint, the shirt could not be worn.
＝The shirt, spattered with..., could not...
(分詞片語緊接著要修飾的 shirt，當然更好)

不能說:

Spattered with..., I could not wear the shirt.

◉ John's hat was chewed to pieces by the dog.
John 的帽子被狗咬成碎片。

◉ John could not wear his hat.
John 不能戴他的帽子。

→ Chewed to pieces by the dog, John's hat could not be worn.

＝John's hat, chewed to pieces..., could not...

不能說:

Chewed to pieces..., John could not wear his hat.
(因為如此一來意思會變成 John 被狗咬得粉身碎骨)

可見,不論是現在分詞片語或是過去分詞片語,都要緊靠著要修飾的名詞或代名詞。

8. 用動名詞(gerund)和不定詞(infinitive)來作為名詞的代替 (noun substitutes)。

例如:

◉ The dog howled and whined at night.
夜晚狗在吠叫和哀鳴。

◉ This upset our neighbors.
這使我們鄰居不高興。

→ The dog's howling and whining at night upset our neighbors.
(把動詞原式 howl 和 whine 變成動名詞,當名詞用)

- Some people believe Japan did not kill 35 million Chinese people.
  有些人相信日本沒有殺害 3500 萬中國人。
- They ignore the true history of World War II.
  他們忽視了二次世界大戰的真實歷史。

  → To believe that Japan did not kill 35 million Chinese people is to ignore the true history of World War II.
  (使用不定詞 to believe, to ignore 作為名詞)
  ＝Believing that Japan did not... is ignoring the true history...
  (Believing 和 ignoring 都是動名詞)

- Mr. Li bought a beautiful house.
  李先生買了一棟漂亮的房子。
- He wanted to impress his friends and relatives.
  他想讓親友們留下深刻印象。

  → Mr. Li bought a beautiful house to impress his friends and relatives.
  ＝To impress his friends and relatives, Mr. Li bought a beautiful house.
  (表示一種目的或期望，多用不定詞)

2-3
容易弄錯的句子

　　本章沒有介紹太多新的文法規則，而是整理並複習一些觀念。這些都是英語學習者容易弄錯的地方。在此，我把相似的詞類放在一起，並舉例說明。

1. 主詞的單複數，不受介詞片語或形容詞子句修飾的影響

例如：

- A box of candies is on the kitchen table.
  廚房桌上有一盒糖果。
  (主詞是 box，不是 candies，所以動詞用單數 is；介詞片語 of candies 只是修飾 box)

- The writer who wrote many articles for the newspapers was born in China.
  為報紙寫許多文章的那位作者在中國出生。
  (主詞是 writer，形容詞子句 who... newspapers，只是修飾 writer 而已，所以動詞用單數 was。其他如 whose, whom, that, which 引導的形容詞子句也是如此，主詞的單複數不受其影響)

2. 主詞的單複數，不受附帶或插入字(parenthetical words)影響

　　最常用的插入字是：as well as, along with, together with, no less than, accompanied by, in addition to 等。

例如：

- John, as well as his parents, is responsible for this new project.
  John 和他的父母負責這個新企畫。
  (主詞 John 是單數，動詞也用單數 is，不受 as well as his parents 附帶字的影響)

◉ Mary, in addition to her two assistants, seems very busy with her work.

Mary 和她的兩個助手，工作似乎很忙。

（Mary 是單數主詞，動詞也用單數 seems，代名詞也用單數 her，不受插入字 in addition to... assistants 的影響）

3. 集合名詞當作一個整體單位時，動詞用單數，但指整體中的成員時，動詞則用複數

這種集合名詞常用的是：class, family, band, jury, committee 等。

◉ The band is making a trip to the Britain.

這個樂團要去英國旅行。

（把主詞 band 當作一個整體單位，是單數，動詞也用單數 is）

◉ The band are bringing their own instruments.

樂團成員會帶著他們自己的樂器。

（這裡的 band，指樂隊裡的隊員，是複數，故動詞也用複數 are。此類集合名詞後面加上 members，可以讓句子更為清楚，但通常都不加）

4. 兩個單數名詞，雖然用 and 連在一起，但一般都放在一起，會有「連帶性」，所以動詞用單數

例如：

◉ Cereal and milk is John's favorite breakfast.

麥片加牛奶是 John 愛吃的早餐。

（因為 cereal 和 milk 被一般美國人視為早餐的一種，所以當作單數主詞，故動詞用單數 is）

◉ Playing the piano and singing at the same time is rather difficult for her.

同時彈鋼琴和唱歌，對她來說相當困難。

(主詞 playing 和 singing 對某些人可同時進行，認為是一個動作，因此可用單數動詞 is；但對某些人是兩個動作，也就是兩件不同的事，故動詞也可用複數 are)

◉ The English teacher and guidance counselor seems very courteous.
這名英文老師兼指導員似乎很客氣。
(這裡的 English teacher 和 guidance counselor 是指一個人，是單數，所以動詞也用單數 seems；如果 guidance 前面加上冠詞 the，即指兩個人，動詞就用複數 seem)

5. 通常指距離、金錢或時間的複數名詞，動詞用單數

例如：

◉ Five hundred miles is too far for me to drive in one day.
一天開 500 英里路程，對我來說太遠了。
(把 500 英里當做一個單位＝a distance of five hundred miles，其真正的主詞是 distance，故動詞用單數 is，但通常都把 a distance of 省略)

◉ Seventy five dollars seems quite expensive for this old chair.
這張舊椅子要價 75 美元，似乎太貴了。
(把 75 美元當作一個整數價格＝the price of seventy five dollars，所以真正主詞是 price，故動詞用單數 seems，不過 the price of 被省去)

◉ When I am on vacation, two weeks goes by very fast.
當我在度假時，兩星期過得很快。
(把兩星期當做一個單位＝a period of two weeks，真正的主詞是 period，故用單數動詞 goes)

6. 主詞是動名詞片語、不定詞片語或名詞子句時，動詞用單數

例如：

⊙ Writing articles and books is Mr. J's favorite way to spend his retirement.

J 先生排遣退休生活最好的方式是寫文章和出書。

（writing articles and books 是動名詞片語，主詞是 writing，故用單數動詞 is，不受動名詞的受詞 articles and books 的影響）

＝Mr. J's favorite way to spend his retirement is writing articles and books.

（主詞還是單數 way）

⊙ To write articles and books remains Mr. J's goal.

寫文章和出書仍然是 J 先生的目標。

（to write articles and books 是不定詞片語，主詞是 to write，動詞故用單數 remains）

＝Mr. J's goal is to write articles and books.

（主詞 goal 還是單數）

⊙ What China really needs is health insurance and better education for its people.

中國真正需要的是提供人民健康保險和較好的教育。

（what China really needs 是名詞子句當主詞，是單數，故動詞用單數 is）

⊙ That languages have many differences seems very obvious.

各種語言有許多不同之處似乎很明顯。

（that languages have many differences 是名詞子句當主詞，為單數，動詞也用單數 seems）

7. 帶有連字符號的複合名詞當形容詞時，最後一個名詞，不用複數

例如：

⊙ Mr. A bought a seven-room house last month.

A 先生上個月買了一棟有七個房間的房子。

（seven-room 當形容詞，修飾 house，不用 seven-rooms）

＝Mr. A bought a house with seven rooms last month.

⊙ Dr. Smith made a two-and-half inch incision in her hand.
Smith 醫生在她手上開了兩吋半的切口。
(two-and-half inch 當形容詞，修飾 incision，不用 two-and-half inches)
＝Dr. Smith made an incision of two-and-half inches in her hand.

⊙ This is a twenty-foot living room.
這是一間寬 20 英尺的客廳。
(twenty-foot 是形容詞，修飾 room，不用 twenty-feet)
＝This living room is twenty feet wide.

8. there 或 here 放在句首時，動詞的單複數是依照後面名詞的單複數而定

（例如：）

⊙ There are several geese in the park.
公園裡有幾隻鵝。
＝Several geese are in the park.
(因為主詞 geese 是複數，動詞也用複數 are)

⊙ There was one issue to be discussed at the meeting.
會議中有一個議題要討論。
＝One issue was to be discussed at the meeting.
(主詞是單數 issue，動詞也用單數 was 或 is)

⊙ Here come my daughter and her husband.
我女兒和她的先生來了。
(主詞是 my daughter and her husband，是複數，動詞也用複數 come)

可見以上例句裡的 there 和 here，都不是主詞，只是一種倒置方式。

動詞也可用其他時態：there went, there might have gone, here came, here has come 等。

9. 主詞是 no one, everyone, someone, anyone, either 時，動詞用單數

例如：

- No one /nobody among the basketball players wants to take a rest.
  籃球隊員中沒有人要休息。
  (主詞是 no one，所以動詞用單數 wants)

- Everyone /everybody in this company has been on strike for five days.
  公司裡每個人都罷工 5 天了。
  (主詞是 everyone，故動詞用單數 has been)

- Either of the students is capable of doing so much work.
  這些學生中任何一位都能做這麼多工作。
  (主詞是 either，故動詞用單數 is)

- Nobody in this office has his/her report ready for the meeting.
  辦公室裡沒有人準備好開會的報告。
  (主詞是 nobody，動詞也用單數 has。現在也有人不用 his/her，而用 their 代替)

10. 指一般任何人時，通常用代名詞 one；指特別一群人則用代名詞 you

例如：

- If one lives in California, one will feel the difference in temperature between night and day.
  人如果住在加州,就會感受到日夜溫差。
  (one是指任何一個人)

- One should fasten one's safety belt before the plane takes off.
  飛機起飛時,每個人都要繫好安全帶。
  (這裡的 one,也是指 anyone 或 everyone。也有美國人用 you 代替)

- If you are over 65, you are eligible for Medicare.
  假如你過了 65 歲,你就有資格加入美國老人醫療保險。
  (這裡的 you,是特指那群 65 歲的人,通常不用 one。)

11. 不定代名詞 all, some, none 當主詞時,動詞的單複數要看句子的意思而定

例如:

- All (that) Mr. A has left in his room is several books.
  A 先生在他房間裡就留下了幾本書。
  (主詞 all 被視為一個集合整體,故動詞用單數 is,形容詞子句 that Mr. A has left in his room 只是修飾主詞。that 也可省去)

- All of the major characters in that novel written by Mr. B were very interesting.
  B 先生寫的那本小說中的主要人物都很有趣。
  (主詞 all 指的是複數人物,故動詞也用複數 were)

- Some of the spectators are getting impatient.
  有些觀眾感到不耐煩了。
  (主詞 some 指觀眾中的某些人是複數,故動詞用複數 are)

- None of the gossip is true.
  這些流言蜚語都不是真的。
  (主詞 none 係指帶有抽象意味的 gossip,故動詞用單數 is)

⊙ None of the books you brought in are useful.
你帶來的書都沒有用。
(主詞 none 指 books 是複數，動詞也用複數 are)

12. 過去簡單進行式是用在強調過去一個動作發生時，另一
個過去的動作正在進行。

例如：

⊙ I was writing an article when Mr. A arrived.
A 先生來的時候，我正在寫一篇文章。
(強調過去動作 arrived 發生時，我正在寫作)

⊙ While we were playing poker, the phone rang.
我們正在打撲克牌時，電話響了。
(指過去動作 rang 發生時，我們正在玩牌)

13. 過去完成式是用在強調過去一個動作，比另一個過去的
動作更早發生

也就是主要子句用過去完成式，附屬子句用過去簡單式。

例如：

⊙ I had finished writing an article when Mr. B visited me.
B 先生來看我時，我已經寫好一篇文章。
(主要子句的 had finished 動作，比附屬句的 visited 動作更早)

⊙ By the time our meeting was over, the rain had stopped.
我們會議結束前，雨已經停了。
(主要子句裡 had stopped，發生在附屬子句的 was 之前)

14. 過去簡單式只指過去某個時間所發生的行為，而現在完成式是指過去所發生的行為，一直延續到現在

例如：

● Mr. A finished his work last night.
A 先生昨晚完成他的工作。
(只指昨晚某一時間裡完成)

● Mr. A has not finished his work yet.
A 先生還未完成他的工作。
(指從過去某一時間開始，直到現在)

● I have known John for ten years.
我認識 John 已經十年了。
(表示從過去某一時間，直到現在，如果說：I knew John for ten years. 意思是已經沒有再往來，或 John 已經去世了)

如果強調現在還要繼續下去，則用現在完成進行式：

● I have been living here for 30 years.
我已經住在這兒 30 年了。
(強調還會住下去)

● I have lived here for 30 years.
我已住在此地 30 年。
(表示住了 30 年，但未必會繼續住)

15. 動詞的進行式，本指一個行為正在進行，但表示心理上或思想上(mental)的一個狀態，這方面的一些動詞通常不用進行式表示

這種動詞諸如：belong, hate, know, need, hear, understand, want 等。

例如：

⊙ This book belongs to Mr. A.
這本書是 A 先生的。
不說：This book is belonging to...

⊙ I need to call my daughter today.
我今天要打電話給我女兒。
不說：I am needing to call...

⊙ His mother wants him to take out the garbage immediately.
他母親要他馬上把垃圾拿出去。
不說：His mother is wanting him to...

16. 表示時間方面的附屬子句(即含有 before, after, when, if, as soon as 等)，動詞通常用現在簡單式，代替未來簡單式

例如：

⊙ Before I go to the library, I will eat something.
去圖書館之前，我會吃些東西。
(before I go to the library 是指時間方面的附屬句，動詞用現在簡單式 I go 代替 I will go)

⊙ If it rains tomorrow, I will stay at home.
假如明天下雨，我就要待在家裡。
(if it rains tomorrow 是附屬句，動詞用現在簡單式 it rains 代替 it will rain 或 it is going to rain)

⊙ As soon as Mr. A comes home, he will start working on his thesis.
A 先生一回家就會開始寫他的論文。
(as soon as Mr. A comes home 是附屬句，動詞用現在簡單式 comes home 代替未來簡單式 will come home)

17. 如要強調未來已計劃好的事，通常用現在進行式，代替未來簡單式

(例如：)

◉ I am staying home tomorrow.
　我明天要待在家裡。
　(表示說話者預先已計劃好，故用現在進行式 am staying 代替 will stay)

一般的說法是：

◉ I will stay home tomorrow.
　＝I am going to stay home tomorrow.

◉ Mr. B is taking a bus to New York next week.
　B 先生下週要坐公車去紐約。
　(表示 B 先生預先計劃好要坐公車去紐約，故用 is taking 代替 will take)

一般的說法是：

◉ Mr. B will take a bus to....
　＝Mr. B is going to take a bus to....

18. 與別人的行為相「呼應」時，前後句的動詞時態要一致

(例如：)

用 and...too 表示肯定：

◉ John likes tea, and Bob does too.
　John 喜歡喝茶，Bob 也是。
　(前面動詞用 likes，後面也用助動詞 does，但不重覆 likes tea)

- John is tired, and I am too.
  John 很累,我也是。
  (前面動詞用 be 動詞 is,後面也用 be 動詞 am,後面省去 tired)

- John has seen this movie, and I have too.
  John 看過這電影,我也看過。
  (前面動詞用 has,後面也用 have,省去 seen this movie)

故形成:「肯定+and+肯定」的形式。

但用 but...表示否定:

例如:

- John likes coffee, but Bob doesn't.
  John 喜歡喝咖啡,但是 Bob 不喜歡。
  (前面動詞用 likes,後面只用助動詞 doesn't=does not,省去 like coffee)

- John has seen this movie, but Bob hasn't(=has not).
  John 看過這部電影,但 Bob 還沒有。
  (前後動詞一致,都用 has)

故形成:「肯定+but+否定」的形式。

同理:前句可用否定,後句則用肯定。

例如:

- John doesn't like coffee, but I do.
  John 不喜歡咖啡,但我喜歡。

- John hasn't done his work, but I have.
  John 沒做工作,但我做了。

- John won't(=will not)be here today, but I will.
  John 今天不會在,但我會。

◉ John isn't here, but Mary is.
John 不在，但 Mary 在。
(以上各句前後動詞時態都一致)

故形成：「否定＋but＋肯定」的形式。

19. 與別人的行為相「呼應」時，前後句子有另一種說法。
(動詞時態也要一致)

用 and so...表示肯定：

例如：

◉ John likes tea, and so does Bob.
John 喜歡喝茶，Bob 也喜歡。
(後句助動詞 does，要放在主詞 Bob 之前形成倒裝句)
＝John likes tea and Bob does too.

◉ John is hungry, and so am I.
John 餓了，我也是。
(後句的 am，要放在 I 的前面)
＝John is hungry and I am too.

可見 and so...與 and...too 意思相同。但用 and neither...表示否定，與 and...either 意思相同。

例如：

◉ Bob doesn't like coffee, and neither do I.
Bob 不喜歡咖啡，我也不喜歡。
(後面助動詞 do，要放在主詞 I 之前)
＝Bob doesn't like coffee, and I don't either.
(肯定句後用 too，否定句後用 either)

◉ John is not here, and neither is Bob.
　＝John is not here and Bob isn't either.
　John 不在這裡，Bob 也不在。

◉ John won't be here today, and neither will Bob.
　＝John won't be here today, and Bob won't either.
　John 今天不會在這裡，Bob 也是。
　(以上前後動詞時態都一致)

◉ John has a new car, but Bob doesn't.
　John 有一輛新車，但 Bob 沒有。
　(句中 has 是主要動詞，所以 Bob 後面不能用 hasn't，要用 doesn't，
　也就是 ...but Bob doesn't have a new car)

兩人對話時，and 可省去：

A: I am tired.
我累了。
B: I am too＝So am I.＝Me too.
我也是。(口語)

A: I don't like coffee.
我不喜歡咖啡。
B: I don't either＝Neither do I.＝Me either.
我也不喜歡。(口語)

20. 指「一般人」的形容詞前，加上冠語 the，是表示複
　　數，動詞也用複數

　(例如：)

⊙ A disadvantage of capitalism is that the rich are getting richer and the poor are getting poorer.
資本主義的缺點就是富者越富，窮者越窮。
(the rich 和 the poor 都是指 rich people 和 poor people，但 people 都被省略，故是複數，動詞也用複數 are getting)

⊙ The young want to grow up fast, but the old wish to live longer.
年輕人想要快快長大，但老年人卻希望活得更久。
(the young 和 the old 都是指 young people 和 old people，故是複數，動詞也用複數 want 和 wish)

⊙ They agree that the homeless have not been well taken care of.
他們同意無家可歸者沒有得到良好的照顧。
(the homeless 是複數，動詞也用複數 have。以上 the young, the old, the homeless 後面的 people，都被省略)

21. 形容詞所比較的事物，必須是同樣的性質才算合理。

例如：

台灣的天氣比馬里蘭熱。

不能說：

The weather in Taiwan is warmer than Maryland.
(因為天氣不能與馬利蘭州相比)

應該說：

⊙ The weather in Taiwan is warmer than that in Maryland.
(用 that 代替 weather，這樣天氣與天氣就能相比了。如果是複數名詞，則用 those 代替)

不能說：

Building houses out of bricks may be harder than lumber.
(houses 不能與 lumber 相比)

應該說：

◉ Building houses out of bricks may be harder than building them out of lumber.
用磚頭蓋房子可能比用木材困難。
(用 them 代替 houses；如果是單數 a house，就用 it 代替)

22. 形容詞相比時，不要把自己本身也包括在內

例如：

不說：

Shanghai is larger than any city in China.
(因為「任何城市」，也把上海本身包括在內，不合理)

要說：

◉ Shanghai is larger than any other city in China.
上海比任何中國城市都大。
(加上 other 後變成「其他任何城市」，上海就不包括在內)

但可以說：

◉ Shanghai is larger than any city in Taiwan.
上海比任何台灣城市都大。
(因為上海不在台灣)

不說：

Mr. A has more seniority than anyone in our office.
(因為「任何人」把 A 先生自己包括在內，不合理)

要說：

◉ Mr. A has more seniority than anyone else in our office.
A 先生比我們辦公室裡任何人都資深。
(加上 else 後，變成「其他任何人」，不把 A 先生包括在內)

23. 動詞 get 後面，可用形容詞或過去分詞

get 後面可接的形容詞諸如：busy, angry, cold, dizzy, fat, hot, hungry, nervous, old, rich, sleepy 等等。

◉ Mr. A got drunk at the party so I took him home in my car.
A 先生在派對上喝醉酒，所以我開車送他回家。
（got＝became）

get 後面可接的過去分詞諸如：arrested, bored, confused, dressed, hurt, lost, tired, worried 等等。

例如：

◉ They got married two years ago.
他們兩年前結婚。

24. 分詞片語當形容詞時，應該修飾正確的主詞

例如：

不能說：

Giving the birthday party, several balloons were blown up.

應該說：

◉ Giving the birthday party, Mrs. Lee blew up several balloons.
在生日宴會上，李太太吹了幾個氣球。
（加上主詞 Mrs. Lee 後，現在分詞片語 giving the birthday 方能修飾 Mrs. Lee，不能修飾 balloons，而且動詞也要改為主動的過去式 blew）

不能說：

Lost in the new area, the post office could not be found.

應該說：

⦿ Lost in the new area, John could not find the post office.
John 在這新地區迷路了，找不到郵局。

(過去分詞片語 lost in this new area，不能修飾郵局，故要加上 John，才是分詞片語修飾的正確主詞)

25. 不可把修飾語(modifier)放錯位置，要靠近修飾的字

(例如：)

不要說：

Mr. A spoke to his friend with a cigar in his mouth.

應該說：

⦿ Mr. A spoke with a cigar in his mouth to his friend.
A 先生嘴裡叼著雪茄煙與他朋友說話。

(介詞片語 with a cigar in his mouth，當副詞是修飾 spoke，不是修飾 friend，故要靠近 spoke)

不要說：

The nurse helped the patient who was on duty.

應該說：

⦿ The nurse who was on duty helped the patient.
值班的護士幫助病人。

(形容詞子句 who was on duty 是修飾 nurse，不是修飾 patient)

不要說：

Rolling down the hill, Bob watched the car.

應該說：

◉ Bob watched the car rolling down the hill.
Bob 看著汽車滑下山坡。
(因為 rolling down the hill 是修飾 car，不是修飾 Bob，故要放在 car 的旁邊)

不要說：

The building had once been the site of a flower shop that is for sale.

應該說：

◉ The building that is for sale had once been the site of a flower shop.
要出售的這棟建築物曾是花店。
(that is for sale 是形容詞子句，修飾 building，而不是修飾 flower shop)

26. 有些副詞單字本身已有否定意味，在句中不能再用其他否定字眼。這種副詞最常用的是：hardly, barely, scarcely, rarely, never 等

例如：

不要說：

Mrs. Chen cannot hardly speak English.

應該說：

◉ Mrs. Chen can hardly speak English.
陳太太幾乎不會說英語。
(因為 hardly 本身已有「幾乎不」的意思，故不再用否定字 not)

不要說：

The old man was not barely able to recognize her.

應該說：

◉ The old man was barely able to recognize her.
老人幾乎認不出她。

(barely 也有否定「幾乎不」的意思，故不用 not)

不要說：

There has not never been so much fun at a party.

應該說：

◉ There has never been so much fun at a party.
派對從來沒這麼好玩過。

(never 已有否定意味，故不再用 not)

＝Never has there been so much fun at a party.

(never 放在句首時，要把 has 放在 there 之前)

27. 小心以下幾個副詞的用法：

◉ Mr. A played well in many kinds of sports.
A 先生擅長多種運動。

(well 是副詞，修飾動詞 played，不能用 good 代替 well，因為 good 是形容詞，不能修飾動詞 played)

◉ Mr. B feels badly right now.
B 先生現在不舒服。

(feel badly 指「生病」)

◉ Mr. B feels bad about her injury.
B 先生對她的受傷感到難過。

(feel 當連綴動詞用時，後面須接形容詞，feel bad 表示「感到遺憾或難過」)

- Maybe he is sick today.
  也許他今天生病了。
  （Maybe 連寫時是副詞）

也可寫為：

He may be sick today.
（may be 分開寫是為兩個動詞）

- John came late today.
  John 今天遲到了。
  （late 是形容詞或副詞，意思是「遲到」。這裡是副詞，修飾動詞 came）

- What are you doing lately?
  你最近在做什麼啊？
  （lately 是副詞，意思是「最近」或「近來」）

- He always works hard.
  他工作一向努力。
  （hard 是形容詞或副詞，這裡是副詞，修飾動詞 works）

- He hardly works.
  他幾乎不工作。
  （hardly 是副詞，意思是「幾乎不」）

28. 使用成對的連接詞 either... or 和 neither... nor 時，通常只
    指兩人或兩件事物，而且動詞或代名詞要與第二個主詞
    一致

例如：

- Either you or John is responsible for this new plan.
  不是你就是 John 要負責這項新計畫。
  （動詞 is 是與第二個主詞 John 一致）

◉ Neither Mr. A nor the Smiths are willing to accept their responsibilities.
　A 先生和 Smith 一家都不願意承擔他們的責任。
　(nor 後面的主詞是 the Smiths，為複數，因此接複數動詞 are，代名詞也用複數 their)

如果是：

◉ Neither the Smiths nor Mr. A is willing to accept his responsibility.
　(用單數動詞 is 和代名詞 his，才能與 nor 後面的主詞 Mr. A 一致)

or 如果單獨使用時，動詞也要與最後的主詞一致。

例如：

◉ Mr. A or I am to write a letter to the mayor.
　A 先生或我要寫信給市長。
　(動詞 am 與第二個主詞 I 一致)

使用成對連接詞時，所連接的詞類，也要相同。

例如：

◉ John usually eats either at home or on campus.
　John 通常不是在家就是在學校吃飯。
　(所連接的都是介詞片語 at home 和 on campus)

◉ Either you are late or I am early.
　不是你遲到就是我早到。
　(所連接的 you are late 和 I am early 都是子句)

29. because 是從屬連接詞，不能代替關係代名詞 that

例如：

不要說：

The reason why he is tired is because he works too hard.

應該說：

◉ The reason (that) he is tired is that he works too hard.
他疲倦的原因是他工作過於努力。
(why 是多餘的，要刪去。用關係代名詞 that 所引導的附屬句，作主詞 reason 的補助語)

也可以說：

◉ He is tired because he works too hard.
(用連接詞 because 連接兩個子句)

不要說：

The reason why Mr. A drives to California is because he is afraid to fly.

應該說：

◉ The reason Mr. A drives to California is that he is afraid to fly.
A 先生開車去加州的理由是他怕坐飛機。
(理由與上句相同)

也可以說：

◉ Mr. A drives to California because he is afraid to fly.
(連接詞 because 連接兩個子句)

30. 有些動詞後面須接「動名詞」作受詞

最常用的動詞是：enjoy, finish, stop, quit, keep, consider, discuss, postpone 等。

例如：

- At this moment, it has not quit raining yet.
  雨現在還沒停。
  （動詞 quit 後面，用動名詞 raining）

- Mr. A has stopped smoking since 2007.
  A先生自2007年起就戒菸了。
  （在動詞 stopped 後面用動名詞 smoking）

但 Mr. A stopped to smoke.是表示他「停下來去抽菸」。

如果動詞 go 的後面用動名詞，通常是指「去參與某種休閒育樂活動」。

例如：

- Mr. A goes fishing every week.
  A先生每星期都去釣魚。

其他又如：go shopping, go swimming, go boating, go camping, go running, go skating, go dancing 等等。

要記得：go 後面不加介詞 to。當然，動詞 go 也可用其他時態：went, has gone, will go 等。

31. 有些動詞後面，通常都用不定詞

最常用的動詞是：decide（to）, need（to）, hope（to）, expect（to）, plan（to）, promise（to）, agree（to）, refuse（to）, appear（to）, seem（to）, pretend（to）, try（to）, want（to）, can/can't afford（to）, would like（to）等。

◉ Mr. A promised never to lie to his wife again.
A 先生答應不再欺騙他太太。
（動詞 promised 後面用不定詞 to lie）

◉ Many people can't afford to buy a house.
許多人買不起一棟房子。
（can't afford 後面用不定詞 to buy）

32. 有些動詞後面，可接動名詞或不定詞當受詞，意思不變

最常用的動詞是：begin, start, continue, like, hate, intend, can't stand 等。

◉ John likes to go/going to the library every week.
John 喜歡每週去圖書館。
（動詞 likes 後面，可用不定詞 to go 或動名詞 going）

◉ I continue to write/writing articles for *World Weekly*.
我繼續為《世界周刊》寫文章。

◉ Mr. Wang can't stand to sleep/sleeping in a room without fresh air.
王先生不能忍受睡在沒有新鮮空氣的房間。

於是，不定詞有時可取代動名詞。

例如：

◉ To climb mountains is fun.
爬山很好玩。
＝Climbing mountains is fun.
＝It is fun to climb mountains.

33. used to 後面接動詞原式，而 be used to 後面則接名詞或動名詞

◉ Mr. J used to work at the university.
J 先生過去在大學工作。
(to 是不定詞符號，故動詞用原式 work，表示過去在大學工作，現在不是了)

◉ Mrs. A used to be afraid of dogs.
A 太太過去怕狗。
(表示 A 太太過去怕狗，但現在不怕了)

◉ Mr. B is/gets used to the cold weather.
＝Mr. B is/gets accustomed to the cold weather.
B 先生適應這種寒冷的天氣。
(這裡 to 是介詞，故後面用名詞 weather)

也可以說：

◉ Mr. B is/gets used to living in the cold weather.
＝Mr. B is/has gotten accustomed to living in the cold weather.
(to 是介詞，後面也可用動名詞 living。以上動詞 get 可用其他時態，如 has gotten 等)

◉ I am getting used to the cold weather.
我越來越適應這種寒冷的天氣。
(be getting used to 表示強調慢慢在適應或越來越適應)

34. would rather 和 had better 可指現在或將來，後面動詞都用原式

◉ Mr. A would rather visit California than（visit）Chicago.
A 先生寧可去加州也不去芝加哥。
（would rather 後面用動詞原式 visit，第二個 visit 可省去；He would rather＝He'd rather）

◉ I would rather have tea than（have）coffee.
我寧可喝茶，不喝咖啡。
＝I like tea better than coffee
＝I prefer tea to coffee.
（would rather 後用動詞原式 have）

至於 had better（＝'d better），不指過去，後面銜接動詞原式。

（例如：）

◉ You had better study harder.
你最好用功些。
（had better 後用動詞原式 study）

35. 介詞 except 和 like，與連接詞 unless 和 as，中文意義頗
有相似，但用法不同

（例如：）

不說：

Bob will not finish up his work except you give（him）the order.

要說：

◉ Bob will not finish up his work unless you give（him）the order.
除非你命令 Bob，否則他不會做完他的工作。
（要把介詞 except，改為連接詞 unless，才可連接兩個句子）

不說：

　　Mr. Wang works very hard like I always do.

要說：

◉ Mr. Wang works very hard as I always do.
　　王先生像我一樣工作非常努力。
　　（like 是動詞或介詞，這裡是介詞，故要改為連接詞 as，才能連接兩個句子。不過，也有人不遵守此文法規則）

36. 連接詞 as... as 是用在肯定句，而 so... as 是用在否定句

例如：

◉ John seems as capable as Bob.
　　John 似乎與 Bob 一樣能幹。
　　（肯定句）

◉ Mr. A is not so honest as his younger brother.
　　A 先生不如他弟弟誠實。
　　（不過，也有人不遵守此文法規則）

37. to be supposed to+動詞原式，表示預料某件事將會發生

例如：

◉ Mr. B is supposed to visit me this afternoon.
　　B 先生今天下午要來看我。
　　（也許早已約好）

◉ The students are supposed to write a paper next week.
　　學生下周要寫一篇文章。
　　（表示規定要寫）

⊙ It is supposed to rain tomorrow.
明天會下雨。
(也許看過天氣預報)

38. 連接詞片語 even if 或 even though 不能用副詞 even 代替

例如：

⊙ Even if it is late, I will stay up to finish my articles.
即使很晚了，我還是要熬夜寫完文章。
(even if 不能用 even 代替，其實 even if 就是連接詞 if 的加強語氣)

⊙ John gave his girlfriend an expensive gift even though he did not have much money.
儘管 John 沒有很多錢，他還是送他女友一個貴重禮物。
(even thought 也可寫作 although 或 though，比後兩者語氣強烈)

39. 泛指一年四季，每天用餐、平時交通工具以及日常通訊方式的名詞前面，都不加冠詞 the, a 或 an

例如：

⊙ Spring is a wonderful time of year.
春天是一年中很棒的季節。
(Spring 前不加冠詞，所以 summer, fall 或 autumn, winter 前也不加冠詞。但 He spent the summer in France.中是指特定的夏天，故用 the summer)

⊙ We had lunch at a nice restaurant yesterday.
昨天我們在一家好餐廳吃午飯。
(lunch 前不加冠詞，還有 breakfast, brunch, supper, dinner 前也不加)

◉ Mr. A came here on foot from his house.
A 先生從他家走來這裡。

(on foot 是片語，要連用，foot 前面不加冠詞，其他如 by bus, by boat, by plane 等也不加冠詞)

◉ We will inform you by mail.
我們會以信件通知。

(表通訊方式，如 by mail, by phone 等都是片語，要連用，mail 或 phone 前不加冠詞)

40. 主要子句裡的動詞表示勸告、建議、決心或要求時，that 子句裡，通常只用動詞原式

表示勸告、要求等，常用的動詞是：advise, beg, command, demand, determine, order, insist, pledge, propose, recommend, request, require, suggest, stipulate 等。(含有"action"意味)

◉ The committee members recommend that John be promoted.
委員們推薦晉升 John。

(在 that John be promoted 的子句裡，動詞只用原式 be，代替 should be)

◉ Mr. B insisted that the meeting begin at 7 p.m.
B 先生堅持晚上七時開會。

(在 that 的子句裡，動詞用原式 begin，代替 should begin)

◉ They demanded that the chairperson follow the new regulations.
他們要求主席遵照新規定。

(在 that 子句裡，動詞用原式 follow，代替 should follow)

例外：

◉ I think that the report should be submitted within a week.
我認為這份報告應該要在一週內交。

(因為動詞 think 或 feel 沒有 action 的意味，故用 should be)

41. 在日常會話中，回答問句時，可把 that 引導出來的名詞子句用 so 代替

例如：

問句：Is Mr. Wang from Taiwan?

回答：I think so.
＝I think（that）Mr. Wang is from Taiwan.
（so 代替名詞子句 that Mr. Wang is...）
或 I don't think so.
＝I don't think（that）Mr. Wang is from Taiwan.

問句：Does Mr. Wang work at the factory?

回答：I believe so.
＝I believe（that）Mr. Wang works at the factory.
或 I don't believe so.
＝I don't believe（that）Mr. Wang works at the factory.

問句：Did Mr. Wang pass the test?

回答：I hope so.
＝I hope（that）Mr. Wang passed the test.
問句：Did Mr. Wang fail the test?
回答：I hope not.
＝I hope（that）Mr. Wang did not fail the test.

42. be 動詞＋形容詞／過去分詞的後面，也可銜接用 that 引導的名詞子句。

(例如：)

◉ I am sure (that) Mr. Lee lives in Taiwan.
  我相信李先生住在台灣。
  (用 that 引導名詞子句 Mr. Lee lives in Taiwan)

◉ Mr. A is glad (that) his son is doing well.
  A 先生很高興他兒子事業順利。
  (上兩句的主要動詞 am, is 都屬 be 動詞，sure 和 glad 都是形容詞)

◉ You must be disappointed (that) your girlfriend is not here.
  你一定很失望你女友不在這裡。
  (disappointed 是過去分詞作形容詞用，表「失望的，沮喪的」)

其他形容詞又如：be afraid that, be aware that, be certain that, be angry that, be proud that, be furious that 等等。

其他的過去分詞又如：be surprised that, be delighted that, be convinced that, be terrified that, be pleased that 等等。

43. 回答問題時，yes 後面要用肯定，no 後面要用否定，並且回答的動詞，要與問句的動詞一致

(例如：)

◉ A: Are you writing an article? 你正在寫文章嗎？
  B: Yes, I am. (No, I am not.) 是的，我是。(不，我不是。)
  (問句的動詞用 be 動詞，回答也用 be 動詞)

⊙ A: Will Mr. Wang be here tomorrow? 明天王先生會來這裡嗎？
B: Yes, he will.（No, he won't.＝He will not.）是的，他會。
（不，他不會）
(問句用助動詞 will，回答也用 will)

⊙ A: Have you seen Mr. Wang recently? 你最近有見到王先生嗎？
B: Yes, I have.（No, I haven't.＝I have not.）有，我見過，（沒有，我沒見過）

⊙ A: Do you know Mrs. Lee? 你認識李太太嗎？
B: Yes, I do.（No, I don't.）是的，我認識，（不，我不認識）

⊙ A: Did it rain last night? 昨晚下雨嗎？
B: Yes, it did.（No, it didn't.）是啊，有下雨。（沒有啊，沒下雨）

44. 問句變成名詞子句時，要注意主詞和動詞的位置以及動詞時態的變換

問句開頭多半是：when, where, why, how, which, what, who, whose, whom 等。

例如：

問句：

⊙ Where does Mr. Wang live?
王先生住在哪裡？

名詞子句：

⊙ I don't remember where Mr. Wang lives.
我不記得王先生住在哪裡。
(where Mr. Wang lives 是名詞子句，問句的助動詞是現在式 does，名詞子句的動詞也用現在式 lives)

不能說：

I don't remember where does Mr. Wang live.

問句：

◉ When did Mr. Chang leave?
張先生什麼時候離開？

名詞子句：

◉ I don't know when Mr. Chang left.
我不知道張先生什麼時候離開。
(when Mr. Chang left 是名詞子句，作動詞 know 的受詞，問句的助動
詞用過去式 did，名詞子句的動詞也用過去式 left)

不能說：

I don't know when did Mr. Chang leave.

問句：

◉ Why is John absent this morning?
John 今早為什麼缺席？

名詞子句：

◉ I don't know why John is absent this morning.
我不知道 John 今早為什麼缺席。
(名詞子句裡的主詞 John 還是放在動詞 is 前面)

不要說：

I don't know why is John absent this morning.

問句：

◉ Whose books are those?
那些是誰的書？

名詞子句：

⦿ I don't know whose books those are.
　我不知道那些是誰的書。

不要說：

I don't know whose books are those.

問句開頭用助動詞或 be 動詞時，也可用 if 或 whether 引導成為名詞子句。

問句：

⦿ Does Mr. Wang work at this school?
　王先生在這所學校工作嗎？

名詞子句：

⦿ I don't know if Mr. Wang works at this school.
　我不知道王先生是否在這所學校工作。
　＝I don't know whether Mr. Wang works at this school or not.

問句：

⦿ Is John at the library?
　John 在圖書館嗎？

名詞子句：

⦿ I wonder if John is at the library.
　我不知道 John 是否在圖書館。
　＝I wonder whether（or not）John is at the library.
　（whether or not 可運用，也可分開）

45. 附加問句(tag question)。如果主要子句是肯定，那麼後面附加問句就用否定，而且動詞前後要一致

例如：

◉ You know Mr. Chang, don't you?
你認識張先生，不是嗎？
（前句是肯定，動詞用 know，後面附加問句否定，用 don't。可回答：Yes, I do.或 No, I don't.）

◉ Mr. Wang is from Taiwan, isn't hc?
王先生來自台灣，不是嗎？
（前句是肯定，動詞用 is，後面附加問句否定 isn't。可回答：Yes, he is. 或 No, he isn't.）

◉ Mrs. Wang can speak English, can't she?
王太太能說英文，不是嗎？
（前面肯定，用 can，後面附加問句用否定 can't。可回答：Yes, she can. 或 No, she can't.）

如果前句是否定，後面的附加問句就用肯定，動詞也要一致。

例如：

◉ You don't know Mr. Wang, do you?
你不認識王先生，是嗎？
（前句是否定，用 don't，後句用肯定 do。可回答：Yes I do. 或 No, I don't.）

◉ Mr. Wang isn't from Taiwan, is he?
王先生並非來自台灣，不是嗎？
（可回答：Yes, he is. 或 No, he isn't.）

◉ Mrs. Wang can't speak English, can she?
王太太不會說英文，對吧？
（可回答：Yes, she can. 或 No, she can't.）

46. 大致有三種情況之下會使用 if 句：即一般條件句、現在
事實相反句和過去事實相反句

例如：

◉ If I have some money, I will buy him lunch.
假如我有一些錢，我要請他吃午餐。
（表示我口袋也許有錢，是一般性的條件句）

也就是：if 句的動詞用現在簡單式（have），主要句動詞用
will 或can+動詞原式（buy）。

◉ If I had some money, I would buy him lunch.
假如我現在有錢，我就會請他吃午餐。
（表示現在我身上沒有錢，故不能請他吃午餐，這是與現在事實相反）

也就是：if 句的動詞，用過去簡單式（had），主要句動詞用
would或could+ 動詞原式（buy）。

◉ If I had had some money, I would have bought him lunch.
假如我那時有錢，我就會請他吃午餐。
（表示過去某個時候我沒有錢，不然我早就請他吃午餐）

這是與過去事實相反。也就是：if 句的動詞用過去完成
式（had had），主要句動詞用 would或could＋have＋過去分詞
（bought）。

47. 動詞 wish 常用來表示一種願望，有兩種情況：對現在
或未來的願望以及對過去的願望

表示對現在或未來的願望時，在 wish 後面 that 引導名詞子
句。

例如：

◎ I wish（that）I knew how to speak French.
我希望我會說法文。（但我現在不會說）
（that 的名詞子句裡，動詞用過去簡單式 knew。that 可省去）

◎ Mrs. A wishes（that）she had a diamond ring.
A 太太希望她有一顆鑽戒。（但實際上她沒有）
（that 的名詞子句裡，動詞用過去簡單式 had）

wish 後面所接的 that 子句中若有 be 動詞時，不論是第幾人
稱、單複數，一律用 were。

例如：

◎ He wishes（that）he were a rich man.
他希望他是位富翁。（但他現在不是）
（that 的名詞子句，用動詞 were）

如果願望是指過去，那麼 that 的名詞子句動詞用過去完成
式。

例如：

◎ I wish（that）I had studied harder.
我希望我過去更用功。（是指過去不用功）
（t hat 子句的動詞用過去完成式 had studied）

⊚ Mr. A wishes (that) he had not attended the party.
A 先生希望他沒去參加宴會。（但他參加了）
（that 子句裡的動詞用過去完成式 had attended）

48. 指願望的 wish，也可用與現在或過去事實相反的 if 子句 表示一部分相同的意義

例如：

⊚ He wishes (that) he made more money.
他希望他能賺多些錢。
（與現在事實相反）

用 if 句表示：

⊚ If he made more money, he would (could) buy a car.
假如他能賺多些錢，他就會（能）買車。
（與現在事實相反）

⊚ He wishes (that) he had made more money.
他希望他過去能賺多些錢。
（與過去事實相反）

用 if 子句表示：

⊚ If he had made more money, he would (could) have bought a car.
假如他過去能多賺點錢，他早就買車了。
（與過去事實相反）

⊚ I wish (that) I were as tall as Mr. A.
我希望我跟 A 先生一樣高。
（與現在事實相反。that 子句裡的 be 動詞，都用 were）

用 if 子句表示：

◉ If I were as tall as Mr. A, I could be a good basketball player.
假如我跟 A 先生一樣高，我就能成為一位籃球好手。
(與現在事實相反)

49. only if 和 if only 意義不同

only if 意思是「只要」或「要是」；但 if only 意思是「但
願……」或「……該多好」。

例如：

◉ He could take a vacation only if his boss approved.
只要老闆批准，他就可以休假。

　＝Only if his boss approved could he take a vacation.
(only if 放在句首時，助動詞 could 要放在主詞 he 之前)

◉ If only I could write better articles.
我要是能寫出更好的文章，該有多好啊！

　＝I wish (that) I could write better articles.
(表示現在還寫不好)

50. 代名詞當主詞補助語，或是表語主格時，要用主格。

例如：

◉ The person may have been he, but I don't know.
那個人也許就是他，但我不曉得。
(代名詞 he，是主詞 person 的補助詞，故用主格 he，不用受格 him)

　＝He may have been the person, but I don't know.

◉ The ones (that) you are talking about are we.
你們所談的那些人，就是我們。
(代名詞 we，是主詞 the ones 的補助詞，故用主格 we，不用受格 us)

　＝We are the ones (that) you are talking about. (that 可省去)

2-4

直接引語和間接引語

　　引語或引文(quotation)可分為兩種：寫作時，把某人所說的話一字不漏地重述一遍(quote speaker's exact words)，就叫做直接引語(direct quotation)，也叫 quoted speech。

　　如果只引用某人所說的意思，而不是一字不漏地直接引用某人說過的話，就是間接引語(indirect quotation)，也叫 reported speech。

　　現分述如下：

1. 使用直接引語，通常是把別人的話，用「某人 say」或「某人 ask」等動詞表達，再加上引號(quotation marks ——""）；但使用間接引語時，只要把別人的話用「名詞子句」表達即可，不必用引號。

　　例如：

　　◉ John said, "I am very tired."（直接引語）
　　　John 說：「我很累。」
　　　(在 said 的後面要加逗點，句尾的句點加在引號之中)

　　◉ John said (that) he was very tired. （間接引語）
　　　John 說他很累。
　　　(that he was very tired 是名詞子句，不加引號，代名詞要改為 he, that 可以省略)

　　◉ Mary said, "The door is not open."（直接引語）
　　　Mary 說：「門還沒開。」
　　　(The 的第一個字母 T 要大寫)

　　◉ Mary said (that) the door was not open. （間接引語）
　　　Mary 說門還沒開。
　　　(that the door was not open 是名詞子句，當動詞 said 的受詞)

除了 say 和 ask 動詞外，當然也可用其他動詞：

- Mr. A announced, "We won the basketball game today." (直接引語)
  A 先生宣布：「我們今天籃球賽贏了。」

- Mr. A announced (that) they had won the basketball game today. (間接引語)
  A 先生宣布他們今天籃球賽打贏了。

2. 至於直接引語與間接引語間的動詞時態變換，也有一些規則。

如果直接引語裡的主要動詞是現在式，那麼間接引語裡的名詞子句動詞時態也是現在式。

(例如：)

- Mr. A says, "I write a letter every week." (直接引語)
  A 先生說：「我每周寫一封信。」

- Mr. A says (that) he writes a letter every week. (間接引語)
  (主要動詞 says 是現在式，所以名詞子句裡的動詞時態不變，仍然用現在式 writes)

- Mr. A says, "I am writing a letter."
  A 先生說：「我正在寫一封信。」

- Mr. A says (that) he is writing a letter. (間接引語)
  A 先生說他正在寫一封信。
  (因為主要動詞是現在式 says，所以名詞子句裡的動詞時態不變)

- Mr. A says, "I wrote a letter to the mayor yesterday." (直接引語)
  A 先生說：「我昨天寫了一封信給市長。」

◉ Mr. A says（that）he wrote a letter to the mayor yesterday.（間接引語）
A 先生說他昨天寫了一封信給市長。
(名詞子句裡的動詞時態仍然不變)

◉ Mr. A says,"I will write a letter by tomorrow."（直接引語）
A 先生說：「我明天前會寫一封信。」

◉ Mr. A says（that）he will write a letter by tomorrow.（間接引語）
A 先生說他明天前會寫一封信。
(名詞子句裡的動詞時態，仍然用未來式)

可見直接引語的主要動詞是現在式時，間接引語裡的名詞子句動詞時態不變。

3. 如果直接引語的主要動詞是過去式，那麼間接引語裡的動詞，也要用過去式。

在此，我們來看不同的動詞時態變化：

◉ John said, "I study hard."（直接引語）
John 說：「我很用功。」

◉ John said（that）he studied hard.（間接引語）
(因為直接引語的主要動詞是過去式 said，所以間接引語裡的動詞也要用過去式 studied。that 可省略。但現在也有人用現在式動詞 studies)

以下間接引語的動詞時態變換理由與上句相同：

◉ John said, "I am studying hard."（直接引語）
→ John said（that）he was studying hard.（間接引語）
(因為主要動詞是過去式 said，所以名詞子句裡的動詞也要改為 was)

⊙ John said, "I studied hard."

→ John said（that）he had studied hard.

（用 had studied 表示「用功」的動作，發生在 said 之前，但也有人只用過去簡單式 studied）

⊙ John said, "I am going to study hard."

→ John said（that）he was going to study hard.

⊙ John said, "I will study hard."

→ John said（that）he would study hard.

⊙ John said, "I can study hard."

→ John said（that）he could study hard.

⊙ John said, "I may study hard."

→ John said（that）he might study hard.

⊙ John said, "I have to study hard."

→ John said（that）he had to study hard.

⊙ John said, "I must study hard."

→ John said（that）he had to study hard.

（助動詞 must 沒有過去式，故用 had to 代替）

⊙ John said, "I should study hard."

→ John said（that）he should study hard.

（這裡助動詞 should 有義務上「應該」的意思，所以不必改變）

⊙ John said, "I ought to study hard."

→ John said（that）he ought to study hard.

（ought to 意思比 must 強些；因為 ought to 沒有過去式，故動詞不變）

不過，也有人為了表示直接引語是「立即」被引述出來，或表示動作「仍在進行」，那麼即使主要動詞是過去式，名詞子句裡的動詞時態仍然不變。

例如：

⊙ John said, "The tide is coming in."
  → John said (that) the tide is coming in.
  (表示漲潮動作在說話過後仍然進行中。所以主要動詞雖是過去式
  said，名詞子句的動詞時態，仍然不變)

⊙ John told me, "I need to go to the library."
  → John told me (that) he needs to go to the library.
  → John said to me (that) he needs to go to the library.
  (表示「去圖書館」，現在還是需要)

4. 直接引語變成間接引語時，亦可使用「釋義」或「改寫」(paraphrase)方式表達

也就是：主詞＋某種動詞＋名詞或代名詞受格＋不定詞。

最常見動詞的有：advise, ask, encourage, invite, order, permit, remind, tell, warn, allow, beg, convince, instruct, direct, persuade, challenge, expect, urge 等。

例如：

直接引語是：

⊙ The judge said to John, "You must pay a fine of five hundred dollars."
  法官對 John 說：「你必須付 500 元罰款。」

可改寫為：

⊙ The judge ordered John to pay a fine of $500.
  法官命令 John 付 500 美元罰款。

也就是：主詞（judge）＋動詞（ordered）＋名詞（John）＋不定詞（to pay）

直接引語是：

- John said, "You may use my computer."
  John 說：「你可以用我的電腦。」

可改寫為：

- John permitted me to use his computer.
  John 允許我使用他的電腦。

也就是：主詞（John）＋動詞（permitted）＋代名詞受格（me）＋不定詞（to use）

直接引語是：

- His wife said, "Make an appointment with your dentist."
  他的太太說：「跟你的牙醫約個時間吧。」

可改寫為：

- His wife reminded him to make an appointment with his dentist.
  他太太提醒他跟牙醫約個時間。

所以上面的例句，只是把直接引語中的意思改寫而已，與真正的間接引語，有點差異。

注意

動詞 suggest 和 recommend，由直接引語變為間接引語時，不用上述的句型，仍用名詞子句。

例如：

直接引語：

⊙ John suggested/recommended, "She should see a doctor."
John 建議／勸說：「她應該去看醫生。」

間接引語：

⊙ John suggested/recommended that she see a doctor.
(名詞子句裡的動詞有 action 的意味，故只用原式 see，不用 sees 或 saw)

但不說：

John suggested/recommended her to see a doctor.

5. 一般直接引語的動詞，可放在句首，句中或句尾。(較常放在句首)

最常用的動詞有：ask, say, reply, wonder, add, continue, announce, inquire, think, volunteer, plead 等。

例如：

⊙ John said, "I have permission to interview the new teacher."
John 說：「我得到許可，可以面試新老師。」

＝"I have permission," John said, "to interview the new teacher."
(或用 said John；因為 John 是名詞，所以可以放在動詞 said 的後面)

＝"I have permission to interview the new teacher," John said.
(或用 said John)

◎ The mechanic said, "The engine ran perfectly."
技工說：「引擎運轉完全正常。」

＝"The engine," said the mechanic, "ran perfectly."
(或用 the mechanic said；因為 mechanic 是名詞，放在動詞 said 的前面或後面皆可)

＝"The engine ran perfectly," the mechanic said.
(或用 said the mechanic)

◎ He said, "The lunch served at this cafe was bad."
他說：「這間咖啡廳供應的午餐不好吃。」

＝"The lunch," he said, "served at this cafe was bad."
(不說 said he，因為 he 是代名詞，不能放在動詞 said 的後面)

＝"The lunch served at this cafe," he said, "was bad."

＝"The lunch served at this cafe was bad," he said.
(不說 said he)

◎ "I can," John volunteered, "come an hour early to help."
John 主動說：「我能提早一個小時來幫忙。」
(或 volunteered John)

◎ "Two heads are better than one," I said.
我說：「三個臭皮匠勝過諸葛亮。」
(不說 said I)

6. 寫文章時，直接引語要用逗點和引號，但說話或演講時，只說 quote...unquote去代替逗點和引號。(因為看不見，只能聽得見)

例如：

寫文章時的直接引語：

- Mr. A said, "I shall not run for office next year."
  A 先生說：「明年我不參選。」

說話時的直接引語：

- Mr. A said quote I shall not run for office next year unquote.
  A 先生說，引文開始，我將不參加明年競選，引文結束。
  (不用逗點和引號)

寫文章時的直接引語：

- John Kennedy said, "Ask not what your country can do for you, but ask what you can do for your country."
  甘迺迪說：「不要問國家能為你做什麼，要問你自己能為國家做什麼。」

說話時的直接引語：

- John Kennedy said quote ask not what your country can do for you, but ask what you can do for your country unquote.

寫文章時的直接引語：

- Ben Franklin said, "Fish and visitors stink in three days."
  富蘭克林說：「魚和訪客三天後就會發臭。」
  (意謂住在親友家，不能久住，否則容易發生問題)

說話時的直接引語：

- Ben Franklin said quote fish and visitors stink in three days unquote.
  (所以 quote... unquote 只用在說話的直接引語)

注意事項：

(1)直接引語開始時，要用逗點和大寫。

（例如：）

◉ Mary asked, "Where do you want to go?"
Mary 問說：「你要去哪兒啊？」
（asked 後面要加逗點；引語第一字 Where 要大寫）

◉ John yelled, "Watch out!"
John 大叫：「小心！」
（yelled 後要加逗點；引語第一個字 Watch 要大寫）

（2）直接引語如果分為兩部分，第二部分的第一個字首字母不必大寫；如果第二部分自成一句，那麼第一個字的首字母就要大寫。

（例如：）

◉ "Will you call me," John asked, "and tell me your decision?"
（第二部分的第一個字 and，不必大寫）

◉ "Where," Mary asked, "did you put your watch?"
（did 不必大寫）

◉ "I will go to the library today," said John. "What time will you come home?"
（第二句自成一句，所以 What 要大寫）

（3）直接引語後面是問號或驚嘆號時，通常後面不再加逗號。

（例如：）

◉ "Who is in charge here?" John asked.
John 問這裡由誰負責。
（John 前面不加逗點，因為問號取代了逗號）

⊙ "Don't throw that away!" Mary yelled.
Mary 大叫著別把那個丟掉！
(Mary 前面不加逗號，因為感嘆號已經取代了逗號)

其他感嘆動詞又如：cry, roar, mutter, warn 等。

(4)如果直接引語是陳述句（declarative sentence），那麼問號或感嘆號要放在最後引號之外。

例如：

⊙ Did you say, "John has been lazy"?
你的意思是「約翰一直很懶」嗎？
(John has been lazy 是陳述句，所以問號放在最後引號之外)

⊙ Who said, "Waste not, want not"?
說「不浪費，就不愁缺」這句話的是誰？
(Waste not, want not 是陳述句，所以問號放在最後引號之外)

⊙ I am surprised that he said, "I am not happy"!
我很驚訝聽到他說「我不快樂」！
(I am not happy 是陳述句，所以感嘆號放在最後引號之外)

但如果問號或感嘆號是屬於引句的一部分，就要放在最後一個引號之內。

例如：

⊙ He asked, "Do I have to housesit for her every day?"
他問：「我每天都必須幫她看家嗎？」
(問號是屬於引句的一部分，故要放在最後引號之內)

⊙ Mr. B complained, "I have tried this too many times!"
B 先生埋怨：「我試這個已經試很多次了！」
(times 後面的感嘆句是屬於引句的一部分，故要放在最後引號之內)

(5)直接引語是問號，而間接引語用動詞 ask 時，那麼後面多半以 if 或 whether 引導名詞子句，而非 that。

例如：

直接引語：

◉ John said to me, "Are you happy?"

間接引語：

◉ John asked（me）if/whether l was happy.
（me 可以省去；後面跟 if 或 whether 的名詞子句，而不是跟 that 的名詞子句）

2-5

談句子不同的開頭

寫文章時，困難的地方，不是寫什麼(what to write)，而是怎麼寫(how to write)。雖然許多美國人為了節省時間而主張多寫簡短易懂的白話文，但老寫「主詞＋動詞＋受詞」此類最基礎的句型，也會顯得單調無味(monotonous)，所以句子也要有些變化(sentence variety)，才可增加新鮮感和效果。

在「句子的組合」一章中已說明過怎樣把短句連結起來，這也屬句型變換的一種。現在再談一些句子不同的開頭(different sentence openers)，讓文章風格更富變化。

最常見的句子開頭，有以下幾種基本方式：

1. 用主詞(subject)開頭

「主詞在先，動詞在後」是最常用的形式。

例如：

⊚ The crowd cheered the visiting president of the United States.
群眾向來訪的美國總統歡呼。
(開頭是主詞 crowd；動詞是 cheered)

⊚ They refused to hear our side of story.
他們拒聽我們這邊的說詞。
(開頭是主詞 they；動詞是 refused)

⊚ The committee chairperson feared a drop in its annual budget.
委員會主席擔心年度預算會減少。
(開頭是主詞 chairperson；動詞是 feared)

⊚ The mayor gave a speech about the city's development.
市長就都市發展情形發表演說。
(開頭是主詞 mayor；動詞是 gave)

⊙ Mr. and Mrs. Wang left on the early morning plane to California.
王氏夫婦搭早班飛機去加州。
（開頭是主詞 Mr. and Mrs. Wang；動詞是 left）

2. 用單字修飾語(single-word modifier)開頭

通常為了加強語氣，開頭會用單字形容詞或副詞當修飾語。

例如：

⊙ Furious, the man threw down the paper.
這個暴怒男子把報紙扔到地上。
（開頭用形容詞 furious，加強描寫生氣的程度）
一般句型（主詞開頭）：
⊙ The furious man threw down the paper.

⊙ Amused, she allowed her boyfriend to finish his story.
她被逗得很樂，而讓她的男友說完故事。
（加強形容詞 amused 的語氣）
一般句型（主詞開頭）：
⊙ She was amused and allowed her boyfriend to finish his story.

⊙ Hungry and exhausted, we sat down to rest under a tree.
我們又餓又累地坐在樹下休息。
（形容詞 hungry 和 exhausted 放在句首，修飾 we）
一般句型：
⊙ We, hungry and exhausted, sat down to rest under a tree.

◉ Normally, the train runs on schedule.
火車通常都很準時。
(把副詞 normally 放在句首)

一般句型：

◉ The train normally runs on schedule.

◉ Proudly, the marchers walked down the street.
遊行者威風八面地走過馬路。

一般句型：

◉ The marchers walked proudly down the street.
(也可把副詞 proudly 放在 walked 前面)

◉ Shy and lonely, Mary did not participate in any social activities.
Mary 害羞孤僻，不參加任何社交活動。
(把形容詞 shy 和 lonely 放在句首)

一般句型：

◉ Mary did not participate in any social activities because she was shy and lonely.

◉ Every evening, the group would meet in Mr. A's office.
這組人馬每天傍晚聚集在 A 先生辦公室。
(把副詞片語 every evening 放在句首，修飾動詞 meet)

一般句型：

◉ The group would meet every evening in Mr. A's office.

◉ Eager to tell about their adventure, the hikers returned as soon as possible.
健行者急著分享他們的冒險經歷，儘快趕回來了。
(把形容詞片語 eager to tell about their adventure 放在句首，修飾主詞 hikers)

一般句式：

◉ The hikers, eager to tell about their adventure, returned as soon as possible.

3. 用介詞片語(prepositional phrase)開頭，當副詞用

例如：

◉ With great difficulty, I opened the door.
我好不容易才打開門。
(把介詞片語 with great difficulty 放在句首，當副詞，修飾動詞 opened)

一般句型：(把主詞 I 放在句首)

◉ I opened the door with great difficulty.

◉ At the end of the graduation ceremony, the auditorium was filled with the sound of cheering.
畢業典禮結束時，禮堂裡響起一片歡呼聲。
(介詞片語 at the end of the graduation ceremony 放在句首，當副詞，修飾動詞 filled)

一般句型：(把主詞 auditorium 放在句首)

◉ The auditorium was filled with the sound of cheering at the end of the graduation ceremony.

- From the very first moment, Mr. A showed interest in her.
  A 先生打從一開始就對她有興趣。
  (為了加強語氣,把介詞片語 from the very first moment 放在句首,當副詞修飾動詞 showed)

一般句型:(把主詞 Mr. A 放在句首)

- Mr. A showed interest in her from the very first moment.

- On weekends, John works on his project.
  John 每周末埋首於他的專案。
  (介詞片語 on weekends 放在句首,當副詞修飾動詞 works)

一般句型:

- John works on his project on weekends.

- At the next meeting, some of our suggestions will be discussed.
  下次開會時會討論一些我們的建議。
  (為了加強語氣,把介詞片語 at the next meeting 放在句首,當副詞修飾動詞 discussed)

一般句型:

- Some of our suggestions will be discussed at the next meeting.

4. 用分詞片語(participle phrase)開頭,當形容詞用

例如:

- Looking up at the blue sky, Mary saw an airplane.
  Mary 抬頭看著藍天,看到了一架飛機。
  (現在分詞片語 looking up at the blue sky 放在句首,當形容詞,修飾主詞 Mary)

一般句型:(把主詞放在句首)

- Mary looked up at the blue sky and saw an airplane.

- Examining the project carefully, Mr. B said that it could not be carried out.

  經過仔細檢查後，B 先生說計畫無法實行。

  (把現在分詞 examining the project carefully 放在句首，當形容詞，修飾 Mr. B)

一般句型(把主詞 Mr. B 放在句首)：

- Mr. B examined the project carefully and said that it could not be carried out.

- Damaged by the storm, the windows needed to be repaired.

  窗戶被暴風雨吹壞了，需要修理。

  (把過去分詞片語 damaged by the storm 放在句首，當形容詞，修飾 windows)

一般句型：(把主詞 windows 放在句首)

- The windows were damaged by the storm and needed to be repaired.

  ＝The windows damaged by the storm needed to be repaired. (較好)(主要動詞是 needed)

- Stunned by the stock market crash, many investors stopped buying.

  許多投資者震驚於股市崩盤，停止買進。

  (把過去分詞片語 stunned by the stock market crash 放在句首，當形容詞，修飾 investors)

一般句型(把主詞 investors 放在句首)：

- Many investors were stunned by the stock market crash and stopped buying.

- Distinguished by nothing more than his good looks, Mr. A had enjoyed a successful career in show business.
  A 先生只靠外貌英俊出色就在演藝圈有所成就。
  (把過去分詞片語 distinguished by nothing more than his good looks，放在句首，當形容詞，修飾 Mr. A)

一般句型(把主詞 Mr. A 放在句首)：

- Mr. A was distinguished by nothing more than his good looks to enjoy a successful career in show business.

- Having been in the U.S. for a long time, Mr. J knows American culture well.
  J 先生長期旅居美國，對美國文化很了解。
  (把完成式的分詞片語 having been in the U.S. for a long time 放在句首，當形容詞修飾 Mr. J)

一般句型：(把主詞 Mr. J 放在句首)

- Mr. J has been in the U.S. for a long time and he knows American culture well.

5.用不定詞片語(infinitive phrase)開頭，當副詞用

例如：

- To learn the English language, Mr. J studies every day.
  為了學英語，J 先生每天都在苦讀。
  (把不定詞片語 to learn the English language 放在句首當副詞，修飾動詞 studies；也可用 in order to learn the English language,...但一般都把 in order 省去)

一般句型：(把主詞 Mr. J 放在句首)：

- Mr. J studies every day (in order) to learn the English language.
  (in order 也可省去)

◎ To correct all the term papers in two days, John worked around the clock.

為了在兩天內改完全部的期末報告，John 不眠不休地工作。

(把不定詞片語 to correct all the term papers in two days 放在句首，當副詞用，修飾動詞 worked)

一般句型：(把主詞 John 放在句首)

◎ John worked around the clock (in order)to correct all the term papers in two days.

(in order 也可省去)

◎ To be checked for cavities and other problems, see the dentist every six months.

為了檢查蛀牙和其他問題，每半年要看一次牙醫。

(把不定詞片語 to be checked for cavities and other problems 放在句首，當副詞修飾動詞 see)

一般句型：(把主詞 you 放在句首)

◎ (You) see the dentist every six months (in order)to be checked for cavities and other problems.

(you 和 in order 都可省去)

◎ To be a good student and to earn high grades, you must fulfill basic requirements.

你必須符合基本條件才能成為好學生並拿高分。

(把不定詞片語 to be a good student and to earn high grades 放在句首，當副詞，修飾動詞 fulfill。也可寫成：In order to be a good student and...)

一般句型：(把主詞 you 放在句首)

◎ You must fulfill basic requirements (in order)to be a good student and to earn high grades.

⊚ To provide for the future as well as for the present, we must develop new sources of energy.

為了現在和未來，我們必須開發新能源。

(把不定詞片語 to provide for the future as well as for the present 放在句首，當副詞，修飾動詞 develop)

一般句型（把主詞 we 放在句首）：

⊚ We must develop new sources of energy (in order) to provide for the future as well as for the present.

6. 用同位語片語(appositive phrase)開頭

進一步說明主詞的意義。

(例如：)

⊚ A friend of her family, the lawyer represented Mary in court.

這名律師是她家的朋友，代表 Mary 出庭。

(把同位語片語 a friend of her family 放在句首，進一步說明主詞 lawyer)

一般句型（把主詞 lawyer 放在句首）：

⊚ The lawyer, a friend of the family, represented Mary in court.

⊚ The new financial director, Mr. A moved his office upstairs.

新任財務長 A 先生把他的辦公室搬到樓上。

(把同位語片語 the new financial director 放在句首，說明主詞 Mr. A)

一般句型（把主詞 Mr. A 放在句首）：

⊚ Mr. A, the new financial director, moved his office upstairs.

⊚ A short, courteous man, the old professor talked with me in his office.

個頭小而有禮的老教授，在他的辦公室跟我聊天。

(把同位語片語 a short, courteous man 放在句首,說明主詞 professor)

一般句型(把主詞 professor 放在句首):

◉ The old professor, a short, courteous man, talked with me in his office.

(talked with me 表示彼此談話;talked to me 表示只有他在說,我在聽)

◉ A writer for the World Journal Weekly, Mr. J has been trying to play a small role in bridging the Chinese and American cultures. 《世界周刊》作者 J 先生試著在連結中美文化方面擔任一個小角色。

(把同位語片語 a writer for the world Journal Weekly 放在句首,說明主詞 Mr. J)

一般句型(把主詞 Mr. J 放在句首):

◉ Mr. J, a writer for the World Journal weekly, has been trying...

7. 用附屬子句(subordinate clause)開頭

在複雜句(complex sentence)內當副詞用。

例如:

◉ After the storm stopped, Mr. B inspected the garage for damage. 暴風雨後,B 先生檢查車庫損害的程度。

(附屬子句 after the storm stopped 放在句首後,加逗號,再接主要子句,成為複雜句)

一般句型(把主要子句放在句首):

◉ Mr. B inspected the garage for damage after the storm stopped. (主要子句放在句首時,後面不加逗號。附屬子句,當副詞用,修飾動詞 inspected)

- If a dog is howling, something strange may be happening.
  如果狗在咆哮就可能會有怪事發生。
  (把附屬句 if a dog is howling 放在句首，後加逗點，再連主要子句，成為複雜句)

一般句型(把主要子句放在句首)：

- Something strange may be happening if a dog is howling.

- Before John came here, I had finished writing my articles.
  在 John 來之前，我已寫好文章。
  (把附屬句 before John came here 放在句首，當副詞用，修飾動詞 had finished)

一般句型：

- I had finished writing my articles before John came here.
  (把主要子句放在句首，再接附屬句，成為複雜句)

- Because the train was moving so fast, it disappeared in seconds.
  火車開得很快，一下子就不見了。
  (把附屬句 because the train was moving so fast 放在句首，當副詞，修飾動詞 disappeared)

一般句型(把主要子句放在句首)：

- The train disappeared in seconds because it was moving so fast.

- Since the volcano was going to erupt, the villagers were evacuated quickly.
  由於火山即將爆發，村民被迅速撤離。
  (把附屬句放在句首，再加逗點)

一般句型(把主要子句放在句首)：

- The villagers were evacuated quickly since the volcano was going to erupt.

◉ Soon after he moved back to Taiwan, Mr. Wang became a famous writer.

王先生搬回台灣不久後，就成為名作家。

(把附屬句放在句首，比較強調搬回台灣後)

一般句型(把主要子句放在句首)：

◉ Mr. Wang became a famous writer soon after he moved back to Taiwan.

(至於主要子句放在句首或句後，要看強調什麼，並無真正好壞之分)

8. 把修飾語(modifier)放在句首

通常句子的形式，多是主詞 + 動詞 + 修飾語(S + V + M)，但為了加強語氣，可寫成 M + V + S，屬倒裝句(inverted sentence)的一種。

例如：

◉ Closer and closer came the thunder.

雷聲越來越近。

(closer and closer 是修飾語 ，當副詞，修飾動詞 came，主詞是 thunder，形成 M + V + S)

一般句型(把主詞放在句首)：

◉ The thunder came closer and closer.

(形成 S + V + M 的句型)

◉ Into his mouth went the big piece of cake.

一塊大蛋糕塞進他的嘴巴裡。

(into his mouth 是修飾語，當副詞，修飾動詞 went，主詞是 the big piece of cake，形成 M + V + S)

一般句型：

⊙ The big piece of cake went into his mouth.
(變成 S + V + M)

⊙ Ahead of the couple ran two noisy boys.
兩個吵鬧的男孩跑到一對夫婦前面。
(ahead of the couple 是修飾語,當副詞,修飾動詞 ran,主詞是 boys,
形成 M + V + S)

一般句型:(把主詞 boys 放在句首)

⊙ Two noisy boys ran ahead of the couple.
(為 S + V + M 的句型)

⊙ Beside the fireplace sat a group of people.
火爐邊坐著一群人。
(beside the fireplace 是修飾語,當副詞修飾動詞 sat,主詞是 group,
為 M + V + S 的句型)

一般句型(把主詞 group 放在句首):

⊙ A group of people sat beside the fireplace.
(變成 S + V + M)

⊙ So boring was the speaker that many in the audience fell
asleep.
演講人太過無趣以致於有許多聽眾睡著了。
(so boring 當形容詞,做主詞 speaker 的修飾語,動詞是 was,形成 M
+ V + S 的句型)

一般句型:(把主詞 speaker 放在句首)

⊙ The speaker was so boring that many in the audience fell
asleep.
(變成 S + V + M)

- Hardest hit by the drought were many Chinese farmers.
  受到旱災影響最鉅的是中國農民。
  (hardest hit by the drought 是修飾語，當形容詞，修飾主詞 farmers。M + V + S)

一般句型：

- Many Chinese farmers were hardest hit by the drought.
  (把主詞放在句首，形成 S + V + M 句型)

- With his safe arrival came a feeling of happiness and relief.
  他的平安到達，令人感到高興與寬慰。
  (with his safe arrival 是修飾語，放在句首，當副詞，修飾動詞 came，主詞是 feeling)(M + V + S)

一般句型(把主詞 feeling 放在句首)

- A feeling of happiness and relief came with his safe arrival.
  (S + V + M。一般美國人主張多用 S + V + M 句型，因為倒裝句不易使人一目了然)

9. 含有否定意思的副詞或副詞片語，也可做句子的開頭

　　句中有 never, seldom, no, not, neither, nor 等，都含有否定的意思，但要把助動詞或動詞放在主詞前面，成為倒裝句型。

(例如：)

倒裝句型：

- Never did I say such a thing.
  我從來沒有說過這件事。
  (副詞 never 放在句首時，要把助動詞 do 或 did 放在主詞 I 的前面)

一般句型：

- I never said such a thing.

倒裝句型：

◎ Never could I have left my good friends.
　我絕不可能離開我的好友。
　(把助動詞 could 放在主詞 I 的前面)

一般句型：

◎ I could never have left my good friends.

倒裝句型：

◎ Seldom is Mr. A here on time.
　A 先生很少準時到這裡。
　(動詞 is 放在主詞 Mr. A 前)

一般句型：

◎ Mr. A is seldom here on time.

倒裝句型：

◎ Not once has John missed my class this year.
　John 今年在我班上從未缺席過。
　(變成倒裝句時，把 not 和 once 連在一起，放在句首，同時把 has 放
　在主詞 John 的前面)

一般句型：

◎ John has not missed my class once this year.

倒裝句型：

◎ Not for anything would I leave this lovely community.
　說什麼我也不會離開這個可愛的社區。
　(倒裝時，把 not 和 for anything 連在一起，再把助動詞 would 放在主
　詞 I 的前面)

一般句型：

◉ I would not leave this lovely community for anything.

倒裝句型：

◉ Not for all the money in the world would I abandon my wife.
即使把世上所有的錢都給我，我也不會離棄我的太太。
（倒裝時，把 not 和 for 連在一起，再加名詞 money）

一般句型：

◉ I would not abandon my wife for all the money in the world.

倒裝句型：

◉ Not until today did John realize his credit card was missing.
John 直到今天才知道他的信用卡遺失了。
（倒裝時，把 not 和 until 連在一起，再加名詞 today）

一般句型：

◉ John did not realize his credit card was missing until today.

倒裝句型：

◉ Under no circumstances will the boy be allowed to drink.
無論如何，那男孩都不准喝酒。
（倒裝時，用 no 代替 not 和 any，再把動詞 will 放在主詞 boy 前面；
也可用 conditions 代替 circumstances）

一般句型：

◉ The boy will not be allowed to drink under any circumstances.

倒裝句型：

⊙ In no case can I make an exception to this regulation.
我決不成為這個規定的例外。
(倒裝時，用 no 代替 not 和 any，再把助動詞 can 放置主詞 I 的前面)

一般句型：

⊙ I cannot make an exception to this regulation in any case.

倒裝句型：

⊙ No way is John going to miss his ex-wife.
John 絕不會想念他的前妻。
(倒裝時，用 no way 代替 not 和 for any reason，再把動詞 is 放在主詞 John 的前面)

一般句型：

⊙ John is not going to miss his ex-wife for any reason.

倒裝句型：

⊙ Nowhere have I been that is as pretty as this city.
我從沒到過像這個城市這麼漂亮的地方。
(倒裝時，用副詞 nowhere 代替 not 和 anywhere，再把動詞 have 放在主詞 I 的前面)

一般句型：

⊙ I have not been anywhere that is as pretty as this city.

倒裝句型：

⊙ Not another penny will I spend on his schooling unless he improves his grades.
除非他的成績有進步，不然我不願再花一毛錢繳他的學費。
(倒裝時，把 not 和 another penny 連在一起，再把助動詞 will 放在主詞 I 前面)

一般句型：

◉ I will not spend another penny on his schooling unless he improves his grades.

10. 成對的連接詞，也可放在句首

(例如：)

倒裝句型：

◉ Not only do carrots taste sweet, but they are also good for you.
胡蘿蔔嚐起來不但很甜，而且對你有益。

(they 指 carrots。not only 放在句首時，助動詞或動詞要放在主詞 carrots 前面，因為 not 有否定的意思。also 可以省略)

一般句型：

◉ Carrots not only taste sweet, but they are also good for you.

倒裝句型：

◉ No sooner had the picnic started than it started to rain hard.
才一開始戶外野餐就下起大雨。

(no sooner...than 意思是「一開始……就……」，no sooner 放在句首時，要把動詞 had 放在主詞 picnic 前面，因為 no 有否定意味)

一般句型：

◉ The picnic had no sooner started than it started to rain hard.

倒裝句型：

◉ Neither does John know Chinese, nor is he interested in it.
John 不懂中文，他對中文也沒興趣。

一般句型：

◉ John does not know Chinese; he is not interested in it either.

總之，倒裝句型多半是為了加強語氣或增加句子的變化，以免過於呆板。

2-6

多寫簡短易懂的字句

在一切講求快速，分秒必爭的文化要求下，美國大學開始推行日常生活上的文章，不用長句和難字，盡量使用白話英語（plain English），寫得愈白愈好，愈短愈妙，使一般人都能一目瞭然，避免誤解。

美國暢銷書 Effective Writing 作者 Dr. H. J. Tichy 也強調：「文章必須做到明白、簡短和易懂，以達到百分之百溝通的目的。」美國大文豪馬克‧吐溫（Mark Twain）也曾說：「我不在字典裡找長字或難字，我能用 city 這個字，為何要用 metropolis 呢？」

以下提出簡短易懂字句的幾個基本原則，供讀者參考。

1. 多用動作動詞(action verb)

把句子裡的名詞或形容詞，設法改為動作動詞。

（例如：）

◎ John is a leader in many research projects.
可改為：
John leads many research projects.
John 主導多項研究計畫。
(lead 是動作動詞)

◎ Our college budget cuts are a threat to several programs.
可改為：
Our college budget cuts threaten several programs.
我們大學預算的削減威脅到幾個計畫。
(threaten 是動作動詞)

◉ New Chinese immigrants have to make adjustments to American ways.

可改為：

New Chinese immigrants have to adjust to American ways.
新來的中國移民必須適應美國人的生活方式。
(用動作動詞 adjust 替代)

◉ Your method would constitute an improvement in this process.

可改為：

Your method would improve this process.
你的方法能改進這個程序。
(用動作動詞 improve 替代)

◉ The dance group gave a performance at our college.

可改為：

The dance group performed at our college.
這個舞團在我們大學演出。
(performed 是動作動詞)

◉ Many people like to place emphasis on special education.

可改為：

Many people emphasize special education.
許多人重視特殊教育。
(emphasize 是動作動詞)

◉ The weather in Maryland is pleasant to many visitors.

可改為：

Maryland weather pleases many visitors.
馬里蘭的氣候讓許多遊客感到滿意。
(用動作動詞 please)

⊙ Mr. Lee was excellent in computer programming.
可改為：
Mr. Lee excelled in computer programming.
李先生擅長電腦程式設計。
(動詞 excel 的過去式是 excelled)

⊙ I have given consideration to your suggestion.
可改為：
I have considered your suggestion.
我已考慮過你的建議。
(用動詞 consider 代替)

⊙ The city will carry out the purification of the water.
可改為：
The city will purify the water.
市政府要淨化水質。
(用動作動詞 purify；the city 就是「市政府」的意思)

2. 多用主動語態和肯定句(active voice and positive sentences)

因為主動和肯定句，比較直接、有力，也可以節省用字。

例如：

⊙ Many species of fish are endangered by industrial waste. （被動）
可改為：
Industrial waste endangers many species of fish. （主動較好）
工業廢物危害到許多魚類。

⊙ Money for the new library was raised quickly by our community. （被動）
可改為：

Our community quickly raised money for the new library. （主動較好）

我們社區很快地就為新圖書館籌到款項。

- Mr. Wang's dog should not be permitted to pounce on visitors. （被動）

可改為：

Mr. Wang should not permit his dog to pounce on visitors. （主動較好）

王先生不該讓他的狗撲向訪客。

- It has been learned that your company will be relocated to New York. （被動）

可改為：

We （I）have learned that your company will move to New York. （主動較好）

我們聽說貴公司將搬去紐約。

- Any information you can give me will be appreciated and discretion will be exercised in its use. （被動）

可改為：

I will appreciate any information you can give me and I will use it with discretion. （主動較好）

我感謝你給我任何資訊，並且我會謹慎使用。

- John is not old enough to carry out this project. （否定句）

可改為：

John is too young to carry out this project. （肯定句較好）

John 太年輕，做不來這項計畫。

- The old man did not remember what I told him. （否定句）

可改為：

The old man forgot what I told him. （肯定句較好）

老人忘了我告訴他的事情。

⊙ He did not have the ability to lead this department.（否定句）

可改為：

He lacked the ability to lead this department.（肯定句較好）

他缺乏能力帶領這個部門。

其他又如：

not stay＝leave 離開
not accept＝reject 拒絕
not the same＝different 不同的
not consider＝ignore 忽略，不顧
not allow＝prevent 防止，制止

3. 避免難字或華麗的字眼(big or flowery word)

例如：

⊙ The rumor has been disseminated all over the city.
謠言已傳遍全市。
(如把 disseminated 改為 spread 會更容易明白)

⊙ He will endeavor to ascertain the result of the test.
他將設法查出測驗的結果。

也就是：

⊙ He will try to find out the result of the test.
(endeavor＝endeavour＝try 努力、設法；ascertain＝to find out 查明、
找出)

◉ The supervisor will have to elucidate this policy to his staff.
上司將會向員工解釋這項政策。
(如把 elucidate 改成 explain，會更容易明白)

◉ To build a new college library will cost in close proximity of 40 million dollars.
蓋間新的大學圖書館要花將近四千萬元。
(如把 in close proximity of 改用 about，更易了解)

◉ We don't know what will transpire when we get a new boss.
當我們有新老闆時，不知會發生什麼事。
(如把 transpire 改用 happen，更易明白)

其他又如：

diminutive＝small 小的
transmit＝send 傳遞
apprise＝inform 通知，告知
cognizant of＝aware of 知道的，察覺的
contingent on/upon＝depend on/upon
subsequent to＝after 在……之後
envisage＝think/see 設想

4. 在正式文章裡，少用俚語或諺語

雖然俚語或諺語等的意義和用法值得學習，但對一般讀者而言，還是使用易懂的字眼較好。

例如：

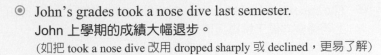

◉ John's grades took a nose dive last semester.
John 上學期的成績大幅退步。
(如把 took a nose dive 改用 dropped sharply 或 declined，更易了解)

◉ We will leave no stone unturned to find a solution to this problem.
我們會想盡辦法解決這個問題。
(如把 leave no stone unturned 改用 do all we can，更易明白)

◉ When my wife saw the big snake, she jumped out of her skin.
我太太看到一條大蛇，嚇了一大跳。
(把 jumped out of her skin 改用 terribly scared，更易明白)

◉ We would like to begin our trip at the crack of dawn.
我們在黎明時開始我們的旅程。
(把 at the crack of dawn 改用 at daybreak 更易明白)

◉ Beyond a shadow of doubt, Mr. B made the complaint to my boss.
毫無疑問地，是 B 先生跟我的老闆抱怨。
(把 beyond a shadow of doubt 改用 unquestionably 更省字、更明白)

◉ Mr. A's cheating was the last straw for his wife.
A 先生的不忠讓他的妻子忍無可忍。

如寫成：Mr. A's cheating made his wife really mad. 不是更明白嗎？
(the last straw＝the straw that broke the camel's back 壓垮某人的最後一根稻草，使某人忍無可忍)

◉ It was a bummer to spend $100 seeing a show that was a total bomb.
花100美元看這麼差勁的演出真是浪費。

更簡單明白的表示法：

It was a waste to spend $100 to see such a bad show.

5. 不寫囉唆或多餘的字眼(wordy or redundant)

例如:

◉ It is a fact that there are dozens of new families that move into our community every week.
每周有好多新家庭搬進我們社區。

可簡化為:

◉ Dozens of new families move into our community every week.
(it is a fact that 是多餘的)

◉ John's attitude in the way that he felt toward his boss changed greatly.
John 大幅改變對他老闆的態度。

可簡化為:

◉ John's attitude toward his boss changed greatly.
(in the way that he felt 是多餘的)

◉ I am of the opinion that this method is more efficient.
我相信這個方法比較有效。

可簡化為:

◉ I believe/think this method is more efficient.
(to be of the opinion＝to believe or to think)

◉ Mr. A asked many questions in the course of the interview.
A 先生面試時問了許多問題。

也就是:

◉ Mr. A asked many questions during the interview.
(in the course of＝during)

⊚ We have received your check in the amount of $100 payable to the order of John Smith.
我們收到你付給 John Smith 的一百美元支票了。

可簡化為：

⊚ We have received your check for $100 payable to John Smith.

⊚ In the matter of professional ethics, it may be said that his action violates the codes.
他的行為違反了職業道德。

可簡化為：

⊚ His action violates the codes of professional ethics.

⊚ In the event that the documents arrive late, please call off the meeting.
假如公文晚到，請取消會議。

也就是：

⊚ If the documents arrive late, please call off the meeting.
(in the event that＝if)

其他又如：

in the neighborhood of＝about 在……附近
with the exception of＝except 除……以外
within the realm of possibility＝possible 或 possibly 可能的，可能地
from time to time＝occasionally 偶而，有時
come to terms with＝agree 同意，達成協議
at this particular time＝now 現在，此刻

| concerning the matter of＝about 關於，有鑑於 |
| in the light of the fact that＝because 因為 |
| in the not-too-distant future＝soon 不久，很快 |
| on the occasion of＝when 當……時 |
| despite the fact that/in spite of the fact that＝although 雖然，儘管 |

以上用法都可減少字數，讓句子更簡潔。

6. 用介詞片語、分詞片語、不定詞片語、動名詞片語或同位語，也可代替子句，減少用字。

(例如：)

⊙ After John has graduated from college, he will be looking for a job.
John 大學畢業後將會找工作。

可改為：

⊙ After college graduation, John will be looking for a job.
(用介詞片語 after college graduation 代替附屬子句 after John has graduated from college)

⊙ When the sun sets, the street lights come on.
太陽下山後，路燈亮了。

可改為：

⊙ At sunset, the street lights come on.
(用介詞片語 at sunset 代替附屬子句 when the sun sets)

● The basketball team which had come from New York was not scheduled to play.
從紐約來的籃球隊沒有安排比賽。

可改為：

● The basketball team from New York was not scheduled to play.
(用介詞片語 from New York 代替形容詞子句 which had come from New York)

● Since I was sitting close to the stage, I was able to better see the tricks of the magician.
因為我坐得離舞台很近，所以比較能看出魔術師的花招。

可改為：

● Sitting close to the stage, I was able to better see the magician's tricks.
(用現在分詞片語 sitting close to the stage 代替附屬子句 since I was sitting close to the stage)

● When the victims were trapped by the earthquake, they waited for rescue.
災民因地震受困，他們等待救援。

可改為：

● Trapped by an/the earthquake, the victims waited for (a)rescue.
(用過去分詞片語 trapped by the earthquake 代替附屬子句 when the victims were trapped by the earthquake)

● After I had finished writing, I read a book which was written by Ms. Chang.
我寫完文章後，看了一本張女士寫的書。

可改為：

◉ Having finished writing, I read a book written by Ms. Chang.
(having finished writing 是完成式分詞片語，代替附屬子句 after I had finished writing；過去分詞片語 written by Ms. Chang 代替形容詞子句 which was written by Ms. Chang)

◉ Mr. B decided to take the bus so that he could save money.
為了省錢，B 先生決定搭公車。

可改為：

◉ Mr. B decided to take the bus to save money.
(不定詞片語 to save money 代替子句 so that he could save money)

◉ I preferred that I would get an early start on my project.
我寧可提前開始我的計畫。

可改為：

◉ I preferred to get an early start on my project.
(用不定詞片語 to get an early start 代替子句 that I would get an early start)

◉ If you take the meat from the freezer now, it will be thawed out in time for supper.
如果你現在把肉從冷凍庫拿出來，就可以來得及在晚餐前解凍。

可改為：

◉ Taking the meat from the freezer now will make it thaw by supper time.
(taking the meat from the freezer 是動名詞片語，當主詞，代替附屬句 if you take the meat from the freezer)

⊙ Dr. Smith who is the heart surgeon will operate on Mr. A.
心臟外科醫師 Smith 要為 A 先生開刀。

可改為：

⊙ Dr. Smith, the heart surgeon, will operate on Mr. A.
(the heart surgeon 是同位語，代替形容詞子句 who is the heart surgeon)

⊙ Mr. B's two children, one of them is a banker and the other
(is) an accountant, work in the same company.
B 先生的兩個孩子，一個是銀行家，一個是會計師，都在同一
間公司服務。

可改為：

⊙ Mr. B's two children, a banker and an accountant, work in the
same company.
(a banker and an accountant 也是同位語，代替子句 one of them is a
banker and the other is an accountant)

7. 有時可用單字代替片語或子句。

例如：

⊙ Mr. Wang replied in a loud voice to every question I asked.
王先生大聲回答我所問的每個問題。

可改為：

⊙ Mr. Wang replied loudly to every question I asked.
(loudly 代替片語 in a loud voice)

⊙ The girl cried in a desperate way when her dog died.
女孩的狗死時，她哭得很傷心。

可改為：

⊙ The girl cried desperately when her dog died.
（desperately 代替片語 in a desperate way）

⊙ It was with great reluctance that I turned in my half-completed report.
我心不甘情不願地交出只完成一半的報告。

可改為：

⊙ Reluctantly, I turned in my half-completed report.
（reluctantly 代替子句 it was with great reluctance）

⊙ Her piano lesson that has been canceled will be rescheduled.
她被取消的鋼琴課將再安排時間上課。

可改為：

⊙ Her canceled piano lesson will be rescheduled.
（用過去分詞 canceled 當形容詞，代替形容詞子句 that has been canceled）

⊙ The forces that were against gun control ran an advertisement that covered two pages.
反槍枝管制團體刊登了兩大頁的廣告。

也就是：

⊙ The anti-gun control forces ran a two-page ad.

　　總之，寫文章要為讀者著想，假如文章能淺顯易懂，讓一般讀者所接受，就是作者最大的心願和喜悅了。

3-1

談片語的種類

片語(phrase)為一群字的組合，沒有主詞，也沒有動詞，只當句子的修飾語(modifier)。

片語通常分為以下幾種：

1. 介詞片語(prepositional phrase)

介詞片語可當形容詞或副詞用。

例如：

- Mr. A walked by the river.
  A 先生沿著河邊走著。
  (by the river 是介詞片語，是介詞 by 和它的受詞 river 連在一起；by＝along)

- You can come into my living room or kitchen.
  你可以進來我的客廳或廚房。
  (into my living room or kitchen 是介詞片語，由介詞 into 和它的複合受詞 room 和 kitchen 組成)

- Mr. B bought two books for John and me.
  B 先生買了兩本書給 John 和我。
  (for John and me 是介詞片語，是由介詞 for 和它的複合受詞 John 和 me 組成)

- In compliance with your request, I will attend the meeting.
  我會依你的要求參加這場會議。
  (in compliance with your request 是介詞片語，是由複合介詞 in compliance with 與其受詞 your request 組成)

- According to my schedule, the project will be finished next week.
  根據我的時間表，此企畫將於下週完成。
  (according to my schedule 是介詞片語，是由介詞 according to 和它的受詞 my schedule 組成)

2. 形容詞片語(adjective phrase)：

介詞片語當形容詞用，就叫做形容詞片語。其功用和單字形容詞(single adjective)一樣，可修飾名詞或代名詞。

由於形容詞能修飾名詞，所以形容詞片語也有同樣的功能。而名詞又能作句子的主詞、受詞、表語名詞等，不過，單字形容詞通常放在名詞之前，而形容詞片語則放在名詞之後。

(1) 修飾主詞(subject)

◉ The man with a mask frightened the little girl.
戴面具的男子嚇壞了小女孩。
(with a mask 本是介詞片語，當形容詞，修飾主詞 man，放在主詞後面)

有時可變成：

◉ The masked man frightened the little girl.
(masked 是單字形容詞，修飾主詞 man，放在主詞前面)

◉ The children from the primary school played baseball.
來自這所小學的孩童打了棒球。
(from the primary school 本是介詞片語，現是形容詞片語，修飾主詞 children，放在主詞後面)

可改為：

◉ The primary school children played baseball.
(把 primary school 做單字形容詞，修飾 children)

◉ A building on our street needs major repair.
位在我們街上的一棟建築物需要大整修。
(on our street 是形容詞片語，修飾主詞 building，放在主詞後面)

但不能改成：

◉ Our street building needs...

因為 street building 意義不通，只能說 street sign 或 street lights 等等。可見要把形容詞片語，改成單字形容詞，也要看句意是否合理。

(2)修飾受詞（object）

◉ Mr. A bought a garage door with a remote control.
   A 先生買了一個有遙控器的車庫門。
   （with a remote control 本是介詞片語，當形容詞，修飾受詞 door。door 是動詞 bought 的受詞）

可用單字形容詞：

◉ Mr. A bought a remote-controlled garage door.

◉ The teacher gave children with good behavior several magic markers.
   老師給品行良好的孩子幾枝魔法麥克筆。
   （with good behavior 是形容詞片語，修飾間接受詞 children）

也可用單字形容詞：

◉ The teacher gave well-behaved children several...

◉ The company offered the job to the person with the most experience.
   公司讓最有經驗的人來做這份工作。
   （with the most experience 是形容詞片語，修飾介詞 to 的受詞 person）

也可用單字形容詞：

◉ The company offered the job to the most-experienced person.

（3）修飾表語名詞（predicate noun）

也叫做表語性主格（predicate nominative），就是名詞和連綴動詞（linking verb）同時出現，說明名詞是什麼。

◉ This is a book with many interesting stories.
  這是一本有許多有趣故事的書。
  （with many interesting stories 是形容詞片語，修飾 book，說明 book 是什麼樣的 book，而 book 又是 this 的表語名詞）

如改為單字形容詞，只能說：

◉ This is an interesting story book.

◉ Today will be a perfect day for a field trip.
  今天是校外教學的好日子。
  （for a field trip 是形容詞片語，修飾 day，說明名詞 day 是什麼，而 perfect day 又是 today 的表語主格）

也可變成單字形容詞：

◉ Today will be a perfect field trip day.

3. 副詞片語(adverbial phrase)

介詞片語當副詞用，就變成副詞片語，其功用與單字副詞（single adverb）一樣，可修飾動詞、形容詞和其他副詞。

（1）修飾動詞（最常用）

例如：

◉ Our tennis team played with great enthusiasm.
  我們的網球隊打得很熱中。
  （with great enthusiasm 本是介詞片語，當副詞用，修飾動詞 played）

◉ After work, Mr. A drove to the fitness center.
下班後，Ａ先生開車到健身房。
(after work 和 to the fitness center 都是介詞片語，當副詞用，都修飾
動詞 drove。不能用單字副詞代替)

◉ By chance, his uncle lives near the busy airport.
恰巧，他的叔叔住在熙來攘往的機場附近。
(by chance 和 near the busy airport 都是介詞片語，當副詞用，都是修
飾動詞 lives。不能用單字副詞代替)

◉ My friend was working on his old jeep.
我朋友在整修他的老吉普車。
(on his old jeep 是副詞片語，修飾動詞 was working。不能用單字副詞
代替)

(2)修飾形容詞

通常修飾緊接著的形容詞。

例如：

◉ The salesperson was not courteous toward his customers.
那位店員對他的顧客不禮貌。
(toward his customers 是副詞片語，修飾靠近的形容詞 courteous)

◉ Mr. Wang has been happy with his new project.
王先生對他的新計畫感到滿意。
(with his new project 是副詞片語，修飾緊靠近的形容詞 happy。不能用
單字副詞代替)

◉ Sometimes the president's building and its grounds are open to
the general public.
總統的辦公大樓及其周遭環境有時會對外開放。
(to the general public 是副詞片語，修飾形容詞 open。不能用單字副詞
代替)

(3)修飾其他副詞

例如：

◉ My boss always arrives early in the morning.
我老闆總是一大早就進公司了。
(in the morning 本是介詞片語，現當副詞片語，修飾另一副詞 early)

如用單字副詞，只能說：My boss always arrives early.

◉ This student came late for class.
這位學生上課遲到。
(for class 是副詞片語，修飾另一個副詞 late)

4. 同位詞片語(appositive phrase)

同位語(appositive)本是名詞，放在另一個名詞後面，進一步說明前面名詞的意義；同位詞片語，就是同位語和修飾語連在一起，進一步說明主詞、受詞或表語主格。

(1)加強說明主詞

◉ Professor Thrash, an experienced scholar of good character, knows every aspect of the English language.
Thrash 教授是位經驗豐富、品德良好的學者，對英語的每一個面向都很了解。
(an experienced scholar of good character 是同位詞片語，進一步說明主詞 Professor Thrash)

◉ The Chinese medicine, a brown liquid with a bitter taste, seems to be effective.
棕色流質帶有苦味的中藥似乎有效。
(a brown liquid with a bitter taste 是同位詞片語，進一步說明主詞 medicine 是什麼)

(2)加強說明受詞

◉ Our college president introduced the keynote speaker, a well-known writer from Taiwan.
我們大學校長介紹主講人,是一位來自台灣的名作家。
(a well-known writer from Taiwan 是同位詞片語,加深說明直接受詞 speaker)

◉ I gave John, an important preacher in our community, a copy of the Bible in Chinese.
我把一本中文聖經送給了我們社區的一位重要牧師 John。
(an important preacher in our community 是同位詞片語,進一步說明間接受詞 John)
＝I gave a copy of the Bible in Chinese to John, an important preacher in our community.

(3)加強說明表語主格

◉ His lifelong ambition is to establish a special school, a training place for the poor.
他畢生的願望就是創辦一所特別學校,一個給窮人訓練的場所。
(a training place for the poor 是同位詞片語,加深說明表語主格 school)

◉ Mr. Wang's plan was a trip, a week in Taiwan and a week in China.
王先生的旅行計畫就是一週在台灣,一週在大陸。
(a week in Taiwan and a week in China 是複合同位詞片語,進一步說明表語主格 trip 是什麼)

5. 分詞片語(participle phrase)

分詞片語是由現在分詞或過去分詞與其他修飾語連在一起,當形容詞用。

◉ Speaking leisurely in a low voice, the professor explained the issue.
教授從容、低聲地解釋問題。
（speaking leisurely in a low voice 是現在分詞片語，當形容詞，修飾主詞 professor）

有人認為把主詞放在句首較好：

◉ The professor, speaking leisurely in a low voice, explained the issue.

◉ Not knowing this community, Mr. Wang had a hard time in finding an apartment.
王先生對這社區不熟，找公寓很困難。
（Not knowing this community 是現在分詞片語，當形容詞，修飾主詞 Mr. Wang）
＝Mr. Wang, not knowing this community, had a hard time...

◉ Known for their mountains and rivers, Taiwan and China are good places for tourists.
台灣和中國都以山脈河川著稱，是遊客的好去處。
（known for their mountains and rivers 是過去分詞片語，當形容詞，修飾主詞 Taiwan and China）
＝Taiwan and China, known for their mountains and rivers, are good places....

◉ Troubled by the terrible news from his friend, John went home immediately.
從朋友那兒得知這個壞消息而擔憂不安，John 馬上就回家了。
（troubled by the terrible news from his friend 是過去分詞片語，當形容詞，修飾主詞 John）
＝John, troubled by the terrible news from his friend, went...

也可用完成式的分詞片語。

- Having lived here for 30 years, Mr. J knows many people.
  J 先生在此住了30年，認識許多人。
  (having lived here for 30 years 是完成式的分詞片語，當形容詞，修飾主詞 Mr. J)
  ＝Mr. J, having lived here for 30 years, knows...

- Having been broken by the storm, the window needs to be replaced.
  窗戶被暴風雨吹壞了，需要更換。
  (having been broken by the storm 是完成式分詞片語，有被動語氣，當形容詞，修飾主詞 window)
  ＝The window, having been broken by the storm, needs...

注意

分詞片語放在句尾不好，因為與修飾的字相距太遠。分詞片語放在句首或句中，都要加逗點，以表示這個片語不是句子的重要部分，只是附加說明而已。但分詞片語特別指涉某人或某物，為句中重要部分時，則不加逗點。

例如：

- The young lady wearing the blue jacket is my daughter.
  穿藍夾克的年輕女孩是我的女兒。
  (因特指「穿藍夾克的」屬句中重要部分，故不加逗號)

6. 動名詞片語(gerund phrase)

動名詞片語，就是動名詞和修飾語或補助語連在一起，當名詞用。其功用與單字名詞一樣，可以當主詞、受詞、同位語和表語主格。

(1) 當主詞

◎ Good writing for a newspaper requires lots of practice and hard work.
要寫出可以上報的好文章，需要許多練習和努力。
(writing for a newspaper 是動名詞片語，是由動名詞 writing 和修飾語 for a newspaper 組成，作動詞 requires 的主詞)

◎ Walking on the grass is forbidden on our campus.
我們的校園裡禁止踐踏草坪。
(walking on the grass 是動名詞片語，當動詞 is 的主詞)

(2) 當受詞

◎ Mr. J has enjoyed writing during his retirement years.
J 先生在他退休期間喜歡寫作。
(writing during his retirement years 是動名詞片語，當動詞 enjoys 的受詞)

◎ Mary has stopped dancing and singing before audiences.
Mary 已不在觀眾面前跳舞唱歌了。
(dancing and singing before audiences 是動名詞片語，當動詞 has stopped 的受詞)

◎ In writing your thesis for graduation, you have to choose the words carefully.
寫畢業論文時，用字必須謹慎。
(writing your thesis for graduation 是動名詞片語，作介語 in 的受詞)

◎ After three hours, I was tired of replying to so many letters.
三小時後，我對於要回這麼多信感到厭煩。
(replying to so many letters 是動名詞片語，作介詞 of 的受詞)

（3）當同位語

◉ Mr. A has a new plan, writing for a popular magazine.
A 先生有個新計畫，就是為知名雜誌寫稿。
（writing for a popular magazine 是動名詞片語，作同位語，解釋 new plan
是什麼）

◉ John designated a weekend activity, running along the river in
the afternoon.
John 指定的周末活動就是下午沿著河邊跑步。
（running along the river in the afternoon 是動名詞片語，作同位語，說明
activity 是什麼）

（4）當表語名詞（表語主格）

◉ My daily exercise has been walking three miles in the park.
我每天的運動，就是在公園裡走三哩路。
（walking three miles in the park 是動名詞片語，當表語主格，說明主詞
exercise 是什麼）
＝Walking three miles in the park has been my daily exercise.

◉ Mrs. Wang's habit remains talking about other people.
王太太一直習慣談論別人的事。
（talking about other people 是動名詞片語，當表語主格，說明 habit 是
什麼。參閱動名詞的用法）
＝Talking about other people remains Mrs. Wang's habit.

7. 不定詞片語(infinitive phrase)

不定詞片語，就是不定詞和修飾語連在一起。其功用與單字
不定詞一樣，可以當名詞、形容詞或副詞。當名詞時，又可以做
主詞、受詞、同位語或表語主格。

（1）當主詞

◉ To walk along the beach seems enjoyable.
沿著海邊走路似乎很有趣。
　　(to walk along the beach 是不定詞片語，是由不定詞 to walk 和修飾語 along the beach 組成，作動詞 seems 的主詞)

◉ To write about the Chinese civil wars requires lots of research.
想寫中國內戰需要做很多研究。
　　(to write about the Chinese civil wars 是不定詞片語，作動詞 requires 的主詞)

(2)當受詞

◉ Mr. Wang hopes to open a small business.
王先生希望做個小本生意。
　　(to open a small business 是不定詞片語，是由不定詞 to open 和修飾語 a small business 組成，當動詞 hopes 的受詞)

◉ Courageous and brave, the man wanted to swim across the sea.
懷著無畏和勇敢的精神，這名男子要游過海洋。
　　(to swim across the sea 是不定詞片語，當動詞 wanted 的受詞)

◉ Under such circumstances, he has no choice but to escape from the danger.
在此情況下，他除了躲避危險外，別無選擇。
　　(to escape from the danger 是不定詞片語，做介詞 but 的受詞。but＝except)

(3)當表語主格

也叫表語名詞，與連綴動詞同時出現，說明主詞。

◉ The response from the government was to cut annual spending.
政府的回應是緊縮年度開支。
　　(to cut annual spending 是不定詞片語，當表語主格，說明主詞 response 是什麼。不定詞 to cut 和連綴動詞 was 同時出現)

◉ My goal has always been to write useful articles for Chinese people.
我的目標向來是寫對中國人有用的文章。
(to write useful articles for Chinese people 是不定詞片語，當表語名詞，說明主詞 goal 是什麼)

(4) 當同位語

◉ Mr. Huang's dream, to write two books on economics, has been realized.
黃先生的夢想──寫兩本經濟學的書，已經實現了。
(to write two books on economics 是不定詞片語，當同位語，解釋主詞 dream 就是寫兩本書)

◉ Mary has reached her goal -- to get into a graduate school.
Mary 已經達成目標──進入研究所。
(to get into a graduate school 是不定詞片語，當同位語，說明主詞 goal，就是進研究所)

(5) 當形容詞

◉ The head of this department was the one to notify us about our proposal.
這部門的主管就是通知我們提案的那個人。
(to notify us about our proposal 是不定詞片語，當形容詞，修飾名詞 the one＝the person)

◉ Mr. J has enough confidence to write better articles for the magazine.
J 先生有足夠的信心為這本雜誌寫出更好的文章。
(to write better articles for the magazine 是不定詞片語，當形容詞，修飾名詞 confidence)

(6) 當副詞

◉ Mr. Lee wants to improve his English conversational skills.
李先生要精進他的英語會話能力。

(to improve his English conversational skills 是不定詞片語，當副詞修飾
動詞 wants)

- Too shy to talk to the audience, Miss B looked at the ceiling.
因為太害羞而不敢跟觀眾說話，B 小姐盯著天花板。
(to talk to the audience 是不定詞片語，當副詞用，修飾形容詞 shy。副詞
too 也修飾 shy)

- This machine is hard to operate at this time.
目前這台機器很難操作。
(to operate at this time 是不定詞片語，當副詞，修飾形容詞 hard)

- The woman came early to find a better seat for the dance
performance.
這位女士提早到是為了要找到較好的座位觀賞舞蹈表演。
(to find a better seat for the dance performance 是不定詞片語，當副詞，
修飾另一副詞 early)(參閱 1-12 不定詞的用法，p. 205)

註：

(1)以下動詞的後面，通常都用不定詞：agree, appear, can/can't
afford, decide, expect, hope, intend, need, offer, plan, pretend,
promise, refuse, seem, try, want,（would）like

(2)以下動詞後面，可用不定詞或動名詞，而且意義相同：
begin, can't stand, continue, hate, like, start,
I like to write letters to my friends.
＝I like writing letters to my friends.

(3)以下動詞後面，通常都用動名詞：consider, discuss, enjoy,
finish, keep/keep on, postpone/put off, quit, stop, talk about,
think about.

(4)習慣上，動詞 go 的後面，都用「有關活動」方面的動名詞，
而且 go 後面不加介詞 to：
諸如：go+fishing, dancing, running, boating, shopping,
　　　swimming, hunting

3-2
談子句的種類

子句(clause)和片語(phrase)雖然都是字群，但並不相同。子句有主詞和動詞，而片語沒有。

子句基本有兩種：獨立子句和附屬子句。

一、獨立子句(independent clause)也叫主要子句(main clause)

有主詞和動詞，並且能表達完整的意思，可單獨存在，為完整句。

二、附屬子句(subordinate clause)也叫從屬子句(dependent clause)

雖然也有主詞和動詞，但不能表達完整的意思，不能單獨存在。所以附屬子句要與獨立子句連在一起，才能表達完整的意思。

⊙ After he completed the job, Mr. A felt relieved.
A 先生工作做完後就放心了。
(after he completed the job 的意思並不完整，故為附屬子句，必須與獨立子句 Mr. A felt relieved 連在一起，才能表達完整意思)

⊙ He missed breakfast because he got up late.
他沒吃到早餐，因為他太晚起床了。
(because he got up late 的意思並不完整，所以是附屬子句，要與獨立子句 he missed breakfast 連在一起，才能表達完整意思)(參閱2-1「句型和結構」P 253和「句子的組合」，p.269)

為了能有更多的表達方式，附屬子句又分為三種：形容詞子句、副詞子句和名詞子句。

1. 形容詞子句(adjective clause)

　　就像單字形容詞或形容詞片語一樣，形容詞子句可以修飾名詞或代名詞。然而名詞又可作主詞、受詞、同位語等，所以形容詞子句也可以修飾主詞、受詞、同位語等。

　　形容詞子句通常開始是用關係代名詞 that, which, who, whose, whom 或關係副詞 before, since, where, why 等來引導。

（1）修飾主詞

例如：

◉ The computer which was bought five years ago still works.
五年前買的電腦現在還能用。
　(which was bought five years ago 是形容詞子句，修飾主詞 computer，which 多半指事物，可用 that 代替)

◉ The man who broke the window is my friend.
打破窗戶的男子是我的朋友。
　(who broke the window 是形容詞子句，修飾主詞 man。who 指人，是主格)

◉ The article whose title I don't remember was written by Mr. B.
我記不起標題的那篇文章是 B 先生寫的。
　(whose title I don't remember 是附屬子句，也是形容詞子句，修飾主詞 article。whose 是指人或事物，是所有格)

◉ The person whom you want to see is my uncle.
你想見的人是我叔叔。
　(whom you want to see 是形容詞子句，修飾主詞 person。whom 指人，是受格；也就是把 the person is my uncle 和 you want to see him 兩句話合併成一句)

⊙ The lake where I swim is very deep in the center.
我游泳的那個湖中心很深。
(where I swim 是形容詞子句，修飾主詞 lake。也就是把 the lake is very deep in the center 和 I swim in the lake 兩句話合併成一句)

⊙ The hour before the party began was a hectic time.
宴會開始前一小時是最忙的時候。
(before the party began 是形容詞子句，修飾主詞 hour)

⊙ The place where I have been living is near the lake and park.
我住的地方靠近湖和公園。
(where I have been living 是形容詞子句，修飾主詞 place)

⊙ The time when I stayed in the mountains, I didn't watch television.
我待在山上時不看電視。
(when I stayed in the mountains 是形容詞子句，修飾主詞 time)

注意

關係代名詞who 或whom 只能代表人；which 只能代表事物。但用 that 有時可代表人或物。句義容易理解時，關係代名詞往往可以省略。

例如：

⊙ The person whom you met in my office is my son.
你在我辦公室遇到的那個人是我兒子。
(whom 在口頭上常被省去；有人用 that 代替 whom，但形容詞子句要與所修飾的字，緊緊靠近，不可分開太遠)

不要說：The person in my office whom you met is my son.因為形容詞子句 whom you met 距離修飾的字 person 太遠。

(2)修飾受詞

◉ We selected Mr. B who was qualified for this position.
我們選擇資格符合的 B 先生擔任這個職位。

　　(who was qualified for this position 是形容詞子句，修飾 Mr. B；而 Mr.
　　B 又是動詞 selected 的受詞)

◉ I remembered the day when I visited this museum.
我記得我參觀這個博物館的那一天。

　　(when I visited this museum 是形容詞子句，修飾 day；而 day 又是動
　　詞 remembered 的受詞)

◉ He stated the reason why he resigned his job.
他說明辭去工作的理由。

　　(why he resigned his job 是形容詞子句，修飾 reason；而 reason 是動詞
　　stated 的受詞。why 在口頭上，也可省去)

◉ Mr. A wrote a book which won a prize.
A 先生寫了一本得獎的書。

　　(which won a prize 是形容詞子句，修飾 book。有人也用 that 代替 which)

◉ I met Mr. Wang whom Ms. Lee wanted to see.
我遇到李小姐要見的王先生。

　　(whom Miss Lee wanted to see 是形容詞子句，修飾 Mr. Wang；而 Mr.
　　Wang 又是動詞 met 的受詞)

◉ My wife writes frequently to her sister who lives in Taiwan.
我太太常寫信給她住在台灣的妹妹。

　　(who lives in Taiwan 是形容詞子句，修飾介詞 to 的受詞 sister)

◉ The sun didn't shine on days when we could enjoy it.
當我們有空享受陽光的那幾天，卻沒出太陽。

　　(when we could enjoy it 是形容詞子句，修飾介詞 on 的受詞 days。it
　　指太陽)

◉ I have thought of a good place where we can meet.
我想到一個我們可以碰面的好地方。

　　(where we can meet 是形容詞子句，修飾介詞 of 的受詞 place)

(3)修飾同位語(appositive)

◉ John is the person whom we appointed to represent our company.
John 就是我們指定來代表公司的人。

(whom we appointed to represent our company 是形容詞子句,修飾同位
語 person,說明 John 是什麼人)

◉ This is the time when he likes to travel.
現在正是他喜歡出遊的時節。

(when he likes to travel 是形容詞子句,修飾同位語 time,也說明了主
詞 this 是什麼)

注 意

在兩個句子中,如果其中一句有介詞,變成形容詞子句時,要把
介詞的受詞改成whom 或which。

例如:

◉ The teacher was friendly. I talked to him yesterday.
這位老師很和善。我昨天跟他說過話。

把第二句介詞 to 的受詞 him,換成受格 whom,就可變成一
個形容詞子句:

◉ The teacher whom I talked to yesterday was friendly.
＝The teacher to whom I talked yesterday was friendly.(較好)

◉ The chair is uncomfortable. I am sitting on it.
這張椅子不舒服,我坐在上面。

把第二句介詞 on 的受詞 it,改用 which,連成形容詞子句:

◉ The chair which I am sitting on is uncomfortable.
(也有人用 that 代替 which,在會話中,which 或 that 常可省去)

＝The chair on which I am sitting is uncomfortable.（較好）
（介詞 on 後面的 which，不能用 that 代替，也不能省去）

⊙ Mary likes her parents. She is living with them.
Mary 喜歡她的父母。她與他們同住。

把第二句介詞 with 的受詞 them 改為 whom，連成形容詞子句：

⊙ Mary likes her parents whom she is living with.
（把介詞放在句尾，有人認為不好）
＝Mary likes her parents with whom she is living.（較好）

⊙ The young lady is over there. I told you about her.
那位小姐在那裡。我向你提過她。

把第二句介詞 about 的受詞 her 改成 whom，形成形容詞子句：

⊙ The young lady whom I told you about is over there.
（whom 也可用 that 代替，會話中也常省去）
＝The young lady about whom I told you is over there.（較好）
（介詞 about 後面的 whom，不能用 that 代替，也不能省去）

2. 副詞子句(adverbial clause)

副詞子句，也像單字副詞或副詞片語一樣，可修飾動詞、形容詞或其他副詞。

副詞子句通常用從屬連接詞(subordinating conjunction)，把主要子句和附屬子句連起來。常用的從屬連接詞有：as, because, since, so that(指原因)，as if, if, in case, unless, as long as, assuming that, in order that（指條件）although/though（指相反），where, wherever（指地點），after, before, since, until, whenever, while, than, as soon as（指時間）

(1)修飾動詞（最常用）

◉ I will help you with your project whenever you need me.
你的計畫需要幫忙的話，我隨時都可以幫你。
（whenever you need me 是副詞子句，修飾動詞 help）

◉ Mr. A listened to the radio because he wanted to know the news.
A 先生聽收音機，因為他想知道新聞。
（because he wanted to know the news 是副詞子句，修飾動詞 listened）

◉ If it rains, I will go to the library.
假如下雨，我就會去圖書館。
（if it rains 是副詞子句，修飾動詞 go）

◉ I write to Mr. Chou even though he seldom answers.
我寫信給周先生，雖然他很少回信。
（even though he seldom answers 是副詞子句，修飾動詞 write）

◉ Before I left on vacation, I asked my friend to take care of my house.
我去度假前請我朋友幫我照顧房子。
（before I left on vacation 是副詞子句，修飾動詞 asked）

◉ You may lose your job unless you listen to your boss.
除非你聽你老闆的話，不然你有可能會失去工作。
（unless you listen to your boss 是副詞子句，修飾動詞 lose）

(2)修飾形容詞

◉ John was happy because he did well on the test.
John 很高興，因為他考得不錯。
（because he did well on the test 是副詞子句，修飾形容詞 happy）

◉ The house was quiet after the party was over.
宴會結束後，屋子很安靜。
（after the party was over 是副詞子句，修飾形容詞 quiet）

◉ Mr. A was disappointed as his girlfriend was not there.
A 先生很失望，因為他的女友不在。
（as his girlfriend was not there 是副詞子句，修飾形容詞 disappointed）

（3）修飾其他副詞

◉ John ran more rapidly than I did.
John 跑得比我快。
（than I did 是副詞子句，修飾副詞 rapidly）

◉ We arrived early so that we would get a better parking place.
我們提早到以便找到位置較好的停車位。
（so that we would get a better parking place 是副詞子句，修飾副詞 early）

◉ The storm struck sooner than the forecasters expected.
暴風雨來得比氣象預報員預期的早。
（than the forecasters expected 是副詞子句，修飾另一副詞 sooner。動詞
時態：strike, struck, struck 或 stricken）

副詞子句，除了能修飾動詞、形容詞和其他副詞外，還能修
飾分詞、動名詞和不定詞，因為這三個準動詞（verbals），都來自
動詞，所以具有動詞的特性，因而可以用副詞子句修飾。

（4）修飾分詞（participle）

◉ Smiling so that he would not seem nervous, Mr. A asked her to
dance.
面帶笑容讓自己看起來不緊張，A 先生邀請她跳舞。
（so that he would not seem nervous 是副詞子句，修飾現在分詞 smiling；
而 smiling 也修飾主詞 Mr. A）

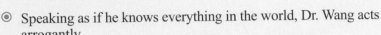

- Speaking as if he knows everything in the world, Dr. Wang acts arrogantly
  王博士說起話來一副無所不知的樣子，行為舉止狂妄自大。
  (as if he knows everything in the world 是副詞子句，修飾現在分詞 speaking；而 speaking 則修飾 Dr. Wang)

- Waving whenever she meets me, our neighbor Mary is very friendly.
  我們鄰居 Mary 非常友善，不論什麼時候見到我，總會揮手致意。
  (whenever she meets me 是副詞子句，修飾現在分詞 waving；而 waving 也修飾主詞 our neighbor)

- Sorrowed by her husband's death, Mrs. A still goes to work every day.
  因老公去世而悲傷的 A 太太，仍然每天上班。
  (by her husband's death 是副詞子句，修飾過去分詞 sorrowed；而 sorrowed 也修飾主詞 Mrs. A)

- Disappointed when he failed the test, John began to work harder.
  John 因考試沒過感到失望而開始更加努力向上。
  (when he failed the test 是副詞子句，修飾過去分詞 disappointed；而 disappointed 也修飾主詞 John)

(5) 修飾動名詞 (gerund)

- Jogging when you are not wearing comfortable shoes may be harmful to your feet.
  不穿舒適的鞋子跑步的話，可能會對腳有害。
  (when you are not wearing comfortable shoes 是副詞子句，修飾動名詞 jogging；而 jogging 是主詞。動詞時態：jog, jogged, jogging)

- Mr. B goes skating whenever the ice is thick enough.
  只要冰夠厚，B 先生就會去溜冰。
  (whenever the ice is thick enough 是副詞子句，修飾動名詞 skating)

- Frequent writing as long as time permits can keep your mind active.
  只要時間充裕就經常寫作可以使你的腦子保持靈活。
  (as long as time permits 是副詞子句，修飾動名詞 writing；而 writing 也是主詞)

- Studying while you watch TV is a bad habit.
  邊做功課邊看電視是壞習慣。
  (while you watch TV 是副詞子句，修飾動名詞 studying；而 studying 也是主詞)

(6) 修飾不定詞 (infinitive)

- I decided to stay after the meeting was over.
  我決定在會議結束後留下。
  (after the meeting was over 是副詞子句，修飾不定詞 to stay)

- Mr. A plans to write as soon as he retires.
  A 先生計畫一退休就寫作。
  (as soon as he retires 是副詞子句，修飾不定詞 to write)

- I will not be able to finish my article while you are here.
  你在這裡，我就無法完成我的文章。
  (while you are here 是副詞子句，修飾不定詞 to finish)

3. 名詞子句 (noun clause)

名詞子句，也是附屬子句，當名詞用；就像單字名詞一樣，可作主詞、動詞的受詞、介詞的受詞和表語名詞或同位語。

名詞子句通常用以下的字引導：that, which, whichever, who, whose, whom, whoever, whomever, how, if, what, whatever, when, whenever, where, whether, why

(1)當主詞

◎ That Mr. B won the writing prize did not surprise me.（主要動詞是 surprise）
B 先生寫作得獎，我並不驚訝。
(that Mr. B won the writing prize 是名詞子句，當主詞用)

◎ Where John can find a nice home has become a problem.（主要動詞是 has become）
John 能在哪裡找到好房子，已成為問題。
(where John can find a nice home 是名詞子句，當主詞)

◎ Whoever comes to his party will need to bring a dish.（主要動詞是 need）
不管誰來參加他的宴會，都要帶一道菜。
(whoever comes to his party 是名詞子句，當主詞用)

◎ What Dr. Lee wants to talk about is always his academic achievements.（主要動詞是 is）
李博士要談的都與他的學術成就有關。
(what Dr. Lee wants to talk about 是名詞子句，當主詞)

◎ Why John dropped the class remains unclear.（主要動詞是 remains）
John 為何退掉這門課的原因仍然不明。
(why John dropped the class 是名詞子句，當主詞)

(2)作動詞的受詞

◎ I wonder which road to the library is shorter.
我想知道哪一條路到圖書館比較近。
(which road to the library is shorter 是名詞子句，當動詞 wonder 的受詞)

◎ No one knows why my wife is so afraid of dogs.
沒人知道我太太為什麼那麼怕狗。
(why my wife is so afraid of dogs 是名詞子句，當動詞 knows 的受詞)

◉ I always give whomever I invite a warm welcome.
我總是熱情歡迎我邀請的人。

(whomever I invite 是名詞子句,當動詞 give 的間接受詞)

＝I always give a warm welcome to whomever I invite.

(warm welcome 是直接受詞)

> **註:**
>
> 指 welcome 時,動詞多用 give;指 hospitality 時,動詞多用 show。

◉ The professor offered whoever presented an oral report some extra credit points.
誰做口頭報告,教授就給誰加分。

(whoever presented an oral report 是名詞子句,作動詞 offered 的間接受詞;extra credit points 是直接受詞)

＝The professor offered some extra credits to whoever presented an oral report.

◉ Mr. Chang gave whoever flattered him a big promotion.
張先生大力提拔奉承他的人。

(whoever flattered him 是名詞子句,當動詞 gave 的間接受詞;big promotion 是直接受詞)

＝Mr. Chang gave a big promotion to whoever flattered him.

(3)作介詞的受詞

◉ Mr. Lee chose to write on/about how politics works in China.
李先生選擇寫與中國政治運作方式有關的東西。

(how politics works in China 是名詞子句,作介詞 on 或 about 的受詞)

◉ I will write to whoever promises to write (me) back.
我要寫信給承諾回信給我的人。

(whoever promises to write back 是名詞子句,作介詞 to 的受詞)

- Many people are seldom pleased with what the government tells them to do.
  許多人不太喜歡政府要他們做的事。
  (what the government tells them to do 是名詞子句，作介詞 with 的受詞)

- We are proud of whatever Mr. Gates does for the good of society.
  我們以 Gates 先生為社會所做的善行為榮。
  (whatever Mr. Gates does…是名詞子句，作介詞 of 的受詞)

(4)當表語名詞（predicate noun）：

也叫表語主格（predicate nominative），就是把名詞子句放在連綴動詞（linking verb）後面，說明主詞是什麼。

例如：

- The difficulty was whether the city would allow the company to build a factory here.
  困難之處在於市府是否允許公司在此建廠。
  (whether the city would allow…是名詞子句，放在連綴動詞 was 後面，說明主詞 difficulty 是什麼；was 也是主要動詞)

- His excuse has always been that he forgot the appointment.
  他的藉口一向都是他忘了約會。
  (that he forgot the appointment 是名詞子句，放在連綴動詞 has been 後面，說明主詞 excuse 是什麼；主要動詞是 has been)

- The question will be whether Mr. A is qualified for this position.
  問題在於 A 先生是否夠格擔任這個職位。
  (whether Mr. A is qualified…是名詞子句，放在連綴動詞 will be 後面，說明主詞 question 是什麼；will be 也是主要動詞)

- The rumor was that Mr. Chen had resigned from his post.
  謠傳陳先生已經辭職。

(that Mr. Chen had resigned…是名詞子句，放在連綴動詞 was 後面，說明主詞 rumor 是什麼；was 也是主要動詞)

◉ The report was that many undocumented immigrants were put in jail.
報告說許多非法移民被捕入獄。
(that many undocumented…是名詞子句，放在連繫動詞 was 後面，說明主詞 report 是什麼；was 也是主要動詞)

(5) 當同位語 (appositive)

就像用括弧一樣，先用名詞子句解釋主詞後，再接主要動詞。

◉ The rumor that Mr. Chen had resigned from his post was mentioned.
關於陳先生辭職的謠傳被提及。
(that Mr. Chen had resigned from his post 是名詞子句，先解釋主詞 rumor 是什麼，再接主要動詞 was mentioned)

◉ His excuse that he forgot the appointment upset his friends.
他忘記有約的這個說辭，讓朋友不高興。
(that he forgot the appointment 是名詞子句，先解釋主詞 excuse 是什麼，再接主要動詞 upset。動詞時態：upset, upset, upset)

◉ The question whether Mr. A is qualified for this position will be discussed.
A 先生是否適任這個職位的問題，將會被拿來討論。
(whether Mr. A is qualified for this position 是名詞子句，先解釋主詞 question 是什麼，再接主要動詞 will be)

◉ The report that many undocumented immigrants were put in jail was published in the newspaper.
許多非法移民被捕入獄的報導已經見報。
(that many undocumented immigrants were put in jail 是名詞子句，先解釋主詞 report 是什麼，再接主要動詞 was published)

> 註：
>
> (1) 名詞子句當表語名詞或同位語，有點相似，多半都是解釋一個 idea, fact, question, report, impression, rumor 等，只是主要動詞的放置位置不同。
>
> (2) 以下動詞後面，通常都接 that 的名詞子句，當動詞的受詞：agree, ask, assume, believe, conclude, decide, demonstrate, discover, doubt, dream, feel, fear, find out, figure out, forget ,guess, hear, hope, know, learn, imagine, indicate, notice, observe, predict, prove, presume, pretend, read, realize, recall, recognize, regret, remember, reveal, say, show, suppose, suspect, teach, tell, understand, wonder 等。

例如：

◎ I think that John is a good professor.
  我認為 John 是位好教授

◎ I hope that you will come to my party.
  我希望你能來我的宴會。

◎ He realizes that he needs to work harder.
  他知道他需要更努力工作。

◎ I dream that I can write better English.
  我夢想自己能寫出更好的英文。
  (以上 that 的名詞子句，作動詞 think, hope, realizes, dream 的受詞；在會話中 that 多被省去)

> 註：
>
> (3) 名詞子句當主詞時，有時可用 it 代替，稱為虛字 (expletive) 或虛主詞。

◉ It is obvious that Mr. A does not have a job.
　＝That Mr. A does not have a job is obvious.
　很明顯 A 先生沒有工作。
　(it 在這裡，只是「填空」的虛字而已，不是主詞)

◉ It is important that you call Mr. B right away.
　＝That you call Mr. B right away is important.
　立刻打電話給 B 先生很重要。

註：

(4) 用 if 或 whether 時，可把問句變成名詞子句，當動詞的受詞。

例如：

◉ Is Mr. Wang at home?
　王先生在家嗎?

可改成名詞子句：

◉ I don't know if Mr. Wang is at home.(or not)
　＝I don't know whether Mr. Wang is at home (or not).
　＝I don't know whether or not Mr. Wang is at home.
　我不知道王先生是否在家。
　(以上 if 和 whether 的名詞子句，都是動詞 know 的受詞。句尾 or not
　也可省去)

4-1

大寫字母的用法

大家或多或少都學過英文大寫字母（capitalization）的用法，本章的目的是把重要的規則再複習一下，以溫故知新。

1. 句首的第一個字、信件地址、信中的開頭稱呼和結尾，
   都要大寫。

   例如：

   ◉ How is everything with you today?
     你今天一切都好嗎？

   ◉ 25 Park Street, Silver Spring, Maryland（地址）

     寫信開頭稱呼：
     Dear 收件人姓名,
     Hello,
     Greetings,

     信中結尾：
     Sincerely yours,
     Yours truly,
     Best wishes,
     With love,
     Respectfully yours,

2. 表示特定的人、地或物的專有名詞或是屬於專有名詞的
   一部分，都要大寫。

   例如：

   ◉ Mr. Wang Dachung was born in China.
     王大中先生在中國出生。

◉ Bob Smith sailed on the Queen Elizabeth for a trip to France.
Bob Smith 搭乘郵輪伊莉沙白號到法國旅遊。

其他專有名詞如：Yale School of Law 耶魯法學院、Declaration of Independence 獨立宣言、The American Society for the Prevention of Cruelty to Animals. 美國防止虐待動物協會等。

> 註：
>
> 專有名詞中的虛詞(冠詞、介詞、連接詞)，如上句的 for, the, of, to，都不必大寫，除非是名字的開頭。

3. 一星期七天，十二個月份，以及假日都要大寫。

◉ The Chens came to see me on Father's Day.
陳家人父親節來看我。

◉ He works on Saturdays and Sundays.
他週六和週日都要上班。

◉ His store closes during January and February.
他的店 1 月和 2 月不營業。

但是春夏秋冬四季，則不要大寫：

◉ Mr. A will stay in Florida next winter.
明年冬天 A 先生將待在佛州。

◉ The fall semester starts in September.
秋季班 9 月開始。

◉ In Maryland July and August are summer months.
馬里蘭州 7 月和 8 月是夏天。

此外，earth 地球、sun 太陽、moon 月亮也不必大寫。

4. 學校的課程名稱以及各國的語文，都要大寫。

例如：

- Her daughter will take Math II and Algebra III this semester.
  她女兒本學期將選修數學 II 和代數 III。

- All new students have to take History 101.
  所有新生都必須上歷史基礎課程。

- Many American students now take Chinese in big universities.
  在大型大學裡，很多美國學生現在都會選修中文。

但是指一般性的課程或一般知識，則不必大寫。

例如：

- Many Chinese students are good at mathematics.
  很多中國學生數學很棒。

- High school students are encouraged to take music and history.
  學校鼓勵高中生選修音樂和歷史。

5. 地理上特有的名稱，如國家、州、省、城市、山脈、湖、河流、公園等都要大寫。

例如：

- Have your parents ever been to Africa?
  你的父母去過非洲嗎？

- His dream trip would be a cruise across the Atlantic Ocean.
  他夢想的旅行是坐郵輪橫渡大西洋。

- We have lived in Maryland for over 25 years.
  我們住在馬里蘭州已超過25年。

◉ The company is located halfway up Fifth Avenue.
公司位於第五大道的中間。

其餘如：Asia 亞洲，China 中國, Lake Michigan 密西根湖，the Black Sea 黑海，the Rocky Mountains 洛磯山脈，Yellowstone National Park 黃石國家公園等特別名稱，還有東、西、南、北地區和位置(region and location)也要大寫。

例如：

◉ Living in the East, I have never seen high mountains.
住在東部的我從沒看過高山。

◉ The North of China is experiencing a serious drought.
中國北部正經歷一場嚴重旱災。

但是 east, west, north, south 只指方向(direction)時則不必大寫。

例如：

◉ Drive south for one mile and you will see the building.
往南開一哩路，就可以看到那棟建築。

◉ Please turn north at the next corner.
請在下一轉角往北轉。

6. 社會上的職位或專業上的頭銜(social and professional titles)包括學位和得獎名稱(award)，都要大寫。

例如：

◉ Professor Lee, Ph.D., is from Taiwan.
擁有博士學位的李教授來自台灣。

◉ Dr. Anderson, M.D., is well-liked by his patients.
醫學博士安德生醫師深受病患喜愛。

◉ President Bush, MBA from Harvard, was a business man.
具有哈佛大學企管碩士學位的布希總統以前是位商人。

◉ Reverend Smith and Father Jackson were both present at the meeting.
Smith 牧師和 Jackson 神父都出席了這場會議。

其他頭銜還有：Sir, Mister, Miss, Madame 夫人，Congressman 國會議員，Senator 參議員，Governor 州長，Mayor 市長，Secretary of State 國務卿，Attorney 律師，Judge 法官，Bishop 主教，Sister 修女，Sergeant 士官，Corporal 下士，Lieutenant 中尉等等。

但是指普通名詞時，則不必大寫。

例如：

◉ He is a professor at a university.
他是大學教授。

◉ The mayor of a large city has a tough job.
大城市的市長難為。

◉ The presidents of many companies attended the conference.
很多公司的董事長都來參加這次會議。
(上面的 professor, mayor, presidents 都是指一般性的)

7. 書名、文章標題等都要大寫。還有短篇故事(short story)，詩(poem)，戲劇(play)，電影(movie)，歌曲(song)，繪畫(painting)，雕刻(sculpture)等名稱，也要大寫。

例如：

- Mr. Wang authored a book entitled *My Life in America*.
  王先生寫了一本書叫《我的美國生活》。

- Did you read the latest issue of *TIME* magazine?
  你看了最新一期的《時代》雜誌嗎？

8. 談到神(God or deity)或宗教與種族(religion and race)時，
名詞及代名詞都要大寫。

例如：

- He said that God will take good care of his wife.
  他說上帝會好好照顧他的太太。

- We pray for God's/the Lord's help and His blessings upon her.
  我們祈求上帝幫助以及祝福她。
  (His blessing 是指上帝的祝福)

- Some people say that the Japanese are more aggressive than
  the Chinese.
  有些人認為日本人比中國人更具侵略性。
  (指種族)

其他如：Roman Catholicism 天主教，Baptist Church 浸信
會，Christianity 基督教，Hinduism 印度教等，首字母都要大
寫。但如果 god 及 goddess 是指古代神話(mythology)人物時，則
不必大寫。

例如：the gods of ancient Rome(古羅馬諸神), the god Jupiter(宙
斯), the goddess Juno(女神朱諾，即主神 Jupiter 之妻)

9. 學校、政府機關、政黨或公司是指專有名詞時，都要大寫。

例如：

◉ Stanford University's business school is well-known.
史丹佛大學的商學院很有名。

◉ She graduated from Parkside High School last year.
她去年自 Parkside 高中畢業。

◉ Are you a member of the Lions Club?
你是獅子會的成員嗎？

其他如：the Republican Party 共和黨，the Democratic Party 民主黨，the Senate 參議會，the Congress 國會，Boy Scouts of America 美國男童軍等等。

但是學校、樓房、公司、機構等，當做普通名詞時，就不必大寫。

例如：

◉ His son will go to a junior high school this fall.
他兒子今年秋天上國中。

◉ This organization was founded in 1995.
這個機構成立於 1995 年。
(high school 和 organization 都是普通名詞)

10. 特別的地方，諸如紀念碑(monuments)或有紀念性的建築物(memorials & buildings)或是標記(trademark)、歷史上的文件、事件或年代，都要大寫。

例如：

- Many tourists like to visit the Washington Monument and the Lincoln Memorial.
  很多觀光客都愛參觀華盛頓紀念碑和林肯紀念堂。

- The Empire State Building is located in New York City.
  帝國大廈座落於紐約市。

其他諸如：the Revolutionary War 美國獨立戰爭，the Middle Ages 中世紀，the Constitution of the United States 美國憲法，World War II 二次世界大戰，the Renaissance 文藝復興等，首字母也要大寫。

11. 國家和城市名字，當專有形容詞(proper adjective)時，也要大寫。

例如：

- There are many Chinese restaurants in our community.
  我們社區有很多中國餐館。
  (Chinese 形容 restaurant)

- My favorite Maryland dish is blue-leg crab.
  我最喜歡的馬里蘭州食物是藍腳螃蟹。
  (Maryland 形容 dish)

- The mild California climate attracts many young people.
  加州氣候溫暖，吸引很多年輕人。

- There were many World War II battles in China.
  二次世界大戰的很多戰役都發生在中國。

12. 第一人稱代名詞 "I" 以及感嘆字 "O"，不論在句子裡
    什麼地方出現，都必須大寫。

例如：

- I told her I will help her and I mean it.
  我告訴她我會幫她，而我是真心的。

- "Today, O my fellow Chinese, we should help and not hurt one
  another," he said.
  他說：「中國的同胞啊，今天我們應該互相幫助，不能彼此傷
  害！」

- Hear my prayer, O Lord.
  主啊，聽我的禱告吧！

13. 直接引句，也就是引用他人真正說過的話，那麼引句裡
    第一個字要大寫。

例如：

- He said, "Here is my project."
  他說：「這是我的計畫。」

- The boss said, "All staff members must be here tomorrow
  morning by seven o'clock."
  老闆說：「所有員工明早七點前要來這裡來。」

- Mr. A announced today: "Five employees will be laid off as of
  July 1, 2008."
  A 先生今天宣布：「自2008年7月1日起，公司將會裁掉五位
  員工。」

- Academic Dean issued this statement: "Foreign students are required to take an English test."
教務長發出通知：「外國學生必須參加英文測驗。」

假如直接引句包括一個以上的完整句子，那麼每一句的第一個字都要大寫。

(例如：)

- "Please distribute these handbooks to everyone," explained the boss, "They show everything you have to know."
「請把這些手冊分給每個人，」老闆說，「這些手冊記載著你們需要知道的一切。」

當一個直接引句被分成兩部份時，只要第一部分的第一個字大寫即可。

(例如：)

- "Helping others," said my wife, "is the foundation for/of happiness."
我老婆說：「助人為快樂之本。」

14. 用主要子句引出另一完整句子時，為了加強另一句話的語氣，冒號後的第一個字，首字母要大寫。

(例如：)

- Let's think about this: Student enrollment is now decreasing.
我們要考慮到：學生入學人數正在減少。

- Consider this: Our business has declined this year.
要考慮這個：今年我們的生意已在下滑。

不過，在冒號後的不完整句子，只是為了解釋前句的意義時，那麼第一個字就不必大寫。

例如：

- The president of our university has given us two reasons: annual budget cuts and faculty retrenchment.
  我們大學的校長告訴我們兩個理由：年度預算的緊縮以及教師名額的削減。

15. 家庭親屬關係的稱呼，如果放在某人的姓名前或直接稱呼時，那麼要大寫。

例如：

- We respect Uncle Chen's opinions.
  我們尊重陳叔叔的意見。
  （Uncle 放在 Chen 之前）

- Is Cousin Sam visiting us for the weekend?
  Sam 表哥週末要來看我們嗎？
  （cousin 放在 Sam 的前面。cousin 可指表兄弟姐妹或堂兄弟姐妹）

- May I attend the dance party, Mother?
  媽，我能參加舞會嗎？（直接稱呼）

- My problem, Dad, is that I am not interested in chemistry.
  老爸，我的問題是我對化學沒興趣。（直接稱呼）

- I am sorry, Son, but you should not do that.
  兒子，抱歉，你不能做那件事。（直接稱呼）

- How long must he stay in bed, Doctor?
  醫師，他要在病床上躺多久？

但是 father 和 mother 前面有所有格時，首字母則不必大寫。

例如：

◉ Your father wants you to be a physician.
你父親要你當醫生。
(所有格是 your)

◉ Her mother will be in charge of this department.
她媽媽將負責本部門。
(所有格是 her)

16. 書籍、文章、戲劇或條文的一部分，如果後面跟隨著縮寫或羅馬數字時，則要大寫。

例如：

◉ This set of the encyclopedia Volume V focuses on human relationship.
這部百科全書第五卷的重點在於人際關係。

◉ I found Act III, Scene II of the play quite interesting.
我發現這齣戲裡的第三幕第二場很有趣。

◉ Maryland Marriage Law, Article V, Section 3 deals with divorce.
馬里蘭州婚姻法第五條第三節處理的是離婚案件。

◉ In this math book, we need to discuss Unit 10, Part 7.
在這本數學書本中我們要討論第十單元的第七部分。

但是書的頁數、行數、段數、句子的數目等，則不必大寫。

例如：

◉ When you look at sentence 5, line 8, you will find a spelling mistake.
你看到第五句第八行的時候會發現一個錯字。
（sentence 和 line 都不必大寫）

◉ Please turn to paragraph 3 on page 25.
＝Please turn to page 25, paragraph 3.
請翻到第三段，第25頁。
（paragraph 和 page 都不必大寫）

4-2
常見的英文縮寫

平時在報章、雜誌、公文或便條(memo)上，常常看到一些英文縮寫(abbreviation)，其中包括某些或許是美國人因為「怕麻煩」而創造出來的「簡寫形式」(shortened form)。這些字在正式文件上，還是少用為妙，最好完整拼寫出來，以免產生誤解，例如，SOS 一般是指 save our ship 或 save our souls 的急救訊號，但如果單獨使用或無上下文對照，也許就變成 senior officers' school、service of supply 或 secretary of state，甚至有人會解釋成 some one special。所以用縮寫時，要盡量避免誤解。

以下列舉一些常用的的英文縮寫：

1. 國際性或全美國通用的英文縮寫

UNESCO (United Nations Educational, Scientific and Cultural Organization) 聯合國教科學與文化組織(也可簡稱為聯合國教科文組織)

◉ (The) UNESCO has made some contributions to the world.
UNESCO 對世界已有一些貢獻。

NATO (North Atlantic Treaty Organization) 北大西洋公約組織

◉ Can (the) NATO members stick to their commitments?
NATO 的成員國能堅守承諾嗎？

SALT (Strategic Arms Limitation Treaty) 限制戰略武器條約

◉ Should every nation join (the) SALT?
每個國家都該加入 SALT 嗎？

NASA (National Aeronautics and Space Administration) 美國國家航空暨太空總署

◉ The success of U.S. space program depends on the performance of NASA.
美國太空計畫的成功與否要視 NASA 的表現而定。
(註：以上縮寫字也常被當作一個單字看待)

WHO (**World Health Organization**)世界衛生組織

◉ Taiwan has been trying to become a member of WHO.
台灣一直試著成為 WHO 的會員。

FBI (**Federal Bureau of Investigation**)聯邦調查局(負責美國境內)
CIA (**Central Intelligence Agency**)中央情報局(負責國外)

◉ Over the past several years, Dr. Lee has worked for both the FBI and CIA.
過去幾年來，李博士為 FBI 和 CIA 工作。

FDA (**Food and Drug Administration**)美國食品藥物管理局

◉ This new drug has to be approved by the FDA.
這種新藥須經 FDA 核准。

USDA (**United States Department of Agriculture**)美國農業部

◉ The USDA supplies a great deal of information on the agricultural market.
USDA 提供有關農業市場的大量資料。

IRS (**Internal Revenue Service**)美國國稅局

◉ IRS employees should be courteous to tax payers.
IRS 員工應對納稅人有禮貌。

NAACP（**National Association for the Advancement of Colored People**）美國有色人種促進會

◉ Many African-Americans join the NAACP.（註：發音為"N-double A-C-P"）
許多非裔美國人加入 NAACP。

NIH（**National Institute of Health**）美國國家衛生研究院

◉ Mr. Wang works at NIH as a researcher.
王先生在 NIH 擔任研究員。

AARP（**American Association of Retired People**）美國退休者協會

◉ At age 50, you are eligible to become a member of AARP.
年滿50歲的人即可成為 AARP 的會員。

AAUP（**American Association of University Professors**）美國大學教授協會

◉ The AAUP has many branches at different colleges and universities in the U.S.
AAUP 在美國各大學有很多分會。

SCORE（**Services Corps of Retired Executives**）退休經理人服務團（美國企業主管退休後免費擔任顧問、協助年輕人創業的團體。）（注意：**corps** 單複數同形，**ps** 不發音，發音與 **corpse** 不同）

 註：

美國人在機構名稱縮寫字前面，有時加冠詞the, a, an，有時不加，不過在正式文件裡，通常都會加上適當的冠詞。

2. 一般考試名稱

SAT（**Scholastic Assessment Test**）學術評量測驗（美國高中生申請進入大學的重要測驗）

◉ The top universities accept new students based on their SAT scores and moral character.
頂尖大學會根據 SAT 成績及操行來核准新生入學申請。

GPA（**Grade Point Average**）學業成績總平均

◉ His GPA is always at the top of his class.
他的 GPA 向來都是全班第一。

AP（**Advanced Placement**）（高中生可選讀的）大學先修課程

◉ His son took some AP courses at high school.
他的兒子高中時修了一些大學先修課程。

GMAT（**Graduate Management Admission Test**）美國為攻讀企管碩士（**MBA**）學生而設的入學考試

◉ In order to enter a MBA program, you need a high score on GMAT.
要念 MBA 要先有很高的 GMAT 成績。

LSAT（**Law School Admission Test**）美國為進入法學院的學生而設的入學考試

◉ He did very well on the LSAT.
他的 LSAT 考得很好。

MCAT（**Medical College Admission Test**）美國為進入醫學院的學生而設的入學考試

◉ Do you think he will do well on the MCAT?
你認為他會考好 MCAT？

GRE（Graduate Record Exam）美國大學研究所對一般研究生的入學考試

◉ Most American graduate schools require GRE scores.
多半美國研究所要求 GRE 成績。

TOEFL（Test of English as a Foreign Language）托福（外國學生想進美國大學的英語能力考試）

◉ Almost all Chinese college graduates are required to take the TOEFL if they want to come to the U.S. for advanced degrees.
幾乎所有的中國大學畢業生想到美國深造的話，大多必須考托福。

CLEP（College Level Exam Program）任何人只要有學識專長，都可參加這種考試，一旦及格，就可取得大學的學分

◉ As long as you pass CLEP, you can earn college credits.
只要你通過 CLEP，就能獲得大學學分。

ESOL（English for Speakers of Other Languages）美國為新來移民及外國學生所設的特別英語課程，也叫 **ESL（English as a Second Language）**

◉ ESOL courses for foreign students are offered on many American campuses.
許多美國學校為外國學生開設 ESOL 課程。

3. 一般生活方面：

EOE（Equal Opportunity Employer）提供平等機會的雇主（美國部分公司行號招考員工時常會表明自己是 **EOE**）

◉ All African-Americans hope that their companies are EOEs.
所有非裔美國人都希望他們的公司是 EOE。

DOQ（**Depending on Qualifications**）根據申請工作者的資歷決定是否雇用

◉ The DOQ policy is being used by our school in the hiring of new teachers.
本校採用 DOQ 政策聘用新教師。

PR（**Public Relation**）公共關係

◉ The college president wants to improve its PR with the community.
大學校長想改善與社區間的公共關係。

CEO（**Chief Executive Officer**）總裁，執行長（多半指企業或公司領導人）

◉ The CEO of this company will resign because of poor health.
這公司的 CEO 因為身體狀況欠佳而辭職。

CPA（**Certified Public Accountant**）美國有執照的會計師

◉ Do you have a CPA to prepare your income tax?
你有 CPA 幫你報稅嗎？

COLA（**Cost of Living Adjustment**）工資隨物價調整方案

◉ Our annual pay raise will be based on COLA.
我們的年度調薪是以 COLA 為準。

STD（**Sexually Transmitted Disease**）＝**VD**＝**Venereal Disease**
性病（現在 **STD** 較常用）

◉ Many teenagers face STD problems alone.
許多青少年獨自面對 STD 的問題。

SOA（**Sexually Oriented Advertisement**）有關性方面的廣告

◉ Don't you feel we have too much SOA in the media?
你不認為在媒體上有太多的 SOA 嗎？

GOP（Grand Old Party）美國共和黨另一稱呼＝**Republican Party**

- The GOP has nominated Mr. Bush as its presidential candidate.
  GOP 已提名 Bush 先生為總統候選人。

PMS（Pre-menstrual Syndrome）經前症候群

- Steer clear of her; she has PMS.
  她有 PMS，最好離她遠一點。

ADHD（Attention Deficit Hyperactivity Disorder）注意力不足過動症

- Tens of thousands of youngsters suffer from ADHD in the U.S.
  成千上萬的美國青少年有 ADHD 的問題。

RSVP（Respondez si'l vous plait）敬請回覆＝**Please reply/ respond**（源自法文，常見於請帖中）

- There is an "RSVP" on the invitation card.
  請帖上面寫著「敬請回覆」。

BYOB（bring your own bottle）自行帶酒（美國人請客時，為了減少負擔或個人對酒類的愛好不同，開派對前常會註明 **BYOB**）

- His parties are all "BYOB."
  他的派對都要「自行帶酒」。

AIDS（Acquired Immune Deficiency Syndrome）愛滋病（後天免疫缺乏症候群）

- AIDS has spread all over the world.
  AIDS 已蔓延全球。

CPR（Cardiopulmonary resuscitation）心肺復甦術

◉ Everyone should learn how to do CPR.
人人都該學心肺復甦術。

EKG（Electrocardiography）心電圖檢查

◉ Her physician has asked her to have an EKG next week.
醫生要她下週做 EKG。

IV（intravenous injection）為病人注射的點滴

◉ In the hospital emergency room, I saw a patient with an IV in his arm.
我在醫院急診室看到一位打點滴的病人。

RN（registered nurse）登記有案的護士（最資深的）
LPN（licensed practical nurse）有執照的實習護士（較資淺）

◉ She is an RN and her daughter as an LPN.
她是登記有案的護士，而她女兒則是有執照的實習護士。

DWI（driving while intoxicated）或 DUI（driving under influence）酒後開車

◉ The police charged my friend with DWI.
警方指控我的朋友酒後開車。

ASAP（as soon as possible）盡快

◉ Please update me on any changes in this matter ASAP.
如果這件事情有新的發展，請盡快通知我。

FYI（for your information）供你參考之用

◉ This is FYI.
這供你參考。

TGIF（**Thank God it's Friday**）或（**Thanks Goodness it's Friday**）感謝上帝今天是星期五（美國人常在星期五說 **TGIF**，因為週末就不用上班了）

◉ Many American people say "TGIF" on Fridays.
許多美國人喜歡在星期五說「TGIF」。

COD（**cash on delivery**）現款交貨或貨到付款

◉ The merchandise will be charged COD.
此商品貨到付款。

4. 簡寫形式(shortened form)

多半用於口語或非正式文件。

info＝information 訊息，資料

◉ The info you provided me last time is inaccurate.
你上次給我的資料不正確。

specs＝specifications 規格（通常用多數）

◉ This set of furniture really fits our specs.
這套家具的規格很符合我們所需。

copter＝helicopter 直升機

◉ The Air Force has acquired more copters.
空軍買了更多架直昇機。
(俚語裡，直升機也叫 chopper)

rec＝recreation 娛樂

◉ Many students learn to dance in our rec center.
許多學生在我們的活動中心學跳舞。

rehab＝rehabilitation 康復（中心），勒戒所（後面的 **center** 或 **room** 一般都省去）

◉ After surgery Mr. Chen was sent to rehab (room).
手術後陳先生被送到恢復室。

gym＝gymnasium 體育館

◉ Our school will spend 20 million to build a new gym.
本校將花兩千萬蓋一座新體育館。

ed＝education 教育

◉ The County Ed. Dept. will offer evening courses for retirees.
縣教育局將為退休人士開設夜間課程。

congrats＝congratulations 恭喜

◉ Congrats grads!
各位畢業生，恭喜你們！
（須注意，grad＝graduate 指「畢業生」，複數是 grads；grad school 則指「研究所」）

doc＝doctor 醫生（複數是 **docs**）

◉ Doc, do you know what's wrong with my stomach?
大夫，我的胃怎麼了？

vet＝veterinarian 獸醫

◉ He took his sick dog to the vet.
他帶他生病的狗去看獸醫。

demo＝demonstration（或動詞 **demonstrate**）示範，表演

◉ The company sent him to demo the new machine.
公司派他去示範操作新款機器。

mike＝microphone 擴音機，麥克風（**hand mike** 就是拿在手上的麥克風）

⊚ As he has a hoarse voice, he has to use a mike.
因為他聲音沙啞，所以他得用麥克風。

veggie(s)＝vegetable(s) 蔬菜

⊚ Parents should encourage their kids to eat more veggies.
父母應鼓勵孩子多吃蔬菜。

veep＝vice president 副總統

⊚ The American veep is now busy with his election campaign.
美國副總統正忙於他的競選活動。

IOU＝I owe you 借據

⊚ He wrote an IOU in front of her.
他在她面前寫好借據。

xing＝crossing 提醒駕駛人過路小心（**xing** 只能寫在牌子上，在句子裡要用 **crossing**）

⊚ Down the road, there is a school crossing.
馬路的那端有一條學童專用的通道。
（美國路牌上常見 School Xing 或 Train Xing，要過往車輛小心學童或火車）

ex＝ex boyfriend, ex girlfriend, ex-wife, ex-husband 前男（女）友、前妻、前夫

⊚ He met his ex yesterday.
他昨天跟他的前妻見過面。

4＝for 為了

- House 4 sale
  欲出售的房子
  (常見於告示牌、標語或非正式用法)

U＝you 你/妳/你們；**N＝and** 和

- U pick N pay.
  你自行採完農作物後再付錢。
  (常見於告示牌、標語或非正式用法)

5. 其他

ca.＝cerca 大約(源自拉丁文，表示不知道正確的年代或世紀)

- This book was written ca. 1840.
  這本書大約是在1840年寫的。

Rx 處方：源於拉丁文，用在醫生處方開頭(**Rx** 也是 **pharmacy** 的縮寫)

Esq.(**Esqr.**或 **Esquire**)紳士，君子，受過良好教育者(通常寫在名字後面)

ib.(**ibid.**或 **ibidem**)＝**in the same place** 出處同上，出處同前：指文章中前文已出現過的註腳(**footnote**)，以免重複寫過的作者或書名，通常只用在書目(**bibliography**)，不用在句子裡。

i.e.(**id est**)＝**that is** 也就是，即(源自拉丁文)

- Some money will be set aside for later needs, i.e., computers, books, etc.
  有些錢要留存以後使用，如購買電腦、書籍等。

etc.（et cetera）＝and so forth, and other things, and so on, and the rest 其他等等（源自拉丁文，多半指物）

⊙ Yesterday I bought shirts, pants, shoes, etc.
我昨天買了襯衫、褲子、鞋子等。
（注意：etc.前面不要加 and）

et al.（et alibi）＝and others 其他人（多半指人）

⊙ This article was written by Jim Smith, et al.
這篇文章是 Jim Smith 和其他人合寫的。
（et al.前面也不加 and）

vs.（versus）相對於，……對……（為介詞，通常以 **noun vs. noun** 的結構出現，如 **the Vikings vs. the Packers**；**criminals vs. the police**

⊙ Who won the boxing match in Jones vs. Smith?
Jones 對 Smith 的拳擊賽誰贏了呢？

⊙ In the case the Federal Government vs. Smith, the judge ruled in favor of Smith.
聯邦政府對 Smith 案，法官判 Smith 勝訴。
（注意：vs.後面要加縮寫點）

a.k.a.（also known as）又名，亦稱

⊙ New York, a.k.a. Big Apple, is one of the largest cities in the world.
紐約又名大蘋果，是全球最大的城市之一。

c/o（care of）代轉

⊙ I mailed（out）a letter to William Smith c/o Mr. Wang.
我寄了一封信給 William Smith，由王先生代轉。

e.g.(**exempli gratia**)例如，比如＝**for example**

◉ Please park your car in the nearest lot, e.g., the lot alongside the library.
請把車子停在最近的停車場，比如說圖書館旁邊的那個停車場。

4-3
標點符號的用法

　　標點符號(punctuation)能使句子更清楚正確,所以不可輕忽。這裡列舉一些主要的標點法,供讀者參考。

一、句點(**period**)

　　句點有以下幾個主要的用法。

1. 用在表示事實(fact)或意見(opinion)的陳述句(declarative sentence)的結尾。

　　　例如:

- ⊚ Ms. Smith is a high school teacher.(事實)
  Smith 小姐是高中老師

- ⊚ There is an active volcano in Hawaii.(事實)
  夏威夷有一座活火山。

- ⊚ I think he is a good student.(意見)
  我想他是個好學生。

2. 用在表示指示(command)或要求(request)的祈使句(imperative sentence)的結尾。

　　　例如:

- ⊚ Show your father some respect.(要求)
  要對你父親表示一點尊敬。

- ⊚ Listen carefully to the instructions given by the police.(要求)
  注意聽警察給你的指示。

- ⊚ Always lock the door before you leave.(指示)
  你離開前務必要鎖門。

3. 用在間接問句(indirect question)的結尾。

例如：

- Bob asked me what time it was.
  Bob 問我時間幾點。

- My son asked me where to turn the car.
  我兒子問我車子要在哪裡轉彎。

4. 用在縮寫字(abbreviation)或起首字母(initial)之間。

例如：

- He is earning a B.A. degree and his wife is earning an M.S. degree.
  他獲得學士學位，他太太獲得碩士學位。

- Mr. H. T. Chen has been our director for years.
  陳先生多年來一直是我們的主任。

5. 用在表示時間和金錢的元和角時。

例如：

- Mr. Wang comes to work at 8 a.m. and leaves at 3 p.m.
  王先生早上8點上班，下午3點下班。
  (也可寫成 A.M.或 P.M.)

- This desk sells for $160; the chair for $58.80.
  這張書桌要賣160元美金；這張椅子則是58.80元美金。

也有一些縮寫字不加句點，例如：YMCA（Young Men's Christian Association）, VA（Veterans Administration）等，以及州名的縮寫，如 CA（California）和 MD（Maryland）等。

二、逗點（comma）：

逗點的功用是讓讀者在閱讀時可以稍微停頓一下（to pause briefly），其用法有：

1. 在複合句（compound sentence）裡，使用逗點和對等連接詞（coordinating conjunction）把兩個獨立子句分開。對等連接詞包括 and, but, for, or, nor, so, yet。

例如：

- John and Bob will play tennis, and I will keep score.
  John 與 Bob 打網球，我計分。

- The game was over, but no one wanted to leave.
  比賽結束了，但沒人想離開。

- I turned on the light, for it was getting dark.
  因為天漸漸黑了，所以我開了燈。

- You may stay here for the weekend, or you may visit me later.
  你可以週末待在這兒或晚點來我家也行。

- He did not seem confused, nor did he ask for help.
  他似乎不感到困擾，也不要別人幫忙。

- Ms. Chen is very shy, so Ms. Wang did all the talking.
  陳小姐很害羞，所以都是王小姐在說話。

- Summer has arrived, yet the weather is still cold.
  夏天來了，但天氣還是冷。

如果兩個獨立句很短，意思很分明，也可省去逗點。

例如：

- He runs and I walk.
  他跑我走。

- I phoned but no one answered.
  我打了電話但沒人接。

假如遇到單字或片語或附屬句,兩邊都有對等連接詞(即 and, but, for, or, nor, so, yet)時,也可省去逗點。

例如:

- Glue or tape will hold the sign in place.
  膠水或膠帶都能固定住那標誌。
  (or 的兩邊都有單字 glue 和 tape)

- I will go to the movies or for a walk。
  我會去看電影或去散步。
  (or 的兩邊都有片語 to the movies 和 for a walk)

- Try to buy a car that has low mileage and that is in good condition.
  試著買輛里程數低、狀況又好的車。
  (and 的兩邊都有形容詞子句 that has low mileage 和 that is in good condition)

2. 在非限制的同位語(non-restrictive appositives)或非主要因素(non-essential element)的字或片語或子句(通常是形容詞子句)之間,要用逗點。

例如:

- Mr. Bob Smith, my math teacher, came to see me.
  我的數學老師 Bob Smith 先生來看過我。
  (my math teacher 只是附加同位語,即使省去,也不會影響主句的意義,故是非主要因素)

⊙ Andy, waiting in the car, asked me to hurry.
Andy 在車裡等著，要我快一點。
(waiting in the car 是形容 Andy 的片語，也是非主要因素)

⊙ We applauded Mrs. Wang, who can play piano well.
我們為鋼琴好手王太太鼓掌。
(形容詞子句 who can play piano well 也是非主要因素)

⊙ Taiwan, which has many mountains, is a beautiful place.
擁有許多山岳的台灣是個美麗的地方。
(形容詞子句 which has many mountains，是非主要因素)

反之，有限制性的同位語 (restrictive appositives) 或會有主要
因素 (essential element) 的字或片語或子句，就不要用逗點。

(例如：)

⊙ I need someone who can play piano well.
我需要鋼琴彈得好的人。
(形容詞子句 who can play piano well 是限定的，是句裡的主要因素，
不能省去，否則意義就不同了)

⊙ The man waiting in the car is my nephew.
在車裡等著的人是我的姪子。
(waiting in the car 是分詞片語，形容 man，也是限定形容子句，不能
省去)

⊙ The famous dramatist Ben Jenson wrote many comedies.
名劇作家 Ben Jenson 寫了許多喜劇。
(famous dramatist 屬於有限制的同位語，不是其他同名的 Ben Jenson)

⊙ The guest who came late missed the dinner.
晚到的客人錯過了晚餐。
(who came late 是限定的形容子句，不能省略，否則意義就不同了)

- The idea that the earth is round fascinated Columbus.
  地球是圓的這個觀念令哥倫布著迷。
  (形容詞子句 that the earth is round 也是有限制性的)

3. 如果附屬子句(多半是副詞子句)放在前面或中間時，要加
   逗點。如果主要子句放在前面，則不加逗點。

例如：

- When the movie began, they all stopped talking.
  當電影開始時，他們都停止談話。
  (附屬子句 when the movie began 放在前面，故加逗點)

- Since there was no bus, I had to walk.
  因為沒有公車，我只好走路。
  (附屬子句 since there was no bus 放在前面，故加逗點)

- Bob has wanted to be a teacher since he was a child.
  Bob 自從孩童時代就想要當老師。
  (附屬子句 since he was a child 放在後面，故不加逗點)

- Andy hopes, if I remember correctly, to become a teacher.
  如果我沒記錯的話，Andy 希望成為一名老師。
  (附屬子句 if I remember correctly 放在句中，所以也要加逗點)

- After he had finished his work, he left immediately.
  他工作做完後就馬上離開。
  (附屬句 after he had finished his work 放在前面，故加逗點)

4. 在分開一連串的單字或片語或子句時，要加逗點。

例如：

- The buffet included chicken, beef, pork, and lamb.
  自助餐有雞肉、牛肉、豬肉和羊肉。
  (分開一連串的單字)

- He ran easily, smoothly, and effortlessly.
  他跑得很輕鬆、順暢而不費力。
  (分開一連串的副詞單字)

- She wanted to marry, to have a large family, and to live a long time.
  她想要結婚、有個大家庭和長命百歲。
  (分開一連串的片語)

- He searched under the table, along the wall, and behind the piano for the missing shoe.
  為了不見的那只鞋,他找過桌下、牆緣和鋼琴後面。
  (分開一連串的片語;piano 後面不加逗點)

- We could not understand why the accident happened, who caused it, and how everyone escaped injury.
  我們不懂這起意外發生的原因、肇事者是誰以及大家是如何毫髮無傷的。
  (把一連串子句分開)

但是在一連串的項目(item)中,如果每個項目都有連接詞 and 或 or 連接時,就不必加逗點。

例如:

- I usually swim or ride or hike.
  我通常不是游泳、騎車就是健行。
- He visited the park and the zoo and the museum.
  他去了公園、動物園以及博物館。

注意

在一連串的項目中,最後一項的後面不加逗點。

例如:

⊙ He wanted a shirt, a tie, and some new shoes before school started.
他在新學期開始前想要襯衫、領帶和一些新鞋。
(shoes 後面不加逗點)

5. 句子裡的開端字或開端片語(introductory words or phrases)後面要用逗點。

例如:

⊙ Bob, I need your kind assistance.
Bob,我需要你好心幫忙。
(Bob 是開端字)

⊙ Well, how shall we begin?
嗯,我們要怎麼開始?
(well 是開端字)

⊙ To play in the band, you have to practice a great deal.
為了要在樂團演出,你需要多加練習。
(to play in the band 是開端片語)

6. 句子裡的插入字或插入片語(parenthetical or interrupting words or phrases)後面,要用逗點。

例如:

⊚ The offer, however, came too late.
然而這個機會來得太晚了。
(however 是插入字)

⊚ The sport fans, no doubt, will be eager to hear the good news.
毫無疑問地，球迷渴望聽到好消息。
(no doubt 是插入片語)

⊚ I believe in his ability, of course.
我當然相信他的能力。
(of course 是插入片語)

7. 遇到對等(equal rank)的形容詞時，要用逗點分開。

所謂對等，就是形容詞之間，如用 and 連接或改變次序，也不會改變句中的意義。

例如：

⊚ He has made a simple, polite request.
他提出一個簡單、有禮的要求。

⊚ Disorganized, illogical, messy term papers need to be rewritten.
紊亂、不合邏輯、亂七八糟的學期報告應該重寫。

⊚ A smooth, round stone was cupped in his hand.
他手裡握著一塊圓滑的石頭。

但是最後一個形容詞後面一般不加逗點。

例如：

⊚ The frisky, young dog ran to greet her.
活潑的小狗跑去迎接她。
(young 後面不加逗點)

- A red, long-stemmed rose lay on the table.
  桌上放著一朵長莖的紅玫瑰。
  （long-stemmed 後面不加逗點）

8. 在地址、州市、年月、日期之間或在信件的開頭和結尾，
   都要用逗點。

(例如：)

- He lives at 125 Spring Street, Salisbury, Md.
  他住在 Maryland 洲，Salisbury 市，Spring Street 街125號。
  （註：門牌號碼後面不加逗號）

- He was married on Monday, May 21, 1980.
  他在1980年5月21日星期一結婚。

- August 29, 1994 was an exciting date for me.
  對我而言1994年8月29日是個令人興奮的日子。

- Dear Uncle Neil,
  （信件開頭）

- Sincerely yours,

- Yours truly,

- With love,
  （最後 3 例是常見的信件結尾）

但只有單一的年、月和地名，就不加逗點。

(例如：)

- The meeting on Monday was very successful.
  週一的會議非常成功。

- I was walking to Spring Street yesterday.
  我昨天去 Spring 街。

- In 1980 a big fair was held in New York.
  1980 年，紐約舉行了一次大型博覽會。

9. 使用直接引句(direct quotation)時，要用逗點。

(例如)：

- Mr. Smith said, "Hold the door open."
  Smith 先生說：「不要關門。」
  (said 後面用逗點，hold 要大寫)

- "I can't," Bob replied, "because my hands are full of books."
  Boy 回答：「沒辦法，我的雙手都拿著書。」
  (replied 接逗點，because 的首字母小寫，因為接續於 I can't 之後)

- He murmured with a yawn, "This is a dull movie."
  他打著呵欠低聲地說：「這部電影索然無味。」

10. 直接稱呼他人時(direct address)，要用逗點。

(例如)：

- Bob, please open the door.
  Bob，請開門。

- This project, John, requires your assistance.
  John，這個企畫需要你的協助。

- When you return from Taiwan, Ms. Wang, you will have more responsibilities.
  王小姐，當妳從台灣回來時將會承擔更多責任。

- There is no need, fellow citizens, to worry about our future.
  同胞們，不需要為我們的未來苦惱。

直接稱呼與同位語（appositive）不要弄錯。

例如：

- Bob, our teacher has arrived.
  Bob，我們老師來了。
  （直接稱呼 Bob）

- Bob, our teacher, has arrived.
  我們的老師 Bob 已經來了。
  （our teacher 是 Bob 的同位語）

三、冒號（colon）：

1. 為了引導出許多項目，冒號是用在獨立子句後面。通常前面接 the following, as follows, these, those。

例如：

- He will visit three states: Maryland, Georgia, and Virginia.
  他將會造訪三個州：馬里蘭州、喬治亞州和維吉尼亞州。

- My favorite past times are these: walking, hiking, and reading.
  我最喜愛的休閒活動是這些：走路、健行以及閱讀。

- You may study any of the following languages: Chinese, French, Spanish, or German.
  你可以學習下述任何語言：中文、法文、西班牙文或德文。

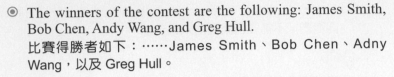
- The winners of the contest are the following: James Smith, Bob Chen, Andy Wang, and Greg Hull.
比賽得勝者如下：……James Smith、Bob Chen、Adny Wang，以及 Greg Hull。

- My reasons are as follows: The store closes too early in the evening, its advertising is inadequate, and the service is poor.
我的理由如下：店家晚上太早關門，廣告不夠以及服務欠佳。

2. 商業上的信件，警告標誌以及表示時間，都可用冒號。

例如：

- Gentlemen:

- Dear Mr. Smith:

- He will come to see me at 3:30 this afternoon.
他將在今天下午三點半來找我。

- Warning: The ice is thin.
警告：冰層仍薄。

- Note: Shake before using.
注意：使用前搖一搖。

- Caution: High voltage.
警告：有高壓電勿近

然而，冒號不能直接用在動詞或介詞後面。

不能說：Some of the features in the magazine are: ...

也不能說：Some of the features in the magazine are about: ...

但可以說：Some of the features in the magazine are the following: ...
雜誌的幾個特色如下：……

四、分號（semicolon）

分號的用法有：

1. 連接兩個或兩個以上意義相關的獨立子句(related independent clauses)，而且沒有被連接詞 and, for, or, nor, but, so, yet 所連接。

（例如：）

◎ Bob said the glass was half full; John said it was half empty.
Bob 說此杯半滿；John 說此杯半空。
（這兩句意義相關，故可用分號連在一起）

◎ I don't want orange; I want apple.
我不要柳丁；我要蘋果。

◎ The book is over five hundred pages long; it is much too long for him.
這本書超過 5 百頁那麼厚；對他而言大多了。

◎ He was a printer; he ran a newspaper in the city.
他是個印刷業者；他在市內經營報社。

◎ Sunday evenings are his time for relaxing; he watches TV with his wife.
星期天晚上是他放鬆的時候；他與老婆一起看電視。

◎ The birds vanished; the sky grew dark; the pond was still.
鳥兒不見了；天黑了；水池靜悄悄的。

假如兩個獨立句意義不相關，不要用分號連在一起，還是分開為兩句。有時候在獨立子句中，分號可以代替逗點與連接詞 and, but, for, or, nor, so, yet 等

例如：

◎ We have made the offer; now we must wait for your decision.
我們已經發出錄取通知；現在我們必須靜待你的決定。

也可以說：We have made the offer, but now we must wait for your decision.

2. 在兩個獨立子句的複合句裡，當第二句有連接副詞 (conjunctive adverb)或語氣轉折(transitional expression) 時，使用分號。

連接副詞包括：also, besides, farther, more, however, indeed, instead, moreover, nevertheless, otherwise, therefore, thus 等。

語氣轉折有：as a result, at this time, consequently, for instance, in fact, on the other hand, that is 等。

例如：

◎ I was impressed with his knowledge of science; indeed, he was remarkably well-informed.
我對他的科學知識印象深刻；確實，他的見識十分廣博。

◎ His analysis was brief; nevertheless, it contained many valuable insights.
他的分析雖然簡短，卻包含了許多寶貴的看法。

◎ He forgot to mail the payment; consequently, the electricity was turned off.
他忘了付費，所以電源被切斷了。

◎ We followed your suggestions; as a result, we have had satisfactory results.
我們遵照你的建議，最後得到了滿意的結果。

五、引號(**quotation mark**)：

引用語(又稱引語)雖然有直接和間接兩種，但只有「直接引語」(direct quotation)會使用引號，也就是把別人真正說過的、寫過的引用出來。(通常跟隨 he said, she replied 等等，而且可以放在句首、句中、或句尾。)

例如：

◉ Jim told his friend, "I had a wonderful time at the party."

◉ Bob said, "Tomorrow I am going mountain climbing."
(引用語符號，要放在句子兩頭的外面，而且句子結尾要加句點。還有，在引用語裡，第一個字母要大寫，如 Tomorrow)

◉ "I guess it's time," said Bob, "to return to work."
(to return...的 to，要小寫，因為它是整個引句的第二部分)

◉ "The Empire State Building is the tallest building in New York," Bob said.
(詳細說明請參閱 2-4「直接引語和間接引語」，p. 333)

4-4

撇號的用法

在英語裡，撇號(apostrophe)是很常用的符號用法，共有下面幾種：

一、單數普通名詞或專有名詞，字尾沒有 s 也不發 s 音），加「撇號 s('s)表示所有格(possessive case)或所有權(ownership)

例如：

◉ The woman's wallet was lost during the dance party.
這位女士的錢包在舞會中遺失了。
(woman 是單數普通名詞，加's 變成所有格)

◉ The teacher's suggestion was adopted at the meeting.
老師的建議在會議中被採納。
(teacher 後面加's 變成所有格)

◉ Each applicant's qualifications have been reviewed.
每位申請者的資格都已審核過了。

但是，遇到字尾有 s 或發 s 音，就只加撇號(')或 's，有時則要看發音是否方便而定。

例如：

◉ Her dress'/dress's quality is topnotch.
她的衣服品質一流。

◉ Dr. Jones'/Jones's new car cost lots of money.
Jones 醫生的新車花了很多錢。

◉ James'/James's opinions on writing are helpful to me.
James 的寫作意見真是讓我受益良多。
(不能用 Jame's)

其他又如：

Adams' idea＝Adams's idea

Bass' children＝Bass's children

Lois' house＝Lois's house

Chris' ability＝Chris's ability

另外舉出一些因「發音不便」而產生的例外：

Charles Dickens' novel（不用Dickens's）

Doris' brother（不用Doris's）

Robert Graves' book（不用Graves's）

但有些專有名稱不加撇號：

例如：

- ⊙ Veterans Administration
  退伍軍人管理局
  （不說 Veteran's 或 Veterans'）

- ⊙ National Newspaper Editors Association
  全國報業編輯協會
  （不說 Editor's 或 Editors'）

註：

過去一般人認為有生命的東西(animate object)可直接加 's，變成所有格；無生命的(inanimate)，則用 of 的片語。但是現在也有老外不守這個規則，他們認為任何東西都可直接加 's，表示所有權，這樣既方便也省字。

例如：

⊙ The garage's wall has been repaired.
　＝The wall of the garage has been repaired.（較好）
　車庫的牆已修繕完畢。

⊙ The tree's leaves are falling.
　＝The leaves of the tree are falling.（較好）
　樹上的葉子正飄落。

⊙ Books' contents are more important than their covers.
　＝The contents of books are more important than their covers.（較好）
　書籍的內容比封面來得重要。

　　至於無生命的單數名詞，含有「許多人」或「一群人」的意思時，現在許多人都直接在字尾加's 變成所有格。

（例如：）

⊙ The city's problem could be solved by the council members.
　城市的問題可由議員解決。

⊙ Many courses are listed in the college's catalog.
　許多課程列在大學課程手冊上。
　（catalog＝catalogue）

⊙ The most heavily abused substance by America's youth remains alcohol.
　美國年輕人濫用最多的東西還是酒。

⊙ My family's friends had a get-together yesterday.
　我們家的朋友昨天舉行一個聚會。

　　以上的 city, college, America, family 都含有「許多人」或「一群人」的意思，所以字後面直接加撇號和 s。

其他又如：Maryland's weather, county's budget, band's/bands' members, committee's proposal 等。

二、複數名詞字尾有 s 或 es 或發 s 的聲音，變成所有格時，只在後面加撇號（'）就行

例如：

◉ A touchy issue was discussed at the governors' meeting.
州長會議中討論了一個棘手的問題。
（governors 是多數）

◉ The relatives' invitations will soon be mailed.
親戚的邀請函即將寄出。
（relatives 是多數）

◉ The club members' fees should be paid by July 1.
俱樂部的會費應於七月一日前付清。

其他又如：ladies' clothes, visitors' suitcases, designers' fashions, candles' light, the Smiths' ideas 等等。

但遇到不規則的複數名詞，字尾沒有 s 或 es 時，則要加 's。

例如：

◉ There are some children's toys in my garage.
我的車庫裡有一些兒童玩具。
（單數是 child）

◉ Some mice's ears are short; others are long.
有的老鼠耳朵短，有的耳朵長。
（單數是 mouse）

◉ The geese's habits are observed by the zookeeper.
動物園管理員觀察鵝的習性。
（單數是 goose）

其他又如：women's coats, men's club, oxen's yokes 等等。

三、複合名詞（compound noun）或一群字（groups of words）形成所有格時，只須在最後一個字的字尾加's 就行

例如：

◉ The Salvation Army's office is located in the downtown area.
救世軍的辦公室位於市中心。

◉ University of Maryland's basketball team is pretty good.
馬里蘭大學的籃球隊很不錯。

◉ The president of China's tour to the U.S. was a success.
中國總理訪美成功。

◉ The American Rifle Association's lobbying of Congress is powerful and influential.
美國步槍協會對國會的遊說活動很有力又具影響力。

◉ I visited the chairperson of the Board of Education's committee yesterday.
我昨天拜會了教育委員董事會主席。

四、有連字號（hyphenated）的單複數的複合名詞，也是最後一個字尾加's

例如：

- The editor-in-chief's comments are normally highly respected.
  總編輯的評論通常受到高度重視。
  （或複數：editors-in-chief's comments）

- Her brother-in-law's car was made in Germany.
  她姐夫的汽車是德國製的。
  （複數是：brothers-in-law's cars）

- His aide-de-camp's opinions were invaluable.
  他副官的意見非常寶貴。
  （複數是：aides-de-camp's opinions）

- The jack-in-the-box's spring broke yesterday.
  驚奇箱的彈簧昨天壞了。
  （複數是：jacks-in-the-box's springs）

其他又如：passer-by's opinion, mother-in-law's hospitality, John Smith, Jr.'s answer 等等。

五、單數名詞指時間（time）、數量（amount）、距離（distance）、價值（value）或後面有 sake 時，通常是字尾加's，如果是複數名詞，字尾只加撇號

例如：

- Mr. A will spend this year's spring break at home.
  A 先生今年春假在家度過。
  （year 是單數名詞，指時間）

- His boss complimented him for a good day's work.
  他老闆誇獎他今天工作表現很好。
  （day 是單數名詞，指時間）

- Please give me a moment's thought on this topic.
  請給我一點時間思考這個問題。

- I dislike to drive over one hundred miles' distance.
  我不喜歡開超過一百英里的路。
  (miles 是複數名詞指距離)

- For heaven's sake, don't do that.
  天哪！你不要那樣。

- This is one dollar's worth of sugar.
  這糖價值一塊錢。
  (dollar 是單數名詞，指價值)

其他又如：two days' wages, a minute's notice, five cents' worth, one quarter's worth, for God's sake 等等。

有時也把 s 省去，例如：for convenience' sake, for goodness' sake。

六、指共同所有權 (joint ownership) 時，只在最後的名詞字尾加's

例如：

- The husband and wife's house was damaged by the storm.
  那對夫婦的房子被暴風損毀了。
  (指兩人共住的一棟房子)

- Mr. A and Mr. B's dentist will be retiring.
  A 先生和 B 先生共同的牙醫將要退休。
  (指兩人共同的牙醫)

◉ You can find John, Bill, and Bob's restaurant in the city.
你可以在城裡找到 John, Bill 和 Bob 共有的餐館。
(指三人共有的餐館)

但指個別所有權時，每個名詞的字尾，都要加's

例如：

◉ John's and Jack's houses were built last year.
John 和 Jack 的房子都是去年蓋的。
(指兩人各有一棟房子)

◉ Either Bob's or Tim's paper could win the essay contest.
不是 Bob 的文章，就是 Tim 的文章應該會贏得散文獎。
(指兩人不同的文章)

七、不定代名詞（**indefinite pronoun**）的所有格，也可用撇號和 **s** 表示

例如：

◉ Someone else's package was delivered to me.
別人的包裹送到我這裡。

◉ Somebody's book was left on my desk.
有人的書留在我桌上。

◉ We considered one another's choices.
我們考慮彼此的選擇。

◉ You may compare each other's homework.
你可以跟對方的作業做個比較。

◉ Everybody's/everyone's heart is so generous.
大家都如此大方。

其他又如：who else's, anybody else's, nobody's business, one's position, other's opinions 等等。

八、用撇號代替縮短詞（**contraction**）

所謂縮短詞就是把一個字母或幾個字母省去。不過正式文章，最好不要使用。

常用的縮短詞有：

1. 用動詞或助動詞與副詞 not 組成。

isn't＝is not	wasn't＝was not
aren't＝are not	weren't＝were not
don't＝do not	didn't＝did not
can't＝can not（或 cannot）	couldn't＝could not
wouldn't＝would not	shouldn't＝should not
won't＝will not	mightn't＝might not
mustn't＝must not	needn't＝need not
oughtn't＝ought not	shan't＝shall not
hasn't＝has not	hadn't＝had not
haven't＝have not	

所以可以說：

◎ Haven't you heard the news?
　＝Have you not heard the news?
　你還沒聽說那則新聞嗎？

◉ Didn't you bring a sweater?
　＝Did you not bring a sweater?
　你沒帶毛衣嗎？

2. 由代名詞與助動詞 will 組成。

I'll＝I will	you'll＝you will
he'll＝he will	she'll＝she will
we'll＝we will	they'll＝they will
who'll＝who will	

3. 由代名詞與動詞 to be 或 to have 組成。

I'm＝I am	you're＝you are
he's＝he is（或 he has）	she's＝she is（或 she has）
it's＝it is（或 it has）	we've＝we have
we're＝we are	they've＝they have
they're＝they are	mine's＝mine is
who's＝who is（或 who has）	

4. 由代名詞和助動詞 would 組成。

I'd＝I would	you'd＝you would
he'd＝he would	she'd＝she would
we'd＝we would	they'd＝they would
who'd＝who would	

九、撇號可用在年代的縮短詞

例如：

1950's＝'50's	1960's＝'60's
The 2008 elections＝'08 elections	The class of 1998＝the class of '98
spirit of 1776＝spirit of '76	

以上縮短詞，不是文法規則，只是一種個人習慣，最好不要在正式文章內使用。

不過年代加 's 也可成為複數：

the 1980's＝the 1980s（即80年代）

during the 1960's＝the 1960s（即60年代）

所以可以說：

◉ Styles of the 1970's/1970s are back in fashion.
  70年代的款式又開始流行了。

◉ The 1990's/1990s were happy years for John.
  對 John 來說，90 年代是幸福的年代。

十、撇號和 s，能把字母（letter）、數字（figure）、符號（symbol or sign）或單字（word）變成複數

例如：

1. 指字母

◉ Your n's look like h's.
你寫的 n 看起來像 h。
(也有人寫成 ns 和 hs。指多數的 n 和 h)

◉ Please dot all your i's carefully.
你 i 上面那一點都要寫清楚。
(不能寫成 is，以免與真正的 is 弄錯)

◉ Mrs. A told her son to mind his p's and q's.
A 太太告訴她兒子小心行事，舉止得當。

◉ We spell Mississippi with four s's, four i's, and two p's.
我們用四個 s、四個 i 和兩個 p 來拼 Mississippi 這個字。

2. 指數字

◉ There were four 2's and five 6's in the phone number.
電話號碼裡有四個 2 和五個 6。
(也有人寫成 2s 和 6s)

◉ John bought two more 8's for his house number.
John 為了他的門牌，又買了兩個 8。

◉ His 6's are upside down 9's.
他的 6 是顛倒的 9。(他的 6 和 9 顛倒了。)
(也可寫成 6s 或 six's；9s 或 nine's)

3. 指符號

◉ Make sure the ;'s look different from the :'s in you article.
你的文章裡，分號與冒號看起來一定要不一樣。

◉ The +'s and -'s represent positive and negative, respectively.
加號和減號分別是正數和負數。

◉ Should I add two ?'s to this paragraph?
我應該要在這一段裡面加兩個問號嗎？

4. 指單字

◉ He wrote five but's and three if's in this letter.
這封信裡他寫了五個 but 和三個 if。

◉ You need to eliminate unnecessary and's.
你要刪去不必要的 and。

◉ In your essay you used many maybe's and therefore's.
在你的文章裡，你用了很多的 maybe 和 therefore。

◉ Instead of and's, John wrote &'s.
John 寫 & 來代替 and。

注意

所有代名詞，諸如yours, his, hers, its, ours, theirs，已經代表所有
權，所以後面不能再加撇號。

◉ The motorcycle is his, but the bicycle is hers.
摩托車是他的，但腳踏車是她的。
(不是 his's；也不是 her's)

◉ Yours is the best article I have ever read.
你的文章是我看過最好的。
(不是 your's)

◉ His car needs its tires replaced.
他的車胎該換了。
(不是 it's。its 是指事物上的所有格，但 it's＝it is，不可弄錯)

4-5

受詞和補語

一個句子中除了主詞和動詞外，往往還要補語作輔助說明，才能使句子的意義更明白。

補語大致可分為：直接受詞、間接受詞、主詞補語和受詞補語四種。

分別說明如下：

一、直接受詞(direct object)

1. 直接受詞通常是放在及物動詞(transitive verb)後面，接受及物動詞(多半是動作動詞)的動作，並且能回答出 what 或 whom。

   只有及物動詞，才能有直接受詞。

   例如：

   ◉ My wife baked a cake yesterday.
     我太太昨天烤了一個蛋糕。
     (baked 是及物動詞；cake 是直接受詞；回答了烤什麼)

   ◉ John is sanding the coffee table.
     John 正在用砂紙磨亮咖啡桌。
     (sand 是及物動詞；table 是直接受詞，回答了用砂紙磨了什麼)

   ◉ Lots of leaves clogged our gutters.
     許多樹葉堵住了我們屋頂的排水道。
     (clogged 是及物動詞；gutters 是直接受詞，回答了堵住了什麼。動詞時態：clog, clogged, clogging)

   ◉ Mr. B writes at least two letters a month.
     B 先生每月至少寫兩封信。
     (write 是及物動詞；letters 是直接受詞)

- After dinner, John gave details of the event.
  飯後 John 說出整件事的來龍去脈。
  (gave 是及物動詞；details 是直接受詞；of the event 只是介詞片語，
  修飾 details)

2. 問句中可把直接受詞放在及物動詞前面。

- Which bus should Mr. A take?
  A 先生要坐哪一輛公車？
  (bus 是直接受詞，放在及物動詞 take 的前面)

- Whom did you meet in the mall?
  你在購物中心碰見誰？
  (whom 是直接受詞，放在及物動詞 meet 的前面)

- Whose bike did your son borrow?
  你兒子是借誰的腳踏車？
  (bike 是直接受詞，放在及物動詞 borrow 前面)

- What effect did the medicine have on your pain?
  這種藥對你的疼痛有什麼療效？
  (effect 是直接受詞，放在動詞 have 之前)

- Which teams will they pick for the game?
  他們要選那一隊參加比賽？
  (teams 是直接受詞，放在動詞 pick 之前)

3. 直接受詞也可以由兩個或兩個以上的名詞或代名詞組合而成，成為複合直接受詞(compound direct object)。

- At the trade fair, Mr. B bought a new jacket, shirt, and pants.
  B 先生在展銷會中買了一件新夾克、襯衫和褲子。
  (bought 是及物動詞，jacket, shirt, pants 都是直接受詞，也是複合直接
  受詞)

◉ Mr. B planted tomatoes, onions, peppers, and cabbage.
B 先生種了番茄、洋蔥、青椒和高麗菜。
(planted 是及物動詞，tomatoes, onions, peppers, cabbage 是複合直接受詞)

注 意

1. 不及物動詞(intransitive verb)沒有直接受詞，也可以說不及物動詞本來沒有直接受詞，但加上介詞後就能有受詞了。
2. 不要把直接受詞和介詞受詞弄錯。

例如：

◉ Soon, they moved into the building.
他們很快就搬進大樓。
(moved 是不及物動詞，不能回答 moved 什麼？building 是介詞 into 的受詞；into the building 是介詞片語，當副詞，修飾 moved)

◉ John walked with his wife through the park.
John 和他太太走過公園。
(walked 是不及物動詞，沒有直接受詞；wife 是介詞 with 的受詞，park 是介詞 through 的受詞。with his wife 和 through the park 都是介詞片語，當副詞，修飾 walked)

二、間接受詞(indirect object)

一個句子中一定要先有直接受詞，才能有間接受詞。間接受詞通常是放在直接受詞之前。在間接受詞前面，最常用的動詞是：ask, bring, buy, do, give, lend, make, offer, promise, sell, show, teach, tell, play, wish, write 等。

例如：

- John bought his wife a birthday present.
  John 買一份生日禮物給他太太。
  (bought 是及物動詞，wife 是間接受詞，present 是直接受詞)

- Our family lent the school our Chinese paintings.
  我們家把一些國畫借給學校。
  (lent 是及物動詞，school 是間接受詞，paintings 是直接受詞)

- John gave his bedroom a fresh coat of paint.
  John 為他的臥室上了一層新油漆。
  (gave 是及物動詞，bedroom 是間接受詞，coat 是直接受詞，of paint
  只是介詞片語，修飾 coat)

- Mr. Chou has not written me a letter for a long time.
  周先生很久沒有寫信給我。
  (write 是及物動詞，me 是間接受詞，letter 是直接受詞，for a long
  time 是介詞片語，當副詞，修飾 write)

可見間接受詞的位置幾乎都介於及物動詞和直接受詞之間。

間接受詞與直接受詞一樣，也可把兩個或兩個以上的名詞或
代名詞連接起來，成為複合間接受詞（compound indirect object）

例如：

- Please bring the guests and me some cookies.
  請拿一些餅乾來給客人和我。
  (bring 是及物動詞，guests 和 me 是複合間接受詞，cookies 是直接受
  詞)

- Education gives men and women more job opportunities.
  教育給予兩性更多工作機會。
  (gives 是及物動詞，men and women 是複合間接受詞，opportunities 是
  直接受詞)

◉ Did you tell your parents, brother, and sister the true story?
你告訴父母和兄弟姊妹實情了嗎？
(tell 是及物動詞，parents, brother, and sister 是複合間接受詞，story 是
直接受詞)

◉ We should give her efforts and suggestion a chance.
看在她的努力和建議，我們應該給她一個機會。
(give 是及物動詞，efforts and suggestion 是複合間接受詞，chance 是
直接受詞)

注 意

間接受詞不可與介詞 to 或 for 的受詞弄錯。

例 如：

◉ Mary gave her teacher a special gift.
Mary 給她老師一份特別的禮物。
(teacher 是間接受詞，gift 是直接受詞)
＝Mary gave a special gift to her teacher.
(這裡的 teacher，是介詞 to 的受詞；gift 也是直接受詞)

◉ At the restaurant, the chef prepared us two delicious dishes.
在餐廳裡，大廚為我們準備兩道美味佳餚。
(us 是間接受詞，dishes 是直接受詞)
＝At the restaurant, the chef prepared two delicious dishes for us.
(這裡的 us 是介詞 for 的受詞，dishes 也是直接受詞)

◉ My daughter read her son a story about a bear.
我女兒為她兒子講了一個熊的故事。
(son 是間接受詞，story 是直接受詞)
＝My daughter read a story about a bear to her son.
(son 是介詞 to 的受詞，story 還是直接受詞；about a bear 是介詞片語，
當形容詞，修飾 story)

三、主詞補語（subjective complement）

主詞補語，通常是名詞、代名詞或形容詞，放在連綴動詞（linking verb）之後，以便說明主詞。

有人把這種的名詞和代名詞叫做表語名詞和表語代名詞（predicate noun and predicate pronoun），也有人把這兩個名詞和代名詞統稱為表語性主格（predicate nominatives），至於形容詞，有人就叫做表語形容詞（predicate adjective）。

這些名稱看起來很容易混淆；不過，說白了，表語性主格就是補充說明主詞意義的名詞或代名詞；表格形容詞就是補充說明主詞意義的形容詞。這三個詞類和連綴動詞，在句中同時出現時，就是要進一步解釋主詞。

1. 用表語性主格為主詞補語。

〔例如：〕

◉ The new school principal is Mr. Smith.
新校長是 Smith 先生。
（is 是連綴動詞；Mr. Smith 是主詞補語，也是表語性主格，都說明主詞 principal）

◉ John will become either a professor or a writer.
John 將來不是當教授就是作家。
（become 是連綴動詞，professor 和 writer 都是主詞補語，也是表語性主格，都說明主詞 John）

⊚ The best qualified persons for these two positions will be he and she.
最適合這兩個職位的人，將是他和她。
(will be 是連綴動詞，he 和 she 都是主詞補語，也是表語性主格，都是進一步說明主詞 persons)

⊚ Peace of mind and a clear conscience are everything in life.
心靈平靜且問心無愧才是人生的一切。
(are 是連綴動詞，everything 是主詞補語，也叫表語性主格，進一步說明主詞 peace 和 conscience)

⊚ We have remained good friends for years.
我們已經當了很多年的好友了。
(remained 是連綴動詞，friends 是主詞補語，也叫表語性主格，說明主詞 we)

⊚ Mary has been a teacher, writer, and philosopher.
Mary 曾當過老師、作家和哲學家。
(has been 是連綴動詞，teacher, writer, and philosopher 都是主詞補語，也叫表語性主格，說明主詞 Mary)

可見，主詞補語也可以由兩個或兩個以上的名詞或代名詞組成。

2. 用表語形容詞當主詞補語。

也就是連綴動詞和形容詞，同時在句子裡出現，進一步解釋主詞。

例如：

⊚ The vegetable soup tastes too salty.
蔬菜湯太鹹了。
(tastes 是連綴動詞，salty 是形容詞，說明主詞 soup，所以是主詞補語，也叫做表語形容詞)

- After writing, my neck felt stiff and sore.
  寫完東西後我的脖子僵硬又酸痛。
  (felt 是連綴動詞，stiff 和 sore 都是形容詞，解釋主詞 neck，所以是主詞補語，也叫表語形容詞)

- Mr. Lee's criticism was both harsh and merciless.
  李先生的批評既嚴厲又無情。
  (was 是連綴動詞，harsh 和 merciless 都是形容詞，說明主詞 criticism，故是主詞補語，也叫表語形容詞)

- The unruly boy grew up to be belligerent and wicked.
  這不守規矩的男孩長大後好鬥又邪惡。
  (grew 是連綴動詞，belligerent 和 wicked 都是形容詞，說明主詞 boy，故是主詞補語，也叫表語形容詞)

- Despite the cold weather, my vegetables outside remained healthy.
  即使天冷，我種在外面的蔬菜還是長得很好。
  (remained 是連綴動詞，healthy 是形容詞，說明主詞 vegetables，故是主詞補語，也叫表語形容詞)

- The colors of the school banner will be white, red, and blue.
  校旗將有白、紅、藍三色。
  (will be 是連綴動詞，white, red, blue 都是形容詞，說明主詞 colors，故是主詞補語，也叫表語形容詞)

所以有人說主詞補語只有兩種：表語性主格和表語形容詞。

四、受詞補語（objective complement）

受詞補語，通常是把名詞、代名詞或形容詞放在直接受詞後面，進一步說明直接受詞。因此要有了直接受詞後，才能有受詞補語。

最常用的動詞是：appoint, choose, consider, declare, call, name, elect, find, make, judge, label, show, select, think 等。

例如：

- I consider John the best candidate for the job.
  我認為 John 是這份工作最佳的人選。
  (consider 是動詞，John 是直接受詞，candidate 是說明 John，故為受詞補語)

- The company president appointed him director of public relations.
  公司總裁指派他擔任公關主任。
  (appointed 動詞，him 是直接受詞；director 是受詞補語，說明 him)

- The parents will name the baby John or Robert.
  這對父母將把嬰兒取名為 John 或 Robert。
  (name 是及物動詞，baby 是直接受詞，John or Robert 是受詞補語，說明 baby)

- The children in my neighborhood think my backyard a playground.
  我家社區的孩童認為我家後院是運動場。
  (think 是動詞，backyard 是直接受詞，playground 是受詞補助，因為進一步說明 backyard)

- My colleagues elected Mr. B committee secretary.
  我的同事們選 B 先生擔任委員會秘書。
  (elected 是動詞，Mr. B 是直接受詞，secretary 是受詞補語，說明 Mr. B)

受詞補語，和主詞補語一樣，除用名詞、代名詞外，也可用形容詞。

例如：

◉ The judge has found the defendant guilty.
法官判定被告有罪。
(found 是及物動詞，defendant 是直接受詞，guilty 是形容詞，也是受詞補語，說明 defendant)

◉ The continuous rain made some people depressed.
雨下個不停讓一些人感到沮喪。
(made 是動詞，people 是直接受詞，depressed 是形容詞，也是受詞補語，說明 people)

◉ He called the young writer brilliant and hardworking.
他稱讚這位年輕作家傑出又努力。
(called 是及物動詞，writer 是直接受詞，brilliant 和 hardworking 都是形容詞，也是受詞補語，進一步說明 writer)

◉ A snobby person, Dr. Lee thinks some patients ignorant and stupid.
李醫師自命不凡，覺得有些病人既無知又愚蠢。
(thinks 是動詞，patients 是直接受詞，ignorant 和 stupid 都是形容詞，也是受詞補語，說明 patients。snobby＝snobbish)

　　明白上述受詞和補語的基本原則後，想要充分描寫事物就易如反掌囉。

Linking English

美國實用英語文法 修訂版

2010年10月二版
2015年3月二版二刷　　　　　　　　　　　　　定價：新臺幣400元
有著作權・翻印必究
Printed in Taiwan.

著　　　者	懷	中爵
發 行 人	林	載爵

出　版　者	聯經出版事業股份有限公司	
地　　　址	台北市基隆路一段180號4樓	
編輯部地址	台北市基隆路一段180號4樓	
叢書主編電話	（02）87876242轉226	
台北聯經書房	台北市新生南路三段94號	
電話	（02）23620308	
台中分公司	台中市北區崇德路一段198號	
暨門市電話	（04）22312023	
郵政劃撥帳戶第0100559-3號		
郵撥電話	（02）23620308	
印　刷　者	文聯彩色製版印刷有限公司	
總　經　銷	聯合發行股份有限公司	
發　行　所	新北市新店區寶橋路235巷6弄6號2F	
電話	（02）29178022	

叢書主編	林	雅玲
校　　對	曾	婷姬
內文排版	陳	如琪
封面設計	Atelier design d'Ours	

行政院新聞局出版事業登記證局版臺業字第0130號

本書如有缺頁，破損，倒裝請寄回台北聯經書房更換。　ISBN　978-957-08-3701-8 (平裝)
聯經網址 http://www.linkingbooks.com.tw
電子信箱 e-mail:linking@udngroup.com

國家圖書館出版品預行編目資料

美國實用英語文法 修訂版/懷中著．
二版．臺北市．聯經．2010年10月（民99年）．
504面．14.8×21公分（Linking Eghlish）
ISBN 978-957-08-3701-8（平裝）
[2015年3月二版二刷]

1.英語 2.語法

805.16   99019978

聯經出版事業公司

信用卡訂購單

信　用　卡　號：□VISA CARD　□MASTER CARD　□聯合信用卡

訂　購　人　姓　名：_____

訂　購　日　期：_____年_____月_____日　　(卡片後三碼)

信　用　卡　號：_____　_____　_____　_____

信　用　卡　簽　名：_____(與信用卡上簽名同)

信用卡有效期限：_____年_____月

聯　絡　電　話：日(O)：_____夜(H)：_____

聯　絡　地　址：□□□ _____

_____

訂　購　金　額：新台幣_____元整

　　　　　(訂購金額 500 元以下,請加付掛號郵資 50 元)

資　訊　來　源：□網路　　□報紙　　□電台　　□DM　　□朋友介紹
　　　　　　　　□其他_____

發　　　　　票：□二聯式　　　□三聯式

發　票　抬　頭：_____

統　一　編　號：_____

※ 如收件人或收件地址不同時，請填：

收　件　人　姓　名：_____□先生　□小姐

收　件　人　地　址：_____

收　件　人　電　話：日(O)_____夜(H)_____

※茲訂購下列書種,帳款由本人信用卡帳戶支付

書　　　　　名	數量	單價	合　　計
		總　　計	

訂購辦法填妥後

1. 直接傳真 FAX(02)27493734
2. 寄台北市忠孝東路四段 561 號 1 樓
3. 本人親筆簽名並附上卡片後三碼(95 年 8 月 1 日正式實施)

電　話：(02)27683708

聯絡人:王淑蕙小姐(約需 7 個工作天)